"This the man does not know,
The warrior lucky in worldly things,
What some endure
Who tread most widely the paths of exile."

(The Seafarer. 10th century poem)

Discard

Wild Field

AN 11ᵀᴴ CENTURY LOVE STORY

JOHNNY
STONBOROUGH

*From the life of Gytha of Wessex
and Vladimir, the river prince*

Published by Black Earth Publishing 2020

Copyright © 2020 JTC Stonborough

All rights reserved. This book or any portion thereof may not
be reproduced or used in any manner whatsoever without the
express written permission of the publisher except for the
use of brief quotations in a book review.

This is a work of fiction. Names, characters, places, events,
and incidents, other than those clearly in the public domain,
are either drawn from the author's imagination or used in
a fictitious manner. Any resemblance to actual persons,
living or dead, is purely coincidental.

Printed in the United Kingdom

First Printing, 2020

ISBN 978-1-8381923-0-3 (paperback)
ISBN 978-1-8381923-1-0 (eBook)

www.blackearthpublishing.com

Original Illustration by Lincoln Seligman

Illustration Copyright ©2020 Lincoln Seligman

Cover Design by Emma Thornton

Book design and production by John Chandler,
www.chandlerbookdesign.com

Editing by Wanda Whiteley and Johnny Burrow

FOR JANE

CONTENTS

PART ONE
THE KING SHALL HOLD THE KINGDOM

PART TWO
AT THE MERCY OF DARK HEARTS

PART THREE
THE LONE WARRIOR

WHO'S WHO
(*From Historical Sources)

Gytha (Ēadgӯða) of Wessex*, Eldest Daughter of King Harold*
(d. Hastings 1066)

Lady Edith (Swan-Neck): Gytha's Mother, Handfast Wife of
King Harold

Lords Godwine*, Edmund* and Magnus*: Gytha's Brothers and
Hilde*, Gytha's Sister

The Mother of Heroes: Danish Born Grandmother – England's
Wealthiest Woman*

Aunt Gunhild*, a nun and sister of King Harold.

Wulfwyn, Radknight of Thurgarton: Life-Ward to Gytha

'Twice Scarred' Thegn Eadric: (The Old Thegn) Friend to
King Harold's Family

The Foundling Pig-Boy, Gytha's Groom.

The Axed and Burnished Roni, (A Danish Huscarl) Commander
of the Hearthguard

Queen Edith*, Wife of King Edward (the Confessor) and sister
of King Harold.

The Towering Mace Monk Blaecman of Abingdon*:
The Family's Priest

The Painted Baladrddellt Rac Denau*, Broken Spear of The South:
A Celt Prince.

The Scented Swetesot, A Qypchaq, Tribute-Daughter to The Grand
Prince of Kiev* (and Boniak*, Swetesot's Son)

Prince Vladimir *, Duke of Smolensk, Titled *Monomakh*
Or Lone Warrior.

Queen Elisaveta★ Vladimir's Aunt, Trophy Wife of The Dane King Sweyn Estrithson★, Widow of King Harald Hardradr★ (d. Stamford Bridge 1066)

The Cold Trader Zhiznomir,

Ailsi, An English Girl, Snatched by Raiders

Jon Jarl★ (Pron. Yonyarl) – Slaver and Ruler of Gotland

Colwenne, English Bed-Wife of Jon Jarl

Tulpan, A Thrall Woman

Prince Oleg★ Cousin of Prince Vladimir Monomakh

The Posadnik Khristofor, Mayor of Novgorod

Ragnwald, A Berserker Dane

Princess Kilikia and Princess Parasha (Evpraxia★) – Child Gift-Brides.

Brother Tancred, a Benedictine monk

Piotr, a Boatman

GLOSSARY

Anglo-Saxons - dominant in England pre the Norman invasion of 1066AD.

Boyar - Knight (Baron)

Celts – dominant in the north and west of the British Isles

Dane - Viking

Handfast Wife – Wife in Common law, also known as a Danish marriage

Hearthguard – Elite retinue

Huscarl – Elite bodyguard, senior warrior

Jarl – Nobleman (Earl)

Kievan Rus, a vast medieval Eastern European principality centred on Kiev

Knarr – Seagoing cargo boat, similar to a longship

Posadnik – Mayor

Monomakh - 'byname' of Emperor Constantine IX of Byzantium Vladimir's grandfather (from Μονομάχος, a lone warrior or gladiator)

Qypchaq - Central Asian warrior pastoralists (Qypchaq-Kuman Confederation)

Qumiz – Fermented mares' milk

Radknight – Minor land owner, mounted soldier

Rus - Viking/Slavic people (see Kievan Rus)

Rusalka - Unquiet water spirit (Slavic folklore)

Terem – Elite women's quarters

Tengri – Shamanic deity, ruler of all the celestial realm (Central Asia)

Thegn – Retainer to the King, landowning warrior, nobleman

Thrall - Slave, servant, or captive

Wend – Germanic term for Baltic Slav peoples (historical)

Wild Field – (Дикое поле) Russian term for the Eurasian Steppe

MAP OF GYTHA'S JOURNEY
1066AD – 1074AD

GYTHA'S FAMILY TREE

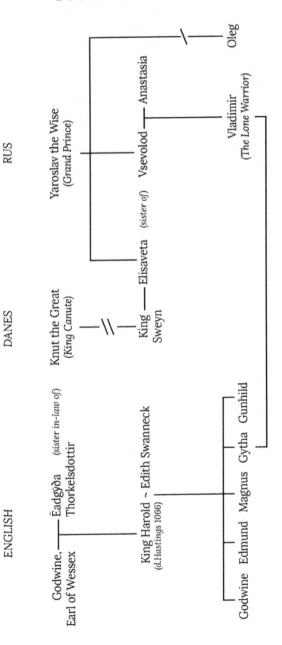

For reference

PART ONE

THE KING SHALL HOLD THE KINGDOM

"William (the Conqueror) ... built castles far and wide throughout this country, and distressed the wretched folk, and always after that it grew much worse. May the end be good when God wills."

(from the Anglo-Saxon D Chronicle)

PART ONE CHAPTER ONE

WILLIAM THE BASTARD

(Waltham, near London, October 1066)

A DOVE WITH MUSIC in its wings fluttered to the rafters in the barn. The message from the slaughter field was fastened to its slender leg. All colour drained from Lady Edith's face. It was as if the air itself had vanished. Then, she uttered such a scream that Gytha clutched her ears, fearing it must split her head in two. Her brothers stood rigid, turned to stone.

The news of Harold's death passed from person to person. As each heard it, they fell to their knees wailing, keening, clasping crosses to their hearts. Their grandmother, keeper of the old ways, whispered prayers to many gods, shaping silent verses of mourning in the rhythms of her Danish tongue. Only little Hilde, too young to understand, kept asking what was wrong.

Gytha ran outside. A small crowd had gathered, farm hands – old men mostly – the young men marched off by her father, King Harold Godwineson, to fight the Bastard Duke. Standing on an unhung bell, Wulfwyn, her mother's life-ward, was shouting to be heard. He pulled off his felted hat as she approached.

'I bring news of the battle. Our King has fallen to an arrow in his eye, snatching victory from him. Around him lie mounds of English dead, the hearthguard, the earls, his brothers, all dead.' His voice trailed away.

Gytha pushed past him into the unfinished church. Her brothers followed, their nail-hard boots ringing on the flags as she ran to the altar and fell to her knees. Above her the Flinty Cross, newly blessed, hung crooked off the wall. Somewhere monks chanted the Paradisum.

The boys knelt beside her, a numbness lying over them. Godwine, the eldest, rose. Lean and muscled in his leather jerkin and belted tunic, his boy-fair beard and long hair framing his face. He had their father's blue eyes like Gytha – the colour, their mother said, of the queen of heaven's cloak. He faced his two brothers.

'Edmund, Magnus, we will avenge our Father, so help me, Lord Jesus Christ.' Calling the priest to be their witness, he grasped his brothers' right hands. 'Say after me, both of you. As the Most High who knows all secrets is our witness, we will avenge our father and kill every one of this Bastard William's men, wherever and whenever we find them.'

Before the boys could answer, Gytha placed her hand on theirs. 'Please Godwine, make the vow again, but with me too.'

Godwine paused, unsure if a girl might make a warrior's vow.

'Please,' she said.

Putting his hand on hers, he began again, Gytha and her brothers repeating his words. 'As God the Great Creator is our witness … we will avenge our father … and kill every one of the Bastard William's men until all England is ours once more. Amen.'

Gytha's voice rang out louder than her brothers'. Then they kissed the Flinty Cross – Gytha, Godwine, Edmund, Magnus – the King's children.

There was a gasp. Gytha turned as the crowd parted for her mother, Lady Edith, whom all knew as Swan-neck. Noble born, handfast wife, mother of Harold's children, she was as graceful as the swan from which she took her name.

Pulling her cowl from her head so that the people might better see the golden circlet of her rank, she cried out, 'Godwine, we will bring your father home. He will be buried here at Waltham in holy ground, not tossed as offal into the fitful sea.'

At this, Magnus and Edmund jumped up, two beardling boys, silver wrist rings loose on skinny arms.

'The king shall hold the kingdom. The king shall hold the kingdom,' they shouted, 'we too will bring Father home with all honour due to the king.'

Their grandmother silenced them. 'You will remain. Take pride that your father and your uncles fell to the cold steel. It is nothing to the cold bed your mother must now endure.'

The crowd was silent, only roosting crows bickered in the trees. 'Mother of Heroes,' said Lady Edith, distraught, 'I have no room in this heart of grief for your hard words.'

Gytha stared at the floor to hide her brimming eyes. Not daring to breathe in case the dam burst inside her. She helped her mother prepare for the ride to the slaughter field, with Godwine chiding them to hurry. The young Radknight, Wulfwyn, would lead them back to the bloody slope from which he had so recently sped.

'Let it be known that I will give the king's weight in gold to this William for the return of Harold's body,' said their grandmother as they set off.

Her brother Godwine, his sword, mail coat and helm tied tight to his saddle, was at the head, then her mother, her cowl loose about her blonde hair, and her life-ward Wulfwyn beside her. Magnus and Edmund raised their fists in salute. 'The king shall hold the kingdom! The king shall hold the kingdom!' they cried. Gytha watched them go, as she had watched her father go to his last battle, and she kept waving long after her mother, her brother Godwine and Wulfwyn were part of the land and sky.

PART ONE CHAPTER TWO

GENTLE SWAN

THE NIGHTS BROUGHT GYTHA joyful dreams. She saw her father waving from his horse, laughing as she played. She called out to him. He answered, his voice deep and loving in reply. But in the autumn realm of daylight there was no father, no king, no mother, only the emptiness. Even the yard was full only of puddles.

Her brother Edmund, always quiet, spoke to his falcon Turul. Magnus, so mischievous, now kicked angry stones at the barn wall or hid in the hay alone. Gytha tried to settle to her embroidery or play with little Hilde, but could not hear the child's questions without tears. And so, the King's children waited a week, until Gytha stood again in the yard with her grandmother, as the procession, led by priests and a single piper, filed into the courtyard.

The Old Lady was muttering in Danish, calling to her elder gods. There were three coffins, three sons, each of them draped with the Golden Dragon banner of Wessex. Gytha dared not look.

Edith Swan-neck stopped and gazed at her, then to the coffins behind. She did not answer her welcome, but slid half fainting from the saddle. Gytha gripped her mother's hand and led her to the Hall, as Godwine ordered the men to unload.

From that day, fair Edith, their gentle swan, was lost to her children. Gytha never again heard her laugh, or felt the warmth of her mother's love, or the succour she craved in her own grief.

They buried their father Harold at Waltham in the new Abbey, beneath the Flinty Cross. At the graveside stood two fighting men, lamenting for their king with their bare heads bowed, and the war-blood still on them. These warriors were Thegn Eadric, whom they called the Twice Scarred, and the axed and burnished Roni, Huscarl and commander of the hearthguard. It was they who had escorted the Lady Edith onto the slaughter field.

After the service the company gathered in the great hall to praise and honour the King and Ring-Giver with feasting. Minstrels sang of Harold's daring, his mighty strength, his fair face and heart. Many spoke of their fallen king, companion and lord, weighing his worth and achievements with pleasing words.

Then the Twice Scarred Thegn called for silence. Addressing the king's children directly, he and the Burnished Roni relived the scene that met their mother as she reached the bloody slope.

The Old Thegn spoke first. 'There are a thousand English bodies still strewn on the field, picked over by the invaders. I saw good English men cut down by Norman swine. The housepriests met your lady mother. With them was the smirking traitor Malet, wearing the Norman helm. On his sword arm was the golden bracelet, the one your mother gave as a love-gift to your father, our King and Ring-Giver on his crowning day.'

The Burnished Roni took up the story. 'Your mother said to the traitor, "If it pleases, it is my heart's hope to carry my king and his brothers to Waltham for Christian burial.' But the traitor dismissed her. He said, "Put yourself in the bed where he now lies, gather his worms to your breast, embrace his corpse. He does not care now for your love, however much he delighted in it while he lived".'

Gytha gasped, and Wulfwyn the Radknight glanced at her kindly. Gytha bit hard on her lip and stared ahead, as her Grandmother did. She would not let them see her cry.

'I would have stabbed him as he stabbed us, but I could do nothing. The duke's men were all around us. Had your mother been our anointed queen, the traitor would not have spoken to her so.' The Old Thegn was shaking in his anger and frustration. 'I could do nothing. Nothing.'.

'The priests took your lady mother,' Roni continued, 'to the dune of looted bodies. All of the badges, helms, war-shirts and weapons of the fallen were gone. If one of those heroes was our king, only the Lady Edith could tell. Calm, erect, her cape and cowl tight about her face, the fairest mother of children in all England searched amongst our fallen thegns and huscarls, stopping only to wipe the tears that smeared her sight.'

He paused, wiping a tear from his eyes. All in the Great Hall were sobbing now; the sweet lutes were silent.

'Your mother kneeled in the mud. She tugged gently at the gore-stained linen shirt and searched your father's throat and shoulder, daring not to look at where the arrow rested. The mark of her love was clear to see. She ran her fingertips over the red-raised bruise. She was weeping, her body bent, her forehead on his bloodied chest. The Normans looked on, their longswords, axes and thrusting spears dipped in respect. The priests too were on their knees, chanting the Viaticum as we prayed for your father's soul.'

'I laid my hand upon your mother's shoulder,' said the Twice Scarred Thegn, his voice husky. "Fair Lady" I said, "let us bring the king to Waltham. He has completed his earthly pilgrimage and departed for the heavenly homeland.'

And so, we gently wrapped our lord and king, Harold Godwineson, in the purple swathing cloth your mother had embroidered with gold figures of the holy saints. We found his fallen brothers, your uncles Gyrth and Leofwine, and covered them in fine cloth. A horse cart brought hasty coffins. The priest placed a crucifix on the king's chest and folded his hands over it, and Lady Edith climbed on to kiss our dead king for the last time. The carter and his son hammered the lids of riven oak tight shut.'

'Our return to Waltham was slow. Your mother, gagged by grief, would neither eat nor drink. We stopped only at the Abbey Church at Westminster to pray, where not a year before we had gathered joyfully to witness our lord, Harold Earl of Wessex, take the sword of justice, ring and sceptre from the archbishop, as the consecrated king of the English.'

'I now feared for your mother's life,' said Roni, but more and more good English men and women gathered, falling to their knees saying, 'the king lives, glorious through his deeds,' as the cart with three coffins moved through them. The Lady Edith Swan-neck rode on, looking neither left nor right, a widowed queen in all but name, his handfast wife of twenty winters.

Try as she might, Gytha could hold her tears no longer. She buried her face in her aunt's black nun's habit, covering her ears to block the words as the warriors finished their account. Standing, heads bowed, still as pond rocks, Edmund and Magnus drew away as their Aunt reached out to them too.

Godwine coughed as he thanked the Burnished Roni and the Twice Scarred Thegn for their duty to his mother and father. The Old Lady said nothing.

*   *   *

The nuns at Waltham took Edith Swan-neck in. All interest in the world and her children ebbed away as she lay curled like a child, facing the rough plaster wall of the little cell. When Gytha begged to see her, they refused.

'Your mother must rest from the journey and the shock.' said her aunt Gunhild

Gytha shouted, 'I must see her! Why won't you let me see our mother? She needs us. We are all she has; she is all I have.'

Feeling Gytha's distress as her own, her kindly aunt relented. She held the door to the little chamber open, telling her she could have a moment. Gytha stopped in the doorway, reeled at the stench and backed away. Her mother was wearing the king's blood-soaked shirt, now black and foetid.

'Your mother is crazed with grief. She will not let us take the shirt from her.' Now, child, you understand why we would not let you see her.'

But Gytha shook her head. 'My mother needs me,' she whispered, 'My gentle swan needs me.' Stepping forward, Gytha knelt by her mother.

'Why have you tied her?' she asked.

'Because she fights all who would take your father's shirt from her.' The Abbot says she is possessed by the darkness and must be restrained.' Aunt Gunhild crossed herself.

'Father would not want his gentle swan so.' Gytha carefully unwound the ropes, all the while talking softly to her mother as if soothing a frightened animal. Edith Swan-neck did not hear or even know her. But Gytha persevered, asking for warmed water with which to bathe her. Then she pressed the cloth over her mother's brow until she was asleep. Gently, Gytha eased Edith's head from the pillow and, with her jewelled wounding-knife, she pulled the putrid rag away in strips. Her mother did not stir.

'There, let her rest and I will return with my brothers in the morning.'

Gytha visited her mother each day, bathing her, urging her to eat, telling her of life in the Hall, or singing as she combed and plaited Swan-neck's long hair, now greying with shock. Edith said little, and barely seemed capable of more than a murmur. Occasionally her eyes filled with tears or she would press Gytha's hand to her lips, holding it tight. Gytha thought her heart would break, but caring for her gentle swan gave Gytha a gift to her father. It was a duty she alone could fulfil.

But how she yearned for the mother she knew. She would climb onto the bed and lie with her, wrapping her slender arms around her, whispering, 'Mother, it is me, Gytha.' Her Mother would mumble and, in that moment, Gytha was sure that she knew her. But if she gazed into that fair face, those pale blue eyes seemed not to see her. They looked beyond, as if to a stranger. Once, Gytha was sure that her mother had said her name, and she prayed that she might again. But she did not. If no one was about, Gytha would talk to her as they used to, asking questions like: 'The lord I marry, what will he be like?', and Edith Swan-neck would think a while and say, 'well dear child, he will be fair faced, tall with blond hair to his shoulders, a mighty warrior, the bravest in the Kingdom, with bright blue eyes, a loving heart, and maybe the scent of honey-mead on his breath.' And Gytha would giggle, and say 'that's father!' And her mother would laugh and hug her and say, 'yes, I wish you a husband like your father.'

Little Hilde, cared for by the nuns, soon stopped wanting to go to her mother, tugging away from her when Gytha led her to the bedside. But Magnus would lie with his mother at Gytha's prompting, brushing away the tears he would have no one see. Quiet Edmund sat wordless at her side, the saker falcon on his arm.

'You may stroke him, Mother,' he whispered, taking her limp hand he laid it on the dapple-firm feathers. 'Maybe you will fly again and be our gentle swan once more.' But Edith did not stir.

Godwine too visited his mother daily to pray with the priest at her bedside, but he would not speak of her to Gytha, saying only that it was the Lord's will.

Wulfwyn, her mother's life-ward was in the yard. Gytha stopped. Nervously, he asked if he too might visit Lady Edith.

'You will have to ask my brother Earl Godwine, it is not for me to grant, Wulfwyn.'

'My lady,' said Wulfwyn, 'He has forbidden it, but it breaks my heart not to see her.' He paused as if struggling for the words. Gytha gave him a small smile of encouragement. She had so little to smile about, but she liked Wulfwyn. She waited as he twisted all life from the felted cap in his hands.

'My lady, your mother spoke to me as we rode from the slaughter field. She ordered me to care for you and to protect you always, as I have cared for and protected her. I hope to tell her that I gladly take this duty.' He stopped as suddenly as he had begun. He was blushing fully now.

Gytha reeled. No words came, such was her surprise. She faltered. 'You must see her, Wulfwyn. I will take you to her now.'

And so Gytha led the young man back into the Priory and to her mother's side. Wulfwyn knelt, his head bowed, to greet his lady. Getting no reaction, he glanced over his shoulder to where Gytha stood. She nodded to him to continue. Biting his lip, Wulfwyn cleared his throat and in a low voice said, 'My lady, this is Wulfwyn, your humble and obedient servant.'

Another long pause. 'My lady, as you commanded me, I vow to serve your daughter the Lady Gytha Haroldsdaughter and to lay down my life before any harm comes to her, from this day forward.'

'So, you are to be my life-ward?' Gytha asked when they got outside.

Wulfwyn, Radknight of Thurgarton, knelt down on one knee. Putting his hand to his heart, he looked up at Gytha and said, 'I am your servant, my Lady Gytha. Your commands are mine and my life is yours. You and your brothers are in great danger from Duke William now your father is dead and the English defeated.'

Gytha only half took in what he was saying. 'The king shall hold the kingdom,' she said defiantly.

'Your brother will be our King and Ring-Giver. With that comes many duties and much menace. My Lords Edmund and Magnus, your brothers, are still too young. That is why your mother ordered me to protect you from peril and guard you through all adversity.'

The autumn of 1066 turned to winter. The east wind scattered yellowed leaves around the yard and with the rain came riders with bad news. One by one, England's leather-caped thegns submitted to Duke William as he torched a bloody path of murder, rape and theft around the south. London could not hold out after Earls Edwin and Morcar swore fealty to William and with London no longer a threat, the Duke led his army north to cross the river Thames unopposed.

PART ONE CHAPTER THREE

TO DENMARK

'HURRY, MY LADY, DRESS quickly. We leave immediately for Denmark.' Wulfwyn was at Gytha's door.

It was still dark. There were shouts in the yard, orders, and the clank of armed men swearing at horses. Gytha blinked awake, bed-warm and sleepy. She tried to clear her head, but could not, as her thrall woman snatched clothing in panic from the trunks.

'No, not those,' said Gytha, pointing at the soft belted robes and tunics. 'Those ones! Clothes for the wave road.'

The woman pulled out Gytha's thickest blue wool kirtle, dark red felt breeches, and cloths to bind her legs.

With the dream of her father still foremost in her mind, Gytha called out for her mother, but Wulfwyn said gently, 'She does not hear you, my lady. You must hurry. Your grandmother and brothers are waiting in the yard.'

Still in a daze, Gytha tugged on rough raw-hide shoes, criss-crossing the leather laces to her knees. Twisting her thick golden hair tight beneath a cap, she wrapped a woollen cowl around her head. Then she slid the jewelled wounding-knife into the sheath at her waist, pulled the felted wadmal cape over her head, the one that smelt of sheep's piss, and fastened it with a silver raven broach at her shoulder.

'I look like a beardling boy, like Magnus,' she thought, snatching a soft fox fur to wrap about her neck.

Godwine stepped into the dim chamber. He was wearing her father's gold etched war-helm, arm rings, the finest Frankish longsword and fleece-lined scabbard high at his side. Gytha, not knowing if she was awake or asleep, knelt in her young confusion.

'Come on, Gytha! We have no time for that. The duke has crossed the river and marches here.'

'Wait'. Turning back, she reached under her bed and pulled out her jewelled treasure box.

Godwine shook his head. 'Leave that.'

'I'm not taking the box, just some precious things. Hand me that cloth,' she ordered the servant woman, 'I'll wrap what I need in this.'

So Gytha gathered her treasures, including the necklace with the red and blue jewel stones like smooth pebbles. That was her favourite. She also packed her needle-work, pins and scissors, the carved walrus-tusk comb which had been a gift from her mother – and the golden crucifix blessed by the Holy Father in Rome himself.

'What about Hilde?' Gytha looked at her little sister, still sleeping – the angel of the rocking cot, her mother called her. 'Is she not coming?'

Godwine shook his head. 'No,' he said bluntly. 'In God's name hurry girl, everyone is waiting for you.'

It was all happening too quickly. Gytha kissed her little sister, pulled the blanket to her chin, and stumbled after Godwine into the yard. All about were men and horses, the air thick with clouds of breath mist. There were carts stacked with war swords, arrows, thrusting spears and axes. The Burnished Roni and the Twice Scarred Eadric wore helms and ring shirts, their bossed and studded shield-boards slung across their backs. Edmund and

Magnus, spear-armed, shivered at their reins, looking as young as
the beardless boys they were. Godwine's mastiff dogs stood keen.

Godwine led Gytha over to her grandmother and Aunt
Gunhild, cowled and fully furred against the cold. She kissed
their hands.

'But where is mother?' Gytha asked, her voice trembling.
looking around her.

'She cannot come, Child. She is too sick. The holy sisters
will care for her here,' said her grandmother.

Gytha was word-robbed, unable even to protest.

'I will fetch our mother and little Hilde as soon as it is safe,'
said Godwine. 'But for now, they stay.'

'They will be safer here,' said Aunt Gunhild. 'We must leave,
child. The duke is close.'

'But,' Gytha stammered, 'father told me to look after them.
I cannot leave!'

'Move out,' shouted Godwine, the nose-wise hounds
bounding at his heels. Men struck the horses with whips. The
heavy carts lurched.

'I must say goodbye!' Grandmother, I must see her!' Gytha
turned and sped back across the yard. Godwine swore.

But the Twice Scarred Thegn blocked her way. 'Gytha!' he
said, grabbing her arm.

She winced, trying to pull away. 'Let go of me!'

'We have no time, child. The Bastard Duke is close. You
will see your mother soon. Now mount your horse.'

Furious, Gytha jumped onto her sturdy mare, ignoring
the Radknight's helping hand, jerked it round, whipped it on,
then pulled up hard beside Edmund and Magnus. The three
of them clattered past the unhung bells, the New Abbey, the
long-thatched Priory, and their mother's chamber. Gytha was
weeping with anger and hurt. Cowled figures wished them
Godspeed. Magnus was too excited to feel grief at leaving or

much sympathy for his sister, but Edmund leaned to comfort her, his falcon fidgeting on his arm. Gytha grasped his leather gloved hand and held it tight.

'Do we have to leave so suddenly without Mother?' she asked, in a loud angry whisper.

'Duke William's army has crossed the Thames. He is at Berkhamsted.'

'Is that close?' asked Gytha.

'A day's ride, no more.'

Gytha was silent while she took this in. 'Will they kill us?'

At this Magnus joined in, indignant. 'Of course not. We have sent word to our kinsman, the Dane King Sweyn. With his Dane men we will throw these Normans out of England.'

'Is that true Edmund?' asked Gytha.

'Yes.' Edmund nodded. 'You saw those carts? There is enough silver, coins and gold to buy men and arms. We will avenge our father's death, as we vowed.' Edmund put his gloved hand over his mouth and, muffled by the leather, added 'we go to the River and then by boat to our kinsman.'

'Across the Middle Sea? Now in winter? We will die out there.'

'The king shall hold the kingdom,' shouted Magnus suddenly, in his high boy's voice.

'The king shall hold the kingdom,' echoed a hundred riders in the darkness, shadowed faces lit by the flaring torches some carried.

They reached the River Lea. Round bottomed river boats awaited them, each with a twisted prow, oars and naked mast laid flat. Here were still more weapon bearers.

'Gytha look, the Godwineson Hoard!' said Magnus as they dismounted.

Godwine and battle-ready thegns in leather capes watched keenly as chests and boxes packed with the golden cups, the crystal monstrance, golden arm-bracelets, silver shillings, psalters, bibles and precious jewels were quickly loaded. Gytha followed, helping her grandmother and aunt from the slippery wooden jetty onto the crammed overloaded boat. Edmund, Magnus and the Radknight Wulfwyn jumped aboard last. Other boats nearby carried their horses, which stamped on the base-boards, their breath smoking, while men sent to guard the noble ladies were in another. Godwine, the Burnished Roni and the Twice Scarred Thegn remained on the wooden quayside. Godwine waved the noble ladies goodbye.

'Are you not coming with us, Godwine?' shouted Gytha.

'No, I will meet you with bigger craft downstream at the Thames, and from there we sail to Denmark to seek help', Godwine called, as lines were cast off.

Gytha was struggling. In one night had she not abandoned her mother and sister? And now her eldest brother, their new crown-bearer, was abandoning her. She stood up, about to scramble ashore. She would not abandon her mother. She would stay, stay with her mother, their gentle swan. She called her brothers Magnus and Edmund to follow. But a firm hand gripped her arm.

'Your brother will meet us downstream with more boats and men, child,' said her grandmother loudly and firmly, 'He is our King and you will obey him. Now sit! Or feel my anger.'

Gytha closed her eyes tight. She knew her grandmother's anger well enough when she raced her mare too fast, beating her brothers, or if she answered back, or fidgeted during Mass. The Old Lady was sister-in-law to King Canute, the greatest Dane king to rule England. The men of the longships lived within her. Gytha flattened her palms to her mouth. 'Lighten our darkness, we beseech thee, O Lord. And by thy great mercy defend us from all perils and dangers of this night;

for the love of thy only Son, our Saviour Jesus Christ. Amen.'
'Amen,' said her Aunt.

Half-heartedly, the dawn nudged the night aside. It was icy
on the river. Gytha was hungry, cold and uncomfortable. Aunt
Gunhild put an arm tight around her, offering a bannock from
within her wadded cape. A man called to them from the shore,
asking where they were bound so early. 'Away, across the sea,'
replied the steersman vaguely.

'Not in that tub?' came the reply.

A friar, squatting in the reeds, his heavy cassock pulled
up to his waist, signed them with the cross as they glided by
him, barely an oar's reach away. The men laughed. Magnus
sniggered. Magnus loved to snigger, relishing all that was foul
enough to make a joke. He was small for his age; Gytha was
now taller than him, though a year younger. But he was strong
and wiry and showed great promise with a sword and axe, and
like Gytha had their father's blue eyes and his fire.

Gytha, a castaway in her own melancholy that dawn, wasn't
thinking about her brother. So much had happened, she could
make no sense of it. The emptiness rose from the middle of
her belly and grabbed her throat as if to choke her. First her
father's death, forewarned by the dread comet, then fleeing
their tapestried halls at Bosham to the southwest, and now
months later fleeing Waltham – without saying goodbye to her
mother. She shut her eyes tight. Of one thing she was certain:
she must trust in God. But though she prayed for strength,
she felt no compass in His love that morning. She felt only
that she was alone.

'Be strong Gytha, in your breast be bold,' she remembered
her father saying, the night he left, the lamp flickering as they
knelt together under the figure of the Virgin in her parents'
chamber. She could almost taste the smell of his tunic, and

touch the rumble in his voice. He had taken her small hand in his rough and jewelled grasp, his arm ring glinting in the lamplight. 'Be strong Gytha, in your breast be bold.'

'Yes father,' she had whispered. 'Be strong, Godspeed Father.' And he had kissed her, pulling her to him. It was to be his last hug, the last time she felt the might of his arms around her, the last time she pressed her soft cheek to his beard.

The land slid past them, the grass, trees, and distant huts all silvered with frost. Growing clouds told of rain. Occasionally an animal splashed under the bank, an otter, maybe, or a water rat; herons stood guard. Men lifted and dipped dripping oars in and out of the black river to the groaning harmonies of squeaking rowlocks. The steersman, scanning for crouching mudbanks, leant on the stern-pole, blowing on his bone-chilled fingers and cursing. In time, copse and meadow yielded to flat marsh, deep drains and mysterious ditches left and right.

'We'll lie here!' the steersman shouted, nosing into the bank to get a line around a willow tree. The other vessels followed, settling flat onto the mud with the falling tide. Ahead was the Thames; beyond that, the grey sea.

The horses shifted and stamped on the bottom boards. Men stoked braziers at the stern, stirring welcome porridge. They waited, tucked into the shore, hidden by the high banks. Gytha looked out at the grey river as it began to rain. A heron, still as stone, suddenly darted forward, plunging its long neck into the water before standing tall once more. An eel, thick as rope, wriggled furiously on the tip of its sharp beak. She watched fascinated as the eel twisted and turned itself in knots to stop its captor from swallowing it. Gytha caught Edmund's eye. The eel knew its fate; they knew its fate. The heron did nothing, expressionless, detached from the struggle. Then, the heron nodded back its narrow head, and the eel was gone.

'Eels don't give up, even when it's hopeless,' said the ever-thoughtful Edmund.

'Stupid, if you ask me,' Magnus scoffed.

'It wanted to live.'

The steersman offered them broth. Magnus and Gytha finished theirs in moments. Edmund fed Turul some scraps, before spooning the hot soup, relishing the taste. The bird on his arm flapped its wings, almost knocking the spoon from his hand. Edmund calmed it with a word. He was always slow to anger. His father would say that he had his mother's temperament. He had given the saker falcon to him and not to the others, because he knew that Edmund alone had the patience to train it and care for it. How right he had been, thought Gytha watching.

Edmund looked up. 'Do you ever wonder why I can hunt with Turul but not with a heron? The heron never misses either.'

'If we are here any longer, you'll be able to try,' said Gytha bitterly, desperate to be away from this dank place that stank of evil itself. 'What are we waiting for?'

'The tide and Godwine,' said Magnus.

'And if he doesn't come?'

'I shall give the order to go without him.'

'You, Magnus?' Gytha looked at her brother, his teeth chattering. 'And go where?' She laughed, which made him angry.

'To our kinsman King and Ring-Giver across the sea.'

Gytha pulled Magnus closer to the brazier. 'I think not,' she said kindly.

The day passed; the rain stopped. Little eddies formed around them, then the laden boats floated clear of the mud with a nudge and a bump, swinging on their mud anchors in the tide. A horse whinnied in the distance, then another.

'It's Godwine!' cried Gytha. But Wulfwyn the Radknight reached for his sword.

Around the bend came not one but a dozen boats of all shapes, laden with men rowing hard against the flooding stream. Godwine was on the first. Gytha shouted to him.

'Is Mother with you? And Hilde?'.

Godwine seemed not to hear. 'The duke's men will find us gone by now,' he yelled back. 'Follow us, we must hurry.'

'But mother is at Waltham. We cannot leave her! What will happen to her and Hilde? What will the Normans do to them?'

'Child,' said her aunt gently, 'we pray that the Lord protects them in this time of danger. There was no choice but to leave your mother. She is sick and your sister is too little. Pray for their safety and the Lord will heed your prayer.'

Gytha turned away as, one by one, the three boats slipped their moorings and headed out into the great river Thames. Curling her legs under her on the hard bench, she stared deep into the water. She prayed for Hilde; she prayed to get off the hateful boat. But most of all she begged the Lord not to punish her for failing her gentle swan.

There was a shout. A cluster of dim lamps low on the shore. It was a creek and harbour. 'Up together, boys, let's not get swept past!' cried a steersman. Men strained on their oars against the stream. Ahead were shadowy buildings and, as they got closer, they could see craft pulled high up the strand.

"Is this Denmark, Grandmother? Is this your home?' Gytha asked, bleary eyed.

'Child,' said the old lady, 'we are still in England, near to London'.

'Why?' asked Gytha in surprise. 'You said Denmark.'

'You ask too many questions, child.'

'Because of traitors, silly,' said Magnus. 'It was to set a false trail,' he laughed.

'I'll explain', said Edmund patiently.

*   *   *

Around them, horses squealed as men tugged and thrashed them over the sides of the beached boats. Their hooves slipped on the planking before sinking into the black ooze. Geese, startled by the uproar of the landing boats, added their honking to the din; gulls roused from their roosting circled, screeching in the darkness overhead.

Gytha stood alone with her grandmother and Aunt Gunhild waiting on dry land, while Edmund, Magnus and the young Radknight helped the other men to stack the hoard clear of the rising water.

"Where are we to sleep?' groaned Gytha, her teeth chattering in the icy wind. How she wished for the hot brazier on the boat.

Suddenly, out of the darkness, burst a cluster of men with sticks. Lit by one lamp they ran from behind a timber shack, across the sandy ground straight at them. On they came, a dozen, no match for the armed men down on the shore, but at that moment the three noble ladies were caught between them and the hoard. Gytha shouted a warning 'Ambush! Ambush! Ambush! We are attacked, ambush!' and pulled her jewelled wounding-knife from her belt, as they ran past her, knocking her onto the shingle. Gytha swore at them.

'My lady, are you hurt?' yelled the Radknight, sprinting to her aid. Gytha scrambled nimbly to her feet. Winded, she brushed herself down, holding the wounding-knife.

The Burnished Roni, charged up the beach, followed by Godwine and the Twice Scarred Thegn. The attackers, seeing the three warriors, froze, feet from the Godwineson treasure.

'Touch that and die,' ordered the Twice Scarred Thegn.

'Who are you?' shouted a ruffian in reply, a man bigger even than the Burnished Roni. In his left hand he held up a mullein lantern, in his right a great blacksmith's hammer. Lowering the Frankish sword, Godwine stepped in front of Roni and the Twice Scarred Thegn. 'I am Godwine Haroldson, the king's son.'

'King Harold's son? The king's son?' the man repeated. 'Here?'

The villagers – no match for lances, swords and axes, hesitated and then bowed.

'Yes, I am Godwine, eldest of the king's sons.'

'Have you come to aid or harm us, Lord?' If the blacksmith was fearful, he hid it well.

'Neither, smithy.'

The villagers watched, trembling with terror, fearful that Godwine would hang them or cut off their hands as common thieves.

'You've nought to fear from us, smithy, though my sister may think otherwise.' The others laughed loudly. The ruffian paused, relieved, but cautious.

'I meant her no harm, I thought her a boy with her wounding-knife.' 'My Lady,' he said, turning to Gytha, 'I meant you no harm my lady, I am your servant.'

'She swears like a boy,' said Magnus, impressed. The Old Thegn ordered him to be silent. Gytha was still angry, but unhurt. She said nothing, but looked straight ahead, seeming to ignore the man.

Godwine took a shilling from his pouch and handed it to the man he would have split in two. 'Stand up,' he repeated, 'you have nought to fear from Englishmen, who need your help. We'll be away soon as you have loaded every cart you have and provided horses and food. Now we seek lodging for the ladies.'

The smithy stood and bowed again. Grunting his thanks at so much silver said, 'Lodging? You'll find nothing here;

the Duke's men took everything and burned our homes. We
have nothing, only bony mud fish caught fresh today and the
rope store for shelter.'

Soon fires were lit, and the attack forgotten. The noble
women, now guests of the smithy, were settled in the rope-
store amid the stink of seaweed and rotten fish. Gytha hastily
joined her brothers where a bowl of thin oat gruel and burnt
mud-fish awaited her.

Men cheered as she arrived at the fire's edge. 'Lady Gytha,
your shout alone stopped that Smithy in his tracks,' said one.
'Aye, Lady,' said another, 'you spoke true as any Englishman.'
Everyone laughed and Gytha smiled proudly, 'I think the sight
of the burnished Roni's axe halted him, not my swearing,' she
answered, laughing as she sat herself next to Edmund.

'Where did you learn that?' asked her brother. 'I wonder
what Grandmother and Aunt Gunhild thought.'

'So why are we close to London, not in Denmark? Is it to
mislead the Bastard Duke?'

'Yes, they think we flee to Denmark. But we go west to
our aunt, Queen Edith, at Winchester and raise another army
under the golden dragon banner,' said Magnus.

Gytha listened, wondering why Magnus knew about this
but not her. But she said nothing.

'Look,' said Godwine, pulling a red and gold banner from
a pouch. 'This will be our standard,' he said it so proudly. 'It
belonged to our grandfather. Now we too fight under the
Golden Dragon of Wessex.'

'The king shall hold the kingdom!' shouted Magnus, but
wearily now.

'Yes, but Godwine, what will happen to Mother? They will
harm her,' said Gytha.

'Be calm, sister, the Lord protects her,' said the quiet
Edmund. 'The Normans seek Godwine, Magnus and me.'

'You don't know that, Edmund!' Gytha was angry now. She never lost her temper with Edmund, but this time she did. 'Do not tell me to be calm, Edmund. They will use Mother to get you. They will harm her to get you!'

Edmund stayed silent, not wanting to provoke her. He loved his sister, and she had done well that day.

'What then, Edmund? What if God does not protect her because of our sins?' She couldn't help herself.

'Gytha,' said Edmund, shaking his head. 'I don't know, you must ask a priest.' He paused. 'You saved lives today.'

'Aye sister,' said Godwine, 'You did.'

'Fisherfolk with sticks,' said Magnus.

'Shut up, Magnus,' said Godwine.

'Now sleep, sister,' said Edmund. 'We can do nothing for our gentle swan but pray.'

Returning to the stinking rope-store, Gytha pulled a blanket tight around her. All about men snored, as she drifted into a troubled sleep. In her nightmare, she saw the river, the heron, minstrels, an ambush, her mother's joy, her father's laughter, the victor in his hall. She saw his body on the slaughter field.

PART ONE CHAPTER FOUR

PIG BOY

GYTHA AND THE NOBLE ladies rode westward, skirting London, unseen, warm in their furs and wadmal capes. Protecting them, with etched helms, ring shirts, shield-boards and the finest Frankish swords were Gytha's brothers, Godwine, Edmund and Magnus. The King's children were all together, beneath the Golden Dragon standard. Wulfwyn, Gytha's life-ward, rode next to her; and behind, with their thick silver armbands and hair down to their leather capes, the Twice Scarred Thegn and the burnished Huscarl Roni.

Behind this company of nobles came ceorls in felted caps and leg hose, armed with clubs and war-shafts, guarding the collar thralls. All moved cautiously, with an eye on the laden hoard-carts and stumbling pack horses, still muddied to their bellies with the river slime. They kept to the high trees, where damp leaves carpeted the chink and clatter of their passing. Smoke hung over burnt parishes close by, the stench lingering in their nostrils. Gytha caught glimpses of London as they moved along the hillside. Edmund pointed to the West Minster where they had watched their father crowned barely one year before. Now, thought Gytha, they skulked like brigands.

She glanced at her grandmother. The Old Lady, mother of heroes, pushing her horse on through the brambly undergrowth, muttering cold Danish oaths when it shied at ducks flighted from a pond. Gytha wondered how it must feel to lose three sons in one battle. Was it three times worse than the pain she felt losing her father? 'How could it be worse?' she thought.

Scouts brought them bleak news. There was no food, they said. Fresh provender for men or horses might be days away. Death was everywhere, they said. The Normans had left a scorch of devastation. From Canterbury to London, the women had been raped, old men killed or cruelly maimed, farmsteads burnt, the harvest stolen and the cattle driven off. With the hard winter upon them, the people wept, not knowing how to survive till spring.

Gytha sat silently as Godwine, her grandmother and the leather-caped thegns gathered in Council to debate whether to press on to Winchester and raise an army, or ride into London to declare Godwine King of the English.

Godwine to be their King and Ring-Giver! Hurrah, she thought and looked eagerly at Magnus and Edmund. They too leaned forward, excited. Then the Twice Scarred Thegn spoke.

'My Earl Godwine, sire,' he said, picking words that none dared say. 'Loyalty must be in the warrior and wisdom in the man. The thegns of England who swore fealty to the Bastard Duke hold the Aethling boy, Edgar, blood-heir to King Edward, as their rightful king.'

Motionless, Gytha watched Godwine's fury over-brim.

'Thegn,' he yelled, leaping to his feet, 'Harold, my father, took the king's helm, consecrated and anointed, as King Edward wished it on his deathbed. Harald Sigurdsson Hardradr, then this Bastard Duke William would seize it, and now you say King Harold's son must stand aside to this Aethling Edgar. We shall ride to London and the people will flock to us, not the foreigners. No, Thegn. God ordained the crown-helm stays with Godwine Haroldson.'

Magnus jumped up shouting 'The king shall hold the kingdom,' 'The king shall hold the kingdom' until Edmund pulled him down, protesting as always. Gytha held her breath, shocked at her brother's disrespect, shocked too at the Old Thegn's words. She knew the boy Edgar, ward of her Aunt Queen Edith. 'He is too young,' she thought. 'Godwine is our rightful King.' She felt it passionately, with vehemence. 'Godwine is our rightful king.'

There was a long pause. The Company of English was silent. Wind rustled the last-leaved trees as crows bickered and squawked high above them. All waited.

'Very well, Earl Godwine,' said the Thegn, holding God-wine in his grim gaze.

The Old Lady, Mother of Heroes, stood, and turning to speak to the Thegn directly said 'none present here doubt your loyalty, wisdom or courage.'

Thegn Eadric, turning to Godwine, said sharply, 'Godwine, do not enter London. A king without an army is no king. Your youth walks you into a trap. The Bastard Duke will spring at his pleasure.'

'Aye, grandmother,' said Godwine, knowing not to argue. 'but I am the rightful king and Ring-Giver.'

She looked at Godwine, understanding his fury and his humiliation.

'Be patient,' said the Old Lady, softening slightly. 'You are too young to take up the mantle of kingship, a task that needs wisdom beyond your years. Let your beard thicken and you will be King.'

Reluctantly, Godwine yielded. They would press on west to Winchester, foraging as best they could. Gytha's heart sank. In London, bed and dry clothes were a ride away.

'The Lord will provide,' said Aunt Gunhild mildly, crossing herself.

'He had better,' said the Twice Scarred Thegn.

'Amen,' the others replied.

Hunger forced them out of the bracken woods and down to the Thames meadows. Here, where the tide-reach ended, boats lay scattered on the bank, each with its planking smashed – the work of William's men. Few buildings remained untorched. There were people; too weak to flee, starving like the dogs sniffing at the carcasses of beasts. The stench of burnt thatch was everywhere, stinging their eyes and catching in their throats. Gytha held her cowl across her face, glad of the jewelled wounding-knife at her belt.

'There is nothing for us here. Press on,' said Godwine, as the Company picked its way past blackened walls that had been homes, swords unsheathed, axes and lances ready.

Something caught Gytha's eye, a sudden movement to her side. Godwine swore as a stone struck him hard on the helmet with a clang. 'Ambush!' he shouted. All turned, looking for the attack, but no ambush came. Instead, an urchin darted from a shed and hurled another sling stone.

This time it was the Twice Scarred Thegn who cursed loudly. He sped off in pursuit and a moment later he was back, a ragged boy with sacking on his feet dangling from his mighty arm like a wriggling worm. Godwine's hounds, their leashes tighter than bow strings, strained to leap at this prey. The Thegn threw the boy furiously to the ground, pinning him with his sword. Dismounting, he pulled the wretch's head back by his hair and pressed his blade to the boy's neck.

'Stinks like a pig!' he shouted. 'And he can die like one.'

'No!' shouted Gytha, jumping from her horse. 'Don't!' The Old Thegn wavered. 'Don't kill him!

'Ask him what he knows,' said Godwine, 'speak boy,' he ordered.

Dragging the boy back on his feet, the Thegn cuffed him hard. The boy grunted, shielding himself with a skinny arm.

'Are there Normans here, boy?' said Godwine, swearing at his dogs.

The boy said nothing. The Thegn struck him again, harder this time. 'Speak, wretch,' he ordered, but the boy only honked and mewed in reply. 'Stinks like a pig and sounds like a pig. He's no use to us, he's an idiot. Let us kill him and be gone from here,' said Godwine.

'If you kill him, we are no better than the Normans,' said Gytha, listening to the strange honking the boy made, opening his mouth wide and pointing a dirty finger at his teeth.

'He's hungry,' Marcus jeered. 'And so am I.'

'No,', replied Gytha. 'Maybe he cannot speak, maybe he's dumb.'

Magnus scoffed, 'You're dumb.'

Grabbing the boy's chin in his fist, the Old Thegn twisted his head this way and that and swore. 'The devil curse them,' he said in amazement. 'His tongue's cut out; with a knife, and not a sharp one.'

Gytha slid from the mare for a closer look and winced. A quivering blood-stump filled the boy's mouth, where a pink tongue should have been. 'Ugh. Why would they do that?'

'So that he can tell no tales,' said her grandmother impatiently. 'Enough. Let us go.'

'Leave the wretch,' said Godwine, swinging his horse around.

'The boy bolted towards the shed. Gytha hesitated. 'Wait!' she called, but the boy sped off between the houses. Kicking her horse on, she followed him as he ran, catching a glimpse as he vanished behind a shed.

Not even waiting for her Radknight and defying shouts to stop, Gytha approached the shed, her wounding-knife drawn, and pulled at the broken door.

'Boy,' she shouted, 'come out, I will not harm you.'

Inside, rosy as cheeks on a frosty morning, was a mound of windfall apples, and from behind the apples came an unmistakeable sound and smell. There, in a hurdle pen, was a fat black sow waffling its nose at them. Hiding behind it was the boy.

They made their camp in the ruined village and set about the butchery. Women went to the river for water and ripped planking from the broken boats for the fire. Some men stood guard; others bound oars with rope to make trestles. Knives were given a last stroke over whet-stones, buckets were readied to catch the scarlet blood-fountain jetting from the sow's neck. As it squealed and kicked its last, half a dozen men, blood to their elbows, forced a sturdy oar through the carcass, end to end. They hoisted the sow – mud, bristles and all – onto the trestles and the roasting began. Others scoured the ruins about them, some returning with flagons of mead and apple wine which the Normans had missed.

The fire smoked, sputtered and hissed. The Company drank. The pig turned from black to gold. Impatient men poked it with their spear tips, their hunger made unbearable by the glorious smell of crisping fat that oozed from within. At last the embers died, the juices ran clear and each man and woman stepped forward according to their rank for their share. The noble ladies and collar thralls chewed the sweet flesh, the scalding, crackling grease running down their chins and dripping on their clothes. All the while the urchin boy, now tied hand and foot, howled like a wild animal, tear-rivers running down each grimy cheek. Gytha felt sorry for him. He was about her age, she reckoned.

'I wonder what his name is?' she said, bending to give the boy meat on the tip of her jewelled wounding-knife. The boy jerked his head away.

'Ask him,' said Magnus, and the others laughed.

'Not funny, Magnus, but he must have a name.'

'We won't ever know,' said Edmund, feeding a sliver of meat to his falcon. 'You know, I think the sow suckled him. How else could he be alive? He cannot live on apples, and I doubt he can chew. He must have sucked at her milk teats. He's small, but he is not starving, is he?'

Looking down at the wretch at her feet, Gytha was stunned.

'You mean,' she said wonderingly, 'the sow suckled him like a whelping bitch, like a mother takes a baby to her breast?'

'That is disgusting,' said Magnus. 'Sucking on a pig's tit.'

'Oh, may the Lord forgive us,' said Gytha as the truth struck her. 'That's why he cries so. That sow was mother to him. He fed her apples and she kept him warm and gave him her milk. That stinking pen is his home. Oh Lord, forgive us!' She crossed herself. 'We've killed and eaten his mother.'

'That's a blasphemy, don't talk so stupid, Gytha,' said Magnus. 'It's not his mother, it was a pig!' But Gytha was thinking of her mother, her gentle swan, her eyes so full of love as she combed the little knots from Gytha's long hair and sang to her as she lay down to sleep. Here there was nothing of warmth or tenderness; just endless rain, blood and harsh men's voices. The sow was all the boy had.

'So why did he try to kill Godwine with a sling shot?' Asked Magnus, 'he nearly got himself killed.'

'He wasn't trying to kill Godwine or the Twice Scarred
Thegn Eadric,' Gytha explained. 'He was calling for help. He
never thought we would stuff ourselves on his sow. We cannot
leave him. He will starve to death.'

She had to make it right. It was her duty as a Christian
woman. Her mother had taught her that.

'We take the Pig-boy with us,' she announced.

PART ONE CHAPTER FIVE

A TRAITOR IN
THE FAMILY

ON THEY PRESSED, PASSING more burnt villages and stead-ings which marked the Bastard William's bloody march. Not all had perished. Ragged men, with nothing save clubs, a sharpened thrusting stick or scythe joined the Golden Dragon of Wessex as the Company made their way westward to Win-chester, Capital of England.

Gytha had lost count of the days.

At a farmstead beneath the chalk ridge, Godwine shouted to halt. 'Let's get out of this rain. We'll ride on to Winchester in the morning.' Tomorrow, Gytha would meet her Aunt Queen Edith, ring-adorned widow of King Edward and sister to her father, King Harold. What would she be like? Gytha wondered whether she would be like her father. She would tell her aunt of the hole in her middle where her heart should be. So recently widowed and with her brothers dead, she would understand the pain.

As they ate, Gytha turned to her brother saying,

'Godwine. Please bring our mother and little Hilde to us.'

'How' snapped Godwine. 'How can we bring them? If we send men back now? I cannot spare any men. They will be killed or worse by the first Norman they meet. It's impossible,

Gytha. Put it out of your head. We will get her when it's safe to do so, I've said it a hundred times.'

Try as she might, Gytha could not stop great tears welling up and rolling down her cheeks. She sniffed hard, wiping her nose on her sleeve.

'Oh, stop your snivelling,' said Godwine, putting a flagon to his lips. There was silence. There was no sympathy, and no support from Edmund nor Magnus either. Gytha was crushed. She stared into the wet logs spitting and hissing in the hearth. Did they not need their mother with them?

It was The Radknight Wulfwyn's idea.

'Lord,' he said respectfully addressing Godwine, 'let me fetch my lady your mother. I would gladly go. I can move swiftly; they will not harm me.'

'Wulfwyn, If they catch you, they will kill you,' said Edmund. 'How will you bring our mother back?'

'I carry the warrant with Duke William's seal I carried for your gracious mother at the slaughter field. God willing, I can pass where others cannot.'

'It's a simpleton's plan,' said Godwine. 'Our mother is safe where she is. The monks guard her, and the holy sisters comfort and care for her.'

Then the Old Lady spoke. 'The Duke may yet take your mother hostage, Godwine. The boy should go and if he dies, so be it.' She crossed herself. 'And may the most high God who knows all secrets go with you, boy.'

'Then I too will go,' said the Twice Scarred Thegn Eadric, 'to bring your lady mother back to us. Death holds no fear for me.'

'Thegn, you stay here and protect us,' said the Old Lady. 'There will be fighting aplenty for you before this journey is done and we return to our home.'

And so, it was settled. Carrying the warrant, the Radknight Wulfwyn would go to Waltham. Gytha gave him her blessing, hardly able to contain her thanks.

'I want you to take a servant,' she told him. Leaving the barn she ran across the yard. Ducking under the awning of a rough shelter Gytha found the Pig-boy curled on the ground, with a dirty cloak for a blanket.

'Get up, Pig-boy!' she chivvied, prodding him with her foot. Reluctantly he got to his feet, his head bowed, cap in hand. 'I saved you, now I have a task for you.'

The next morning, as the Company of the Golden Dragon of Wessex prepared for the last leg to Winchester, Wulfwyn made his farewells and promised to return from Waltham with the Lady Edith Swan-neck and little Hilde. Gytha watched him mount his small horse and swing it around. He bowed to her grandmother as he passed, then to Aunt Gunhild, who signed the cross and wished him Godspeed, and to Gytha too. She opened her mouth to wish him well, but no words came, usurped by a burning in her cheeks. And he was gone. She watched as he disappeared back up the road with the Pig-boy on a mule and wondered if she might see them again, perhaps, and she closed her eyes tight, with her gentle swan. 'Oh Lord, keep them safe,' she prayed.

At Winchester lay the mortal remains of King Alfred of Wessex. Here too were the bones of her grandfather, Earl Godwine, the shrewdest warrior lord in all of England. Gytha looked across the small valley at the city wall and watch towers. The great Minster was in the centre, with their thatched hall next to it and many smaller buildings huddled around.

'The mother church with whelps at her teats,' said Edmund, Turul on his arm. Magnus laughed. The rain had moved off behind them and the sky was the palest washed-out blue. There was still a spiteful breeze from the north-east and she was glad of her wadmal cape.

Between them and the town earth wall was a bridge and track to the gate.

'Look,' said Magnus, 'the gate is closed! And the wall manned.'

'As I feared,' said the Twice Scarred Thegn, calling the company to halt.

Godwine conferred with his Grandmother, saying he and Edmund would ride forward alone to ask the Queen their aunt permission to enter. But as he spoke, the great gate swung open. Gytha watched a party of horsemen clatter over the bridge and up the steep slope towards them, one wearing a rich cape and brightly coloured leggings. A priest rode with him. The Old Lady watched as the party slid from their horses and bowed low to her.

'Great Lady, I bring you greetings from our Queen Edith,' said the fine-looking townsman. 'He looks so clean,' Gytha thought, 'But we are dirty and road-weary.'

As she admired his fur-lined cloak, calves bound in fresh strapping over new hide boots. A Frankish longsword hung low from a buckler studded with coloured stones of great worth. He wore no war-shirt, and at his neck there was a large silver broach with a circle of figures to clasp his cloak.

How she dreamed of shedding her damp, mud-spattered lice clothes for a flaxen slip and a clean wool smock.

'My lady,' he was saying 'Duke William of Normandy has shown mercy to the people of Winchester and to our Queen your daughter.' The man paused, waiting for all about him to fall silent. 'and we, the Byrh of Winchester, and our lady the crowned Queen Edith, have sworn fealty to the Duke as rightful heir to England.'

There was a gasp. Gytha glanced at Godwine. His hand was poised over the jewel stone of his sword.

Fury flashed across Old Lady's lined face. 'And the Treasury that is ours? Is that forfeit to the Bastard William?

'No, Great Lady,' said the Townsman defiantly, 'the Queen keeps that which is hers.'

Gytha listened intently, knowing something terrible had happened but struggling to grasp what it meant for her.

A second man, a black-robed monk, stepped forward. He addressed the Old Lady with a bow. 'Greatest Lady, Eadgytha Thorkelsdaughter,' he began, calling her by her full name. 'Most noble ring-adorned wife to Earl Godwine, may his soul rest in peace, kinswoman to King Cnut the Great, mother of our late King and our Queen. We have suffered untold deaths in the service of your son, King Harold. Our most holy abbot and twelve of our order, most gallant brothers, also died at the Senlac slaughter field defending these shores from the Norman raiders. Few Wessex men returned from that service. Now homes are hollow without their menfolk, filled only with the wails of women and hungry children. Canterbury, Dover, and London have surrendered.' There was a murmur from those around. The monk raised his voice. 'Great lady, against every wish and sinew of our hearts, Winchester too swore fealty to the duke, in sacred ritual of Christian men. The duke, on his part, has confirmed all land and dignities remain to our crowned queen, Edith.'

None spoke at the monk's words. The gravity of the betrayal weighed heavy.

'We came to our capital as friends and brothers seeking sanctuary. We leave as foes,' said the Twice Scarred Eadric and spat on the ground.

The Old Lady, wife of Godwine, Earl of Wessex, barely paused. Winchester had been her home. Her husband was buried in the Minster in front of them.

'My daughter! My daughter has sworn fealty to the Bastard William to keep herself in furs and jewels, when the finest men in England lie dead? My daughter has done that?' She was shouting. 'And you,' she cried, arching a jewelled finger at the townsman, 'you have sworn fealty to save your lily skin. I don't doubt you all flocked to bend your knee like flies on an oozing sore. You are traitors, and you will die a traitor's death. Now leave, before I have your eyes put out and your heads on a stake, and drown your kin in the river where they belong. Go!'

The two hounds at Godwine's side stood rigidly alert. The Old Thegn put his hand to his longsword, but Godwine stopped him. 'No,' said Godwine, 'we give them safe passage. Let them wait a little longer to feel our steel on their necks, so help me God. We will go to the Queen. I am the rightful heir to the throne of England. She will support me, not this foreigner.'

'Thegn Eadric, Roni, take the hearthguard,' said the Old Lady.

'No, Mother of Heroes,' said Godwine, 'we go alone. The Queen will not harm us, her kin, and risk the wrath of all English folk. Edmund, Magnus you will be my hearthguard.'

'What about me?' blurted Gytha. She hadn't meant to speak; it just came out. 'She is my aunt too and we vowed, remember?'

'Take her,' said the Old Lady.

Gytha's heart leapt. A roof, and a roaring hearth awaited her. She would meet the Queen, her aunt, her father's sister, and maybe talk to her of him. She wanted to do that. She needed to do that.

'Beware, young lords,' said the old Thegn. 'there is no warmer welcome than the smile of treachery. We keep this insolent townsman until you return to us safely. '

Gytha's joy soon turned to fear as they rode into the walled town. There was no welcome, no guard of honour to escort them. Just barbs, jeers and insults from the wall. 'Be gone,' shouted a woman. 'have we not suffered enough?' asked another as Gytha passed, nervously peering into alleyways. They had been cautious, fearing ambush before, but this was different. Here she was among her kin, this was their town, yet were hated. Magnus swore under his breath, adjusting his helm-strap nervously, but Gytha said nothing as they approached the carved and plastered hall, the finest in all the South that had been her Grandfather's when he ruled all Wessex. Guards greeted them coldly, in a manner unbefitting of the king's sons and his oldest daughter. The priest left them to wait outside.

'My Lady,' he said to Gytha on his return, 'Our anointed queen, your aunt, wishes you to attend her now. My Lords, our Queen will summon you.' Godwine was about to speak, but Gytha touched his arm and said 'fear not, brother.'

The queen had grey-blonde hair, visible beneath her cowl, and she wore a woollen over-mantle of virgin blue, thickly bordered with golden thread. Two golden broaches were linked beneath each shoulder by a rope of precious stones, and around her waist was a slim golden belt to cinch her tunic. Her arms were hidden beneath full sleeves and her hands were heavy with rings. She looked like her father. Gytha stared, then shifted her glance to take in the queen's chamber. Each wall was draped in heavy tapestries worked with gold. There was a window at one end, not vellum, but with glass panes the colour of the sea and honey. There was no smoking hearth, instead a bake oven of clay heated the room and golden dishes glistened on an embroidered altar wrap beneath the crucifix. It was so lovely. She wanted a chamber like it.

'You know who I am, child.' Gytha nodded nervously, tearing herself back to the moment, conscious of her shabbiness amid the splendour, 'I am your Aunt Edith Godwinesdaughter,' said the queen. Her speech was low and measured. Gytha froze, all courtesy owing to the consecrated dowager queen of the English, anointed wife of King Edward, failed her.

'God willing,' said the queen, 'you will stay with us here, child, where you will be safe. Your mother and your little sister Gunhild will join us soon,' Gytha's heart leapt at this, 'but your brothers and grandmother, Mother of Heroes, must leave immediately, for they are neither welcome nor safe.'

Gytha still said nothing. The older woman went on, resting her jewelled hands on her lap. 'Your father, my brother, was,' she hesitated, as if picking her words carefully, 'a great king, from whom greatness was snatched.' She paused a moment, staring at Gytha, and getting no answer she changed the subject. 'You have no clothes, so we have plenty for you to wear, though you are taller than I remember. Like your mother.'

'Thank you, Noble Aunt,' replied Gytha. There was a long pause while they stared at each other, searching as kin do for the little secrets of affinity. Her eyes, as cerulean as Gytha's own, the set of her chin, the tall forehead, were all so familiar.

'Is Aethling Edgar to be king, now father is dead?' asked Gytha, awkwardly.

The queen smiled grimly. 'No, child. Some wish it, but he is too young. Not so much older than you. What are you, thirteen?' Gytha nodded. 'There is to be a new king and Ring-Giver of all English folk. He will be crowned in the West Minster at London this Christmas Day, where my husband Edward and your father too were crowned.'

'Who?' asked Gytha, innocently.

'Duke William of Normandy.' The Queen replied.

'The man who killed father is to be king of the English and crowned in our Great Minster where father was crowned not a year back.' Gytha felt the hurt rise, gripping her by the throat. She clenched her fists, steeling herself not to show it.

'Yes, child, I am bidden to bear witness. But let us not contend the will of God, the great creator, for that is not our place.'

Anger reddened Gytha's cheeks. 'Grandmother, Mother of Heroes, said you swore fealty to the foreigner to save your skin and our estates for yourself.'

Anger flashed across the queen's face. 'Child, you don't know of what you speak, be gone, there is no room for you here. Take your brothers.' And with that, her Aunt Edith Widowed Queen of the English, waved Gytha from her golden chamber, back into the winter rain.

PART ONE CHAPTER SIX

THE PAINTED
CELT PRINCE

GYTHA WAS OVERWHELMED WITH guilt. She felt all eyes were on her as Godwine described the jeers and taunts of the townspeople,

'Not all,' said Edmund. 'Some bowed as we passed.'

'Not many, I thought they would tear me from my horse and beat me to death,' said Magnus, turning his fear into a boast.

'It was my fault. I made her angry. Mother of Heroes, I said what you had said and she got angry with me,' said Gytha.

The Old Lady glanced at her. Gytha's heart was pounding. She knew her grandmother would berate her. But she didn't.

'Child,' she said icily, 'my daughter the Queen has betrayed the memory of your father and her father my husband and every Englishman who died to rid this island of the Bastard Duke. You, child, gave voice to her conscience.'

'Out of the mouth of babes and sucklings,' Growled the Old Thegn.

'Amen to that,' said Godwine bitterly. 'Let us talk no more of it. Gytha, stop snivelling.'

The situation was grave. The wealth of English kings, The royal treasury itself, was now lost to the Bastard Duke, leaving

Gytha, a child woman aching for her lost mother; the three fatherless boys bent on vengeance; and the Old Lady, reaved of four sons, betrayed by her royal daughter, thwarted even in her wish to pray at her husband's grave in Winchester, the city she had enriched with offerings for his soul. With all hope of raising an army now gone they could not remain as outlaws on that hillside. Exeter to the west was their best hope.

'By the grace of God,' said Godwine, 'we did not put our trust in the people of London.'

The irony was not lost on Edmund. 'It was you who had suggested it,' he said mockingly. 'Didn't he, Turul?'

'Shut up, Edmund,' said his elder brother. 'And get that crapping thing out of here.' Edmund ignored him.

Gytha shuddered and scratched her head. She had been dreaming of fresh clothing, a soft woollen tunic, a light green mantle with a broad ribbon of embroidered white meadowsweet and flecks of gold thread at the neck and cuffs. And of washing her hair, combing it dry in front of a crackling hearth, and having a thrall woman plait it for her. Instead ten more days on the road in filthy louse-filled clothes was all she had to look forward to.

'The Bastard Duke is to take father's crown-helm for his own on Christmas Day,' she said 'Queen Edith is to be witness, she told me.'

'Wife, sister, traitor,' said the Old Lady bitterly. 'She is an *obstinate and malevolent queen who will do anything she can against her lord and whole people*'.

'Grandmother, Mother of Heroes,' said Magnus, 'what if we find the gates of Exeter closed to us too and traitors on that wall?'

The Old Lady cleared her throat. 'Child, my people of Exeter, High Byrh of the West, will not swear fealty to the Bastard William.'

'Great Lady,' said the Old Thegn, 'a painted warrior from the West has joined our company.'

'Fetch him,' said Godwine, 'He will tell us if Exeter will stand with us or kneel to the Bastard.'

A stranger entered. Under the thick blanket draped across his massive shoulders, Gytha could see he was covered in swirling tattoos. He stopped, bowed, and waited. He had thick black hair, yet his eyes were green, set deep in his square head. But for the wounding-knife at his slim waist, he was unarmed. If he was nervous in the presence of the Old Lady and her noble sons, he hid it. What he lacked in height, he made up for in the sturdiness of his legs, and the sinewed strength of his forearms which were encased in silver bracelets.

Gytha stared at him, fascinated. This was not a mouse haired Saxon or red-blond Dane. This was a painted Celt. She had heard much of these wild warriors but had never seen one. She watched as he stood easily in front of her grandmother, legs set apart, laughter lines about his eyes. He was beautiful, she thought.

'My name is Baladrddellt rac Denau, Splintered Spear of the South son of Petroc Baladrddellt ap Clemen.' His voice seemed to rumble up from his broad chest. Gytha caught Magnus' glance, both of them astonished at this powerful fighting man.

'Well, Prince Baladrddellt rac Denau,' said the Old Lady, 'welcome. Tell me, do the people of Exeter not have a special relationship with the widowed Queen Edith, my daughter?'

The fighting man from the west thought for a moment before answering. 'Great lady,' he said, 'an absent queen is less without her dwelling place.' Exeter, High Byrh of the West is full of zeal. Rich, numerous and valiant. All ranks are joined to withstand the stranger to the utmost.'

'Well spoken,' said the Old Thegn. 'We should go to Exeter, now. We cannot stay here on this open down, my lady. The Normans can attack us from behind or from the coast and all will be lost before it has begun.'

'Aye,' said the burnished Roni, 'we can move quickly if we follow the stone road of the giants to Sarum or else we will drown in the white mud.'

'Wise counsel, Thegns,' said the Old Lady. 'There is danger here now. I thank you, Baladrddellt rac Denau. With God's will, your trust in the people of Exeter will be justified.'

'I place myself and my men at your service, my lady,' he said formally, bowing deeply to the Old Lady and nodding to Godwine. Gytha lowered her eyes, embarrassed at her dirty, travel-worn clothes, and hoped the Celt Prince would not notice her.

As if reading Gytha's mind, The Old Lady said loudly, 'clean clothes, fresh washed hair and feather bedding must wait, child. We leave at dawn.' The Celt Prince guffawed. Gytha blushed crimson.

That night she lay awake awhile, her heart heavy. Humiliated not once, but twice, when neither had been her fault. In the morning there was only the road and the rain. How would the Radknight and her mother ever find her if they left Winchester now? Gytha pulled her rug over her head, overwhelmed once more. The nun, her aunt Gunhild, knelt by her as she slept. 'The Lord bless you and keep you, the Lord make his face to shine upon you and be gracious to you, the Lord lift up his countenance upon you and give you peace.' And with her thumb she made the sign of the holy cross on Gytha's smooth brow and wiped away a wisp of golden hair stuck to her grimy, tear-tracked cheek.

*   *   *

Their defeat, more bitter than the bitterest herbs in Exodus, was made worse still by the jeers and taunts from the wall where once their Golden Dragon of Wessex flew. King Harold's family, his mother, daughter and three sons, did not look up as they passed the barred gate of their former capital, at the head of a rabble of Englishmen, their families, and a handful of painted Celts. Leafless beech, oak, elm and alder of the valley gave way to lifeless scrub gorse and thistle. Ahead was the priory at Wilton. The weather was brighter, but where the rain had soaked them, now a rude wind bit at their clothes with icicle teeth. A dusting of snow lay on the rough grass, and chalk mud sucked at the feet of each man, woman and laden beast till all were smeared in a hard-grey paste as the burnished Roni had warned. In places, smooth flagging stones and cobbles from ancient times hurried their progress as the track rose onto the high downland, with its wind-smooth tops, hidden coombs and the soundless mounds of long-dead kings.

'Look, Gytha,' said Magnus, 'I'll wager you don't know what those are.'

'Don't know and don't care,' replied Gytha, her teeth chattering. 'I want to get to a hall like the queen's and get warm.'

'Graves of heathen kings,' said Magnus knowledgeably.

There were snow dusted mounds to her left and right. There were so many that Gytha wondered how many kings there had been in heathen times.

'But not real kings like father.'

'None compared to your father,' said the Burnished Roni. 'None so great, so warlike or greatly feared as your father.'

A winter white hare jumped from between Gytha's horse's legs and sped away. In a flash Edmund pulled off Turul's plumed hood, eased her jesses and, with a skyward sweep of his left arm, let the falcon fly.

Thegn Eadric, his beard streaming like his horse's mane, watched as the magnificent bird jinked low after the fleeing hare, matching every darting turn and finally in a lightning assault, struck it from behind, sending the hare rolling over and over. Turul banked round again, white underfeathers flashing, to plunge her talons into her prey which was now twitching and quivering its last. It never stood a chance. As Edmund galloped up, Turul was atop her quarry with her wings and tail outstretched, picking at the thick fur with her curved beak to snap its spine. The stress of the road was no place for Turul and she pecked harshly at Edmund's outstretched hand, so he left her to enjoy her winnings in the blood-speckled snow, before summoning her to his glove once more.

'Glory of Kings, that was a fine sight,' said the Twice Scarred Thegn, breathless at the fury of the kill. 'This saker your father gave you is a fine gift, boy, more deadly even than the stooping Peregrine, though not as swift perhaps. You have trained her well, young Lord.' Edmund beamed his pleasure and stroked the now sated bird on his forearm. Turul's kill lifted all their spirits.

'Father said she comes from the Wild Field, a treeless land, far from here, where horsemen shoot arrows backwards,' said Edmund

'This is a wild field,' said Gytha, looking about her at the treeless hills.

'Shoot their arrows backwards!' said Magnus.

'Aye,' said the Old Thegn, 'The wild field beyond the end of Christendom.'

Magnus scoffed. 'There is no place beyond the end of Christendom, only hell itself, Thegn Eadric.'

'If you don't believe it, ask Turul where she comes from,' said Gytha, her teeth chattering.

'Don't be silly,' said Magnus, 'that stupid bird cannot talk.'

'Crows can speak, and magpies too,' said Edmund. But Gytha's thoughts had turned to the message dove that brought the news of her father's death, and no more was said of birds.

They left the snow ground, dropping to a stream and causeway over a marsh. Here there were fish traps of withy-wood and a collar thrall to mind them. Talk turned from their betrayal to sport, as men who live to fight will do.

'I fancy angling here on a summer's evening,' said the Twice Scarred Thegn Eadric. 'This must be the clearest gravel stream in all England, with trout as thick as an arm.'

'Whose arm, Thegn?' asked the painted Celt warrior with a deep chuckle, 'mine or the Lady Gytha's?' The men laughed and talked of feathered decoys and furtive hooks to beckon a trout from its weed bed. Magnus, his boy-brain hungry to every detail pestered the Old Thegn about knots, flies, catgut and canes. Gytha listened. There was nothing else to do and nobody to speak to. Her Grandmother was lost to her silent gloom, and Aunt Gunhild prayed as she rode.

Gytha day-dreamt of her other life, which faded with every mile west. She watched the painted Celtprince chatting easily with her brothers and noticed he had glanced at her a twice at least. She stopped looking at him.

'Horseman behind!' A shout from the rear of the Company stopped the talk of fishing. Godwine, Edmund and Magnus swung their horses back, followed by the painted Celtprince Baladrddellt, his battle-scarred shield-board at his arm, readying his lance as he galloped.

Bellowing, the Burnished Roni and the Twice Scarred Thegn ordered some men to the rear, and others to surround the noble ladies and the laden Hoard carts.

Gytha waited, all her senses sharp, the wounding-knife at her waist. Were they under attack? Who were these horsemen?

The guarding circle of fighters tightened, as some struggled to settle nervous horses. There was a squeal. Gytha's mare took fright and, throwing up its bridled head, struck her full in the face.

She struggled to stay in the felted saddle, but her muddied foot slipped from the stirrup. The whole incident lasted a moment. Gytha tumbled onto the track, striking her head on an ancient cobble. Half blinded, with her eyes streaming from the blow and crimson blood spattered on her cloak, Gytha passed out.

When she came to, Wulfwyn, her Radknight, was kneeling over her, pressing a bloody wad of tussock moss to her head. Gytha cried out, the pain forgotten, 'Is mother here?' But the young life-ward said nothing. She asked Wulfwyn again, panic rising inside her. Still he said nothing.

'No, my Lady,' he answered awkwardly. 'Your fair mother remains at Waltham.' At first, Gytha did not understand. If Wulfwyn was here, then her mother must be too. He wouldn't return without her. Then his words struck home, more cruelly than any blow.

'But why?' she sobbed faintly, 'Where is she? Why isn't she here?'

Kind arms took her, lifted her and placed her most gently into a cart where she lay as if dead beneath a sheepskin.

They took Gytha to the Great Priory at Wilton. The nuns tended her wound with balm of camomile, feverfew and goldenrod. Whether it was the blow to her head or to her heart they didn't know. But she did not stir the whole night nor the next day. Her brothers came to the vaulted cell, but Gytha could not be comforted despite Magnus admiring her two black eyes.

*   *   *

'Come,' said a novice, no older than her. 'Let us wash the blood from your hair and get you dressed. You must be starved. We must hurry, it will soon be Vespers.'

Gytha, her swollen eyes still barely open, spent the evening in the guest hall with her brothers. She sat quietly near the great hearth with Godwine's dogs crowding her for a share of stewy broth. The boys too were subdued. Godwine buffed the hilt of his longsword while Edmund and Magnus played draughts without the usual whooping and taunts. They knew the respite would be brief. They were in danger and they had to move on.

The Old Lady looked up from her embroidery. 'Child,' she said, looking at Gytha. 'you will stay here in the company of nuns at the abbess's invitation.' Gytha's mind raced. Was she not to leave with the boys?

'Mother of Heroes, am I to be left here at Wilton, now?' She asked meekly, fearing the Old Lady's anger.

'Aye, Child, it was your father's wish for you and your little sister to be schooled in mathematics, astronomy, Latin, poetry and needlework.'

'But Grandmother, things are different now.' Her voice trailed away. Gytha knew better than to argue. She knew of her father's plan for her schooling, but she had no wish for the cloistered life with its plain food, scratchy clothes and hours of silent contemplation. Her dream was to splash in the stream, to gallop the green downs with her brothers, to wander past the fishing boats pulled up the strand, the air rich with gull cries and hot tar. Above all, she longed to be that girl again, back in the High Hall with its tapestries and treasures, laughing, complaining, and yelping as her mother combed the knots from her hair.

Everyone was dressed for the road but her. Gytha, wearing the borrowed tunic, was summoned back to the Hall by Wulfwyn, her loyal Radknight, A sickening pang engulfed her. They would leave her. She was so caught up in her distress that she did not notice the towering monk in a ring shirt, bearing a fearsome mace.

'Look who's here,' whispered Edmund.

It was Blaecman of Abingdon, priest and shoulder-friend to her father, a man of God and a warrior. But for the black cassock, he looked like no other priest Gytha knew. He smiled at her with a nod of his sheep-shorn head.

'Welcome Father Blaecman of Abingdon. I thank you for your courage and fealty to my father that brings you here to us today,' said Godwine, hailing him stiffly.

'Father Blaecman has something to share with you,' said the Old Lady. 'It concerns your mother.'

Blaecman pulled a torn vellum from his belted tunic and unrolled it. It told a devastating story. Their noble mother Edith Swan-neck, it said, had not recovered since they left Waltham. She had sunk deeper into the black contemplation that had overcome her since her return from the bloody slaughter field. The nuns were caring for her but she had not spoken, nor did she show interest in the world, not even in her youngest child Hilde, their sister.

The Towering Mace Monk paused, thanked the Radknight for bringing the message, then read some more. 'The duke came to Waltham in search of the brothers. His men had killed all who opposed them, even those who sought sanctuary in the new church. Then the duke honoured their father's grave with prayer even as his men stole from the glebe barns, fired them, and have left all to starve this winter.'

Blaecman paused again. 'There is more. "Then further disaster befell us. He ordered that as unanointed wife, the Lady Edith Swan-neck's lands and farms were given to their new Lord at Waltham, the Breton count, Ralph de Gael."'

Edmund put his arm around his sister. Magnus, so full of frustration and anger, blurted something about returning to avenge his mother, but Godwine held his counsel.

'Will our mother be safe?' asked Edmund, turning to the Radknight Wulfwyn.

'Yes, Lord,' he replied. 'With God's will no harm will come to her; the duke swore it.'

Godwine sneered. 'The Bastard Duke need not keep our mother safe. He has stolen all that is hers, she has nothing more to live for.'

'But she has us!' cried Gytha. 'You should never have left her there, Godwine!'

She buried her head in Edmund's shoulder. Godwine flinched at her words.

'We had no choice,' said Godwine, composing himself.

'Is there nothing to be done? Can we not repurchase what is ours? There is gold enough in the Godwineson Hoard.' Asked Edmund.

'Yes,' said the towering mace-monk. 'Forty golden crowns will get you your lands back, but only if you swear fealty to the duke.'

The logs on the hearth crackled and spat. No one spoke.

'Gold?' said the Mother of Heroes, 'Our gold? Never. Let him feel the tip of a Godwineson sword.'

The group stood. Godwine gave the order to leave, Gytha recovered herself enough to blurt, 'Grandmother, Mother of Heroes, am I to be left here?'

The Old Lady turned – she was no taller than Gytha – and looked her directly in the face. 'It is best you remain,' she explained, 'until your mother is whole again.'

'As hostage? Grandmother, Mother of Heroes,' Gytha grabbed her veined hand.

'Here you will learn all the arts and skills of a lady.

How else will you make a good marriage, child?'

'But who am I to be married to? If you leave me here, you will make me the ring-adorned wife of a Norman. I would rather be dead.'

'Hush, Child,' said the Old Lady. 'We cannot take you. You will wait here for your sister and mother.'

Gytha stared at her grandmother, word robbed, her blue eyes wide. She didn't know what to do: wait for her mother among her father's enemies or leave with her brothers and not see her mother. She turned to her brothers, pleading for help. 'Why do you say nothing?'

Magnus shuffled, then shrugged his shoulders. Godwine wore the rigid mask of kingship. 'It is Grandmother's wish,' he said coldly.

'Edmund?' Her eyes met those of her brother beseechingly. 'You promised. We all four made a vow at Waltham under the Flinty Cross, before the Wielder of Glory. You cannot leave me here. You cannot. We vowed. You cannot break a vow.'

She was seized by terror now.

'If you raise an army against the duke, he will have me killed when he finds me here. Please, Godwine, take me with you!' Then, turning to Edmund, she pleaded, 'Would you leave me here alone, a postulant's veil over my head?'

'It is not my decision.' he answered lamely. 'Father wanted the nuns to educate you in the ways of womenfolk here at Wilton.'

Suddenly Gytha felt a deep anger swell within her. Composing herself, she spoke calmly, not begging, her voice low.

'Did we not vow to avenge the death of our father together? You abandoned our mother and sister at Waltham, and now you would abandon me also.' She breathed deeply as she chided them.

'Gytha! quiet your mouth,' said Godwine, but she would not be quiet.

'If you would cast me out, why not leave me with Queen Edith, to betroth me to a Norman?' She was shouting now. 'A Norman's wife! What will you do then, Godwine? Nothing!'

'Gytha!' said Godwine again, more sharply.

'Child, your tongue fights battles far hence,' said the monk, trying to calm her.

But she would not be calmed. 'Father, what does the Holy Church teach about vows?'

The warrior-monk looked at Gytha, slender as a willow, her braided plaits hanging straight down over her pale-green mantle to her waist, and met her sharp blue eyes.

'Why do you ask?' he said, but there was kindness in his voice.

'I want to know what the Holy Church teaches us about vows, father,' she repeated, her jaw set, bright spots of colour in her pale cheeks. Her gaze never left the warrior-monk's face as he spoke.

'Well, Gytha,' he said, 'a vow is a promise to God and the promise is binding.'

The boys were silent, listening, waiting.

'But what if we break a vow, father? What will God the Creator do to us?' she asked.

The monk pressed the tips of his fingers together and touched them to his lips. Again, his reply was cautious. 'A vow can be commuted but only to something equal or better.'

'So, you cannot break a vow, or you will be sent to eternal damnation?' This was more statement than question.

The Towering Mace Monk Blaecman was guarded, hesitant. 'Many, with all good intent, when they are young and zealous, make a vow to God who knows all secrets, intending to keep it for life.'

Gytha felt the frustration rising in her. Why would he not give a straight answer?

Edmund interrupted. 'Is it true a broken vow caused all that has happened to us?'

The warrior-monk nodded gravely. 'It is said your father forswore, on oath, the crown of England to Duke William. Then seized if for himself. "HAROLD SACRAMENTUM FECIT WILLELMO DUCI" Vows are broken. Man is fallible.'

'That's not true!' said Godwine, anger erupting as he spoke. 'My father swore no such thing. It was a lie to get the Pope's support for an attack on our English land. Ask my grand-mother, the Mother of Heroes. She will tell you.'

'But,' said Edmund, not to be side-tracked, 'if he broke his word, will father's soul be eternally damned?'

'He didn't break his word!' shouted Godwine, striking out at Edmund with his fist. Edmund jerked his head aside and the blow missed.

The monk stepped between them. 'Stop this,' he ordered. 'Your father had no choice. He was the prisoner of the duke. And the crown was not his to give. King Edward on his deathbed gave the crown of England to your father and the Witan upheld it. I was there.'

He paused, before continuing. 'However, the testament teaches us that if a man makes a vow in the presence of the Lord, he shall not break his word. The Apostle Matthew tells us "You shall not swear falsely, but shall perform to the Lord what you have sworn".'

'There!' Gytha said, getting the answer she wanted. Turning to Godwine, 'And you will go to hell if you break our vow. If you leave me here, you will be cast into the fiery pit.'

Godwine was word-robbed.

'Well?' Gytha demanded.

'Father, I will speak to our grandmother, Mother of Heroes,' said Godwine, turning to the Towering Monk. 'the girl is in danger if she stays here alone. We cannot protect her.'

'Gytha is right,' Edmund had been watching his sister, impressed. 'We have not protected our mother from the Norman outlanders, we must not repeat our failure with her now.'

Gytha's heart leapt at their words. She tried to hug Godwine, but he pushed her away.

The warrior-monk smiled. 'I hazard Gytha will ride with us and, with God's will, she will live free of this lustful invader. I too will speak to the Mother of Heroes.'

But when the monk informed the Old Lady of the threat to the child and offered his opinion that they should take her to Exeter, the Old Lady refused.

'She will make sanctuary here. It was her father's wish that she be schooled by the Wilton nuns. The abbess awaits her now.'

'Noble lady,' said the monk, 'it is not for me to gainsay the wishes of our departed King Harold for his daughter, but our mortal enemy is days away. We must not leave your granddaughter here at the Priory in the care of one who has betrayed our English cause and yielded to her brother's foe. What will befall her if we do?'

The Old Lady stared at the Towering Monk, her face expressionless. 'The Lord has seen fit to take all whom I loved. My only daughter Edith has turned against me. Good father, the three boys and Gytha are all that remain of my kin on this earth and you would talk to me of Gytha's safety?' She glared at the monk, but he did not stand down. 'Very well, I will relent, though her fate is no surer if she remains with us than if she stays here with the nuns. Come, we must leave. But think on this: who will take Gytha for their wife, without lands, her father dead, her mother robbed and now unschooled? Maybe better the wife to a Norman than no wife at all.'

Dressed like her brothers once more, Gytha walked her horse to the great priory gate, before mounting and turning west with the rabble Company of the English, under the Golden Dragon of Wessex, around her. She passed a laden cart on which was scratched *ego servus sum* in rough letters on the side. Standing on the shaft, reins in hand, was the Pig-boy. Bowing low, his mouth agape, he was making a strange honking sound. Gytha, embarrassed, looked away.

'I think he's honouring you, Gytha,' said Edmund, as Magnus laughed.

'That's stupid,' said Gytha. 'Make him go away. He sounds like a throttled goose.'

'Don't judge him so harshly, child,' said Aunt Gunhild. 'You saved him.'

Gytha, feeling chastened, rode on without saying much for a while,

'You help Pig-boys and Pig-boys help you, Gytha.' said Magnus. The brothers laughed; Gytha stared ahead and said nothing. They might mock her, but she would not grace them with a reply.

'But few Pig-boys can write "I am your slave" in the holy tongue of monks and clerks, can they?' said Aunt Gunhild softly.

The Bastard Duke, William of Normandy, was readying for his coronation as king and Ring-Giver of England and all English folk in London. The two days of rest at the Priory were quickly undone. The rain and the chill wind found the Company once more, for there was no shelter in the chalk hills. Here were few steadings, nor churches, nor barns to sleep in. Men slipped and fell in the churned muck; wheels came off; the carts, heel chains, quarter straps, shafts and traces snapped; the Golden Dragon of Wessex faltered, but, no matter how impatient they became, they could move no faster than the slowest cart. The Godwineson Hoard was all that remained to them. In time, the high chalk gave way to the folded coombs of the wood-green west, and the ancient stone roadway dwindled. Here there were villages, and dangers lay in wait. Baladrddellt rac Denau, Splintered Spear of the South, counselled them in his deep, musical voice to beware, 'lest the sight of so much gold and treasure in the hoard carts prove too tempting.' Guards were doubled, and thegns, fighting men and collar-thralls prayed that this devil journey might end. Then the rain that had been at their faces for a week eased. A watery sun appeared. It was a false friend, too weak to dry them, but it lifted their spirits. The temperature dropped and by morning the mud and puddles were frozen hard.

'I am done with riding and the road,' the Old Lady announced as they slipped and struggled up yet another slope and saw the white-waved sea for the first time. 'I tire of ruts and mud, framed between this nag's ears. Let us sail west, as is the way of my Spear-Dane people. Let a serpent headed knarr-boat rush us to Exeter to celebrate the twelve days. God provides us with His fair wind before the claw-hand Aegir, the storm bringer, returns.'

Gytha giggled, shocked at her grandmother's talk of Lord God in Heaven and sea gods beneath. Her Aunt Gunhild looked away, crossing herself, The Towering Mace Monk said nothing.

So, the Company split: Godwine and Edmund marched the main hoard west with the painted Celt, the Twice Scarred Thegn Eadric and the few hundred Englishmen who followed the Golden Dragon. The noble women would sail with

Wulfwyn the Radknight, Magnus and the Towering Monk Blaecman in a heavy sea knarr, now drawn up the beach. The Burnished Roni and the Hearthguard following in what boats they could buy or steal.

Gytha, her blood stirred, was frightened too. Desperate to leave the road, she now eyed the grey water with its curling tops and lost her nerve. To her surprise it was her Grandmother, the Old Lady, who mumbled words of comfort.

'You are the daughter of Ran, my child,' she said in Danish. 'The wave-strife will not trouble you. Brine is the blood of Northmen, the wet-cold sea is our road.'

The short daylight was fading as Gytha's boat lifted to the tide, and the last rowers tumbled in, fixing their shield-boards to the gunnels, as the faded brown square sail, fat as a friar, clasped the east wind to its round belly. Suddenly, the knarr began to plunge. The sea hissed by as the rip-race tide swept them faster and faster past the slicked rock cliffs of Portland in a fury of banging waves, wind and spray.

Thrill turned to terror. Gytha shrieked and nearly flew over the side. Wulfwyn grabbed her, held her, as wave after wave crashed onto them. Behind them men on the steering oar, feet braced against the thwart, fought the kicking beam shouting oaths at the sea gods. And then, as quickly as it had started, it was over. The racing tide and the overfalls quieted, and Gytha marvelled how the sturdy boat now charged on into the black night, scattering the water left and right beneath its serpent prow. Even the ice-chill wind seemed banished to a breeze in the lee of the land falling to their stern. But with the swell-roll of the ocean came sickness. Aunt Gunhild, praying and groaning, turned away to heave and choke her vomit to the water. But neither Gytha, buried under wadmal and beaver pelt, nor her grandmother in her sable-fur, a gift from the forest king of Permia, were troubled.

There was not a light anywhere, rendering the land invisible. Gytha's eyes grew used to the blackness, feeling the rhythm, smelling the damp ropes, the caulking tar, hearing the creaking mast. The brazier at the back glowed dull red, lighting the steersman. She watched as he put a flagon to his mouth, spat and belched loudly, his arm never leaving the shuddering sweep. Occasionally, one of the huddled folk spoke, or an oarsman moved on the row bench. Some filled their bellies with broth and bannocks, others took turns at the bucket, the night shielding them from stares and jeering of sea men braced at the stern. The time passed slowly.

'Do I have brine for blood, as the true Northmen do?' Gytha wondered, now cautiously enjoying the boat, while the people tightly packed around her slept as best they could. She wanted to ask about Ran, wife of Aegir, goddess of the drowned dead. But Aunt Gunhild and the monk would permit no talk of any gods save the Lord God the Great Creator, Wielder of Glory, and Jesus Christ his only son. Gytha shuddered at the thought of the drowned dead and crossed herself in the darkness.

In time the moon rose, bright white, dimming the winter stars which the warrior-monk said were the jewels of heroes. Gytha watched the welling-waves heave and froth around them. Wulfwyn, her loyal life-ward, had his head against the tarred clinker side. He was not asleep. She was glad he was there. He had started a straggly blond beard, not much, and the men teased him for his rose fresh cheeks. She trusted him without knowing why. Perhaps it was because her mother had trusted him too.

Plucking up courage, she called to him quietly. 'Wulfwyn, Wulfwyn, tell me about seeing mother.' Magnus stirred.

Pulling his felt hat down against the wind, the young Radknight began with how he and the Pig-boy crossed all of

London without problem. Nobody had taken any interest in them. Trouble started as they neared Waltham. Norman soldiers had stopped all who passed. They were savage men, their heads shaved bald at the back, fully armoured in hauberks and bearing swords, lances and the long shield-boards. They spoke roughly in their tongue to Wulfwyn, ordering him from his horse and demanding to know his business. He did not answer them. Stiff backed, holding his head proudly as befitted his status, he pulled Duke William's seal from the purse at his belt

'I said that I was going home to Thurgarton to my father, mother and my sister Ailsi, and they were about to let us go when this Pig-boy suddenly honked in terror, pointing at one of Normans and trying to get away.'

Gytha gasped. 'Why? why did he do that?'

'My Lady, it was the man who had cut out his tongue. All changed in the beat of a heart. We were herded at spear-point into the great barn and there and, fearing for our lives, we waited. More Normans arrived then, including the Breton count, Ralph de Gael, whose cruelty is as great as his swagger.'

'He who has robbed us, and holds mother at Waltham?' asked Magnus.

'Aye,' said Wulfwyn, 'he demanded to know where I got the warrant. I told him truthfully, but he clouted me across the head with his mailed fist, sending me bleeding to the threshing floor. 'You're a liar, boy," he shouted. 'scum, like your dead master, King Harold Godwineson," he jeered. I spit daily on his grave and would fuck his handfast bed wench, were she more pleasing to me beneath.'

Gytha gasped, sticking her nails hard into Magnus's arm. Wulfwyn apologised.

'Silence, Radknight' said the Mace Monk from the bench behind them, 'you distress Lady Gytha and Lord Magnus with your tale.'

'No!' cried Gytha. 'Speak, Wulfwyn. I must know'.

Wulfwyn swallowed hard but continued, reluctantly. 'The Breton kicked me again and again, accusing me of stealing the Warrant and demanding to know my business at Waltham. But for the warrant he would have killed me then. I could not breathe for pain, but I said I had a warrant from his lord duke William and he must let me pass. "Why?" the Earl demanded. I told him that I must pray with my Lady Edith Swan-neck, beneath the Flinty Cross, as one who rings the lazars' bell.'

'You didn't say that! Do you, do you have leprosy Wulfwyn?'

'No, my Lady, I do not, God have mercy!' chuckled Wulfwyn. 'I said it. You never saw a Norman run faster.'

Wulfwyn was now laughing gleefully, and Gytha and Magnus joined in his mirth.

'Those swine boast no fear of swords and axes, but this Breton count, Ralph de Gael, near died of my lie,' chucked the Radknight. Even the Mace Monk laughed at that.

'But this Breton count, Ralph de Gael, has stolen our mother's lands,' said Magnus, serious for once.

'Yes,' said Wulfwyn. 'He did great harm at the slaughter field they call Senlac, and the Bastard rewarded him with your mother's land and with it all the fees, liberties and customs of the manor.'

'What does it mean, Senlac?' asked Gytha.

'The bloody lake,' said the Radknight. Gytha shuddered. 'Go on.'

'My lady, I feared they would torch us or slit our throats within the barn. The shave-head Normans were everywhere. Their horses were stabled in the new mead-hall, under your mother's tapestries.'

'Yet the good nuns stay to care for our mother and Hilde. They are blessed,' said Gytha. She paused, lowering her voice to a whisper. 'But why can mother not come and bring our sister to us?'

'Lady Gytha, it saddens me so, but your mother is mortally sick in her heart,' said Wulfwyn. 'I fear she will die of grief. I visited her in her chamber, her head on the pillow, her hair undressed. The abbess said my name, but she did not stir. Then the abbess said that I came with news of you, Lady Gytha, and you, Lord Magnus, and of your two brothers. Your mother looked at me, her blue eyes full of sadness, enough to fill the sea with tears.'

Gytha bit her lip; she was not going cry again. She had cried enough. There were no tears left in her.

The Radknight continued. 'Your mother looked at me a long time, and I rejoiced that she recognised me. I kneeled before her and she put out her hand and touched the wound, still fresh with blood, where the Earl struck me.' Wulfwyn stopped and Gytha could see him touch his head above his brow. 'But still my most fair lady did not speak, though she held my gaze. There was such bleakness in her I felt I must speak in case the black silence overcame me too. I told her of our escape from Waltham and how you, Gytha, had saved the urchin Pig-boy's life, and how we feasted on pork and apples sufficient to burst that night. I told her of her sons and the fine army they lead and how together we will avenge her king's death. And still she looked into my face without a word, but I knew, I know, she heard me. Eventually the Abbess nodded for me to leave, so I kissed my lady's hand, then rose and left the chamber.'

Gytha was crying deeply again, pressing the beaver pelt into her face to muffle the sobs. She could not stop. Her heart was ripped in two. Next to her, Magnus was staring straight ahead, moist-eyed, trying his hardest not to do the same. The Radknight waited; Gytha cleared her throat.

'Thank you, Wulfwyn,' she half-whispered. 'You risked your life for the love of our mother.'

'Can we not fetch her?' said Magnus. 'I wish she was with us, not hostage to that Breton Earl. What will happen to her?'

'With God's mercy,' said the Towering Mace Monk from the bench behind them, 'your fair mother, Eddeva Pulchra, will find peace once more and the love that kills all feeling will again one day be the love that fills her life with joy. Let us pray for her safe return to those who love her and whom she loved and will again.'

Drawing Magnus and the Radknight towards her, there, on that icy Christmas night of 1066, as the serpent headed knarr surged, banged, shuddered its way over the night-sea to Exeter, Gytha knelt on the planking and prayed for her mother.

'Oh Lord, hold my gentle swan in my heart, if not my hands.'

EXETER, HIGH BYRH
OF THE WEST

THE MOTHER OF HEROES, Godwine and the leather-caped thegns would gather each day as more news of the invader's oppression reached the green-banked Byrh. Minstrels came to the hall, but their songs were sad. Anger soaked every breath, and pain bathed each utterance. Land-lost English nobles, fleeing with only their families and thralls, came to Exeter. Each new story of forced tribute or death left one question unanswered: when would they be next? Their numbers grew. Over the weeks of 1067 they were joined by the last of the huscarls, hearthguard of kings. Once three thousand strong, few had survived Stamford Bridge or the Senlac slaughter field. These ring-shirted battle men now chafed at their exile in the west. The mead-hall at the Irlesbyri echoed with their bitterness. Godwine struggled to keep axes and swords at rest in their sheaths when the Elders of Exeter talked of kneeling to the invader, rather than fighting.

One Sunday, returning from St Olave's church, Gytha spied Pig-boy lurking. A grin nearly split his face in two. Out of his gape-mouth he honked a wordless greeting. To her embarrassment, he sank to his knees, snatched off his felted bonnet, bowed his head and reached out his hand, which held something wrapped in a dirty cloth. Gytha pulled her cowl about her face and looked away.

It was Towering Blaecman, the Mace Monk from Abingdon, who ordered Pig-boy to his feet.

'Allow me to show you something, child,' he said to her. Snapping his finger, he gestured the Pig-boy to hand him the bundle. From within, he pulled a wax tablet. 'Read it, my lady,' Blaecman said with a flourish.

Gytha hesitated.

'Read it, child,' said the Towering Mace Monk, his breath mead-sour.

She'd had her fill of wax tablets under the nuns' tutelage; another did not excite her.

Gytha read a few words, and found that it was in Latin.

'Here in the year of our Lord 1052 was given Pig-boy to Aelfstan the Monk.' She paused and looked up. 'What is it?'

'It's a chronicle,' said Blaecman.

'Why must I read it?' she asked. 'I have had enough of Latin today, Father.'

'Because, child, it is this Pig-boy's chronicle.'

'So?'

'Whoever cut out his tongue has not silenced him. The foundling Pig-boy, as you call him, was schooled by friars. He can write Latin. He was baptised Baldred. His mother, a virgin of fourteen winters, ravished, left him, a foundling on a church step. He carries still the cross she gave him and a plaited strand of her hair.'

'He writes all this?' scoffed Magnus. 'It's lies. He is a swineherd who lived in the pigsty where we found him sucking on that sow's tit. Very good she was too,' Magnus laughed, too loudly.

'His story is no different to countless others,' said Godwine. 'spare your sympathy.'

'I hazard his mother was high born,' said the monk, continuing. 'A free woman, shamed. He is her bastard. Who knows if she still lives? But if she does, he is lost to her now.'

'And what shall become of this high-born swineherd, who hoots and honks for speech, Father? They will not have him on the mead-bench in the hall, if that is what you think,' said the Old Lady.

Gytha wasn't listening, she was thinking. She was confused, upset. It was something about this Pig-boy losing not one mother, but two. She knew it was stupid, but that sow was a mother to the boy, and they killed her.

'Mother of Heroes,' she said firmly, pointing at Pig-boy, 'I wish this Pig-boy to be my stirrup guard. I shall have him live in the stable and attend my horses. When I ride out, he will run at my side. He needs no weapon but his sling, and no voice but his whistle.'

'Ha, that I have to see,' said Magnus. 'When he does that donkey bray, your stallion will mount him.'

There was much laughter. Gytha ignored him. Pig-boy fell to his knees again.

'So be it,' said the Old lady. 'Father Blaecman, see that this boy continues his study.' She turned to walk away and then added a thought. 'You say he is clever and well born. I see a silenced boy who sees and hears all. He may yet be of use, Father Blaecman. Let him serve the maiden as she asks. This town is thick with rumour, and there are voices that trouble me greatly. This Elder, the Reeve, would fix the Byrhgate key to his lance tip and gift it to the Bastard. So it was at Winchester. We must all see he does not.'

Gytha's days were not her own between all the schooling in the holy bible, singing, plucking the gentle lyre, dancing and needlework. With Aunt Gunhild she learnt to draw figures of men, horses and birds with charcoal, on strips of linen. Then with slender fingers she overstitched the coloured yarns she had dyed herself, with woad, madder and weld.

The days grew longer. Dabs of colour painted the hills around the town. Wisps of white hawthorn blossom speckled black branches, then the willow on the riverbank turned from russet to the palest green almost overnight. In the orchard, birds sang furiously. The moment she was free, she loved to run to the barn where orphan lambs, tails waggling furiously, suckled at her fingers. Sometimes she, Magnus and Edmund would climb to the highest part of the wall overlooking the river and to the sea beyond where Edmund flew his saker falcon. Its doomed quarry clouted from the sky, showering feathers like snow around them. Magnus would shoot at any bird with his bow, missing mostly, or shin up a tree to steal eggs. Sometimes he'd drop triumphantly with a whole nest of blue or speckled eggs, before discarding it. That troubled Gytha. She could see no point to taking it and then throwing it away once he had it. Challenging him once, he rounded on her 'why not?' He said. 'It's a bit of fun.'

Gytha paused, unsure what to say.

'Because,' said Edmund quietly, pointing at the distressed parents tweeting their pain from the branches, 'that nest is the basket of their hopes.

Magnus was about to say something rude about Turul.

'Why not put the nest back?,' said Gytha. 'See, the eggs are not broken.'

The place Gytha liked best was the market by the Cathedral and the narrow lanes around it. Here, where the Celt folk lived, were minstrels, jugglers, jostling thieves, and danger too.

These were the people of the handsome Celtprince, Baladrddellt rac Denau, Splintered Spear of the South. There was no love lost between these Brython and West-Saxon folk, but the women welcomed Gytha. Clustering round her, touching and chattering, they felt her embroidered dress, her soft woollen cowl, the great broaches of her mantle cape, marvelling at how tall and slender she was, her waist no thicker than the Celt prince's tattooed arm. They called her 'Myrgh-teg.' Her golden curls and pink cheeks could not have looked more different than these wild women. Some had hair the colour of polished sunset, their noses spotted with carroty freckles. Others, the ones with green eyes deep as rockpools, let their black manes hang free to their waists.

'Myrgh-teg? What does it mean?' Gytha asked the Celtprince.

Baladrddellt laughed his rich, deep laugh. 'Wouldn't you like to know, little lady! Well, I'll tell you as long as you promise not to be offended.' He laughed again and his eyes crinkled.

'Is it bad?' asked Gytha.

'It probably means stupid,' said Magnus, brushing off a hand that stroked his beardless face.

'Well, you'd be wrong, boy-man,' said the Celt warrior. 'Myrgh-teg means "beautiful girl" in our language.'

Magnus scoffed, and Gytha felt suddenly shy.

As they were leaving, a boy stepped from a doorway. Confronting Magnus, he hissed, 'go, English!' and prodded a finger into his chest. Magnus pushed the boy away; he was no older than Magnus. But he was broader, and like the Celt Prince, there were tattoos up his arms. In a moment the boys were fighting on the ground in the dirt.

Gytha shrieked as the boy grabbed at the wounding-knife Magnus kept at his waist. Magnus punched him, landing hard blows. Over and over they rolled like dogs, neither winning.

'Stop!' ordered Baladrddellt, stepping roughly between them. Dragging the boy to his feet, he cuffed him so hard with his gloved fist that the boy pitched into a shit-puddle. Then the Celtprince pulled him up by his ear and cuffed him again before thrusting him at the watching Celt women with a brutal kick.

Gytha, shocked at Baladrddellt's ferocity, pulled Magnus to his feet.

'Are you hurt? She asked, as he shook his head as if to clear it. There was a little blood.

'Why did he attack Magnus so?' she asked the Celt Prince.

'It was nothing,' said the warrior.

'Nothing!' said Magnus. 'I am the king's son. He wanted to kill me, only I was too quick and strong. Have him brought to me. You bring him to me. Better still, kill him now.'

Baladrddellt laughed, drily this time. 'No, king's boy, I shall not kill him for little more than a finger-prod, even when the boy he poked is the king's son. You fought him well, but you let him grab your wounding-knife.' The Celt Prince bent to pick it up. Magnus was livid, but something about the Celt Prince cautioned him not to speak too hastily again.

'Magnus, you must earn respect if you are to lead my people against the Bastard Duke. Killing a boy for a prod will win nothing. Come Myrgh-teg, let us go. Tomorrow we will return for you to charm them with your beauty.'

Gytha blushed. 'Who was that boy, Prince Baladrddellt?' She asked as they returned to the hall.

'My eldest son,' he replied.

'Your son!' She answered, 'and your wife, where is she?'

'She died of fever and is with the blessed Mary, mother of God and the Apostles.' His voice distracted and Gytha, thinking of another boy without a mother, she said, 'what was her name?'

'Brighid,' he replied. 'She was radiant of beauty, no older than you, when we became betrothed. My son carries the pain, as do I.'

*   *   *

By late spring of 1067, Godwine and his grandmother had
sent messengers to towns throughout the west, to Ireland,
and to their kinsman Sweyn Estrithson, king of the Danes,
begging support. But none came. The Bastard William, was
now crowned King of England.

All the while merchants arrived at Exeter from across the sea.
Barbary slavers, Levant tin traders, Frankish armourers but none
were more fascinating to Gytha than the turbaned perfume
seller and his scented slave-girl; black haired, her skin the colour
of golden leaves in autumn, her eyes slanting up from cheeks as
fresh as rosy apples. Little bells sown into the hem and cuff of
her crimson smock tinkled as she moved, and from the golden
brow-band that framed her perfect face hung two tiny golden
vessels wafting sweetest honeysuckle. Gytha was enchanted, lost
to the merchant's salves and balms, oils and aromas.

There was purple soft lavender from the sun rock hills
above the mistral sea, ambrosia and nectar, lily of the valley,
myrtle, and oak of Cappadocia, priceless ambergris, the
fragrant musk of monsters that sing across the vastness of the
deep. Then, keeping his best till last, the turbaned merchant
offered Gytha the scent of wild roses, her English beauty
captured in a flask, he said, hands out, palms up, his life's work
complete if only she would accept this one gift. The scented
slave girl stepped forward to press the tiny carved bone bottle
to Gytha's nose. Their eyes met, the girl searching her face for
a fleeting moment, and then dropped her gaze. Gytha smiled.
The slave girl was unlike anybody Gytha had ever seen before.

Perfumes and oriental compliments caressed the throats of
many pale skinned noble ladies in the hall that evening, only
Aunt Gunhild, naming vanity as the worst of the seven sins,

dismissed the heathen stench-man who cared not for God, 'neither is God in all his thoughts,' she said.

Gytha protested. 'Well God is in all my thoughts, Aunt; I took no heed of his words. He and his scented slave girl sold many bottles here in the Irlesbyri today. He called each lady beautiful, both young and old alike. Though none are so beautiful as the scented slave girl. Did you see her, Aunt? I never saw one stranger. She peered into my soul.'

Her Aunt frowned at her words. 'Such nonsense. Her eyes are slits. Come now, child. We must eat.'

The meal over, minstrels played to the packed hall, with its sour smell of mead and smoke. Fighting men, fired by the liquor, told more stories of brutality, taxation and lands stolen. Gytha needed no reminding of torched houses, starving people, the sickness and the smell of rotting animals all around, so she was relieved when the Old Lady summoned the turbaned perfume seller to her that she too might sample essences and aloes for her infirmities.

The pair approached. Gytha saw that all eyes were on the scented slave girl. They kneeled in unison to beat their foreheads on the straw-dirt floor. Then they stood, the perfume seller offering her grandmother exquisite vials from his tray, speaking all the while in the common language of the Danes.

'From where do you come, stench-man, that you speak my Dane tongue?', asked the Old Lady.

'Mother of Heroes, I come from the sand lands. I travel winter and summer to honour mighty halls with elixirs for fair ladies, though there are none so fair as you and your grandchild the Lady Gytha,' He added.

'And the girl with slits, where God places eyes in our heads, from where does she come? I never saw one like that before, save demons from the great fire beneath,' said the Old Lady, both impatient and curious.

'Great Lady, she too is a princess; from the Wild Field, with two eyes and a tongue in her head,' said the merchant. There was a rumble of laughter in the hall. He paused. 'Aye, her father is Khan of all the grass ocean, her kin saddle-born. Suckled on mares-milk, they live and die on stallions. Angry and quick-tempered, these Qipchaq fear nothing, but all men fear them.'

'A wild princess? And how did you gain such a prize, little stench man?' asked the Mother of Heroes, mocking him.

'She is a barter-gift from the Land of River Princes, which they call Rus, given to me by the Grand Prince himself.'

The warriors in the hall were guffawing now. Even the Twice Scarred Thegn Eadric ceased his spitting and cursing to join in. But Gytha was spell-bound. A princess? From the Wild Field? Where was this Wild Field, and who were these Qipchaq and River Princes?

'Do you believe in God?' asked The Towering Mace Monk Blaecman, his voice booming through the din.

The little stench-man bowed. 'Peace be upon you priest. I believe in the blessings of Allah, the most beneficent, the most merciful.'

'And in the teaching of our Lord Jesus Christ?' demanded the Monk.

'In the name of Allah, I follow the holy scripture revealed by the angel Gabriel to his messenger Muhammad, peace be upon him. And the one book which unites the sons of Ham Shem and Japheth.'

The growl exploded in the hall; 'heathen, heathen,' they chanted, until the mead-hall beat to the hilts of drumming wounding-knives on the wooden table-boards. Gytha's eyes darted to her brother and grandmother. Something was about to happen. Something bad.

'Heathen! Heathen!'

The perfume seller fell to his knees. But the scented slave girl remained standing, a pillar in a crimson shift, the nostrils in her round face flaring as a deer scenting peril on the wind.

'Godwine, don't let them die,' Gytha begged. 'Godwine, stop them.'

'Silence! There will be no murder in the Irlesbyri,' Godwine shouted, his sword unsheathed. Still the hall drummed to the cries of 'Heathen! Heathen!.

The Radknight, the Twice Scarred Thegn, and the Painted Celt were on their feet now, swords in their hands.

'I, rightful King of all English folk,' yelled Godwine, 'place this man under my shield. Now go in peace, stench-man. You, good father Blaecman,' he said, turning to Monk, 'cease this before men die.'

The turbaned perfume seller stumbled to his feet, gathered his tray of bottles and fled the hall, but not the scented slave girl. She paused, her hands folded over her belly, glancing at Gytha, this time not as a thrall but as her equal. It was a look, and perhaps an acknowledgement. Gytha looked back in wonder at the courage of this bartered princess from the Wild Field.

'What is your name?', said Gytha hurriedly

'Swetesot,' said the girl, and she was gone.

If Gytha rode out beyond the town with Wulfwyn the Radknight and the Pig-boy at her stirrup, the Celtprince Baladrddellt now rode in attendance too. While Gytha was flattered by his interest in her safety, after the incident with his son, Magnus and the Radknight were not.

Sometimes Edmund would join them to fly Turul, or she would follow the hunting dogs as they stalked deer and otter. Gytha thought fishing boring, but Magnus loved to join the Twice Scarred Thegn and stalk the duckling-snatcher pike or lure slip-sinewed trout to his fly.

What Gytha hankered after was to join the boys in their battle play. But as a girl that was denied her. While she embroidered, Baladrddellt rac Denau schooled Magnus and Edmund in war craft, with longsword, lance and battle-axe.

One morning when Gytha was in the courtyard watching them skirmish, she could keep silent no longer. Defiantly, the willow slender girl confronted the painted warrior. 'It's not fair,' she said, making herself as tall as possible. 'Why do you leave me to grieve? Is it not better to avenge than to mourn? But how can I avenge my father's death, Splintered Spear of the South?' she blurted. 'I too took the vow beneath the Flinty Cross at Waltham to avenge my father, but you do not teach me to break open a Norman's skull with this axe, or pin his heart to a tree with that spear. Tell me, Prince, how can I avenge my father if you do not teach me these things as you teach my brothers?'

The boys looked on, not surprised to hear their sister speak her mind so passionately.

Baladrddellt rac Denau took off his helmet, slipped his long-edge sword into its scabbard and looked hard at Gytha. She did not move. The laugh that rumbled from his chest died as he met her gaze.

'Lady,' he said, his deep brown voice kind, without hint of mockery. 'We could clothe you in the golden ring-shirt and your father's silver helm. We could arm you with your brother Godwine's finest Frankish longsword, given by the king of Hungary himself, but a Norman knight, trained in battle work, venom in his veins, would part your head from your slender shoulders. And for what lady, for what? How would this avenge your noble father? Better Lady Gytha to bear the fruit of kings. That royal English blood will live generation after generation. That is how you, noble maiden, can best avenge your father's death.'

Gytha did not interrupt his speech, but nor did she back down. Trembling, she asked, 'Bear the fruit of kings? What kings, Celtprince? All royal English blood was lost at Senlac slaughter field. Or do you mean for me to marry the Aethling boy king, Edgar, whose fealty is now to the Bastard foreigner William? Do as you say, and I will have avenged nothing!'

Baladrddellt rac Denau said thoughtfully, 'The time for all to avenge your father will come, noble Lady.'

Gytha would not be dismissed. 'Then let me help God. Teach me the swordplay, the arrow and lance, as you drill the boys. Magnus will be my spar partner, as only he will not fear striking me hard as if I were a boy.'

'I will not,' said Magnus. 'You won't teach her, will you, Baladrddellt rac Denau? She is a girl, not a warrior.'

'Why not?' said the painted Celt, laughing now, impressed by Gytha's determination. 'With your grandmother, Mother of Heroes' approval, I will teach you to fight as a man, Gytha Haroldsdaughter.'

Gytha was elated and ran to find her grandmother.

'Well!' said Baladrddellt rac Denau to Magnus after Gytha had left. 'She is your father's daughter, no doubt about that. The blood of warriors flows in her veins.'

'And in mine also,' said Magnus, piqued.

'Come,' said the older fighter, slapping Magnus hard on the shoulder with his gloved hand. 'Back to men's work.'

Gytha's demand to learn to fight as her brothers was so serious that it came before the gathering in the mead-hall that evening. Support came from the east thegns, who spoke of shield maids and of Boudicca; Aunt Gunhild talked of gentle Esther. Another spoke of Penthesilea at the gate of Troy.

'Yes,' said the Mace Monk Blaecman. 'Achilles struck Penthesilea to the ground with one blow to her breastplate. She begged for mercy, but he laughed and killed her.'

'But Achilles did not know she was a woman when he killed her,' said Aunt Gunhild.

'Noble lady, good sister in Christ, even knowing the maid Gytha was a woman would not stop a Norman killing her. They show no mercy to man, woman or child. She would be killed, and to what purpose?'

'Yes,' said the Celtprince. 'I told her she can do what no man can.' He was smiling as he recounted the confrontation with Gytha in the yard. 'I said "bear the fruit of kings," but she would have none of it.'

And so it went, back and forth. The Old Thegn Eadric drew much laughter, saying no husband would sleep safe abed knowing his wife Gytha could add longsword and spear craft to her wounding words. Then, as the mead flowed and argument grew more heated, the Old Lady stood and the hall fell silent at her raised hand.

'These are dangerous times. Who knows what we will all be called on to do before the crown of the English is once more on the head of Godwine, Harold's son?' She paused, looking at the men about her, the firelight on her face. Then, her voice loud, hands out, as if addressing the gods themselves, 'I am of the blood of Shield Maidens, the daughter of Hervor who carried the sword Tyrfing, and of his wife Brynhild, with the body of a woman but to whom nature gave the soul of a man. I, Thorkil's daughter, say the maiden Gytha may fight. Baladrddellt rac Denau will be her Sword master. My husband, Earl of Wessex, and my kinsman Knut the Great King would wish it so.'

No one moved. Not the monk, not Aunt Gunhild, nor the boys. All froze at her heathen words. It was the Twice Scarred Thegn who broke the silence.

'Mind you don't mark her fair face though, Celt,' he warned with a laugh. 'She'll not thank you to look like me.' And with that it was settled that Gytha would learn the battle craft.

As Gytha's sword-play drills progressed, marked by nicks up either arm, the boys watched her dodge the stinging blade. Resentful mostly, impressed only when the Celtprince cursed her in his Celtic tongue.

'Diawl bach Myrgh-teg, I would sooner pin a fairy to a cloud of dandelion seed,' he would say in mock anger, his green-brown eyes and barrel chest full of laughter as she willow-danced about him.

'Catch me if you can!' she taunted him back. But only once. As lightning from a stormy sky, as a wasp's sting, his blade tip found her. Gytha gasped and pressed the blood wound to her lips. The boys cheered as he handed her the pot of blue wode to staunch it. It hurt, but she would not cry.

'You have much to learn, willow girl, or die. Come, let me show you once again.' And so, as he often did, he slipped his painted right arm around her shoulder from behind and pressed her to him, 'let it feel as if we are one,' he would say with his mouth in her hair. She could feel the sour-sweet sweat of his muscled body hard against hers. His left hand would find her waist to grip her like the puppet master. Instinctively, she would try to pull away. 'No Myrgh-teg,' he would say, 'give your body and will to my command.' Then he would order Magnus or Edmund to attack, with Gytha in his arms as if he was a dancer. So nimble, so quick, lunging, parrying. It was exciting, but when she mentioned to Edmund that the Celt Prince held her too tight, all Edmund said in his calm way was that she had asked to be trained and he was the trainer.

'But Edmund,' she replied, 'he doesn't press his body to yours when you practice. Does he?

Edmund replied, 'well I kiss and stroke Turul when I train her, so what?'

Gytha shook her head and said no more about it. She remembered the sting of his fearsome anger towards his motherless son, but he was always friendly towards her and if she was learning, so be it. Gytha learnt much and heard much from the painted Celt Prince Baladrddellt rac Denau in the weeks that followed. She neither asked him to treat her differently to her brothers, nor did he. He chided her as he did them. The same tasks, the same challenges, the same drills, the same goals – all were shared. Some said he drove her too hard, and would have him stop, but Gytha insisted. Even Magnus, normally quick to sneer, was fired by her pluck.

PART ONE CHAPTER EIGHT

COMING OF AGE

ACROSS THE MARKET FROM the Irlesbyri, thralls wrestled the midsummer pole upright, with bunten ribbons for the dancers snaking in the breeze. There were stalls with loaves and cheeses, chicken and tender goat, salt-fish and live eels, and a giant bone fire that would light up the night's merrymaking. In alleyways women stirred reeking broths over coals or buried perch and carp wrapped in damp leaves in the embers, while others cast spells, or sold temptation, saying 'man shall not live by bread alone.'

Gytha watched happily as the mead-hall, with its embroidered tapestries of stags and dragons, was dressed in greenery. Fresh boughs draped the roof beams to make a forest glade fit for revelling elven folk. The floor was swept and new straw laid, the settle-benches straightened, facing the carved high chair where Godwine, the Feast Giver, would sit, and the Mother of Heroes next to him. For the first time, Gytha would take her place to serve her brother Godwine and the greatest thegns mead in silvered horns. She was fourteen.

On the afternoon of the feast, Gytha's grandmother summoned her.

Fresh from the sword play, Gytha's golden hair was tamed. The day was warm, and so she chose her favourite dress, the pale blue belted tunic her mother had embroidered. It was too short now that she had grown so tall. Her mother had called it her magic dress and when Gytha asked why, she had said 'because when you wear it, it will make your eyes bluer, your hair blonder and your cheeks rosier.' Hugging it to her face, Gytha smiled. She fumbled with the beads at her neck, pinned the silver clasp at her shoulder and adjusted the slender golden circle of the king's daughter on her head. Both nervous and excited, she was dressed for the feast.

'Sit, child,' ordered Gytha's grandmother as she entered the hall. Godwine, the Twice Scarred Thegn, the Burnished Roni and the Mace Monk Blaecman stood next to her. There was no sign of the painted Celtprince. Gytha kissed her Grandmother's hand. There was an awkward pause. Gytha fidgeted, unsure of what to do as her grandmother measured her with her eyes.

'Eadgytha Haroldsdaughter, maiden of Wessex,' said the Old Lady, addressing Gytha formally. 'Tonight, you enter the mead-hall a child but leave as a noble woman in the eyes of our people.' She paused. 'Eadgytha, your father's death will have no compensation, no wergild will ever be paid. All is gone. But for the Hoard and the lands that are mine here in the west, all is lost. All, except you. You, child, you are an adornment to the greatness of our people.'

Gytha knew not to speak. An adornment? Her embarrassment turned to alarm.

'Now that you are of marriageable age, you are to be the peace-weaver for our people,' her grandmother continued.

'A peace-weaver?' Gytha whispered. 'With whom, Mother of Heroes?'

A peace-weaver? There had been no talk of it in the hall. There were no suitors for her hand. She would rather cut her own throat than be wed to a Norman.

The Old Lady called out. 'Fetch Baladrddellt rac Denau, the Splintered Spear of the South.'

In he walked, cocky and sure of himself as always. Gytha smiled at him, relieved that he was still wearing the clothes he had worn for the swordplay. He would let no harm come to her. But he did not look at her. Instead, he walked up to her grandmother and knelt before her, his handsome head bowed low.

'Stand, Prince' said the Old Lady. 'Child, our sturdy, spirited Celt, son of kings, great leader of his proud people, and friend to the House of Godwine, has sought God's blessing and my permission to take you for his ring-adorned wife.'

The blood ran from Gytha's face. Panic grasped her chest and squeezed her throat; She took a rough breath, but it lodged in her throat. She could feel her heart pumping and a roaring like the wild-sea in her ears. Her Grandmother, Mother of Heroes, was still speaking, but Gytha heard nothing of the words as she gasped for air. The Hall was lit by tallow-lights even on this summer's evening and, with the sun and the birds singing outside, it seemed unbearably hot. Gytha wished to run far away, to feel cool air, not to remain here where the ground beneath her feet rushed up towards her.

It was Aunt Gunhild's voice she heard as if in a tunnel, 'Poor child,' her Aunt was saying, 'she is overcome. Come, child, drink this.' She pressed a little honeyed cider to Gytha's lips.

'Is she not too young, Mother of Heroes?' asked Aunt Gunhild, cradling her niece in her lap. 'She is still a child who would talk with dolls, were she not riven from her mother.'

'Gytha does not speak with dolls, Aunt Gunhild,' Scoffed Magnus, who was now kneeling by her. 'She fights and spits like a wild cat in a gin-trap. The Celtprince will have his hands full.'

'Let us have no talk of dolls, draw straws or peek-a-boo in this time of suffering and hardship. We all must serve, Gytha too. What do you say, Monk?' asked Godwine. 'Is she child or woman?'

'Noble Lord, Gytha the child has departed. Her betrothal to this sturdy warrior Baladrddellt, in this time of suffering and hardship, will weave peace between Brython and Saxon to unite us against our common foe. It is God's will,' pronounced the Towering Mace Monk.

'Gytha. Stand up, or have you lost your voice and your legs?' said her Grandmother.

'No, Mother of Heroes,' she replied, swallowing hard as she struggled to stand. 'No, Grandmother,' she repeated, smoothing her dress, 'Will mother come to see me betrothed and bring the gifts she gathered for me?' her voice stronger now. She glanced at her three brothers. Godwine was stern, Edmund smiled, and Magnus's eyes and mouth were wide open. The Radknight Wulfwyn stared at the ground. They were no help.

For a fleeting moment she remembered how the princess from the Wild Field, the scented Swetesot, had stood where she was standing. Yet she had shown no fear. Gytha stiffened her back. She too was a princess. She too would show no fear of the man next to her. She clenched her fists so tight that the nail-marks would last a week. Betrothed to a painted Celt. She could smell him, but she looked only to her front.

Baladrddellt glanced at her, his prize, Gytha, daughter of the English king, and laughed, his fine voice booming, eyes crinkling. 'Methinks, Great Lady, Mother of Heroes, that the child-lady Myrgh-teg keeps herself for a greater warrior, like her father King Harold Godwineson and his father, your husband. And would not marry this man of the west'.

The Old Lady was in no mood to banter with the Celtprince. 'It is the law of my kin-brother Canute, King of all the North folk, that no maiden can be forced to marry any man or be given for money.'

'Come now,' he answered boldly, turning to Gytha. 'Myrgh-teg here does not dislike me. Why, today we were laughing with the swordplay. You near sliced my ear off, did you not?'

Gytha stared ahead in silence, not trusting herself to speak.

'There will be no more sword–play. That will cease,' said the Old Lady. 'You ask if your mother will come. Well, it is time for you to break your mother's strings and take this man as your husband. It is God's will.' She paused. 'Do you take him gladly as peace-weaver, to unite Saxon and Celt by the children you bear him?'

Gytha, dazed, bewildered, terrified, nodded her assent.

'Speak, child, so that this Company can hear you.'

'Yes, Mother of Heroes,' Gytha whispered.

'Gladly?' said her Grandmother.

'Gladly,' whispered Gytha.

Taking Gytha's shaking hand in her jewelled fingers, the Old Lady opened a hard wood box inlaid with silver and precious gemstones. Out of the box she picked two golden rings, one shaped as a Bishop's mitre decorated with winged dragons; the other wrought with a golden cushion on which stood the Lamb of God.

'Baladrddellt, Splintered Spear from the South, place this Royal finger-ring on your finger as a symbol of the friendship between our two peoples. With Eadgytha come rents of tin-streamers, tanners, renderers, salt makers and smelters and one fifth of all my moor, forest, pasture and plough here in the west.' There was a gasp in the hall. This bride gift would make the painted Celtprince the richest man in all the West. 'And for you, Eadgytha Haroldsdaughter, mother to many

sons. Take this golden ring of the lady Aethelflaed, daughter
to King Alfred the Great as a symbol of your English blood
and the royal house of Wessex,

Gytha felt as if her grandmother was speaking from a
distant place, a hollow cavern. She heard her ringing words,
but found no meaning in them.

'For now, you will both remain here in this city whose
holy places I have enriched in the memory of the Half-
King, my husband.' Then, looking fiercely at the Towering
Mace Monk Blaecman in case he thought to object, said,
'Bless this betrothal Father, and let us sanctify this marriage
before God this St Erbin's Day after we have restored the
crown to my grandson Godwine Haroldson, the rightful
king of the English. All must play their part. Battle comes to
the West. You, Baladrddellt, will raise five thousand painted
Celtish men and place them under the command of my
grandson Godwine.'

Baladrddellt rac Denau looked pleased at this, and several
around him thumped their knives on the table-tops. Glancing
at Gytha he replied, 'Noble lady, my people serve you and
will stand with you against the Bastard King. St Erbin's day is
right enough, the feast day of my people, and what a feast we
will give them.' Then they knelt as the Towering Mace Monk,
Blaecman of Abingdon, blessed them saying 'what is joyfully
begun may in its own time be joyfully completed.'

News of the betrothal of Gytha, daughter of King Harold
and Edith Swan-neck, the fair, the gentle, to prince Baladrddellt
rac Denau, Splintered Spear of the South, flew around the
Byrh. That midsummer feast was the wildest ever. Time and
again English and Celt raised the carved cup to the pretty
maiden who had turned the head of a Prince. Gytha, sitting
in their midst, honoured above all others, prayed over and over
that they would stop.

'Look cheerful, sister,' said quiet Edmund. 'Why else did you join us at the sword-play if you did not want the painted Celt's attention? You wanted him to notice you, well he has now, and you must be happy?'

Gytha felt only horror at his words. Could Edmund, always so sensible, be right? Had she brought this on herself? She shook her head to wake herself from this nightmare of her making, made still harder by her grandmother's cruel order to break her most precious bond, the only bond that sustained her. The bond to her gentle swan.

But the feasting was soon forgotten as they readied for the coming siege. Barns were stuffed with weapons, food, water and wood for the fires. The Byrh walls and palisades were braced and patched with stone and fresh timbers. Fat-bellied ships stole up river by night, laden with supplies. But, while masons and carpenters laboured day and night, Gytha struggled with a problem all her own. The painted Celtprince had changed. He was distant now. His jokes and charm he kept for others; but no longer for Gytha. All playful teasing stopped along with the sword-play. Before he would laugh, now he dismissed her, without a friendly word. She was his willow girl no more. And the more distant he became, the more upset she became. On one particular he had confronted her, as she returned from riding. 'Have you ever even bled?' he asked. Gytha was so surprised, no words came. He stood there, arms crossed, waiting for her reply. What should she answer?

'Yes, my Lord,' she nodded weakly. 'At Wilton,'

'So Myrgh-teg is a woman,' he said. With no warmth in his voice at her discomfort, and walked away.

*   *   *

One evening, as the setting sun bathed the town in gold light and black swifts screamed round and round the yard, Gytha was alone with her Aunt Gunhild. With no other to confide in, she found the courage to ask the one question that haunted her, while not wanting to hear the answer for fear that it was true.

'Is this God's punishment for seeking his admiration?' she asked, 'he looks at me with hatred now and speaks only cold words.',

Aunt Gunhild thought a while, laying down her needlework on the bench. 'Men's passions overwhelm them. They worship what they desire until it is won. Child, the Lord has blessed you. You are a gift of God's grace, a reward of victory, an honourable and worthy prize. You have your father's fire and your mother's beauty. The Celtprince has your bride gift, yet he may not take it nor you, not yet.'

'Take me? Take me? He has me for his betrothed. I will gladly serve, honour and obey him and will swear on St Erbin's day to be the peace-weaver of our peoples What do you mean, he may not take me, Aunt?'

Her aunt Gunhild, virgin bride of Christ, folded her hands and sighed. 'Would that your mother was here. I am unschooled in the ways of *muliebritatem*. But the Lord can ease your burden, child. Pray with me.' Aunt Gunhild crossed herself, and reciting the testament, said, 'come unto me, all ye that labour and are heavy laden, and I will give you rest.'

But Gytha could not pray. She found no comfort in God. She must face the trials of her womanhood in silence.

PART ONE CHAPTER NINE

THE SCENTED
SWETESOT!

'WHAT DO YOU WANT with her?' Gytha demanded.

Pig-boy was at her halter, the Radknight beside her as they clattered past the guards through the iron-stud oak-gate into the town. inside was a group of crawing Celt women. In the middle of them stood Swetesot, fighting them off, jerking her head back and forth as they grabbed at her golden brow band and scented pendants. She was alone, with no servant or man to guard her. Gytha stopped her horse.

'We mean her no harm, Myrgh-teg,' said one. 'She's a lyblac witch and has no need of eyes,' said another. 'She says she's a princess, but she stinks worse than a hog's whore.' The crowd laughed. 'They had Pig-boy, now they have a pig girl.' At this the Celt women shrieked. 'piglets with no tongues and no eyes, piglets with no tongues and no eyes.'

A fury engulfed Gytha. 'Leave her be,' she shouted, but they ignored her. Swetesot had dropped her basket and was clutching her head. 'I said leave her be,' Gytha cried again, louder that time. 'Radknight!' she called, waving him forward. The painted women, harridans all, drew back, shouting insults and curses in their tongue.

'Come,' said Gytha, beckoning Swetesot, 'jump up'. Leaning down, she seized her arm and pulled the scented princess of the Wild Field upwards in front of her. 'Heathen demon,' the women shouted, as they rode away. 'Heathen demon, Myrgh-teg devil friend!'

'Thank you, Gytha Harold's daughter,' said Swetesot, gasping for breath 'a second debt I cannot repay. You give me life not once, but twice.'

At the stable, the young woman dropped feather-lightly onto both feet. Absently, she patted Gytha's horse on the neck, running her hand inside the bridle. She was calmer now. 'Lady, with what do you command your horse?' she asked, her accent like none that Gytha had heard before.

Then Gytha, Pig-boy and the Radknight watched Swetesot speak to the horse in a high whisper, adjusting everything – saddle, bridle, girth and stirrups – with skilful fingers. The horse was motionless, with only its ears swivelling to hear her better.

'There,' Swetesot said. 'Now he is yours to command with thoughts and milk-soft hand.'

Gytha was startled, remembering the words of the turbaned stench-man. 'She is princess; from the Wild Field, with two eyes and a tongue in her head. Aye, her father is Khan of all the grass ocean, her kin saddle-born. Suckled on sour qumiz milk, they live and die on stallions. Angry and quick-tempered they fear nothing, but all men fear them.'

Gytha slipped from the saddle. 'Who was this princess of the Wild Field?' she wondered. Seizing Swetesot's hand, she ordered Pig-boy that this was how she wanted her horse saddled in future.

'Swetesot? I have never heard such a strange name. None here are named Swetesot,' said Gytha.

The young woman paused warily, then her eyes vanished as she laughed. 'It means one hundred flowers. And your name, what does Gytha mean?'

Gytha shrugged, 'I don't know, my father named me after his mother. My full name is Ēadg⁻yða, Gytha for short. My father was king of the English for forty weeks and one day.'

'And my father is the great Khan, ruler of the nine clans,' said the scented Swetesot.

Gytha could contain herself no longer. The questions tumbled out: 'who are you? Is the stench-man kind or does he beat you? Where are you from? How did you get here? Are you a princess or a slave? How can you still see when your eyes vanish?'

Swetesot giggled. 'I see as a hawk sees a mouse.'

'I think it's funny,' said Gytha. 'Does everyone look like you in this Wild Field?'

Swetesot nodded. 'My people, yes. My people think me beautiful. Do you think me beautiful?'

'Yes, I think so, do you think me beautiful?' .

Swetesot chuckled, her mouth turned down at the corners. 'What use is golden hair and pond blue eyes if you would not see the white-furred fox until he bit your long nose off?'

'My nose isn't long!' said Gytha, affronted, touching the end of her nose.

'Yes, it is,' said Swetesot. 'All English have long noses; red turnip faces and straw for hair,' and she rocked with laughter. Gytha joined in, loving the fun of talking to this girl not much older than her. Yet, while everything about the scented Swetesot was different, her hair, her skin, her eyes, her clothes, she felt a warmth, a fellowship that surprised her.

The two girls soon became inseparable, the scented Swetesot slipping away from her turbaned stench-man, and meeting Gytha in the barn. Sometimes they rode together, picking their way across the water meadows and galloping over the green hillside, with larks trilling above them. It seemed to Gytha that even the fieriest, newly broken horse, freshly corned and bucking, would do Swetesot's bidding.

'I swear you have limed your arse to the saddle,' said Gytha, watching as her horse leapt sidewise at a startled hare.

One sun filled day, Gytha and her heart friend were out riding, guarded as always by the Radknight and the Pig-boy. Swetesot had a short bow across a shoulder, and arrows in a quiver. Gytha, only a jewelled wounding-knife at her belt. Her youngest brother Magnus and her middle brother Edmund were hawking and they galloped to join them. With worthy prey eluding the boys, and nothing for Swetesot to shoot with her arrows, the two girls quickly bored.

'How many falcons do you have?' asked Swetesot, as she watched the matchless Gyr and Saker, tugging to be sky-free.

'Only this Saker, which was a gift from my father,' answered Edmund.

'And this Gyr that was my father's also,' said Magnus.

'My father has one thousand hunting hawks,' said Swetesot, 'where sky neither ends nor earth begins. Where a million flowers bloom and riders steer by heaven's unweary stars. Where numberless pink flamingos rise as one from white salt lakes, where giant aurochs graze, and lions tear on antelopes, a land where wild partridges leap skyward to tell of danger before any man can know it. My father is the mightiest Khan with a hundred wives, one thousand camels and ten thousand horses.'

Gytha could not imagine so many horses or wives or flowers or camels, whatever they were. A million flowers. She wanted so much to see a million flowers in the Wild Field, but the boys rolled their eyes at such boasting.

'What shall we do now?' Gytha asked, jumping off her horse to seek the shade of a knarling oak. The others joined her. 'I don't want to return to the Hall and hear more talk of the Bastard. May God strike him and cast him into the fiery furnace,' she said bitterly.

At the mention of that name all the joy vanished from their day; young lives, upended in the tumult from which there was no escape. That was until Swetesot jumped to her feet. They watched her tuck her tunic in her belt, kick off her boots, undo the girth-strap, and lay the saddle on the grass. Then, as her horse's questing lips and the lush grass were joyfully re-acquainted, she stepped lightly over its mane. Up went its head in surprise, lifting Swetesot into the air, before sliding backwards down its neck, onto its back, from where she kicked and whipped the beast into a full gallop. Then, swinging round to fly past them, she climbed under its neck, clinging as a monkey to its mother, then up onto its back again. Hawking forgotten, Edmund and Magnus were open-mouthed at such a trick, but there was more to come. Tugging an arrow from the quiver at her back, Swetesot galloped past them firing not once but twice at the tree above their heads and then as she galloped away, she twisted and fired a third time, the arrow hissing to its mark. The mute Pig-boy jumped up and down, honking in delight. Boasts forgiven, the Radknight and Magnus shouted oaths of admiration. Only quiet Edmund, comforting the flustering bird on his arm, said nothing as Swetesot, now standing on the little stallion's rump, brought it to a shuddering halt by them, laughing all the while as she jumped down.

'Teach us, teach us,' said Magnus, 'teach us your tricks!' Swetesot, nimble as an elf, grinned triumphantly, standing in front of him, her legs slightly apart and her arms crossed.

'What would you learn, Lord Magnus, to stand, to loose a parting arrow, to cling beneath its neck as a drowning man clings to a branch? But first return to your crib,' she replied.

'Crib?' asked Magnus, not understanding.

'She means she was born to it. Saddle born, the Wild Field is in her blood, as brine flows in the veins of Northmen,' explained Gytha.

Swetesot giggled. 'Sour qumiz milk is in my blood. Come Magnus, try this,' and the rest of the afternoon they each stepped across their horse's necks and let themselves be lifted.

So Gytha learnt about Swetesot's world beyond the sea. 'Tell me more about the Wild Field,' she would say, and Swetesot would answer in her own language, rocking gently, in a low wavering chant, not singing, but not talking either. Gytha would ask her to translate.

'The air was filled with the notes of a thousand different birds. On high hovered the hawks, their wings outspread, and their eyes fixed intently on the grass. The cries of a flock of wild ducks, ascending from one side, were echoed from the distant lake. From the grass arose, with measured sweep, a gull, and skimmed wantonly through blue waves of air. And now she has vanished on high, and appears only as a black dot: now she has turned her wings, and shines in the sunlight. Oh, steppe, how beautiful you are!' Swetesot would pause. 'Pond eyes, our Wild Field is without trees. Just the sky and the black earth and the grass. In the north it is so cold that monsters with tusks longer than the tallest man must live underground. In the south, the heat is so great that no man may endure it, but a camel can walk a week without water, yet spit in your eye! And when my people move to fresh pastures, our herds, ox-carts and loaded camels stretch from horizon to horizon. The dust lifts into the sky in such a cloud, that all the world knows we Qypchaq, the people of the Wild Field, come, and they are afraid.

Gytha would sit motionless, her blue eyes wide with wonder. Sometimes her brothers Magnus or Edmund would listen. Edmund was always eager to know about her father's hawks, and Magnus would ask about the horse-warriors in the Khan's army. But Gytha liked it best when the two of them were alone and Swetesot talked and talked.

'You are safe here now, Swetesot. My brother Godwine, as rightful King, has given his word to protect you and your master the turbaned stench-man,' said Gytha. Swetesot took her hand, her almond eyes filling with tears. 'No, pond eyes, you are my friend and I yours, for we are both the daughters of great kings. But your green grass hillocks are not my Wild Field and we are not safe, nowhere is safe, neither for you nor I. Your brother Godwine is young, and this enemy of whom you speak, the Bastard William, may bide his time. But he will come and I am here in England farther from the Wild Field than ever before and more in danger than ever before.'

Gytha could think no more of the danger that lay ahead. To do so filled her nights with dread. Instead, she day-dreamed of the River Princes and the grass ocean and longed not to be at Exeter, not to be betrothed to the painted Celtprince, and wanted so badly to see her mother, her gentle swan, again.

'Tell me about your mother,' asked Swetesot one day. 'You talk with such love and sorrow, where is she, does she live? I have not seen her. Only your aunt and your grandmother. Oh, how I fear the Mother of Heroes, she is kin to the Queen Ingegerd, wife of the one they called Wise who treated me so cruelly. She was a Dane-bride sent from the Dane lands, through the forests and the marsh to the River Prince, and she mothered many beautiful daughters.

Gytha shook her head, uncomprehending, unsure how to begin her own story. It had all happened so quickly. 'My mother is not here, she is a prisoner, sick from grief after my father was killed. But she will come. I pray each day she will come.' She paused, and cleared her throat of the tears that had gathered there. 'She is beautiful. Her name is Edith, Edith Swan-neck, she is my gentle swan.'

The slender Swetesot took Gytha's hand. 'Edith Swan-neck, it is a beautiful name. I see her in my mind's eye, beautiful like you. I still see my mother and hear her tears as they took me away. I wake in the night and feel her near me. I smell her breath on my cheek, her kiss, her gentle voice …,' Swetesot's voice tailed away. The two young women hugged each other. There was no need for words.

'But you have your brothers,' said Swetesot finally.

'Yes,' Gytha replied. 'I have my brothers.' And she told Swetesot how they had fled Waltham after her father was killed.

'And these people of the River, do they believe in God and in his son Jesus Christ?'

'Aye,' said Swetesot, her face alive with laughter. 'They cross themselves and kiss paintings, over and over, every day, like this. Their priests have big black beards and they sing deep songs. But Gytha, they smell and say my gods are devils.'

'What gods? Of what gods do you speak?'

'The gods of my people,' said Swetesot thoughtfully.

'There is only one God and Jesus Christ is his son,' said Gytha.

'No, dear sister, treasure of my breast,' said Swetesot, 'You have only one God but there are seven times seven. Perun, God of Thunder, maker of lightening with his axe, and Volos who lives beneath. Dazhbog, Khors, Svarog, Mokosh and the three headed Triglav. Each day I give offering to Tengri, the blue eternal sky and to the thrice bright Sun and to the moist mother earth.'

'Enough, you speak sorcery. There is only one God in Heaven, and our Lord Jesus Christ is his son.'

There was silence between them. A silence neither wanted. Gytha broke it first.

'Mother of Heroes has her gods too: Odin, Thor and Loki.'

Swetesot smiled, her almond eyes crinkling once more. 'It is not the first time people of the book attack my gods. You said nothing wrong.'

'What people? What book?' Gytha asked. 'You speak in riddles.'

Swetesot laughed, 'I don't know, let's talk of other things. Tell me about your betrothed, this painted man, who stirs his voice from syrup in his barrel chest.'

Swearing Swetesot to secrecy or eternal damnation, Gytha talked of her hurt and hatred for the Celtprince. How as the Serpent beguiles, the muscled Baladrddellt had turned her head with his hard attentions, but now discarded her. Gytha was shaking her head, struggling to make words for what she knew in her heart to be true.

'Oh Swetesot, he has disregarded me. He speaks no more kindness nor cares for me now. I am to be the peace-weaver between his people and mine. The Mother of Heroes has ordered it and St Paul says it is better to marry than to burn. But I fear life with this man more than I fear for my people. I fear it even more than I fear the Bastard William himself.'

Swetesot nodded. 'I too have feared for my life, Gytha. I feared as war-men named me heathen in your Hall, and as screeching hags tore at this scent band around my brow, I thought my life must end until you saved me, a second time.'

'Oh Swetesot, I pray every day to be brave as you. To have the courage of St Perpetua, ground in the teeth of lions, but denying the howling throng her terror with her silence.'

'We, womankind, have within us quickness and valour. Weapons enough for the life-road of our nobility, Gytha.'

'On this life-road, Swetesot, I have no slaughter-field where my valour is weighed, as my father's was. What use is quickness, when the painted Celtprince will toss me to a nunnery for ever?'

'He will not. I'll wager he waits. The turbaned stench-man meditates daily how he might enjoy delights that I deny him. You might do the same with your betrothed.'

Gytha was stunned at Swetesot's words. 'But you are his barter-bride, princess and slave. Does he not beat you?'

As all humanity drained from her face, Swetesot asked 'and have the morning sun dismount at our dwelling as he lies gurgling in his blood-bed?' She snorted, 'I am Qypchaq. I fear no man.'

'You are brave and wise, but enough of troubles,' said Gytha. 'Tell me about the home of the River Princes.'

'Ah, Kiev,' said Swetesot, 'there is a mighty church above the river with twelve golden domes which shine bright as twelve suns in the sky. The great river is like your sea, with the shore far distant and the Wild Field beyond. In the spring, countless boats bring blond giants from the North Land who ride the snow melt with the harvest of collared grinding-slaves, furs, warm amber-stone with living flies within, and sweet honey from the endless forest. And from the scorching sun land of the south, come brown men on camels tied head to tail led by turbaned traders with gold, silks, perfume and spices, for the princes and their jewelled wives. And in winter, when the snow is deep enough to lose a horse and the great river freezes thick, the poor people must fish through ice-holes and drink firewater to stay warm.'

On and on the stories came, Swetesot weaving a realm for Gytha that was beyond her imagining in the soft green folds of Wessex.

'And why are you bartered to the Stench-man?'

Swetesot's narrow eyes over-filled with tears. She told how she was torn away from her brothers and her mother as tribute-daughter to Grand Prince Yaroslav, wisest of all the River Princes, and how with gold, jewels, fine clothes and servants she had lived, captive in Kiev among the river princes in the land they call Rus.

'I had never lived in a Hall, and I cried every night to return to my people, where children ride free to hunt rabbits and quail, or pin an eagle to the sky with arrows if they wish, and where my mother gave us bowls of soured mares' milk and honey cakes to eat,' said Swetesot.

'These River Princes mocked me, saying I was the daughter of horses and had a horse's tail for hair. They laughed when I spoke and when I cursed them in my tongue.' She told Gytha how the River Princes would gather in a great camp of tents and carpets, to hunt and to talk of war and peace. And how each might offer a daughter for marriage. It was from here too that traders were sent far and wide to seek brides for the sons of these men of war.

'The River Princes take wives from the four corners. But the princes shunned me, a tribute daughter from the Wild Field. None took me for his bride and on his return to Kiev, the Grand Prince expelled me from the royal hall above the river.

'But why?,' Gytha asked.

Swetesot paused, 'Because I was with child!'

'And so, the stench-man bought you as his collar thrall?' said Gytha quietly, as Swetesot's story, so much worse than hers, sunk home.

Swetesot nodded. 'I, tribute princess, daughter of the Khan, Ruler of the Grass Ocean, was bartered for odours.' There was fury in her voice. 'He purified me for six months with myrrh and six months with oils. On we journeyed, west from Kiev for many days through forests so dark and marshes so dank, I doubted I would again see the sky or green grass, until I could ride no further and my son was born in a dwelling near to Paris.'

'And your son lives?' Asked Gytha.

Swetesot smiled radiantly. 'Yes! Come, pond eyes, my heart-dear friend, to my lodging tomorrow, but tell no-one. The turbaned merchant forbids it.'

The next day, schooling over, Gytha slipped away with the Radknight, unnoticed, to escort her. They walked to where Swetesot and the stench-man lived in a low bothy like any other in the Byrh, but the inside was unlike any Celt or English hearth. There were rugs on the walls, and sheepskins and bright patterned carpets covered the floor; there were no stools next to the fire pit. Around the side were low sleeping shelves, and in between open chests with candle trees, silver cups and slender, polished metal jugs. There was a lion's pelt draped over a camel saddle. Swetesot whispered to her to sit on it, next to a crib.

'Here is my breast-treasure,' said Swetesot, pulling a blanket aside to reveal a little boy, asleep, his thumb in his mouth.

'Oh, he is so beautiful, he looks like you!'

'His name is Boniak. He will be a great warrior. I will teach him to hunt, to horse war, to shoot with arrows as my people do, and never to yield even to death itself. He will howl as a wolf in the night and many wolves will answer him with their howls. He will strike terror in his enemies and plant his standard in their hearts.'

'And the child's father, what of him?'

Swetesot said nothing, pain crossing her face.

'Prince Oleg, favoured grandson of Grand Prince Yaroslav, whom they call Wise.'

'It is written that love is the greatest virtue.'

Swetesot snorted. 'Love! Prince Oleg beat me, battered down the gate of my virginity and tore my maidenhood from me. Nobody answered my cries, nor saved me when I begged him to stop. The other princes were no better, except one. I thought him beautiful. His name was Vladimir. They called him the Lone Warrior and his mother was an Imperial Princess, the purple blooded daughter of the Emperor in Byzantium! He showed me kindness, but when he spoke for me, his grandfather banished him to Suzdal, far from Kiev. But let us not speak of it. My son will avenge me. He will kill his father.'

Gytha hesitated to let Swetesot's pain and fury pass.

'Your home is so different from the Irlesbyri Hall,' she said, 'where we have hard benches, tables, weapons, shields and hunting dogs, you have only rugs and carpets and chests.'

'My home is as a hollowed tree,' Swetesot replied. 'All can be carried away if we must leave quickly. We are wanderers, never knowing where or how long we stay.'

They talked and Gytha watched as Swetesot fed her baby and settled him once more in the crib. Next to him was a chest, the lid pushed back. Inside were clothes.

'I think you have seen this before,' Swetesot said, lifting out the crimson dress she had worn the first day, its tiny bells tinkling.

Gytha took it. The feel of it amazed her. 'Is it fur?' she asked, pressing her face to the soft cloth. Her own tunic seemed so coarse.

'My people call it "barkhat". the Franks say "velors". These are the slippers.' She pulled out a little pair which curled up at the front, tied in a blue ribbon.

'I would love to have such slippers,' Gytha sighed, clutching them to her chest.

'Only princesses wear red slippers in the palace on the river. No others may wear them.'

'I am a princess' Gytha said. 'Though my father is dead, he was King in this land.' She paused. Outside they heard the Radknight cry halt, then the turbaned merchant called sharply for Swetesot. Swetesot stiffened. The stench-man stopped as he entered, catching sight of Gytha. 'Ah, fair lady,' he said, surprised, his anger giving way to the oiled tones of trade. 'You are most welcome in our modest lodging, great lady.' Then, turning to Swetesot, he shouted 'they will not let us leave. No stranger from distant lands may leave! It is you who wished we stay, now none may leave the Byrh.' He then stopped shouting as quickly as he started. 'But I forget myself, great lady. Will you join us, fair lady, in the name of Allah the merciful the wise, to eat? You are most welcome in our lowly abode.'

'Yes, stay,' said Swetesot, smiling. 'You bless us with your company.'

So Gytha stayed, fiddling nervously with her cowl. A sudden longing overwhelmed her. Swetesot glanced at her, smiled, and took her hand. 'You are most welcome, Princess.'

Gytha's brothers, Godwine, Edmund and the beardling boy Magnus, together with her betrothed, Baladrddellt, had left to hunt stags on the high-moors. So, she went to the barn, calling for the Pig-boy. He was brushing her horse and stopped when he saw her, bowing deeply. But this time there was no welcoming smile on his face. Beckoning Gytha to follow, he walked swiftly to the door that led out to the steaming midden and the orchard. Here he stopped, touching his dirty fingers to his lips and gesturing for her to wait. Gytha was curious, unsure what was happening. Quickly Pig-boy lighted a tallowed mullein plant with a flint, waving it left and right till the smoky flame held. Wrapping his hand in a cloth, crouching as an animal, he hurried to the domed beeskeps that stood deep in the orchard grass beneath the trees.

Gytha watched as he waved the smoking torch near the mouth of the closest hive, before lifting it and snatching out something that lay within, yelping as the bees attacked. Quickly, he bounded back to the barn and doused the flame in a trough. He was holding a wrapped oilcloth. Another bee stung him. Gytha took the bundle and was about to unwrap it. But Pig-boy, agitated, stopped her, signalling her to leave, to flee, half pushing her from the barn.

Once back in her chamber in the Irlesbyri, she unfolded the oilcloth. Inside was a simple writing slate. Her heart throbbed in her ears; her fingers rose to her open mouth in shock. The message was clear enough. It said 'burn the Stench-man out' written in the hand of her betrothed, the painted Celtprince, Baladrddellt rac Denau, Splintered Spear of the South.

The midday meal came and went but she lay face to the wall saying only that she had a woman's cramp. Her mind was racing, but she made herself think. There was no time, she had to save them. Over and over she asked herself how they could do such a thing to Swetesot and her tiny baby. Finally, she called the Radknight to her. Swearing him to secrecy on her psalter, she showed him the message slate.

'Where was it?' he asked, when he had read it. Gytha explained about the message-hive.

'It is a good place to leave messages, guarded by the swarm. The Pig-boy must have known what the message said before he showed you.'

'He is cleverer than all of us.'

'But why, my lady, would your betrothed risk death, defying Earl Godwine's command that the turbaned man and Swetesot not be harmed?'

'Who would care or question it? You heard them in the Hall. But Swetesot is my heart-friend. I have held her baby in my arms. I have shared the bread at their table. She cannot die. She must not die,' said Gytha.

'We must warn her to flee at once – tonight – though to where I don't know,' said the Radknight.'

'I will fetch Swetesot and the stench-man. You, Wulfwyn, think how best they might escape. Find them clothes. Let Swetesot wear a boy's clothing. Her husband will pass as an old washerwoman, and they can hide the baby in the washing.'

Wulfwyn the Radknight looked surprised and nodded. 'Yes. Yes, my lady you have thought of everything.'

'But it may not work,' Warned Gytha. 'We must hurry. No one must know, not my brothers, no one. Be sure to have a knife for each to hold and, Wulfwyn, tell Pig-boy he must return this slate to beneath the wicker where it lay. The burning must go ahead or we will be found out.'

That night, near the fresh-earth wall, flames leapt, embers rising like a million stars over the town. No one dared approach the scorching fire that consumed the small bothy, the stench-man's oils and fragrant unguents nourishing the pyre. The next morning all that remained of her hollow tree, as Swetesot called it, was a smoking pile. A charred crib lay on its side and in a blackened chest some tiny bells remained.

No one had given much heed to the blind boy with only slits for eyes, nor the stooped washer-woman with her heavy bundle, who shuffled unchallenged past the weapon bearers at the Byrh gate and made their way towards the new dock.

Wulfwyn the Radknight and the Pig-boy sauntered along the shore, idly shying pebbles at the gulls as a boat left the river Exe on the falling tide. On board the washerwoman gave the Flemish steersman two silver pennies. A baby whimpered.

For Gytha, there was no triumph, only sadness and confusion. Her heart-friend Swetesot was gone, lost to the

Wild Field. The handsome Celtprince whom all admired had betrayed her beyond redemption, but she had deceived him and her brothers. And still worse, she had placed the Pig-boy, the Radknight and herself in the greatest danger should anyone suspect the measure of their conspiracy.

As Gytha had foretold, the matter was swiftly forgotten. No tears were shed for the stench-man and his scented barter-wife. None who rummaged for the rumoured gold in the smoking ruin remarked at the lack of bodies or crackled bones. Only Gytha grieved for Swetesot, tribute princess from the grass ocean where the horizon never ends, shamed by a River Prince, bartered to a stench-man, and now betrayed by the man to whom Gytha was betrothed.

PART ONE CHAPTER TEN

BESIEGED

SLIP-SILVER FROST GREYED the battlements and the stamping, shivering sentries in rime. An ice haze lingered in the valley. Every hall, barn and shed was stuffed with weapons, grain, apples, salt meat, smoke meat, live cattle and sheep. When news reached them that The Bastard King now demanded a tax of eighteen pounds of gold from Exeter, promising brutal retribution if this levy went unpaid, an urgent meeting of the Council of Elders was called. Gytha took her place next to her grandmother for the first time.

The Reeve shouted to get his voice heard. 'I say give this William tribute and the oath of fealty, as London did, as Winchester did, as do the free cities of Lombardy to their Emperor, in return for being left in peace, it is the choice of wise men.'

Fury burnt in the Old Lady's breast at his words. 'Wise men? Cowardly men who would be guilt-brothers with the enemy. Hear this, Reeve: we will give no oaths, no fealty. We will not receive this William within our walls. We pay to him no more than was due to Kings in former times.'

The Reeve shifted his gaze to Gytha; 'Your wise aunt, our Queen Edith, knew that if Winchester defied the duke, there would be no rescue. Your father was defeated and dead, and your kinsman Sweyn Estrithson the Dane King offered no help. Yet your grandmother would have us defy King William still.'

Gytha needed no reminding of torched houses, starving people, the sickness and everywhere the smell of rotting animals, as his army was harrying the South, but said nothing.

Blaecman stood up, calling for calm. 'We are divided. The devil sows dissent among us. The Bastard William's men harry and slaughter our miserable people. That is why you Elders here at Exeter prefer tranquillity at any price.'

Baladrddellt rac Denau stood. 'Noble lady, my people serve you and will stand with you against the Bastard King.'

Gytha gasped to hear this weasel tongue offer his people to the defence of Exeter. She knew it was a black lie, and he would betray them all. She could feel the anger swelling inside her, until she could scarcely stop herself from calling out 'he lies, do not trust him, he would murder one most dear to me, and thought nothing of it, and he will betray you.'

She sat still as others about her spoke, her mind in turmoil. If she spoke to her brothers, they would not believe her, or worse, they would ask why. But she would have her revenge. Then a thought came to her and Gytha made herself a promise.

'I must marry, but he will never lie with me,' she swore to herself. 'They will have to bury me first.'

After the meeting that had ended in uproar, the painted Celt was in fine humour as men thumped him across his broad shoulders and praised him for his words.

'I drink to our Painted Celt Prince,' growled the Twice Scarred Thegn Eadric, raising a carved cup, 'who choses our rebellion and disorder over their peace and tranquillity. May the end be good when God wills it!'

'And what does my betrothed wife-child say, so that the bard might pluck a song as you pluck at my heart,' said Baladrddellt rac Denau, his eyes crinkling, his deep laugh, that had been so attractive to her, making her shudder at its insincerity. The assembled family and shield warriors called out, 'yes, let us hear a song of fair Lady Gytha and the prince Baladrddellt rac Denau.'

Gytha sat stiff-backed and un-moving, staring straight ahead as the bard sang, 'Venus set him alight with her blazing brand.'

The Company of men and women shouted out in reply, laughing, banging their knife hilts on the wooden table-tops. 'His heart and body seared by the fire of love.'

Gytha blushed crimson and pulled the cowl across her face. Everyone was staring at her.

'The thought of his Splintered Spear has silenced her,' slurred the Twice Scarred Thegn Eadric, his voice full of mead. Some about him laughed, but one look from the Old Lady silenced them all. Baladrddellt rac Denau was now standing, his eyes blazing, and with a look of fury at Gytha he stormed from the Hall.

Let him be angry at her. She did not care. 'I must marry you but you will never lie with me,' she repeated under her breath. 'They will bury me first.'

'Are you mad!' shouted Godwine the moment her brothers were alone with her. 'The Celtprince pledged to us his people. Yet you shamed him.'

Gytha was defiant. 'I did not shame him. I said nothing.'

'Yes, you said nothing, Gytha,' said Edmund, 'but words were not needed. Your face betrayed you.'

Gytha thought hard for what seemed like an age, leaving the boys waiting. Should she tell them all that she had learnt?

Should she tell them that the stench-man and Swetesot had not perished in the fire? That it was Pig-boy who had found the message from the prince to his Celtish folk under the watchful guard of the bees?

'Of course!' Wulfwyn had exclaimed. 'The Prince uses the dumb Pig-boy to carry secret messages from the Hall! Who would ever question him? He can squeal no more under torture than at the bee's sting.'

'Yes, and Pig-boy reads every one before he slips them to the hive-mouth, don't you Pig-boy?' Gytha had said in amazement. 'And you have learned the Celtish tongue, yet you have no tongue to speak it. I have a tongue but do not know one word beyond my name. Nor will I ever,' she added darkly.

'You speak more than he ever will.' The loyal Radknight prodded at Pig-boy with a finger. Gytha laughed. Pig-boy gave a kind of bray.

Should she tell them that from then on, Gytha and the Radknight had Pig-boy be their eyes and ears? News had not been long in coming. Baladrddellt rac Denau's men beyond the wall kept him informed, and he told them of the divisions in the town between the Elders who sought peace with the king and Godwine's hearthguard, who would fight. 'Save yourselves,' Baladrddellt rac Denau had told his people in one message. 'No one comes to aid the sons of Harold or their grandmother, not from the West, from the mountains in the north, nor the Dane king in the east. None are more alone than they at Exeter,' he told them. 'Give fealty to William or die.'

'If he thinks our cause is lost and Godwine too young, why does he stay at Exeter, and swear his battle-axe and sword to my grandmother?' Gytha had said, furious at the Celt prince's treachery.

'To seize your bride gift, my lady,' replied the Radknight. 'He will bring all the West to the Bastard king, when it his prize to give.'

'If I am to be his ring-adorned wife, why does he need to seize the bride gift from me? My father had no wish to seize my mother's lands, as you well know.' Gytha had shaken her head, trying to understand. 'They are hers, or they were.' Her voice tailed away.

'Yes,' the Radknight had said, 'You, lady Gytha, are his prize. But if he waits, and deceives the Mother of Heroes, into thinking his loyalty is unquestioned, then he has both lands and beauty.'

Gytha had blushed at his words.

So, when Godwine was shouting at her, she had no answer, but to tell him all she knew.

But first, her face and jaw set grim, looking older than her maiden years, she made them swear by the Cross-oath that bound them, not to say a word. For if they did, she told them, Baladrddellt rac Denau would kill the Radknight and Pig-boy and beat her most cruelly.

To Godwine it was nonsense, but Edmund said to let her speak. Even Magnus was quiet as Gytha spelled out all she knew – about the hive and the messages – and how with her help, the turbaned stenchman and his bartered wife had got away on a galley bound for Flanders.

By now her brothers were silent, hanging on her every word. 'Where is Wulfwyn? I want him here,' said Godwine, who then listened as the Radknight repeated the Celt prince's plot to steal all their estates and their tin mines and swear fealty to the Bastard King.

'That Celtish thief will die before he gets one hide of ours,' was all Godwine could say, he was so angry.

Thoughtful Edmund, calmer than his brother, added, 'It explains a lot too. I had doubted why his kind would side with us English folk. Now I understand.'

'But what of Gytha?' asked the beardling boy Magnus. 'She is to marry him not forty days from now.'

'Yes', said Gytha, looking at each one of them. 'What of me? I would die than lie with him.'

But the brothers had no words for her. Godwine looked at her dispassionately, with irritation, even. 'Gytha, you are betrothed before the Most High who knows all secrets. The marriage gift is forfeit. It is our grandmother's will.'

'Will you speak to her, please Godwine,' begged Gytha. 'I was joyful. She betrothed me to a friend, to save me from a Norman's bed. Spear-valiant she called him but I must now wed a traitor, an enemy worse as any who ploughed the sea from Normandy to kill us.' She faltered, overcome by the fate destiny had tossed her. 'Please, Godwine.'

But fate had other plans for Harold's children. The weather turned evil cold. Rain-soaked gales raged in from the west, then as winter gripped them, the rude north wind returned, stiffening the deep puddled tracks, while armed men froze.

The bastard King William was marching west with an army of English traitors, harrying, torching, and raping, as was the Norman way. Town after town – Dorchester, Bridport, Wareham and Shaftesbury – implored in vain to be spared his wrath. Bridport was laid waste; in Dorchester few houses remained – the price they paid for siding with Harold's sons.

Godwine decreed that the marriage of his sister to Baladrddellt rac Denau would be delayed and ordered that whoever hoarded food would be killed. Out on the high-wall, look outs and archers stamped and shivered and swore, the frosted air heavy with their shouts, their breath-smoke

and their fires. Some let loose an arrow at a rabbit or a rook
to pass the time. Other men huddled at the braziers, playing
dice, drinking and soaking up heat to sustain them through
their watch. Weapons of every shape and size were polished,
sharpened and ready. Not four miles away, William's soldiers
were gathered.

Harold's sons and the leather-caped thegns made ready.
Still there was no agreement between the defenders, ripping
Exeter apart from within. Led by the Magistrate, the Elders
prevailed over Godwine and his grandmother, Mother of
Heroes, to seek peace.

The Twice Scarred Eadric, the Old Thegn, the Burnished
Huscarl Roni, and the leather-caped thegns urged Godwine
to have the traitor killed. But a wiser counsel prevailed. The
Towering Mace Monk Blaecman, now joined by the abbots
from the monasteries of Somerset and Dorset, warned that
to kill the Elder now would turn all the people of the west
against them.

'It is not for us to do the work of the enemy,' the Towering
Blaecman told the Old Thegn. 'Fear not, this king will reject
their peace offer, he will accept no contract, no bargain, only
submission or death.'

And so, the ladies watched from the walls – Gytha, her
grandmother, and Aunt Gunhild – as the Elders of Exeter
went out to meet the advancing King, offering themselves
as hostages.

'Death to Traitors!' shouted Godwine. 'Death to Traitors!'
echoed his leather-caped thegns. The piper Thorgood played
a dour tune.

Suddenly the Norman army parted. Through the gap rode
King William the Bastard, followed by cavalry, the armoured
knights of Senlac field, driving the hostages before them.
None at Exeter had seen the Norman before. How they stared

at the figure in the glinting corselet of silver rings. The man who, in one year, had stolen their lands, butchered their men and their animals, burnt their crops and their churches, and set brother on brother. The piper Thorgood stopped mid breath.

A knight stepped forward. 'Open your gate. The King of the English commands the gate to be opened. He will grant safe passage to all the people of Exeter, High Byrh of the West, to the kin of Harold Godwineson, to the leather-caped thegns of the west, so too the men of God. No harm will come to them.'

'Tell the Bastard we know not what he says nor care,' shouted Godwine.

'The king of the English commands it,' came the reply. 'See how he leads an English host.'

At this, a great roaring and booing erupted on the Byrh-wall, the defenders banging weapons on the wooden parapets. 'Traitors!' they shouted.

'Fear for your lives, Normans. Traitors chew at any hand,' shouted the Twice Scarred Eadric.

'An English war-shaft up your arse!' yelled the axed and burnished Roni, who had stood with Harold at Stamford Bridge.

Then a hostage was marched to the dead ground before the gate. He was young. 'Save yourselves. Give tribute and fealty to the lawful king!' he shouted to the deaf ears of rebellion.

Godwine's men jeered. William the Bastard waited no longer and ordered the hostage to his knees. A low growl ran along the rampart. Both armies, attacked and attacker, waited. It started to rain. A brazier on a cart drew up, smouldering orange against the grey of armed men and the winter sky.

Blaecman, seeing quickly what was about to happen, shouted, 'NO! Free him, Norman, in God's name or hear the devil hail your soul at the mouth of hell.'

With one last look towards the battlement where Gytha stood, the Norman King swung his horse away. A knight took an iron from the fire and, holding its golden tip up for the English to see, thrust it hard into the hostage's face. His screams were drowned only as the men of Exeter roared in fury, clattering swords and war-shafts against the wooden battlement, the air filled with English defiance.

The screams of the young man on the ground could still be heard as a large Norman stepped across him and plunged a merciful longsword through his heart.

'See,' said Baladrddellt rac Denau, 'how they pin him to the soil of his fathers. He did not need to die for you, Godwine Haroldson. I knew him well; he was my kin. He did not need to offer himself. He was a boy.'

Hands went to hilts at the Celt prince's words. Godwine said nothing.

Then, suddenly, there was laughter and a great cheer from the archers and slingers on the battlements. On the highest point above the East Gate stood a tiny figure of a man, his back to the Hoard. Bending over, he hauled down his breeches and, gripping his arse cheeks with his hands, he wiggled this way and that. It was Pig-boy.

'Pig-boy, Pig-boy, Pig-boy, Pig-boy!' they shouted, pointing with their thrusting spears, a tempest of farting that grew to a jeering, cheering roar. Others jumped up and they too pulled down their breeches, baring white rumps at the French. An arrow flew and then another, then hundreds, most falling short. Amidst the laughter at the Pig-boy's welcome, as it soon became known, there were urgent calls to take cover and get the woman below. Pipers played. The siege of Exeter, High Byrh of the West, had begun.

*   *   *

The wounded and the dying were not long in coming to the Irlesbyri. Gytha and the women heard the crashing rending of the flying rocks that topped the rampart, so recently rebuilt, finding a moan, a curse, or scream at the finish of their flight. Sometimes a cry would tell an arrow found its quarry, and a man would be rushed to the Hall like a baby in the arms of friends as he called out to his Maker and his mother in pain. Aunt Gunhild and the other women smeared the wounds with poultices of comfrey, feverfew, the bitter hyssop and rosemary, which Gytha ground to a paste with scalding water and honey.

In an echo of her own father's death, Gytha held the hand of one who had only a bloodied arrow shaft where his eye should be. She could not look as the man's life faded. She drew her cowl across her face and wept for him as for herself. The friend that had brought him stood, then said, 'Look closely, my lady. It was an English arrow.'

From time to time there was a cheer as the defenders found their mark, but they knew this fight would not be quickly over. There was no escape, no prayer or curse that shielded them. Only ox-hard leather or iron rings might save a man from an arrow, but not the ballista bolt.

Norman siege towers and war machines appeared on the ridge. Mangonel buckets, flinging stones and red-hot irons that arched into the sky, thumping down and splintering the parapet, men's bones and homes, striking terror till, in time, the English learned to bob up after each strike to jeer and taunt and swear blasphemies at the enemy.

Soon there were bodies in the street, children in search of water for their families or women bringing their menfolk food at their posts. On her way to the chapel with her aunt, Gytha stepped across one corpse, a young woman not much older than her. A stray dog was lapping at the dead woman's hand, which still gripped a wooden pitcher. Beer for a father or a brother, perhaps, Gytha wondered. Aunt Gunhild crossed herself and tugged at Gytha to hurry on.

The clamour of the siege never let up. The men, and her brothers, would come in to the Hall demanding food day and night. Nobody smiled, nobody talked, everyone prayed for deliverance. Their food grew greyer – broth, bread and stinking dried fish – and when they had eaten, they returned to the wall in silence. Gytha could do nothing but wait and listen to the muffled war outside, heed the shouts of thegns, and the groans of the dying in the foetid hall.

Gytha stifled a gasp when she saw the blond tousled figure lying on the dirty floor, his hose dark-soaked in blood. Wulfwyn, Radknight of Thurgarton, his face pale as chalk, was breathing quickly; she could hear him panting. Then a shudder swept through his body and his head twitched. He opened his eyes and seemed to stare right at her, as if begging her to ease his pain.

Suddenly there was yet another crash and voices calling, 'Fire! Fire!' A man ran in shouting that they needed help. Gytha remained crouching by Wulfwyn, refusing to leave him, as Aunt Gunhild summoned all the women to follow her. Now The Hall was dark and empty but for her, alone with the groaning injured. She knelt on the bloody floor beside the young man raised on their estates, who had sworn to her mother always to protect Gytha. Laying her hand on his forehead, she pushed the sweat-sodden hair back from his face. His skin was clammy. He opened his eyes and she smiled at him. 'What happened, my lady?' he asked so faintly.

'Shhh, you've hurt your leg.'

He gave a groan. 'How bad is it?' His voice was a whisper.

'I don't know. Let me look,'

'It burns so,' he hissed, the breath gulping in his throat, fighting down a scream. Taking her jewelled wounding-knife from the scabbard at her belt, Gytha cut the thongs that held his chain war-shirt and pulled it up from the blood-sodden breeks beneath. Near the top of his thigh on one side, there was a rip and she could see the torn gape of red muscle beneath as the crimson blood ran onto the floor. Bunching her cowl in her hand, she forced it onto the wound, scraping away the tumbling hair that fell over her eyes with the back of her arm.

'I need to get your breeches off. Can you lift your arse?' she asked, but when Wulfwyn tried to speak a strangled gargle sound came out.

'Very well, I need to cut the cloth away from the wound.' Holding the bandage with one hand, she ran the knife carefully up the inside of his thigh, pulling at the bloodied fabric. The wound, as wide as a man's fist but not deep, stopped in the Radknight's manhood hair. Gytha hesitated, unsure of what to do. With nothing to hand but her shawl, she pushed his manhood aside, covering him as best she could. Then, using beer from the jug on the bench she doused the wound, sliced the remaining cloth into a long strip for a poultice, then reaching her arm beneath his thigh she pushed bandage gently under him to tie it firmly in a knot at his groin.

'What are you doing?' Baladrddellt rac Denau, his face and tunic blackened by the fire, was striding towards her. Gytha, without raising her head, continued what she was doing.

'Stop that!' he yelled. The young Radknight groaned. 'Stop!' Baladrddellt rac Denau repeated, even louder this time, his deep voice ringing in the gloom of the Hall. Still, Gytha ignored him.

'I'm tying his wound. He will bleed to death if I don't.' Her voice sounded tiny in the great hall, but her loathing of her betrothed and the love she felt for life-ward Wulfwyn Radknight of Thurgarton gave her strength. She turned a scarlet gore-glistened palm for the Celtprince to see the blood. 'There, see, he bleeds.'

'I said you are to stop!' hissed the Celtish prince, even more furious now. He stepped forwards and grabbed Gytha by her hair, jerking her so roughly she called out in pain. 'You will not gainsay me. Do as I order, go to your place.' Then he hit her violently across the face with the back of his gloved hand. Gytha was stunned, day-stars dancing in her head.

'Go before I tell your grandmother how you have fouled your maidenhood,' he said, 'and my betrothal is refused. You will be damned and the bliss of heaven denied you.'

'Go, Lady Gytha,' said Wulfwyn in a whisper. 'I will not die yet a while.'

'You're a Celtish pig. I hate you! All my earthly and heavenly bliss is forfeit that I must marry you!' she shouted, dodging his raised arm.

'Go, Lady. Quickly!' It was one of her collar thralls, a black-haired woman, who had followed the tattooed prince into the Hall. 'I will clean and bind the wound. Go, Lady, now. I beg you.'

Gytha ran back to the women's quarters and threw herself onto her bedding pelts. The Celt's words were searing like a whip, making her gasp. What had she done that he would say such a thing to her? How had she befouled her maidenhood? She had tried to stop the bleeding and bind the wound. Would she be damned for that? In time, her anger turned her fear and pain harder than any keystone in the byrh-wall. How dare he say the bliss of heaven would be denied her! Only the warrior-monk could say that, not him! She hated Baladrddellt rac Denau more than any words she knew. She hated him with every sinew of her being. She hated him for hitting her; she hated him for trying to trick them all, and she hated him for plotting Swetesot's death. But he had failed in that and he would fail to steal their land and he would fail to wed or bed her. With the stinging in her skin subsiding and the brim-tears drying on her cheeks, she would rather kill him rather than let him hurt her again. She, the daughter of Harold Godwineson, King of all the English, and he a marsh prince. She got up to splash cold water on her face, her resolve swelling in her heart. How she would escape her vowed troth to him, she did not know. Perhaps a Norman beyond the walls had an arrow for him.

The collar-thrall came to her. 'Lady, have a care,' she cautioned. 'He is nearby still, and may return.'

'I do not care,' said Gytha, more to herself than to the slave woman. 'How is the Radknight?'

'With all the power of heaven and of the Lord who owns us he will live, Lady. It is the leg meat, not the bone, that is torn away. It will heal.'

'Will he walk? Will he ride again?'

'Yes, the ballista bolt passed between his legs. By God's hand it did not stop to rob him of the fleshy lusts of bed. He will ride and sire many fine sons, fine as him.' The thrall woman cawed, then stopped, seeing Gytha's fear for the boy on the floor.

'Tell me when it is safe, and I will make him broth and go to him.'

'Nothing is safe, Lady. They are ten thousand and we only a few. We are trapped and there is no more safety here than for a rabbit with a ferret at his hole.'

'Earl Godwine Haroldson, my brother, says our archers will withstand all attack. None will dare to cross the open field and hope to live.'

The collar thrall paused, not wanting to set herself against her master's word. 'If you please, my lady, my menfolk say the foe will wait for the raw rain to blind our archers and then ram-charge the East Gate. No drenched archer finds his mark with cold wet fingers and rain slicked shaft.' And so Gytha learnt what the men on the wall were saying from a slave-woman. She repeated it to Magnus, who had heard Baladrddellt rac Denau had struck her and came to find her.

'I hate him,' Gytha told him, fighting back a sob, anger and hurt welling in her again. 'He said all heavenly bliss would be refused me, but I don't know why.'

'How dare he! The Celt is no priest or monk, nor even your husband yet.' said Edmund wisely. 'Go to grandmother, Mother of Heroes, before he does.'

The Old Lady scowled as Gytha repeated the Celt's harsh words. She paused, pursed her lips, her wrinkled face grim like a man's, her blue Danish eyes hard as ice. Then she spoke, her voice low so that none should hear her. 'Child,' cupping Gytha's chin tightly in her ringed hand and pulling her face closer to her own. 'Your betrothed is a brave warrior who fights our enemy even now. You, Gytha, will be the peace-weaver and I will hear no more.'

'But grandmother, Mother of Heroes,' replied Gytha, shaking her head free of the Old Lady's hand, 'that's not fair. You demand I be the peace-weaver. What peace? The Splintered Spear is a bad man and his people also. He is biding his time till they ram the gate. He will betray us!' Her voice was rising. 'I'll not weave peace between his people and ours even if the thread is the hair of Jesus Christ our Lord himself!'

In an instant, her grandmother had cuffed Gytha across the same cheek the Celt had hit only hours before. 'Child!' she barked. 'Were you not the daughter of my King, I would send you and your blaspheming tongue to the stocks. Go to the chapel and beg His forgiveness!'

Gytha's face was afire, but she would not cry out. Standing up, so she stood over her grandmother, she glared at the old woman, the red mark on her down-fair cheek glowing red. 'I hate him and I will not lie with him, nor give him what his lust demands. Ever.'

A hand took her arm. It was Aunt Gunhild. 'Come, Gytha,' she said firmly. 'That is enough.' Then she turned to the old Lady. 'Be calm mother, Gytha has suffered today. She doesn't know what she is saying.'

Gytha paused, as if about to speak, but were no words for the unfairness or the despair she felt, so she said nothing. When the enemy made it to the byrh-wall, as the collar thrall had foretold, Gytha did not care. Nor did she care when a rock crashed from the sky through the East Chapel roof, those trapped beneath a hill of beams and straw set alight by the altar lamp, cooked to death. Even the wall breach held no fear for her, for if they took her captive her life would be no worse than having to suffer this betrayal. She had done no wrong, but every hand was turned against her. She had helped the Wulfwyn the Radknight, her friend and companion, as the other women in the Hall cleaned and wrapped the wounded men as best they might. But she was punished, and not one of her brothers had sided with her.

The collar thrall begged her to seek safety in a cellar, but she refused.

Her brothers had plans for Gytha. While she lay in her cot, the bolster pulled over her head to drown the braying battle horns, they had gathered with their grandmother in the Hall to meet with people of the town.

'Lady,' said one townsman, 'we cannot defend the walls much longer. Already they dig below it and soon a part will fall.'

'You wish that we surrender?' said the Old Lady. 'You saw the fate of your brother-cowards. He will kill you too.'

'No, Lady,' he replied. 'He is a King who will pardon the people of the town, if we,' He faltered.

'If you what?' said the Twice Scarred Thegn Eadric, his hand moving to his longsword.

'If they hand the sons of Harold Godwineson and my lady to the king,' said Baladrddellt rac Denau, who had been listening to the exchange from the shadow beyond the fire-glow. Stepping into the light, his hand was also ready on his hilt. The air was thick with the smell of burning, but the battle beyond fell silent. Baladrddellt rac Denau looked at the Thegn, Godwine and the Old Lady. 'There will be no more killing and the king will spare the town and its people if you surrender to him.'

'That has been your plan all along, devious Celt!' shouted Godwine and, drawing his father's Frankish blade, he lunged at the Celtish prince who deftly stepped aside, his own longsword now in his hand. Holding the tip at Godwine's chin, he growled, 'I said there will be no killing.'

Godwine lowered his longsword. There was a crash; a rock smashed down, and another, and another. The men glared, but the moment had passed. Duty called them to the wall.

'Godwine,' said the Old Lady. 'Put aside your sword and your anger. Prince, you have a plan?'

'Grandmother, Mother of Heroes,' Godwine protested, his eyes still bulging with fury, 'this man betrays us, to steal our lands.'

'Calm yourself, boy,' said Baladrddellt rac Denau. 'I steal nothing. I am betrothed to your sister, Gytha. Exeter will fall, and if you care for the lives of the townsfolk, then you must surrender.'

'We will not surrender,' said Edmund, placing himself next to his elder brother. Then the beardling boy Magnus, too, came to stand beside him, the three royal boys side by side.

Feeling emboldened by the support of his brothers, Godwine spoke again, steadily and implacably. 'Do not trust this man with his silver tongue, grandmother, Mother of Heroes. We know of his plans to rob us. We will not surrender. We are the sons of Harold Godwineson. We will fight.'

'Lady, Mother of Heroes — now grandmother of heroes. No Norman ship blockades the river. Flee while you can.'

'But what of Gytha?' said Magnus.

'Your sister stays here,' said Baladrddellt rac Denau.

'And seize all that is ours. Well, you shall not have Gytha!' The normally quiet Edmund was spitting with the anger that welled inside him. 'Father Blaecman? Our law says no woman must marry against her wish, and Gytha does not wish it. We withdraw from the betrothal.'

'And if you hothead boys try to reclaim her, betrothed to me or not, I will kill her and you,' said the Celtprince.

'We know about your secret messages in the hive and how it was you, Celt, who ordered the stench-man burned to steal his gold.'

'Never mind the heathen. My betrothal is sworn before God. This warrior-monk cannot rupture the engagement. Traditio Puellae, that much I know. Just as your father took your unanointed mother, Edith Swan-neck, I will keep Gytha in the secret places of my bedchamber, or if it pleases me to offer her to King William for more lands in the west. He will reward me well for a Haroldson wench. Now go, English pups! Get back to your posts on the wall before I change my mind about letting you flee my birth-land with your lives.'

Godwine spoke. 'You call our mother a whore! Our mother, whom the true King of the English loved exceedingly. On my vow before God, harm our sister, Celt, and your head will top the splintered spear I plant in your heart.' The Hall was silent;

a dog whined and the Old Thegn spat loudly. Godwine stared at the Celtprince.

'Huh,' sneered the Celt, 'I have no fear of you, King Without a Kingdom, king of nothing and of none. The Lord protects me. Flee downriver now or die here.'

'Lady, he has us. The fox is sniffing at the coop,' whispered the Twice Scarred Thegn Eadric as the Irlesbyri emptied. 'It is a trap. The enemy will know our escape by morning and seize us in the river. And were the Lord in his mercy to grant us passage, where might freedom be? There is no safe harbour to the east – our enemies lie on every shore, left and right – nor have we time to make ready for the stormy sea path to the High King Diarmait in Ireland.'

'Yes, Thegn, I am troubled by his treachery. I thought of him as a son and gave my granddaughter to him to weave peace between the Celt folk and our people.' She shook her head grimly. 'There is no ship. He needs only to seize us for ransom. We would make him a fine bounty.'

'Lady, I have a burning-hate for this Celtish ceorl and his folk. I pray my knife will find a warm home in his heart. No, he has no need for a ship, but if we board one and are then captured, he can say he tried to save us but failed.'

'He is the devil himself. Now I see the cunning of the man,' said the Old Lady. 'We must be more cunning. If we are captured, my sons' deaths will not be avenged and Godwine will never be the rightful King of the English. We go tonight. We'll be clear of the Byrh by dawn. Call Godwine, Roni, and the warrior-monk to me now. Exeter, High Byrh of the West, can be our home no longer.'

'And go where?' asked Godwine.

'We will ride north to Athelney and hide out in the marsh-fort as King Alfred did. We will be safe there,' said the Old Lady, 'Roni, gather my hearthguard. Thegn Eadric, the

Godwineson Hoard. Edmund, the Golden Dragon banner of Wessex. Godwine, your sister. She is in the greatest peril from the painted Celt. Guard her well or he will seize her from us. Good Father Blaecman, you will be my tower. Your axe and your cross will shield me.'

Godwine objected. 'We must fight, not run, Mother of heroes!'

'Harold's-spawn,' said the Twice Scarred Thegn Eadric, 'feel my boot up your arse or your days on earth will be numbered on one hand. By God's will, we will tread on their proud necks. But there is a time to fight well and act manfully and a time to run. And you won't know which, if you have no head nor beating heart. He spared you today, but will not do so again.'

The battle for the wall renewed its fury. The Normans were now beneath the East Gate, ramming at the wooden planks; ladders were raised as quickly as the defenders could spike the climbers with their thrusting spears, and the ditch beneath soon filled with dead. And all the time they dug below the wall to breach the ramparts, rushing in and killing any who stood against them.

Amid the noise of terrible battle, Godwine, son of Harold Godwineson, his dream of kingship shattered, took the beardling boy Magnus, the quiet Edmund and two of his most axe-handed fighters to fetch his sister. Gytha, huddled on her cot, barely raised her head as the four of them entered, though her thrall woman – needle and thread in hand – jumped. The sour smell of battle sweat filled the little room.

'Hurry!' said Magnus, shaking Gytha's shoulder violently.

'Go away,' she moaned from beneath the piled fur.

'One word of this and you die here,' Godwine said to the thrall-collar. 'Now, get her clothed.' He dragged the covers from his sister's cot. 'Gytha, move now!'

'Why?' clutching the bedding.

'We flee Exeter.'

'Flee where?' she asked, sitting up, blinking at the armed men.

'To the river. The byrh-wall will fall and we must be gone. Hurry, bring only what you can carry.'

As Godwine turned to leave, Gytha stopped him. 'What of the Radknight? We cannot leave Wulfwyn. He lies in the Hall.'

'There is no time, said Godwine 'Leave him.'

'But they will kill him!'.

'Better a wound to the heart than a slow death on the mead-hall straw,' answered Godwine. 'Come girl, you are in much danger.'

'No! Wulfwyn comes with us. I will speak with Grand-mother, Mother of Heroes.'

'Gytha!' This time it was Magnus who spoke, and he wrenched her by the arm. 'Baladrddellt rac Denau plans to keep you here and barter you to the Bastard for all land in the west. Come now!'

She winced, pulling her arm from his bruising grip. 'Not without these.' Reaching under the bed, she took the box that held the gifts her father and mother had given her.

It was raining again as they gathered in the pitchy darkness of the Irlesbyri courtyard. All were fully cloaked for the winter road – the three boys, Gytha, her grandmother, Aunt Gunhild, the Towering Mace-Monk, the Twice Scarred Thegn, some wives and children. The burnished Roni and a dozen axed huscarls, leather-caped hard mailed helmeted men –the hoard loaded on ponies. Others stood by readying axes, war-shafts, swords and shields, should Baladrddellt rac Denau try to stop them.

The order came to mount. The Towering Mace- Monk raised his hand. 'Wait. Let us pray.' He shouted, 'Oh God, our heavenly Father, whose glory fills the whole creation, and whose presence we find wherever we go, preserve those who travel, surround them with your loving care, protect them from every danger, and bring them in safety to their journey's end, through Jesus Christ our Lord. Amen.' The Company crossed themselves, their eyes momentarily tightly shut,

Baladrddellt rac Denau, the Reeve and twenty armed townsmen rushed from out of the darkness. They ran straight to where Gytha sat astride her horse, Pig-boy at its head. The mare reared, hurling Gytha onto the rubble strewn ground. She felt hard hands grab her and pull her to her feet. Baladrddellt rac Denau shoved Gytha behind him. Holding a battle-axe from which red blood dripped, he challenged the English.

'She stays!' he cried. 'Myrgh-teg stays!' The sound was like a bear roaring at dogs.

'I, Reeve to Queen Edith, Elder of Exeter, High Byrh of the West, have terms for your surrender,' shouted the magistrate. 'All lands and the Godwineson Hoard are given to the king. Leave the Hoard, flee with your lives, else you will have no mercy.'

Godwine charged first, hacking and slashing at the Celt's men. The English, better trained and better armed, quickly forced them back, until only the painted Baladrddellt rac Denau, Splintered Spear of the South, stood against them.

'Release her,' ordered the Twice Scarred Thegn Eadric, stepping forward, his battle axe raised.

'Come, Gytha!' shouted Godwine. 'Run!'

'Come, child,' ordered the Old Lady.

'No!' bellowed the Celtprince, elbowing Gytha behind him. The Thegn's blade bit, striking the metal ring-shirt, crushing the bone and muscle of his massive neck and shoulders beneath. Knees buckling, Baladrddellt rac Denau sank to the ground, his head lolling to the side. Freed of his grip, Gytha's slender form stood over him, shuddering with both fear and rage;

'Release me from my troth, Traitor Prince,' Gytha yelled, her jewelled wounding-knife in her hand, her golden hair uncovered from the fall, catching the light of the burning buildings beyond.

Baladrddellt rac Denau opened his mouth. Gytha raised the dagger. 'Release me from my troth, Baladrddellt rac Denau,' she repeated, her voice carrying above the noise. The painted Celtprince stared up at her as if to speak, but in the bubbling blood-drool no words came.

Gytha crouched close to his once handsome face 'My heart-friend Swetesot lives and you do not,' she whispered and spat at him. 'God have mercy on your soul.'

The Twice Scarred Thegn Eadric raised his blood-axe and split the Celt prince's head in two. 'You are released, my lady.'

PART ONE CHAPTER ELEVEN

ATHELNEY AUGURY

BEFORE THERE HAD BEEN hope. Defiance had been their watchword. Defeated, never crushed, they said. Now, on the eighteenth day of the siege of Exeter, the Company of English slunk singly through the postern gate. The High Byrh of the West was lost and burning. The English crown helm still on the Norman head.

Their hoard-laden ponies slipped and slid down the side of the ravine under the walls. All else that was theirs was now the enemies. To their right, his army was so near, they could smell the cooking fires. To their left, the river Exe was in full winter flow. To be trapped here between slope and flood meant death by spear and arrow or drowning.

Two day's ride to the north-east was the marsh-fort at Athelney. That way lay safety,

Gytha, bruised, her clothes soaked in the shit mud of the Irlesbyri yard, was in despair. She should have been elated, barely daring to believe the hated painted Celt prince was dead. God had delivered her from her betrothal, but the price was too high. A treasured life had been snatched from her: the Radknight whom she had left to die in the mead-hall. The thought of him on the dirty straw consumed her heart. Loyal Wulfwyn, the last thread that bound her to her mother. He had seen her gentle swan last; he had brought her news and nearly died for it. He had ridden in the meadows with her, eaten the same broth as her, played the same games as her, known the same danger as her, conspired with her, protected her every waking hour. Now he was lost to her. Gytha sank into a deep melancholy. Was this God's will? Must she walk through the valley of the shadow of death, as her grandmother had with four sons dead?

The day passed and no pursuers came. But none could lower his spear or rest his horse with the Godwineson Hoard more inviting than a windfall apple to a wasp. They knew the safer path lay to the far side of the river Exe, but had no way to cross the brown flood. Damp, hungry and eager to reach Athelney, they passed a dank night in a hamlet, keen to press on, ever wary of watchful eyes.

The land rose; the rain turned to sleet. Ahead lay the green mires on the High Moor, which could swallow a horse; beyond, the flint-grey valley of rocks. With no shelter from the cold and little for the horses to eat, it was no place for the Company to linger in winter. Only goblins, elves and landwrights lived here on the High Moor, the Twice Scarred Thegn told them. So, on they hurried, the air full of cracking and splashing as smoke-breathed ponies broke through the ice-rimed puddles. Each rider, huddled in damp wadmal wool and fur, wondered if the next step was into the abyss.

At last the bogs, strange rocks and tussocks yielded to alder hazel and ash, as they left the grim moor and rode down an endless valley. Hunched in her saddle, teeth chattering under a watery blue sky, Gytha asked the Old Thegn, now riding near to her, 'What is this Athelney, Thegn Eadric?'

'It is a place to hide,' he answered. 'A low island that rises from the level waters of the sedge marsh, with a shield-wall and a deep-delved dike. To reach it there is a narrow causeway over the bog. It's an evil place for the unwary, but we will be safe.'

'They call it the Prince's Island,' said the Towering Mace Monk. 'In the bygone years, King Alfred hid there from Guthrum, the heathen Spear Dane King they called the Oak of Odin.'

'I would happily eat one of King Alfred's burnt cakes now, I'm so hungry,' said Gytha.

The Old Thegn agreed. 'Yes, Lady Gytha, the thought makes my belly rumble like a cart on a bridge.'

'But much louder,' said the Burnished Roni, wiping a swig of mead from his mouth. The Twice Scarred Thegn let the jibe pass, and they rode on in silence.

Later, the Towering Mace Monk described how England had been seized by the great heathen army of Spear-Danes under the Raven banner and their King Guthrum.

'Just as our land is taken and our people killed by the Bastard Duke of Normandy,' he said. 'And in the all the west, only Athelney was free. There, in that lonely place, King Alfred raised an army with earls, reeves and leather-caped thegns of the west. They forged new weapons and beat the Oak of Odin in battle at Erdington. King Alfred, merciful to his foes, spared the heathen King, making him his God-son, and receiving thirty of his men of the Raven into God's holy church. He ordered the Oak of Odin, dressed in the white cloth of submission, to quit his sinful nature and never to return.'

'How those heathen Spear-Danes must have chafed,' said the beardling boy Magnus.

'Boy,' said the Towering Mace Monk, 'no man chafes who has repented his sins and turned to Christ for his salvation. For it is written, "We have heard that the kings of Israel are merciful. Let us go to the king of Israel with sackcloth around our waists and ropes around our heads. Perhaps he will spare your life".'

'Yes, but,' said Magnus. Gytha flashed him the look, and he was silent.

'My grandmother, Mother of Heroes, is of the royal line of the Raven folk too, Father,' she said.

'Yes,' he replied. 'Raven and Dragon are brothers now, but not then.'

A warrior began to sing and, as all who knew the words joined in loudly, their spirits lifted.

'When the enemy comes in a roarin,' like the flood,
Coveting the kingdom and hungering for blood,
The Lord will raise a standard up and lead His people on,
The Lord of Hosts will go before defeating every foe.
Defeating every foe.'

'Some say that King Alfred himself wrote that,' said the Towering Blaecman.

'King Alfred had a daughter,' said the Old Thegn. 'Her name was Aethelflaed. They called her Lady of the Mercians. She was a warrior queen, mighty like her father. They attacked the Celtish King of Brechnock and she captured his wife!'

'What happened to her?' '

'Who, the wife of the Celt king?'

'No, the Lady Aethelflaed, Lady of the Mercians. I bear her ring, a gift from my father.'

'She lies at her priory over by Gloucester, next to her husband.'

Gytha rode on. She tried to imagine Lady Aethelflaed. Would she have been like her grandmother, the Mother of Heroes, with ice in her veins? Or like her mother, her gentle swan? Maybe she had been both. 'I want the bards to sing of the Lady of the Mercians, I want to know her.'

'Yes, Lady,' said the Old Thegn. 'They will sing of her beauty and courage when we rest at Athelney.'

'I would like to have folk sing about me one day.'

'Yes, little lady,' he said, mocking her ever so slightly. 'What would you have men sing of you?'

'Well, the Lord knows I am no warrior queen nor shield maid,' she replied.

'When you stood over the Celtprince with your jewelled wounding-knife raised, some might not agree, my lady,' said the Burnished Roni.

The beardling boy scoffed. 'She was pretending,' he said.

'I was not,' said Gytha with such clench-tooth venom, his next words stuck in his throat.

She was back in the courtyard, the wounding-knife raised. She could taste her hatred for the tattooed Celt, sour in her mouth. She could see him at her feet. Should she kill him? She wished she had. Then she pushed the memory away and the moment passed.

No one spoke until the Old Thegn called out, 'Look! Athelney.'

'Where?' Gytha asked, seeing only brown reeds ahead.

'There,' said the Thegn, pointing.

In the distance, the grey-green land lifted slightly above the sparkle-black water and swaying reeds. It was not the fort that Gytha hoped for, but a grass knoll with gale-sloped trees. There was a stone chapel at the far end no bigger than a bothy. Behind, Gytha could see a great earthwork with stakes, which stretched from one side of the islet to the other. She shivered. Ducks, thousands of them, and black-and-white geese dotted the wind-ruffled surface. A cluster of dwellings, a hamlet they called Lyng, lay close by; sodden nets hung limp and upturned coracles were pulled up the shore like round bannock buns.

'Is that it?' said Magnus, more in shock than enquiry. 'It's a tussock. How can we defend that? I thought Athelney was like the High Byrh of the West, the way everyone speaks of it.'

'Yes, it's small, right enough,' said the Old Thegn. 'But the sedge marsh is stronger than any byrh-wall, and it is a hard place to reach, even by pole-boat. Guthrum's Dane wolves searched but never found Alfred's camp. There is grazing, and peat to melt iron in the furnace. There are reeds to thatch roofs, carp and bream for the table. Even ducks if you can catch them. It may not look much, Magnus, but the Lord has provided a place like no other for us to lick our wounds and forge new weapons.'

'One day, God willing, a great church will stand to rival Ely, where there is only that chapel now,' said the Towering Monk.

Gytha and Magnus looked doubtful, A dank, damp swamp-mist shrouded them and it grew unearthly still. Athelney vanished as if it had never been. The Company stopped.

'How do we get there?' shouted Godwine from the front. 'We have no boats and can see nothing.'

'Follow the shore to the causeway and cross there, Earl Godwine,' the Twice Scarred Thegn shouted back. 'But give the order to walk the ponies. Don't ride.'

So, they set off to the causeway, wary as the evening approached, always fearing an attack. At the village, the welcome smell of peat fires hung heavy in the still air. Nobody stopped them, and the Company pressed on. The Burnished Roni, his huscarl's axe ready, stood as Gytha stepped onto the narrow path, which waited to break a horse's leg or pitch her into the black ooze.

As they approached Alfred's chapel, the Hermit Priest of Athelney. a sheepskin around his naked shoulders, welcomed them.

'Are there are no lodgings here? There is talk of a monastery?' asked the Old Lady haughtily.

The man waved them to some gap-roof bothies, with floors covered in shit, home to sheep, cows and crows. It stank as the midden stinks, thought Gytha, pressing her cowl to her nose. And so, as fires were lit in the ancient smelt pits and a meal of gruel prepared, they pitched their tents and found what shelter they could. And there they stayed, with nothing but the wind and the complaining mere-fowl for company.

The grey days gave way to watery sunshine, copper withies turned to tender green, moorhens tucked new nests beneath the banks, snowdrops yielded to primroses, and the leafless blackthorn blossomed white. The air rang to the sounds and smells of the smith's furnace; new arrowheads glowed in their moulds. But hunger was with them constantly, fish were few and ducks hard to snare.

'They've got cannier since I was here as a boy,' said the Twice Scarred Thegn, returning empty-handed yet again.

'Where's Turul?' asked Gytha as Edmund slid from his horse, his arm-kin nowhere to be seen. Edmund shrugged, his eyes were red.

'She flew off,' said the Old Thegn. 'We called and called for her but she's gone.'

Edmund sniffed and wiped his nose with the back of his glove. Gytha hugged him and for once he didn't pull away.

'She's gone, Gytha, back to the Wild Field. It is where she came from, where the horizon never ends, and horsemen shoot arrows backwards.'

'Like Swetesot, and we will never see either again.'

'Nor mother,' said Edmund. Gytha hugged him tighter, wiping the tears from his cheeks. She had never seen him so distraught.

'Nor the Radknight. nor the Pig-boy too,' said Gytha. It troubled her that she had no memory of Pig-boy in the tumult of the painted Celt's attack. He was there holding her horse one moment and gone the next.

'But we have each other,' said Edmund softly. Gytha nodded, but could not find any more words.

For her, not knowing the Radknight's fate was worse, even than losing Swetesot. Was he alive, or had they killed him when they found the Company gone? She prayed was swiftly delivered to God's holy hill of Zion. But most of all, she begged God for forgiveness for abandoning him.

'So, what do we do, Mother of Heroes?' Gytha asked over a meagre meal of sprats and bread.

'We have no choice but to flee, Child,' said her grand-mother bitterly. 'With word out that we are trapped in the sedge sea, they will come.'

'Flee again, Mother of Heroes? Where to?' Gytha asked, as she resigned herself to another journey into the unknown, yet further from her gentle swan.

'North to the coast, and from there to Ireland. We have no shield brothers left in England now.'

'But are we not safe here? Can we not raise an army as King Alfred did?' asked the beardling boy Magnus, ever hopeful. 'Can we not raise the Golden Dragon of Wessex as he did when England was lost to Norseman Guthrum and the great heathen army? The king shall hold the kingdom! Mother of Heroes!

'King Alfred's men of Wessex – earls, leather-caped thegns and reeves – are dead, Magnus,' said Godwine. 'Now these men of Wessex swear fealty to the Bastard. We are few. Too few. We go to the High King Diarmait in Ireland.'

'Ireland? But we have no boats, in fact we have nothing!'

'There will be boats,' said the Twice Scarred Thegn, 'to sweep us from the brimming Severn across the sea to Ireland, and silver enough to raise an army there.'

'And when will I return from Ireland, Thegn Eadric,' Gytha asked, 'I yearn for home and my gentle swan? I think my heart will break. And now we go still further, like Israelites wandering in the wilderness.'

'Be strong, sister,' ordered Godwine.

'I know I must be strong, but for whom must I be strong, Godwine?' Gytha asked. 'It makes no difference if I am strong or weak. All is lost. I am lost.' The Twice Scarred Thegn squeezed Gytha's arm and to his surprise she buried her face in his shoulder.

'You must pray and with God's mercy we will all return, child,' said the Old Thegn, gruffly, patting her hair. 'But when only He can decide.'

That night, in her cot, Gytha could not pray. Then as nearing sleep approached, Aethelflaed come into her heart. The Lady of the Mercians was there with her, a simple crown on her cowled head, a jewelled longsword at her waist. Had she lain here, Gytha wondered, in this forgotten mere, as Gytha was now lying? Did King Alfred's eldest daughter suffer such hopelessness as she felt?

'We are forsaken, Queen,' said Gytha.

Aethelflaed answered her. 'Gytha, eldest daughter of King Harold, forsaken by God? No Gytha, God has not forsaken you.'

Gytha cried out to her 'Oh Great Lady of the Mercians, did you despair as I despair, here in this terrible place? They say I must be strong, but for whom? What is strength, if you cannot be strong? All those I have loved are lost to me. My strength did not save my mother, nor Wulfwyn, my Radknight. Strength brings only grief.'

'Gytha,' said the lady, 'despair is the enemy of hope. You, Gytha, bear my ring, you will survive, you must survive. You will be a great queen. Let hope fill your soul, and banish despair, Gytha.'

'Halt, who are you? What business have you?' The shouts from the shield-wall woke those men nearest to it and they jumped up, gathering their weapons.

'What is it?' shouted the Twice scarred Thegn Eadric, battle-axe in his hand. 'Are we attacked?'

'No,' said one of the younger huscarls. 'There was a lantern. There! Look, there it is again!'

In the blackness they could see a dim light out on the water, swinging, as if it were a signal. Then it vanished as quickly as it had appeared.

The Old Thegn shouted, 'Up! Up! All to the shield-wall. We are attacked!'

Godwine ran past Gytha, slipping his sword-sling over his shoulder and grabbing a war-shaft. 'Magnus, Edmund stay with your grandmother!'

Aunt Gunhild fell to her knees and began to pray out loud. Gytha pulled on a cape, took a spear and followed her brother.

'What are you doing?' he yelled.

'I will fight as Aethelflaed the Lady of the Mercians fought.'

'Gytha, get back here at once!' her grandmother ordered, but she took no notice and ran after her brother to the shield-wall.

'There was a light on the water, but it is now gone again. I knew this was a bad place,' said the Old Thegn. 'We are attacked by spirits and marsh demons. They decoy us here with their fairy light as men decoy the duck and will attack on the other side. It is their way.'

'Hush,' said Blaecman the Mace Monk who now stood with them, staring into the inky night. 'Talk no more of demons, Thegn. The wall is defended. None, neither man nor evil spirit, can approach unseen across the water.'

Time passed slowly as they waited, some at the dead fire-pits stoking up embers, others grim and silent, staring outward. All were watchful, but for what they knew not. Dawn came dull as slate to the Polden hills beyond, and the grey-green earth was returned to their sight.

'Look! There!' shouted a watching archer, pointing to the reeds on the far-side shore. There were men − two, maybe three, not more − visible through the drizzle rain, in a bannock coracle, poling toward them. For an age they were hidden by the reeds. Only a cloud of black-and-white geese honking and flapping into the sky, cried out their passing.

The men on the shield-wall waited, their weapons lowered but not cast aside. Eyes scoured the reeds, circling all the shore about them to see if there were other men, other boats, but the marsh was still and the ever-watchful fowl floated in their hundreds, untroubled.

'Pity we cannot have geese to guard us always,' said the Twice Scarred Thegn with a rough laugh. 'They think nothing of being wet and cold all night. I could be warm abed, not standing here half soaked.'

'Who are they?'

'We don't know,' said one.

'Look!' Gytha shouted as her heart leapt in her chest 'Look, it's Wulfwyn the Radknight, and Pig-boy with him!'

Godwine swore, 'By all that's good, she's right. It's the Radknight and the Pig-boy. Hurry, pull them in.'

Gytha could see Wulfwyn, teeth chattering, waving feebly, only raising his hand slightly. Pig-boy honked loudly as a goose in his joy at seeing Gytha and nearly tipped the little craft

over in his eagerness to jump ashore. The men steadied the
coracle and lifted the Radknight out. Carefully they carried
him through the shield-wall and brought him to the chapel
beyond the tents. Gytha came up to Pig-boy and touched his
arm, smiling. The Pig-boy brayed with pleasure and fell to his
knees in front of her.

Gytha did not leave the Wulfwyn's side as he slept, with
Pig-boy crouching nearby. When the Radknight woke, she
cradled his head as he sipped broth from her spoon and in
time, he found the strength to whisper his story.

He had heard the fighting in the yard at the Irlesbyri
but could not move. The Hall was in darkness and there was
nobody there; the only light came from the flames. Then
the sound of fighting stopped. He waited through the night,
wondering what was happening and what he might do. Finally,
despite the waves of pain that made him gasp out loud, hunger
forced him to his feet. Outside came the sound of cheers and
the clashing of shield on weapon. Stepping over the injured
and dying men on the floor, he went to the doorway to see
the Norman King himself. Wulfwyn had melted back into
the shadows as the victorious William passed by him, a spear
jab away. At his shoulder the king wore the Golden Dragon
brooch of Wessex, as big as a man's hand.

'It was your father's,' said the Radknight.

Gytha's hand went to her mouth. 'And my grandfather's
before him.'

'You should have killed him. You had the chance,' said the
beardling boy Magnus bitterly.

'I could not,' whispered the Radknight. 'I fainted from
pain and loss of blood.'

Sometime later – he did not know how long – he had felt
a rough hand. Opening his eyes, there was Pig-boy, kneeling
over him, signalling to be quiet. He then told how Pig-boy

had pulled him up and half carried him out to the stable. There were so many injured, no one noticed them. Unseen, they hid for two days. The Pig-boy smeared the gaping wound with honey from the message-hive, stinging onion and wild garlic. They had nothing to eat but muddied turnip and honey, washed down with mead from a flagon stash. The Radknight made a grimace as he described it and for the first time in an age Gytha giggled.

'But,' he went on, 'we knew we could not stay. We would be discovered and killed. So, with the Lord's guidance and a measure of luck, here we are.'

'But how did you flee the Byrh?' asked Magnus, hanging on every word.

The Radknight smiled wanly. 'The same way Swetesot and her master left. Out of the main gate. Pig-boy put a sack over my head and laid me over your mare's back, my lady. He carried me out of the main gate at nightfall, under the eyes of the Norman soldiers, to the burial pits with the other dead.'

'Lucky he didn't tip you in!' Pig-boy brayed with glee, rocking back and forth, clutching his sides.

'And you rode here on my horse?' asked Gytha. 'With that wound?'

'That is where the Lord took pity on us,' said the Radknight. 'We did not know where you had gone – by boat or by land, and if so where. The river Exe was too fearsome to cross, so we could only strike north. My lady, we never felt more alone. The enemy all about us. Our company missing from this middle-world.'

'Oh Wulfwyn, dear faithful Wulfwyn, I thought you were dead!'

'Well, not quite,' said the Radknight. 'But I could neither walk nor ride, so we traded the mare for a broken cart and the farrier's barn-sour nag.' He laughed and winced as a wave of pain swept over him. 'He told us you had passed by and were headed to the High Moor. He said you would die there; it was so bitter cold.'

Gytha grinned. 'Well, we didn't die either! And we are all together again. We have much to be thankful for. And you, Pig-boy, I don't have the words to thank you.' She stopped awkwardly and Pig-boy brayed all the more, smiling from ear to ear.

'Sleep now, good Radknight. And good Pig-boy too. We leave before daybreak.'

The din started long before daylight returned to the marsh. The geese on the far pond rose into the night as one, the air full of their objections. Then another flock, spooked by the first, sped from the water, circling low, the beat of their threshing wings 'like the host of angels overhead,' said Aunt Gunhild. 'Or the demons of hell,' said the Old Thegn.

Men all about swore and cursed, hawked and stumbled. Those who had slept were now awake, reaching for weapons and helms. 'We are attacked?' they cried, more a question than fact. Godwine ordered two huscarls back down the causeway to spy on what had so spooked the geese. But the Hermit Priest of Athelney counselled against it, saying they would break their legs in the dark and their cover would be lost at the first startled coot or duck.

'I hazard these are not King William's men but thieves who follow the young Radknight and his braying ass. Take the womenfolk, Lord, and your Hoard. I will show you a way. Hurry.'

'Another way?'

'Yes, Lord,' he answered. 'But no horses can pass, nor more than can be carried on a man's back. But you must go now. I am not the only one hereabouts who knows of it.'

The faint day began in-filling the deepest shadows and, with it, a dank mere-mist hid them from watching eyes and ears as each man, woman, child and thrall was given a bundle to carry. Some lugged food, some the Godwineson Hoard of golden cups, bracelets, silver shillings and jewelled treasures; others bore the new weapons, and two carried the Radknight on a stretcher of rough branches, knowing that to slip into the marsh was to die.

'The mist shrouds friend and foe equally,' said the hermit. 'The north calls our watchful geese. They will not furrow our ponds till the autumn storms return.'

So, they left their ponies and the forge at Athelney. A line of bent men and women, using staves and war-shafts to steady them, trudged to the little chapel. Here they stopped and, gathering in a circle, the Towering Monk Blaecman led them in prayer for God the Great Creator to protect them on their journey and to renew their solemn oath to defend Godwine, heir to the Crown of Harold and his family.

'If God should give, as by his angel,' his voice boomed out, loud on the wind, 'that we should come into those lands and make that pilgrimage where Thou dwellest. If we could hear the living words from Thy mouth, how sweet would be Thy eloquence.'

Gytha added a small prayer of her own. Holding the ring, she asked Aethelflaed, the Lady of the Mercians, to give her the strength and courage and to watch over her and her brothers, and her mother, wherever she might be.

Then, unbalanced by their loads, the English slithered down a sheep track, behind the hermit, down to the swamp itself. Before them, hidden by the clumps of alders and reeds, appeared a narrow path – rough boards no wider than a man – that led over the stagnant, stinking mere. Moving carefully, they would stop now and then to ease their aching backs and let the stragglers catch up, Godwine chiding them to hurry.

'I wonder if King Alfred and the thegns of Wiltshire, Somerset, and Hampshire trod these boards beneath the Golden Dragon of Wessex as we do,' said quiet Edmund, still pining for his falcon .

'Maybe Aethelflaed too.'

'We are his war party on our way to battle at Eddington,' said Magnus, stabbing and slashing as if attacking the heathen army. 'The heathen Danes hastened to the hall of hell. The king shall hold the kingdom!' 'Shhh Magnus, stop saying that! We hold nothing,' Gytha hissed.

After about eight furlongs, they could go no further. The marsh had widened into a lake, its centre now a black and swirling stream. The board walk was swept away. With no way back nor forward, the Companions of the Golden Dragon were trapped in the sedge.

Only the Radknight, half dead from his ordeal, was relieved to be stopping. Gytha brought him food and a sip of mead. 'Now what?' he whispered.

Gytha shrugged her shoulders. 'The Hermit Priest said we must wait and has vanished into the marsh.'

All day they waited, until the guards warned of men approaching. Seizing their weapons, the Companions stood, the women and the Hoard at their centre. Nobody spoke. Gytha drew her wounding dagger from its sheath and waited next to her grandmother, her heart thumping, scarcely breathing. Down the stream came men in punts and coracles dragging rafts of bloated sheep bellies tied with willow stems and rope. In the first boat was the bony Hermit Priest of Athelney in his sheepskin cape.

Before nightfall, as bitterns clacked and mewed their tuneless love, all the English Companions were safely across and on firm footing once more. Ahead were the Godwineson estates. Here was the Hall at Blaedon, built by Earl Godwine and bride-gifted by him to their grandmother. Here was lodging, provision and safety.

That night, in yet another steading, the wind blew out the feeble tallow flame. In the darkness, Gytha thought of Aethelflaed who had delivered her, her brothers and the Radknight from the foul swamp. Whatever lay ahead, she knew the Lady of the Mercians would guide her steps. From the bottom of her heart, she thanked her.

But safety here was not to be. The Burnished Roni, sent out to spy the land, returned with bad news. The Constable Eadnoth, in whose charge their father Harold had left his estates, was for the Bastard William now.

At the news, the Old Lady's voice was clouded with anger. 'I know this Eadnoth well. He may steal my lands and would steal the Godwineson Hoard.'

'But Grandmother, we are too few to fight,' said Godwine. 'We can return to kill the traitor another day, when we are more dreadful than a few coracles of warriors and women.'

'Godwine,' said his Grandmother sternly, 'You are not yet your father, and perhaps never will be, you have much to learn. We escaped Exeter because of gold. Our gold. As long as we hold this treasure, we have power, boy. Without the Hoard, my Hoard, we are doomed. Our corpses will float on the Severn's bore unremarked. No, you will not yield one silver penny of my Hoard to this traitor constable. He will not have it. Never! Do you hear?'

'Grandmother, Mother of Heroes,' said Godwine in some exasperation, 'we cannot defend the Hoard here. We must escape to Dublin and seek the help of the High King of Leinster as my grandfather Earl Godwine did. He returned to England and so shall we.'

'And let that ruddy-faced rascal King Diarmait have custody of us?' the old lady replied. 'Yes, Godwine, the High King will help us. And his price will be equal to the Hoard, no more, no less.'

Godwine was right. They could not remain in this place with the sea to their left and the level swamp behind. They were as trapped as if they had remained at Athelney. The traitor, Constable Eadnoth, had only to wait and starve them out.

It was the burnished huscarl, Roni the Dane, who first voiced the idea. 'Time is running out and we have few options.' The Dane pushed his long fair hair from his bearded face, the little hammers of Thor at his neck. He paused, staring at the Company gathered around the evening fire. Gytha sat with Edmund and the beardling boy Magnus. The Radknight was propped near them against the wall. 'Eadnoth will come for the Hoard. Or if we flee to Dublin, the High King will take it. But, brothers, there is a way to guard it and all that is dearest to us, which frees all but a few fighting men.'

'Yes, you would steal it and share it out amongst your heathen friends,' said the Twice Scarred Thegn Eadric, who had little time for the Burnished Huscarl Roni or his kind. The leather-caped thegns grunted their agreement.

Roni ignored him. 'I know of one that can better guard the Hoard than one thousand men. It needs no food, no sleep, no arms, yet like the devil himself is the master of malevolence.'

'This is no time for riddles,' growled the Thegn.

The men around the burning logs stopped their whittling, laid down their whetstones. A jug of mead passing from hand to hand paused its progress as the Companions listened.

'Hear me, Thegn. It is no riddle. I speak of the Severn flood,' Roni said, holding up his hand to silence those who would interrupt him. 'There is an island in the Severn Sea they call Flatholm, where the tide-rips churn the water into brown broth. Six hours by six since the birth of time itself. Let us warriors sail to Dublin and seek the help of the High King, but leave our women with the Hoard on Flatholm rock, guarded by that stream. It is a forsaken place, but they will be safe until we return.'

The Old Thegn Eadric rose in fury. 'You, Dane, who have lived amongst us, shared our barley bread, drunk our mead, would stay with the Hoard while you send us to Dublin, I suppose? A good plan, a very good plan, thief.'

'Come, brothers!' It was the Towering Mace Monk Blaecman on his feet now. 'Remember the old saying? "This the man does not know, the warrior lucky in worldly things, what some endure who tread most widely the paths of exile".' He held out his arms in supplication. 'Brothers, we are the warriors not lucky in worldly things, and we must now endure the paths of exile. But together, united. This company of brothers cannot afford discord. Trust in God and in your fellow man, great Thegn. And you, Dane, if you seek to trick the Hoard from our protection with this plan, the Lord God in Heaven will strike you down and the Hall of hell will take your soul.'

'I'll strike down the pagan first,' said the Twice Scarred Thegn. But before he could say more, Godwine placed a hand upon the old warrior's shoulder.

'The monk has spoken well. The Dane, Roni, served my father, as did you, Thegn. be brothers in arms, for time itself is all the foe we need.'

The Old Thegn nodded. 'Aye, Earl Godwine. Time is no friend to us, but I'll not befriend this heathen in its stead.'

'Then you will stay with the Hoard and Roni will bring the huscarls with me to Dublin.' The Old Thegn shook his head. 'No, Lord. My place is with you.'

'I order it, Thegn, as your rightful King. On my father's life, you will stay with the women and the Hoard,' said Godwine, nodding to Roni to continue. But the mighty huscarl did not; instead, he bowed low on one knee. Into the firelight stepped the Mother of Heroes. Around her head she wore a woollen cowl, in her hand a glistening Frankish sword. Pointing it directly at Roni, she spoke in the North tongue.

'What is she saying, my lady?' whispered the Radknight to Gytha.

Gytha was transfixed. 'Shhh. She is saying, take up Gungnir, spear of Odin, it never misses its mark. Take Skidbladnir, fill it with armed men, hoist its sail, urge it forward, and unflawed gold will be yours.'

And so, the next morning, the main party went to seize boats drawn up on the beach while the others went to the great tythe barn at Bleadon, their former Hall, and emptied it of anything that would sustain the women on the island. Sides of pork, mutton, sacks of rye and barley, barrels of ale, and chickens were packed up, then they waited for their men to return for them.

Their work done, they set the barn alight and a great plume of smoke revealed their presence to any who sought them.

Within a day, all was ready, and there was still no sign of Eadnoth and his traitors. With the Dane Roni the Huscarl shouting orders, the Companions of the Golden Dragon – the last hundred free English on English soil – gathered at the mouth of the River Axe. The Godwineson Hoard was stacked on the sand, clear of the sweeping tide of which the heathen warrior had forewarned. On the horizon, a league away, possibly two, was the grim grey shape of Flatholm island.

Waiting for light-fall, Blaecman the Monk, revealing to the Company the gold and jewelled cross for the last time, blessed all the men and women kneeled around him with a prayer for those about to undertake a holy pilgrimage into the unknown.

'Amen,' they replied, crossing themselves, for none but God could say what lay ahead for them, whether they would come home, live or die, only that they could not linger in England where a Bastard king held their people in hatred.

The crack-tarred knarrs were loaded with many good men's wives and their children and their collar thralls. Leather-caped thegns hung shield-boards to the gunnels and bade each other well, shouting, 'when God wills, may the end be good,'.

Into one of these boats, heavy tunics and thick wadmal mantles pulled up to their waists, stepped three women, the Old Lady, Aunt Gunhild and Gytha Haroldsdaughter.

Of the greatest in all England, nothing remained. In London, Matilda, the ring-adorned wife of William the Bastard, was now crowned Queen of the English.

With the Ladies went the Towering Mace Monk Blaecman and the Twice Scarred Thegn, Eadric the Proud. Only Wulfwyn the Radknight, propped on a staff wedged beneath his armpit, hung back on the beach. Gytha beckoned him to join them, but he would not. He would remain, he said, with the warriors.

'Pig-boy,' ordered Gytha, 'bring him.'

Pig-boy jumped back over the side, seized the Radknight in his strong arms and, braying with effort and pleasure amidst much laughter, lifted him as a sack over the gunwale before scrambling aboard himself.

The wicked tide lapped silently into the Axemouth, lifting all keels. Darkness came. Few would witness their departure or the heading taken in their plundered boats. But Gytha found no joy; her eyes were on the shore, where her three brothers stood bathed in the last of the sunlight, grim and unmoving as they watched their grandmother, aunt and sister depart. Great tears rolled down Gytha's cheeks as she raised her palm to them; not a wave but a reaching out as if she could touch her brothers with her fingertips one last time.

Next to Gytha stood her grandmother.

'The way is clear for you, O warriors,' she shouted. 'Hasten to the battle! God alone knows how things will turn out.'

'How long will you be?' Gytha screamed, but her voice was lost as Roni, in full armour, with his battle-axed huscarls and all the Company roared, 'the king shall hold the kingdom! The king shall hold the kingdom! The king shall hold the kingdom!'

It was deafening. Clattering swords and spears sounded on shield bosses and the Golden Dragon banners thrummed like hornets in the wind. The piper Thorgood played his fiercest war-tune. Godwine raised his sword aloft. At his side, leather-caped and helmed, Edmund and Magnus raised theirs too. The last salute to their grandmother, Mother of Heroes, and to their sister, Gytha.

Gytha stood at the stern, watching as long as she could. These few men would now sail to the west across the storm sea to Diarmait, the High King in Leinster. With them was enough silver to buy men, weapons and the rescue of their womenfolk. If they failed, she knew – they all knew – all memory of their House would end on that beach, the Company of English thegns slain or scattered, her brothers dead. And she, who had vowed to avenge their father's death, would be killed or exiled, or a forgotten prisoner like her mother in a nunnery.

The boat, carrying all that they had, nosed carefully past the Brean, and out into the bucking flood. Clutching her crucifix to her breast, Gytha had never prayed so hard. 'Lord,' she repeated over and over, 'deliver Thy lowest handmaid.'

Finally, as the deck heaved and mast and rigging snagged and jolted over her head, she welcomed a wretched half-sleep, only to wake abandoned in the howling night to the sickness that evicts all will to live.

PART ONE CHAPTER TWELVE

CASTEAWAY

A FORSAKEN BOULDER LOBBED into the cruel Severn stream. Nowhere in the middle world was more desolate. Gytha surveyed this tide-lashed islet that marked the beginning and end of her England. All she, and those with her, possessed was in chests and sacks stacked on the beach. With her were the wounded Radknight, Pig-boy, the Towering Mace Monk and the Twice Scarred Thegn. Her three brothers and all the menfolk had scraped their oak keels down the shingle and were gone to Ireland. Gytha stared after them, bereft.

'Gytha!' said the Old Lady sharply as they dragged their few possessions clear of the tide. 'Your brothers in the long boats have nothing to shield them from wave, wind and rain. This island is at anchor. No waves break over our bow. We will build shelters, free of the needless burden of jewellery and fine clothes, and await rescue.'

Bruised at the rebuke, Gytha dug her nails into her palms. What had she meant, free of the needless burden of jewellery and fine clothes? There was nothing here. The clothes she stood in were damp as if sucking the salt-sea from the air itself. There were no trees, no songbirds sang here, only the mocking seagulls, the stink of seaweed and the undying buffeting wind.

*   *   *

Gytha, along with the other noble wives and Thegn's daughters, built tiny bothies from the rocks and boulders that lay all around, finding driftwood for the roof beams and piling it thick with rough grass and slimy seaweed held down with stones. These shelters, rougher than any pigsty, kept the rain off, but rude gusts found new gaps as quick as the women could plug them.

There were signs that others had lived here before them. There was a crude well and next to it a chapel, barely large enough for a man of God as big as their Towering Mace Monk. He announced it was built by St Cadog the Wise himself. Gytha cared not who had built the chapel, or even how he knew, trusting only that God was present and would hear her.

'Lord who knows all secrets,' she prayed, 'do not forsake your handmaiden. Take me from here. Bring me to my home, to my mother and my brothers, that we can be together again. Amen.'

The days lengthened and it was warmer. Clumps of tiny yellow flowers hid in cracks between the rocks. Gytha gazed to the west, her heart lifting if she saw a distant sail, waiting, hoping it might be her brothers. But mostly, she was helping the noble women at their chores under her grandmother's watchful eye and stern tongue. Hunger was soon nagging at her belly, and blisters stung her mouth. Their precious food, snatched from the great barn at Bleadon, went down and down. Mostly they ate dark rye bread or barley porridge mixed with the brackish well water.

Arrows were too precious to waste on rabbits. They had no hawks to stoop on them and the dogs ate any they caught and bit anyone daring to take them. Even Pig-boy's skill with a slingshot was useless in the rough ground. But he did occasionally get one. Roasted or in a stew, flavoured with nettles and wild leaks, it made a welcome change from the oysters, cockles and mussels, wet eels or a chance fish.

There were a few wild sheep. Ragged, half-starved and savage, when Gytha and the noble women tried to pen them they would kick violently. But they needed the wool, so they bound the flailing hooves and wrapped the fearsome horns before taking their sharpest wounding-knives to shear them. The air was soon thick with blaring sheep, swearing women and blood.

When the weather allowed, they fished off the rocks in the brown sea, knocked barnacles from the rocks with stones or ate mottled green gulls' eggs stolen at their peril, until the sight revolted her and the gulls drove them away.

To her surprise, Gytha quickly adjusted to this new life, so different from the one she knew. She had never thought she would, but she did. Soon it was as if she could imagine no other. Excitement and joy were rare, but there was comfort in the daily chores of baking, gathering drift wood, fetching water and, when they had time, mending their tattered clothes.

One day, the Pig-boy was standing outside her bothy clutching a trap he had made from a basket. Beckoning her to follow, they went down the path to the beach and along the shore to the rocky arch that stuck out into the water like a bridge to nowhere. From his tunic Pig-boy took something wrapped in a filthy rag. It was a stinking mess of rotting oysters and cockles. Gytha gagged at the smell. Above them the gulls swooped and shrieked till Gytha feared they would be overwhelmed and waved her wounding-knife wildly above her head. Glancing up, she saw Wulfwyn watching from the cliff top.

Pig-boy stuffed the putrid mess into the basket, then hurled it far into the water on the end of a roughly woven rope.

Pointing to the sun, then the horizon, and cupping his hands to his cheek as if sleeping, she knew they must return the next morning. Then she and Pig-boy climbed back up the slope, leaving the gulls circling the water in vain. When Gytha looked up at the cliff, Wulfwyn was nowhere to be seen.

Next morning, as soon as she could get away, Gytha found Pig-boy waiting on the beach. Picking their way over the rocks, now soaked with spray, they retrieved the rope and pulled. In the basket, flapping its fury, was the fattest blue lobster she had ever seen.

'Oh, Pig-boy, It's twice the size of father's boot! It's a giant!'

Pig-boy brayed his pleasure and Gytha clapped her hands in joy, so hard she would have slipped had Pig-boy not caught her. Carefully to avoid the lobster's fearsome claws, Pig-boy drew it from the basket. Placing it on the rock, Gytha plunged her wounding-knife downwards, crunching through the blue specked shell till it was still. Her gleeful shrieks as she ran back to her grandmother and Aunt Gunhild, waving her prize, had all the noble women stop their tasks and gather round. There was enough meat on the beast to feed her, her Grandmother, Aunt Gunhild, the Towering Mace Monk, the Twice Scarred Thegn and more. Pig-boy was sent back to the beach to catch more giants while the biggest pot was slung over the fire to boil.

It was the foods of summer that Gytha most craved: the berries, fruits and honey. There was nothing sweet to eat on that island; everything tasted of the sea.

'There is goodness in fish liver,' said her grandmother. 'We people of the north know that fish livers save us in the winter darkness.'

'If it's like this now in the welcome warmth of summer, what will it be like in winter?' said the Twice Scarred Thegn Eadric as Gytha brought him a feast of dense white lobster.

'If we are still here on this cursed rock, child, when the storms howl unwelcomed up the channel, we will not see the spring.'

'The lord will provide,' said Aunt Gunhild, crossing herself as the monk said a short blessing.

'Ah, but will the Lord provide mead and ale?' said the Thegn, spooning food into his mouth with obvious delight. 'We need to get provisions now while we can, somehow.'

'Then we need a boat, Thegn Eadric. The Celtprince spoke once of wreckers who lure boats on to the rocks. Maybe we can lure a boat here. Will the Welsh King help us?'

The old warrior shook his head. 'May the Devil take him,' he growled, poking at the meagre fire of gorse scrub that crackled and spat but gave little heat for the oat biscuits Gytha was making for the morning. 'There is no need to lure boats, child. The Welsh King knows we are here, be sure of it. Every day I look north to the mainland fearing an attack. What can women do against men who rape and murder? We are trapped here with the Hoard, defenceless!'

'The noble women will drive any raider away, Thegn. Go make spears and sharp arrows from driftwood, enough to protect ourselves and the Hoard,' said the Old Lady. The Twice Scarred Eadric said nothing, but the two great wheals on his red face gave a voice to his feelings clearly enough.

But something else was troubling Gytha. The Radknight spoke to her less and less. If she spoke to him, he answered, but nothing more. There was a melancholy about him, and it was getting worse. Now he didn't smile, he only glowered, his blue eyes sullen and accusing.

Keeping to himself, he would not sit with them at their meals nor join in. His tasks done, he limped away, stopping to gaze from the cliff or scrape at cockles on the wide silvery beach when the tide released it to him each day. Gytha could stand the silence that hung between them no longer.

She missed his earnest face, his reluctant grin, the pause before he spoke.

Her grandmother too noticed the gloom that hung over him. 'The black cat comes three times and brings bad luck with it,' she announced.

Gytha was shocked. 'Wulfwyn is wounded, Mother of Heroes. He is suffering. He cannot be blamed for the bad luck that is our fate. He is noble and good and kind, but his wound is not healed.'

The Old Lady said nothing. Aunt Gunhild laid her needle-craft aside, giving Gytha a warning glance to bite her tongue.

'It's not the wound, child. Maybe being picked up by the Pig-boy and dumped into the noble women's boat in front of all the Company is what's eating at him.'

Gytha put her hand to her open mouth. 'Oh, Aunt, it was I who ordered Pig-boy to lift the Radknight on board. Does he blame me that he is here?'

'If the black cat visits a third time, he will die,' said the Old Lady.

Aunt Gunhild, realising that Gytha was distressed, took her hand. 'Wulfwyn has much to be grateful to you for, child. I know the groin wound troubles him greatly. We must see to it.'

Gytha found him raking cockles far out at the edge where beach and sea skirmish and the sanderlings scurry. The sun was shining and the smooth sea-face shone silver. Gytha took off her broken leather boots. The sand was soft and brown and squelched between her toes. Wulfwyn glanced up at her approach but went on raking.

She stopped a few paces off. 'Wulfwyn,' she asked, 'do you hate me?'

He stopped raking and leant on the long shaft, easing the wicker basket at his shoulder. Reluctantly, he pulled off his felted cap. A mocking seagull swooped low. Wulfwyn swore at it. 'No, my lady, I do not hate you, how could I after all that you have done for me?'

'But why won't you speak or even look at me, Wulfwyn?'

He paused. 'I mean you no harm, my lady.' He paused again.

'My lady, I am a Thegn's son, but all that I am is lost to me. My father, my mother, my little sister, Ailsi. I know that you grieve as I do for your fair mother and your noble father but, my lady, I am half a man here!'

'No, you are not half a man. You have your manliness.' Gytha turned crimson as she spoke.

'But not a warrior. I am a prisoner. My life, my loyalty, belongs to you, my lady, but you are my gaoler. Am I so wounded that I can only be with the womenfolk and never again stand with your brothers, with the axed and burnished Roni, and your father's thegns?'

'Oh Wulfwyn,' said Gytha, stepping closer and touching his arm, surprised at what she was feeling. 'Don't be angry with me. I brought you here because you were wounded, but you are still a man and a warrior, nor are you alone with the womenfolk. The Towering Blaecman, the Twice Scarred Thegn Eadric, none are braver and truer in battle, yet they are here among the womenfolk. They see no shame and nor should you.'

She looked at him, searching for the man she knew, the old Wulfwyn. He returned her look, fiddling with his hat, then putting it back on his head.

'Wulfwyn, my heart is heavy and I cannot rest until I see my brothers again. Please don't be angry with me anymore. Please.' Her heart was beating in her chest.

The Radknight, his blue eyes narrowing as he pondered her words, said nothing. He mumbled vague thanks, coughed and walked away. Gytha stared after him, reading his sadness in the set of his shoulders. Had she failed? He was like a brother, yet not a brother. She stood and watched him, resisting the urge to call out or run after him as he reached the path from the beach and disappeared from view. Then a wave broke and wet her dress and she turned away, desolate.

That night there was a gale. Gytha lay in the black dark hut that was now her home and listened to the wind buffeting and gnashing at the seaweed roof. She heard its howl, but her thoughts were elsewhere. Over and over the Radknight's sad words played in her head, his blue eyes staring at her accusingly from the darkness. She wanted so much that he shouldn't be angry with her. Was she wrong to have the Pig-boy bundle him onto the boat? Was he not fit to fight yet? In truth she wanted him to stay. She needed him. Melancholy stole into her heart and her thoughts turned, as ever, to her mother Edith, her gentle swan, and she thought she heard her voice above the storm and Gytha called her name.

The storm over and the well brim-full of fresh drinking water, Gytha went to seek privacy in the gorse near the cliff edge. Glancing down, she spied fifty or more seals sheltering from the surf on the rocks below her. The sight of so much wonderful meat sent her into a frenzy and she ran full tilt back to the huts.

'Wake up, wake up! There are seals – lots of them – on the rocks. We can shoot them. But hurry, they won't stay.'

The Twice Scarred Thegn, tousled from his bed, joined them, along with the Radknight and some of the noble women. Gytha waited impatiently. 'Hurry, the rising tide will clear them from the rocks. They are so fat,' she said, holding her bent arms out.

'Now listen, child,' said the Old Lady. 'Many times, I joined my brothers and my uncles on the seal hunts in my childhood. A seal's ears are small, but their eyes and noses are finer than any hound's. At the first sign of danger, they will slide beneath the waves and not return if they believe that danger lurks. So, you must be stealthy.'

'So how do we hunt them, Grandmother?' asked Gytha.

'You cannot stand,' said the Old Lady. 'If they see you against the horizon, they will vanish. Fetch your bows, crawl to the cliff edge and then, on a signal, shoot lying down.'

'But the mocking seagulls will give us away with their cries,' said Gytha as she grabbed her short bow, the one Swetesot had used. She had three arrows left in the quiver. Each one must count.

'We must call the gulls away,' said the Old Thegn. 'You,' he said, pointing at the Pig-boy, 'you take that basket of oysters and cockles and throw them over there.'

'But the Radknight collected them all!'

'It's nothing, my lady,' said the Radknight. 'There are more in the sea.'

And so the little seal-hunting party of Gytha, the Rad-knight, and three of the noble women who could shoot an arrow true to the mark set off, crouching low.

Gytha put a finger to her lips. 'They are below us here,' she said. 'Spread out.' Inching forward, not to dislodge a stone, Gytha slid to the cliff edge on her belly, the arrow ready in her bow. Lifting her head imperceptibly, she peered over. Only a few seals remained; the tide was lapping at them now. Two more slipped into the waves even as she watched. In a moment they would all be gone. Left and right she heard the snap of bowstrings. Steadying her gaze at a fat bull seal directly below, she shot. The bull seal shuddered and hurled its head up with a roar as the arrow buried itself in its neck. Frantically, it headed for the water, but Gytha had another arrow loosed in a second. In her haste, she missed. She fumbled in her quiver to draw her third and final arrow and saw the Radknight rise from the grass, step to the very edge of the cliff, and with one smooth spread of his brawny arms he aimed and shot the seal in the heart. He turned and grinned. Gytha jumped up and hugged him without giving it any thought. Wulfwyn the Radknight's blue eyes and grin were alive again. Her servant, protector and companion was back. Gytha was jubilant.

Then came the women and the children, the Old Lady, the Towering Mace Monk and the Twice Scarred Thegn, clapping and thumping Gytha and the Radknight. Now they would have meat and fat and fur enough to feed them all. For now, their hunger was over.

But it was not to be. The cliffs were steep; by the time they ran down to the beach and worked their way around, the tide had washed still higher. Pig-boy, a rope around his waist and another in his hand, inched his way out across the slime-covered rocks, slipping and falling, hoping to get the line around a fresh dead seal. But the waves were too strong, the danger too great. Again, and again a thunderous breaker nearly swept him to his death. Then, daring one final lunge, he seized the last of them. The brown sea took all the others.

Pig-boy too was the hero of the hour and everyone gave thanks that he was alive; because of him, Gytha and the Radknight, they had something to roast over a fire. But there were no songs, and a gloom hung over the little community for days. Nobody mentioned seal hunting again. Yet every day Gytha still watched for them, but they did not return. She had done her best. They needed a boat.

One morning, up with the light, there was no sign of the Radknight. Gytha went in search of him. He wasn't on the beach, nobody had seen him, so she walked to the bothy he and Pig-boy shared. She called his name. There was a groan.

'Wulfwyn?' Gytha called again, alarmed. She ducked under the low lintel and went inside.

'My lady, I have yellow poison and the wound burns livid red. The pain is so bad,' he said, and again he groaned.

Kneeling next to his pain-wracked body, she put a hand to his forehead. 'You are on fire! Oh Wulfwyn, why not tell me this before? Let me look at the wound. Peeling the putrid cloth away, she gasped. 'We must clean this or you will die! I will fetch my aunt. She will know the best remedy, and the Towering Mace Monk must pray for you.

'My lady,' said the Radknight, 'it is too late for broth, pungent leeks and prayers. Nor is there honey to smear on it, nor leaches to eat the poison. I am dying.'

She dashed outside, calling for her aunt to come quickly. Gunhild ducked into the hut, followed by the Old Thegn, his bulk filling the space inside. Calling for a tallow lamp, he examined the raw wound.

'Oh God have mercy,' he said. 'Look at those maggots. The red blade will sear the wound. I will heat my wounding-knife or he will be dead by nightfall. We cannot wait.'

Wulfwyn groaned, 'My lady,' he whispered,' I fear the pain of the searing blade more than death.'

'Thegn,' said Aunt Gunhild, 'fetch the firewater you have hidden. It will dim his senses as it does yours.'

'I've none left,' said the Old Thegn.

'You do!' blurted Gytha. 'I've seen it when I brought you biscuits.'

'Only because they are so dry,' said the Twice Scarred Thegn lamely.

'Eadric,' said Aunt Gunhild, 'the Lord have mercy on you. Get it!'

The wounding-knife was in the fire, the blade growing red, as Gytha fed the young Radknight the firewater sip by sip. They waited, and sure enough after about an hour he fell into a drunken sleep. Packing wet rags all round, leaving only the putrid wound open, Gytha placed a stick between his teeth and wedged his head between her knees. The Pig-boy and the Old Thegn held him down as Aunt Gunhild crouched between his out-bent legs and, telling to the others to hold him, pressed the red-hot tip onto the wound. Gytha would never forget the Radknight's scream, how his back arched, the sound of searing flesh, the smell of meat on a roasting spit.

Gytha and Pig-boy nursed Wulfwyn, Radknight of Thurgarton through that night and the next. Outside the bothy, the Towering Mace Monk led the little group in prayer. The Twice Scarred Thegn mourned the loss of his precious firewater to Aunt Gunhild, unsurprised by her rebuke. Only the Old Lady remained aloof, untouched by the young man struggling to live. In his delirium, Wulfwyn shouted and mumbled of his mother, his sister Ailsi and his mistress Edith Swan-neck, the fair, the gentle. Then suddenly, as Gytha held the young warrior's hand, he opened his eyes wide. Looking at her as if seeing a spirit, he said 'I am your servant, my lady Gytha. Your commands are mine and my life is yours.'

Kneeling at his side, holding his hand to her chest, Gytha whispered over and over. 'Don't die! Please God in heaven and all the Apostles have mercy. Don't let him die.'

'I will call the Father that he may administer the rite,' said Aunt Gunhild, rising to leave.

'No,' whispered the voice in the bed. 'I am not ready.'

Wulfwyn recovered slowly, Gytha bringing him any morsel of food that she thought might give him strength, but the long days awaiting rescue by her brothers had become months. It was high summer; slow-worms slid between the rocks and bees touched each flower. The islet was tinder dry; the risk of wild fire ever present. Any spark would set the rough grass alight. More than once they had to stamp and beat the flames.

One day they were too late. The ever-wind caught the flame and fire raged across the rough meadow, eating all bothies in its path. Frantically, they freed the penned sheep, grabbing their few belongings, dousing what they could save with precious water. Smoke hung over the island for days like a flag. Gytha and the noble women, their blackened bothies reeking of the blaze, waited for pirates or the Bastard William to kill them all and thieve the Hoard. But the few boats they spied passed without stopping until the feared shout of a boat on the beach had them all grabbing any weapons they could.

It was one boat, upturned, and next to it, on the tide-line, three bodies, still as sacks. The noble women gathered silently on the clifftop as Pig-boy and the Twice Scarred Thegn, both fully armed, went down to inspect. All scanned the horizon for more boats but saw none. To their relief, the Old Thegn waved them to come quickly. Gytha, leading the way, stopped in surprise to find the three sacks were half-drowned boys, no older than her brothers. Their clothes told her they were Welsh, not English. They were alive, stirring as eager hands lifted them, bedraggled and sun scorched, half carrying, half dragging them to where Gytha's grandmother waited.

'Who are they, Thegn?' asked Gytha, watching.

'Let the devil take them,' said the Twice Scarred Eadric. 'Feed them to the fishes. It's that boat we want.'

'Not the pirates we feared,' said the Old Lady.

'Who sent you? Tell me before I kill you,' said the Old Thegn. Shivering, the half-drowned boys looked at him, uncomprehending.

'Well? Who sent you?' said the Old Thegn, more loudly this time. Still no reply. One said something and the other two fell to their knees, crossing themselves over and over.

The Old Thegn repeated himself a third time.

'Try Welsh?' said Aunt Gunhild. 'They don't understand your English.'

The old man swore.

'May I try?' asked Gytha, turning to the boys. 'I am Myrgh-teg,' she said in the tongue the Celtprince had taught her. 'Don't be afraid.' The boys stopped their praying. 'Food?' asked Gytha, pointing to her mouth and belly. The boys nodded furiously.

'She speaks the tongue of thieves,' said the Old Lady. 'Come Thegn, that one,' pointing to the eldest of the boys, 'holds himself nobly, nor is his tunic rough like a fisherman's. I guess they are sent to spy on us.'

The boys fed; Gytha spoke to them again. They were fishing, they said, there was a gust, the sail tore, the steering pole snapped and they broached, half filling their boat with water. All their gear was lost. Had there not been three of them bailing, they would have sunk, said the eldest. For two days and two long nights the tide swept them, helpless, out to sea and back again until the Lord delivered them to the island.

'Feed them to the fishes,' said the Old Thegn. 'They come to spy.'

The Towering Mace Monk rebuked him. 'No, you may not. These Christian boys come not as pirates or spies but shipwrecked, as St Paul was shipwrecked. The Lord has brought them here to us. If they do not return, others will come in search.',

'Nobody will look for them,' said the Old Lady. 'They will think them dead. Drowned in the brown sea. We cannot keep them, there is no food!'

'Great lady, Mother of Heroes,' said the monk. 'It is summer, there was no storm, the boat is sound and the boys healthy. Somebody will look for them, and soon.'

Sensing their danger, the three boys repeated an urgent response over and over.

'They say,' translated Gytha, trying to understand them, 'If we let them go home unharmed, they will ask their father to send us food in gratitude for their safe return. And a boat.'

'And you believe them, child? said the Old Thegn, snorting. 'These Welsh weave a pleasant tale with their mellow voices.'

'Yes, I believe them, Thegn,' said Gytha, listening to the boys. 'There is more!' She paused, her cheeks flushed, her father's fire in her eyes, her anger only tempered by her respect for the great warrior. 'They are not the sons of fisher folk, Thegn, they are of noble blood, as noble as my own three brothers. Their mother is kinswoman to the Welsh King Blethyn and she will grieve for them, as my mother grieves for me and my brothers, and we for her.'

'Oh, merciful Lord! The Lord be praised,' said Aunt Gunhild, crossing herself. 'We are saved. Send the boys back to their mother.'

The Old Lady, the Twice Scarred Thegn and the Towering Monk Blaecman were now listening to Gytha intently. Her rebuke of the Twice Scarred Eadric was forgotten. Gytha felt proud. Proud not to be dismissed, proud she done something no others could do.

'Yes, all in good time,' said the Old Lady. 'The Welsh King Blethyn was friend and vassal to your father, child, but there are many among his kind who would thieve the Godwineson Hoard and slit our throats for it, kinsman or vassal. Hold two of the boys here hostage. No harm will come to them. And let us send one as messenger. Good Father Blaecman, Towering Monk and friend, you will go. Take the young Radknight with you. Seek the Welsh King's protection and have them send food. I am heartily sick of biscuits and oysters.'

'Yes, I shall eat roast pig and crackling fat, followed by venison,' said the monk.

'But Grandmother!' Gytha cried, 'Wulfwyn cannot go. The wound is open still. He cannot walk more than a few paces.'

Without looking at her, the Old Lady said, 'Make ready to leave, Monk.'

Gytha was about to protest again, clenching her fists in anger and frustration, but her words dried in her throat.

With a new steering pole, the sail stitched and the waning moon easing its grasp of the tide, the Towering mace Monk, the pale and limping Radknight, and the eldest boy – the only one of them who knew the perilous brown waters – set off to bring help. Gytha watched them go, her heart in her throat as the little boat struggled to clear the rocks and head out to the distant shore.

'Don't fret, child,' said her aunt.

'Oh aunt, why did the Mother of Heroes send Wulfwyn? He is still hurt.'

'It is not for you, child, to question your grandmother,' said the nun. 'I am sure she had good reason.'

'What reason? We saved him and now he will die and I will never see him again!'.

Days passed, but finally a cry went up that a brown sail was approaching. The women gathered. All watched, weapons in their hands, as the boat cut a raw path towards them, butting and lurching over the brown stream, sometimes almost vanishing, always reappearing. The Welsh boys were shouting with excitement. 'It is our father! It is our father!' they yelled, and Gytha followed as they bolted to the beach. With the Severn flood sweeping it sideways, for a long moment all feared the craft would miss the islet altogether, but as the stream slacked, the sail was dropped and the oarsmen soon had the sturdy war-boat crunching the shingle. At the bow stood a black-haired man as broad as he was tall. He wore a golden helm, a kilt, burnished ring-shirt, and a green cape with a great broach at his shoulder. Two silver-handled wounding-knives hung at his waist, one long, one short. In his hand he gripped a war axe.

Gytha felt a moment of fear at this Celt, so similar to the terrible Broken Spear of the South. She watched as he jumped easily over the side and hugged his boys tenderly. Then he strode to the Old Lady and the Twice Scarred Eadric, followed by his eldest son and the Towering Priest. Then Gytha ran to the boat. Wulfwyn, ashen-faced, had raised himself and had half fallen over the side, nearly landing on her. She struggled to grasp him, dragging him upright.

'Oh, my lady,' he said, 'again I am as a baby. My shame knows no measure.'

'I am happy to see you safely returned, Radknight,' she replied, fighting the urge to hug him. And then she whispered, glancing at the Welsh warrior, 'Wulfwyn, he is so like the wicked painted Celt prince. His voice, his manner, everything.'

'No, my lady. Fear not. He is nothing like Baladrddellt, and he has much to be thankful to you for, as do I. I told him how you had saved his boys from the Old Thegn.'

'Lucky the man whose sons are returned to him alive,' the Welsh prince was saying loudly in English, looking at the Old Thegn, his thick, braceleted arms around his boy's shoulders.

Gytha glanced at her grandmother. The Old Lady was expressionless.

'Great Lady, wife to Earl Godwine, Mother of Kings, I am Rhiwallon ap Cynfyn,' the Welsh prince said. 'I bring gifts and food in gratitude for the safe return of my boys whom the Lord washed onto your shore. And, my lady, I offer you and all the noble ladies my Hall and all that you lack here on this rock.'

To Gytha's dismay, her grandmother refused the prince's offer. 'I thank you, Prince Rhiwallon. To rule an island, even this, is better than being captive at the kindly stranger's hearth. Before long, my grandsons will come and we will return to our stolen kingdom. We have waited. We will wait. But I thank you.'

The Welshman nodded. 'The king shall hold his kingdom! I thought nothing else, Great Lady. I knew and honoured your sons. My brother King Blethyn gave them fealty on land and sea. Harold was the most merciful of kings – openhanded, terrible in war, but in peace, beloved.'

For the first time since they had left Waltham, the Old Lady smiled. 'Yes, and he spoke well of you, Prince, and of the courage of your Welsh people. Now unload, before the tide lifts your keel too far up the beach and you remain here captive on my rock until a new moon releases you.'

The Old Thegn laughed loudly and the Welsh prince, seeing no harm, laughed too. Then they all joined in – the noble women, the monk, Pig-boy and Gytha – their mirth louder even than the mocking seagulls and the buffeting wind. For now, their starvation was over and they would feast.

The boat was quickly unloaded and, to the Old Thegn's delight, out came flagons of ale and mead. There was no mention that he would have killed the boys had it not been for Gytha. 'My thanks,' he said, holding a flagon like a flag above his head. 'I knew your brother, King Blethyn. Let us drink to him and to the Welsh!'

'Thegn, my brother fights the Bastard William at Hereford with the one they call the Wild,' the Welsh prince said, his eyes darkening. 'But the Bastard triumphs at every battle.'

'Well let us drink to the sons of King Harold, who raise a mighty army in Ireland to drive this Bastard into the sea. Will you join us when they return, Prince?'

'Great Thegn, Great Lady, I await their sails each sunrise as you do.' He looked out at the brown flooding water. 'See, my boat is unloaded and the tide lifts it. We must get away while we can. I will send more boats to you with food and provision enough to last the winter.'

'My grandsons will return,' said the Old Lady.

'God have mercy on you all,' said the prince. 'I pray your grandsons return quickly to free you from this prison rock you call England.' He laughed without mirth.

As the Welsh prince turned to climb back on board his ship, Gytha wished she could go with him.

'Wait, Prince,' ordered the Old Lady. 'Take this silver arm ring, it was my son's. In his name, the true King of England, we thank you.'

Pig-boy was waiting outside Gytha's hut. Pulling off his cap and bowing low as he always did, he tugged at her sleeve in his eagerness to get her to where the Radknight had collapsed. He was on the beach, doubled over, supported only by his clam rake which he held in one hand; the other clutched his groin.

'I cannot walk, my lady. The wound has opened.' The once strong boy with his slow smile was now ashen with pain.

'Oh Wulfwyn, we must get you back! Get help, Pig-boy, quickly!' She was suddenly filled with anger at her grandmother – it was she who had sent him off before he was fit. 'You should never have gone on the boat.' helping him to hobble towards the path.

'My lady, it was your grandmother that sent me on the boat.'

'I know, I tried to stop it but I couldn't. She would not listen. I don't understand it.'

'I do,' said the Radknight. 'She wants me off the island, away from here, away from you, my lady.'

'Away from me! what have I done?'

'Cared for me, my lady.'

Gytha was word-robbed. First the painted Celt and now her grandmother.

'Why?' She repeated, 'because I cared for you!'

In the days that followed, small craft arrived as the prince had promised, the crews lingering, bringing news to the noble women until tide and weather permitted their return. All the while, Gytha's heart and head were in turmoil. This was not anger but another feeling, a yearning, harder to explain. The only path open to her was not to see him, anything else would only make it worse. So, she found reasons not to dress his wound and had Pig-boy take food to him. But his name, his hard-won smile, his earnest brow, his Mercian accent were always in her mind, in her thoughts, till she thought herself possessed. She could not shake them from her: he was everywhere, in everything. She could not sleep nor eat. When the monk asked her why she had not been to see the Radknight, Gytha shook her head, sniffing back a stinging tear, one of many that came unwelcome, uninvited, if they spoke of Wulfwyn to her.

'I know what ails her. It is what ails every silly young girl. He is a man,' said the Old Lady. 'I have tried to put a stop to it. You, Gunhild you encourage it. Make sure she does not see him anymore.'

A red dawn. A freshening wind out of the south-west spoke of rain, the brown stream turned to muddy blue. Marching lines of ocean waves, monuments to distant storms frothing at their crests, stretched from horizon to horizon. And on those waves, racing as if chased by wild animals, sailed the English war fleet.

The noble women gathered on the cliff and marvelled. Boats as far as they could see, surging longships with round shields fastened to their sides, smaller boats struggling in the steeping swells. Everywhere sterns lifting and then, as each wave passed beneath them, the dragons at their bows reached up and up with open mouths to challenge the sky in a rhythm as grand as the sea itself. It was magnificent.

'It's Earl Godwine, he's come at last! How many do you count?' they shouted, each reaching different number.

'Sixty boats, maybe more.'

'Two thousand men!' said the Twice Scarred Thegn.

'Two thousand seasick men. Look at those swells,' said the Towering Monk.

'The king shall hold the kingdom!' they yelled, waving furiously. 'The king shall hold the kingdom!' The words of their battle cry were snatched by the wind. The warriors on the boats waved back.

'Will they rescue us now?' Gytha was so excited, she was jumping up and down.

'No, they cannot take us to the fight,' said the monk. 'With God's will, I see an end to our exile. But we must be a patient a little longer. They will come for us.'

'Amen,' said Aunt Gunhild. 'Not a day too soon.'

The tide slowed, then changed direction until it flowed hard the other way. The fleet of sixty boats, still under bulging wind-full sails, halted as if bound by chains.

'They are snared by the Nine Daughters,' said the Old Lady. 'Snared with invisible threads to the seabed.'

'Oh look, grandmother!' shouted Gytha. 'That is God-wine's boat!'

A longship, the Golden Dragon of Wessex swelling on the taut sail, changed course towards the island until it was barely clear of the tooth rocks. Godwine, Edmund and the beardling boy Magnus, together with the axed and burnished Roni, stood by the steersman, legs braced as the great boat rose and fell, spray soaking the rowers. Gytha waved furiously at her brothers. The Towering Mace Monk blessed them, making the sign of the cross, his great right arm sweeping up and down like a windmill. On board the three helmed boys crossed themselves in reply, bowing deeply to their grandmother, the Mother of Heroes. And Gytha and all the noble women gathered on the cliffs shouted, 'The king shall hold the kingdom! The king shall hold the kingdom!' at the tops of their voices, until they were so hoarse, they could no longer speak. But they were happy for the first time that they could recall.

With a last wave, the longship turned away to return to the heart of his fleet; the last few leagues to the mainland beckoned, and the battle ahead. Gytha, exhausted, windblown, joyful, returned to the mean hut that had been her home for almost half a year. The longing to be rid of the islet and all that reminded her of it suddenly became more acute. She had only to wait a little longer and her brothers would be back to save her. It would be over; she would go to the Hall, she would sleep in her bed, have her clothes, ride with her brothers, but most of all she would see her mother. She could barely contain the excitement that welled up inside her at the thought.

Pig-boy interrupted her, bowing and beckoning, as was his way. At first Gytha refused to follow, but he was begging her, making his strange noises and tugging at her sleeve. 'Why?' she asked him.

He pointed a circling finger to his temple and rolled his eyes. Gytha was intrigued. 'Is Wulfwyn gone mad, crazed? Pig-boy nodded vigorously, but he did not laugh. Instead, he tugged her sleeve more.

As she approached the Radknight's hut, there he was, a shield strapped to his shoulder, long-sword at his belt, his ring-shirt rusted by the sea air, his helm tight on his head.

'What are you doing?' said Gytha in alarm.

'I go to join your brothers. The Welsh are making their boat ready now. We will catch the fleet before the tide turns again if we hurry.'

'But you cannot! You mustn't!' Gytha blurted. 'You are too weak, Wulfwyn. The wound could still open.'

'No, my lady,' he said, 'I am a warrior, son of the great Thegn of Thurgarton, outstanding for his courage among outstanding men. I serve your brother Godwine, to fight or fall as only God alone can say.'

'No, no, no!' wailed Gytha. 'You serve me!' And she turned and ran to her grandmother's hut where the old lady sat in the half-darkness.

'Oh, Mother of Heroes,' she said, bursting in and explaining what Wulfwyn was proposing to do. 'You must stop him. You cannot let the Radknight go to the battle. He is still sick. He will die before he sees an enemy or they him. He carries his enemy with him and it will kill him!' She was weeping openly now. 'You cannot let him, grandmother.'

'My child,' said the Old Lady, 'on that longship ride the finest jewels of our English kingdom. Your brother Godwine has furnished a fleet. Let the current bear them to the Bastard William, monster of evil, to be heroes under heaven. Let the Radknight with them, for he is eager for sailing and can lie no longer lie on women's straw.'

'But Grandmother, he is not ready for battle. It was I who brought him here to the women's isle and in my care he lives. Now you speed him to the bed of death.'

'Child, there was no man in England stronger or more courageous than your grandfather, Earl Godwine, who fathered the many sons of my body. Never once did I plead with him to spare them from battle. Child, you must endure your sorrow at this parting, for it is nothing to holding a son cold in your arms even as they build his funeral pyre, as I have done five times. Gytha, to be a King's daughter bears a weighty commission.'

Gytha knew all protestation was in vain, but she could not bring herself to say goodbye to the Radknight. Her heart was breaking, but she could not tell him and he would never know. She ran to the farthest point of the cliff and watched in agony as the little boat that was carrying him away lurched and stumbled over the waves to clear the rocks and chase after the English fleet. Had he seen her? she wondered on the cliff. She turned, crying openly, and there, a few paces from her, tears rolling down his muddy cheeks, stood Pig-boy. For a fleeting moment, Gytha touched his hand, neither able to speak, united in their love of the Radknight.

Flatholm was now an insufferable agony for Gytha. Her grandmother's words fought with her heart as she lay in her hut, refusing all food, wishing only to be a mocking seagull or vigilant hawk, to peer beyond the east horizon to where their battle for England raged.

Then lookouts shouted, 'Longboats returning!'

The cliff watchers stood in silence, the wind tugging at their ragged clothes. Something was amiss. These boats told of defeat, not victory, the warrior shields no longer orderly along the side, but gapped like broken teeth. In twos and threes, they came, the pride of the advance now straggled across the great brown seaway, not bound for the islet but turning to the mainland.

Gytha watched, her beating heart in her throat. She tried to swallow but could not, knowing she must be calm, knowing to breathe, but feeling as if she would choke on worry itself. Everything told of a failed attack. She scoured the horizon, squinting her eyes against the salt-wind, searching for the Golden Dragon sail. It was not there. There was no Golden Dragon.

Gytha remembered that first time at Waltham; the waiting, and how the message dove had come. Now once more she was waiting, as her mother had waited for news of the one most dear to her. Gytha's only comfort was threadbare prayers, patched and darned like the ragged smock that she, the daughter of a great King and Ring-Giver, now wore.

Night fell. Gytha was deaf to the talk around the fire, refusing food and answering only in single words when spoken to. At dawn she rose, her belly empty, and walked once more to the cliff's edge. Pig-boy was there, smiling and pointing. Godwin's longship, the dragon sail furled tight to the mast, was waiting out the slackening tide before daring to nudge the shingle strand.

All ran down to the beach to seize the hemp line. Godwine, with a bloody bandage around his head half hidden by his helm, made his way forward to the dragon prow as the oarsmen lifted their great oars like wings to the sky and stowed them noisily.

'What happened?' shouted the Old Thegn above the clatter.

Godwine shook his head. 'The folk of Bristol will not rise against the Bastard William. They said we drew his wrath to them and attacked us when we would not go.'

'Not a skirmish, a battle. I can see that from the damage,' growled the Old Thegn. 'So, you were attacked by Englishmen.'

'Yes, traitors,' said Godwine. 'We come to honour our dead.'

'What dead do you honour that brings you here?' said the Towering Mace Monk. Gytha put her hand to her mouth, knowing that the next words her Lord and brother Godwine would utter would be "Wulfwyn, Radknight of Thurgarton".

Gytha felt the breath in her body rise to choke her. Blood pounded in her ears.

'Our brother Magnus, son of Harold, fell to a Norman arrow as our father did. Bury him here on this Island that is England still and let us build a high mound over him for all passing sailors to say, "there lies an English hero".'

Magnus, her dearest brother. Gytha slumped to the shingle with a scream dead in her throat. She heard him teasing her, laughing fit to burst; she felt the rough hay of their lair where they played, saw his pride as he buckled his first ring-shirt, Magnus the rascal, her rascal, her cheeky one, gone, a boy-body in a bloody sail.

Godwine gathered the noble women to him. 'Edmund and the Burnished Roni lead the Company of Heroes now to seize what is rightfully ours from the traitors in Somerset. Then they return here to the island to bring you, the Hoard, to safety in Dublin.'

'No,' said the Old Lady. 'We will not go. We are under the protection of the Welsh prince, Rhiwallon ap Cynfyn. I trust him more than the High King Diarmait in Dublin.'

'But Grandmother, the Welsh Prince cannot protect you from the Bastard William's men. Many English traitors fight under his banner now. Nor can I stay here to protect you, but must return to Ireland,' argued Godwine

'Then,' said his grandmother, 'The Twice Scarred Thegn and The Towering Mace Monk we will seek sanctuary with my kinsman King Sweyn Estrithson in Denmark. He will receive us and hold the Hoard and send seafarers to rid England of this William. We shall sail now before the winter storms drive us to our direst foes.'

Finding a quiet moment Gytha, her heart breaking, sought news of the Radknight. 'He lives?' she asked, unable to hide the tremor in her voice.

'Yes, he lives, said Godwine. 'he stood with our brother Edmund and the Companions of the Golden Dragon of Wessex to avenge our father.'

They buried the beardling Magnus on the island, scraping a shallow grave, as best they could, piling rocks and earth on it, the Towering Mace Monk, shouting against the wind.

'Now, gracious Lord, as never, I need your grace, that my soul may set out on its journey to You, O Prince of Angels, that my soul may depart into Your power in peace. I pray that the devils may never destroy it.'

And then the Mother of Heroes asked that a drift-wood pyre be lit and the story of Magnus's short life be told, as was her Danish way. The fire burnt long into the night. By morning the hopes and dreams of the Harold's kin were embers on that that gull-plagued rock.

END OF PART ONE

PART TWO

AT THE MERCY OF DARK HEARTS

Having escaped from Flatholm Island, Gytha reaches Denmark via Flanders, hoping for sanctuary at the hall of her cousin King Sweyn Estrithson, the last of the Viking kings. Her Grandmother, the Mother of Heroes and her Aunt Gunhild remain in Flanders. With no husband, no dowry, and no kingdom to call home, the future is bleak for King Harold's daughter, her two remaining brothers Godwine and Edmund and the last Companions of the Golden Dragon of Wessex.

PART TWO CHAPTER ONE

THE COLD TRADER

HE GLANCED AT HER and nodded as men do, sizing her like a
bargain horse, his bearded mouth-corners twitching downwards.

The script of hardships that lay deep within Gytha had laid
little mark upon her beauty. She had her father's summer eyes
and cheeks of ripening rose-hips. Her golden hair, gifted by
her fair mother Edith her gentle swan, peeped from beneath
her cowl as she watched the trader weigh her value as the
usurer weighs gold.

He had an angled face, high bones beneath grey eyes; the
cruel Wendish look, not the turnip heads of England. He
greeted her with a flourish of insincerity. His name, he said,
was Zhiznomir. Gytha said nothing as she handed him the
brimming silver welcome horn.

He wore fine clothes, but smelled worse than any spear
Dane. He had brass folding-scales dangling from his waist, the
slaver's mark. On his head was a sable hat, a sable collar on his
cape. A curved scimitar was tucked through the green-and-
gold sash at his waist.

'Gytha Haroldsdaughter!' Elisaveta spoke, shrill trophy queen
of her kinsman King Sweyn Estrithson, 'friend Zhiznomir
brings news of my heart-home on the River. He comes from

my brother in Kiev to search the Danelands for a bride of beauty and royal blood for my nephew, Prince Vladimir. We will make him most welcome at our bord, will we not?' Gytha felt bristling danger spiking at her neck as the queen told the trader it was King Harold of the English, who had killed her first husband, the Viking king, Hardradr.

'The girl-haired English cowered like slow-wit trolls beneath a bridge,' she was saying, 'such was their terror of my husband, Hardradr.'

How Gytha hated the trophy queen.

'Is it true, Thegn Eadric? Did we hide as trolls beneath a bridge?' Gytha asked the Twice Scarred Thegn as soon as she could flee the Queen and the Wendish trader.

'No, my Lady Gytha,' said the old man. 'I was at Stamford Bridge with your noble father. I saw with my eyes the furious Hardradr die, and the traitor Tostig with him. I saw twenty longships flee where three hundred had come to fight us. No trolls nor demons fought at Stamford, only the victorious flower of the English and your father always where the fight was fiercest.' He paused as if reliving the battle, 'Though one fine Englishman did press his spear from beneath the bridge, up a Dane giant's arse. It is that of which she speaks.' He guffawed with joy at the memory.

'And that is why she hates us so?'

'With reason,' said the axed and burnished Roni the Dane. 'Her husband Hardradr was a mighty king and poet. This queen imprisoned him with her beauty. And then your father killed him.'

'Beauty?' said Gytha. 'What beauty? God gave Hardradr a whelped-out bitch for a wife. If he had not attacked my father, he'd be alive and she still with him, not trophy wife to my mead-aged kinsman Sweyn and tormenting me.'

'Well-spoken,' said the Old Thegn. 'I'll wager she is jealous of you, fair Gytha. These Rus princesses have an eye for kings and kings for them. But fear not, this Queen Elisaveta cannot barter you to traders with silver and jewels to exchange without your nod.'

Gytha put her hand on his arm and thanked him. 'You are as a father to me, great Thegn. We have shared so much since fleeing Waltham that dark December. Your words comfort me, but I am afraid. I know in my heart this Wendish trader favours me over all others, and the Queen wishes me gone from her hall. All will praise her generosity to her nephew, and his cunning to get a king's daughter for less than the curved scimitar he wears at his side.'

'Is there no jarl nor kinsman,' said her ever thoughtful brother Edmund, 'here in the North to whom we can betroth her, as our grandmother, Mother of Heroes, was betrothed to our grandfather, Earl Godwine? Are we to let the trophy Queen send Gytha beyond the Baltsea, beyond the limitless forest? God knows what dangers there are on such a journey and what fate awaits her there.'

'My lady,' said Wulfwyn her Radknight, 'the scented Swetesot spoke most bitterly of her captivity in Kiev in the palace of the River Prince and how she yearned for the grass ocean she called the Wild Field.'

'I will not let them send Gytha to this Vladimir. I will forbid it,' said Godwine. 'You say these River princes are rich and will pay the Dane king well for our vow-sister Gytha, but we have the Godwineson hoard still, and shall match the trader's price.'

'Dear brother of my heart, No!' Gytha cried. 'We have nothing, the Hoard chests are empty. Do not give the last of what we have for my freedom alone. If it is the Lord's will that I must be betrothed to this river Prince, His will be done.

I will not bring destitution on the Companions, God will walk beside me in the dark places, his rod and his staff will comfort me and I will not be afraid.'

Gytha's brothers, Godwine, a king without a country and the quiet Edmund, The Twice scarred Thegn Eadric, the Towering Mace Monk Blaecman, the Radknight and others of their dwindled Company stood on the edge of the throng in the King's hall that night. They were unsettled, wary, tugging at their beards and letting idle fingers feel the handles of their wounding-knives. All was not well.

'Look,' said Godwine, 'Normans!'

The Dane-King rose from this throne-seat, his speech faint. 'We welcome yet more newcomers in the hall. This knight and sage bishop visit us with tribute (he paused) from King William of England,' A murmur went around the hall. Some turned to look at the Companions.

Blaecman caught Godwine's eye and gestured to leave; Godwine nodded back, beckoning the Old Thegn.

'They come with gifts from the Bastard to turn this foolish king against us,' said Godwine, the moment they were outside.

'And I hear,' said the Twice Scarred Thegn Eadric, 'there is a ransom on all our heads.'

'I fear we are to discover if we are guest or prisoner.' Said Godwine.

'Guest or prisoner,' said the Towering mace monk Blaecman, 'all guests are prisoners and all prisoners guests. Which, cannot be known until the day you wish to leave.'

'Yes, well spoken,' said the Old Thegn. 'As a bucket of water douses the brightest fire, the Bastard's silver will kill the welcome this king has shown us. We are hunted and must leave without delay.'

'If we leave, every man's hand will turn against us. Let us stay as guests of our kinsmen Sweyn but be vigilant,' said the burnished Roni.

'Are you with us or with them, Roni?' growled the Old Thegn. 'why should we trust your counsel? I say seek a boat for our escape and vanish into the night storm with the lady Gytha and what remains yet of the hoard.'

Roni, the axed and burnished Huscarl, could not conceal his anger.

'Shame on all your kin, Thegn Eadric. I gave my blood oath to King Harold and for you to doubt me now, makes only you my enemy. Seize a boat? where would you have us go? To the west, and perish in the winter-grey seas, east to the forests of the Wends, or perhaps to hide once more on an island and starve. No, old man, I will not follow your plan. We must stay and wait our moment.'

'Hush, put aside your enmity, you both serve me well. We will wait until tomorrow,' said Godwine, 'and in the meantime, I will speak with the king and learn his mind.'

'You'll be lucky to learn his mind, for his mouth speaks the queen's mind,' said the Old Thegn.

The king was still talking, now welcoming the Trader from the East, when they slipped back into the hall.

'And this Zhiznomir comes to us,' he said, 'to find among us a wife for the Prince Vladimir, nephew to our Queen, for it is our tradition that we and the River people beyond the forest offer our daughters. It is a sign of lasting peace and brotherhood with the River people.'

The warriors in the hall beat their mugs and wounding-knives on the wooden table-tops as a sign of their approval. They knew that, above all else, were it not for the friendship of the River people, all trade of grinding-slaves, wax, fur, honey and amber with the empires in the sun-lands of the south would cease.

'We have among us,' the king went on, 'such a gift, brothers.' The Dane King Sweyn Estrithson turned to where Gytha was standing, expressionless, save for the panic in her blue eyes which darted to her brother Godwine. 'Come, lady Gytha, and stand before us.'

The cheering and drumming grew deafening. The queen took Gytha tightly by the arm and pushed her forwards. Head lowered, a strand of golden hair showing from beneath her cowl, Gytha stepped in front of the gathering.

Turning to where the Wendish trader sat, the king declared, 'You have come far in search of your prize in the service of your great prince, brother to my wife. Look now at the daughter of a mighty warrior, my fallen kinsman Harold of England, in whose Virgin heart is the blood of Kings and whose beauty has been the talk of our Northland since she came to us with her brothers and sought safety in our hall. Eadgytha Haroldsdaughter, Princess of Wessex will grace the hall of the mightiest warrior, and your Prince Vladimir will be the envy of all. I offer her to you on the promise that you cherish and protect her, as we do. You must ensure that on her great journey to your land no harm befalls her. Take her and her brothers, that they can be in the service of your prince, for they too are mighty warriors.'

Godwine leapt to his feet. 'My lord and kinsman,' he shouted, but ten spear men rose to step between him and the king. Others grabbed Gytha. The Companions now were on their feet.

'My lord,' Godwine repeated, his hand dropping to his dagger. 'You have not the right to bargain my vow-sister to this man against her will. It is the law of Knut the Great. It is the law of the English and the Dane. Nor may you offer my Company into the service of the River people without my agreement as their rightful king and Ring-Giver.' But Godwine's voice was drowned out by the jeers of the Danes.

The Trader turned and raised his hand as he spoke, as if giving a solemn undertaking. His accent oil-thick, he said 'King, I receive from you this fair orphan maid to plant as a rose within the walls of the River Fortress in Smolensk to bear the fruit of Prince Vladimir's seed. Your gift and generosity know no bounds. No harm will come to her, I will deliver her safely to Smolensk to Prince Vladimir alone. Accept my meagre gifts of fur, spice and silver as small recompense for your loss of your English rose. Who knows what desires women harbour? But she shall have all and more in the Red Fortress on the river at Smolensk.'

The words turned Gytha's heart to ice in her chest. All she could think of was England, the home she would never see again, the brook behind the Hall where she splashed with Magnus, the hay-barn where they played, or brushing her mother's long hair, the smell of her cheek, the love in her eyes, her father's voice, his tight embrace. England and all it meant to her was now a flickering lantern, a fading memory to light the darkness ahead.

The dread deal was struck. King and trader, Dane and Wend, spat into their hands and shook. 'The monks shall prepare the betrothal, with the great seal of Sweyn Estrithson,' said the king, his once mighty presence now bleared with age.

Godwine, elbowing the warriors aside, tried once more to object.

'Silence,' said the Old King, his reedy voice querulous. 'Godwine Haroldson, when the storm abates, you will leave this hall and escort your sister to Prince Vladimir in Smolensk. King William has placed a ransom on your heads. Do not defy me. Any man here may claim it should I decree your life forfeit.'

'King,' shouted Godwine, 'we fear no one, and will not run from a fight, no matter what the odds,' as the King's hearthguard pushed him backwards. 'Fine words but empty words,' said the king. 'Escort your sister to the Prince on the River. Better you guard her, boy, than threaten us. Spring is not far off; the geese fly northward. Take your sister and your Companions. Sail the Baltsea to Gotland and from there to the lands of the River Princes. This is my command, Godwine Haroldson. Till then you are banished from this hall. Your sister will remain here with the Queen for her safety, should misfortune visit you and your men.'

'Say nothing,' hissed the queen and before Gytha could cry out, hidden hands pulled her backwards, and another covered her mouth. She tried to fight but could only squirm in the spear men's grip. 'Take her, guard her,' said the queen. 'Her foolish brothers will try to rescue her.'

The emissaries of the Bastard William, the knight and the bishop smiled, savouring the moment of Godwine's humiliation. Any harboured hope the Golden Dragon might fly over England once more died in that hall that night. Their mission was complete.

And so was Gytha betrothed, with spit on clasped hands, a virgin bride to an unknown prince in a strange land. A prisoner, hidden within the queen's lodging. Snatched from her brothers, Gytha sank again into a dark place. She stared at the wall of the room, not seeing the fine tapestries, refusing all food. Her golden hair was lank about her face; her eyes, once a brilliant blue, were drained of their colour. Yet again, every man's hand was turned against them – a blood price on her brother's heads – and this time, there was nowhere for them to run. She had never dreamed it might come to

this, and her heart ached. She was valueless, not even to be
given as wife to a heathen noble of the Northland; Instead,
she was to be traded to the east like a collar thrall to the
fortress of ransackers and marauders and never heard of
again. Darkness swept over her; an emptiness so profound
that were it to swallow her she would welcome it rather than
face life locked with the devil in his lair. No longer guest but
prisoner, as the towering priest had foreseen. The brimming
coffers of the Godwineson Hoard near empty. Where once
were chests of golden cups, the crystal monstrance, bracelets,
silver coins, tapestries and the jewels of her grandmother,
now nothing but a few boxes of silver ingots and shilling-
coins remained. A royal bride without a dowry; her brother
a king without a country. He was nothing. She was nothing.
They were nothing.

Banished from the Hall by the Dane King and a ransom on
their lives, the Companions mounted guards, as if an enemy
was at hand. Of Gytha they heard nothing.

A week passed. Snow still lay on the roofs and on the boats.
Ice clogged the bay. Word went around that Gytha was starving
herself to death. Concern growing each day, the brothers
demanded they visit her, but the queen refused, nor might the
Towering Mace Monk Blaecman hear her confession. None
were more fearful for Gytha than the Radknight and Pig-
boy. Walking together to the Queen's hall, Wulfwyn engaged
a guard.

'Let this Pig-boy, her groom and servant without a tongue,
serve his mistress. He cannot speak, he has only the voice of
an ass.' A message was sent to the Queen and she agreed. And
so, Pig-boy would scurry back and forth between his mistress
and her brothers, bringing her food and little scraps of news
on a tablet hidden beneath his tunic. To everyone's relief she

ate, but the melancholy lay on her heart. From Pig-boy she
heard that the Wends were eager to return to their homeland
in the great forest beyond the sea. She heard rumours of the
Trader and was filled with dread. For beneath his fine clothes
of eastern cloth, the silk shirt with flecks of gold that was
the envy of the king's women, there beat a cruel heart. Her
mousing cat that lay where it was warmest, disappeared; its
body pierced through by a knife. They said it jumped into
the Trader's lap. Then a slave girl whose screams woke the
Hall was found in the snow with the blood of rape bright
on her torn clothing.

Gytha grew more alarmed at these stories, sending messages to Godwine.

'Yes,' said the Towering Mace Monk, 'she has cause to be
afraid. The king has placed our fair Gytha's life in the keeping
of a devil, whose heart beats black beneath his honeyed words
to that age-dimmed King and his weasel wife.'

'I fear that once we enter the great forest,' said the
Radknight, 'he will slit our throats and seize not only the
prize of English beauty but the Hoard too.'

'Bears or wolves are as nothing to the danger of this
Wendish trader,' said Edmund.

'Pig-boy,' said Godwine, 'tell your mistress my sister that
we will guard her every move. No Wend will harm her, nor
bear attack her. The Radknight will never leave her side day
or night.'

'Tell her, too, I will have that trader cold in his grave if one
golden hair of my lady's head is ruffled,' growled the Twice
Scarred man of war, and nobody doubted it.

And from then on, Zhiznomir was known as the Cold
Trader, in anticipation of his death.

*   *   *

Pig-boy scurried across the mud-snow yard to his Lady, the guards calling out as he passed, 'Here comes the Pig-boy! Sing us a pretty song, Pig-boy.' Pig-boy feigned a laugh, pushing past their kicks and punches. Gytha's pleasure at seeing him never failed to make the ordeal worth it.

Once in her quarters, she placed a hand on his shoulder, which he took and kissed, bowing deeply. Then he reached deep into his shirt and pulled out a small waxed tablet. On it he had written in Latin, 'trader bad. Pig-boy and Radknight protect you always.'

'Oh, Pig-boy!' Gytha cried, 'I am so frightened. We came here to the north for safety among our kinfolk, but now all would harm us.' Her blue eyes melted, she touched Pig-boy's hair. 'At least I still have you.' She put her hand under his chin to lift his bowed head. Pig-boy grinned and nodded his head so vigorously that Gytha began to laugh. Pig-boy laughed with her until his braying had people run in to see if all was well. He quickly buried the tablet in his shirt and, bowing hand to heart, left Gytha, prisoner in her kinsman's hall.

At last the thaw started and boats were readied for the English to leave, their destiny no longer theirs to decide. For Godwine and Edmund, sons of a great Kingdom, all hope and dreams of returning to England were rubble. Their purpose was now dimmed to watchful escort to their sister and their few coffers on the long journey East.

Nowhere in the middle world was there a more forlorn company than the Companions of the Golden Dragon of Wessex the night of their departure. The king had summoned them to a farewell feasting in the great longhouse. Fearing a trap, the Companions entered warily. Catching sight of Godwine, the old king hailed him. 'Come,' he said, shouting. 'Godwine, sit with us here. Drink and feast, as we pray for your safety on the long journey to our friends the River Princes.' Gytha, freed from her imprisonment, rushed to her brothers and her hearth companions.

'Sit all of you, my lady Gytha, sit here to my left and my queen to my right. Come, give me your hands. A fair Lady from the beyond the grey west sea and a Queen with the golden necklace of the east. See how the King of Danes holds all the middle world in his hands and we are friends with all.

There was a guffaw from the Jarls who sat close by. 'Yes, King,' said one, a fearsome warrior, holding up his mead mug, made of a man's skull. 'Most welcome we are in all lands. There is no bluster headland, no creek nor cove, where Danes are not welcome.' The others around him doubled-up laughing. The king joined in and, furiously, the men banged their mugs on the mead board.

Last to arrive was the Cold Trader. He was wearing a long, silken coat of ochre, flecked with gold stars with a thick green cloth belt around his middle. Heavy gold rings weighed down each hand. He greeted the king and queen with the leer of one whose mission is complete, the prize secured, the matter closed to his best advantage.

Turning to Gytha, he said 'what revel tonight, what joy I feel at the match made between you and my master prince Vladimir.' Gytha refused to look at him and said nothing.

The trader reached out to Gytha, tilting her head up by her chin. 'Are you not grateful to the king and queen that you will be a queen in the East?' Gytha tried to pull her head back, but he gripped her tightly.

'You hurt me,' she exclaimed. In an instant, Wulfwyn the Radknight was at her side, jewelled dagger drawn.

'Back away, River dog,' he snarled in English. The trader turned, The Radknight, with the speed of a striking adder on a vole, buried a fist in the Trader's nose. The blood splattered

onto the ochre silk like dark islands in a golden sea. 'Touch
my lady and you die where you stand.'

The Cold Trader wiped his bleeding nose on his silken
sleeve. 'You will live to regret this, boy,' he hissed. 'The princess
will come to no harm in the forest days ahead. But much can
else happen. Beware, boy.' Then he turned and pushed his way
through the drinking Danes.

'Thank you, brave Wulfwyn, my life champion, but next
time let me kill him first,' said Gytha. Wulfwyn laughed and
she whispered, 'Go quickly.'

'Fine blow,' said the Towering Blaecman as the Radknight
nursed his knuckle. 'I fear the next.'

'I do not,' said the boy, the anger still in him. 'I welcome
it, may Christ blind him, for I shall kill him.' And as soon as
they could, the Companions of the Golden Dragon of Wessex
slipped away from the Hall to make ready for the morning.

It was a short ride from the beach to where the trader's laden
boats lay anchored. Gytha, bundled in a fur, guarded by the
trader's blank-faced Balts, joined her brothers on board. The
Trader holding a cloth to his nose boarded another and gave
the order to sail.

Gytha shivered. Once more the future and her part in it
was in God's hands alone. She pulled the pelt about her and
turned to the west to where England lay – to her mother, her
gentle swan, whose soft voice and smiling eyes had bathed
Gytha in her love.

She felt an arm tighten around her shoulder and looked to
see Edmund staring too. Neither spoke. Gytha leaned her head
against her brother's shoulder as they felt the rhythmic surge of
the rowers as the longship gathered speed down the creek and
pointed its prow towards the east. There were no tears within
her, she would survive. Four days sail lay the island of Gotland.

*   *   *

The steersman, long in the service of King Sweyn, had visited the River People, or Rus as he called them, and lived among them. He told them of Kiev, of St Andrew the Apostle, and the church he built which stands above the river. He spoke of the riches of the feuding princes, and he spoke of the blond harvests of the north, destined for the great slave market in Constantinople.

'The snow will linger and the rivers will clog with melting ice until the spring turns to summer, he told them, 'and where the river smokes and roars over rocks and boulders they haul the boats from the stream and drag them on a road of logs through the silver forest and the marsh.'

'What is the silver forest?' asked Gytha.

'It is as if enchanted. Trees as tall as oak, elm or beech, but slender with white unblemished bark. And in the summer their leaves shimmer and rustle in the breeze and sunlight dances on the green-glade forest floor beneath them.'

'Oh, to walk in such a forest,' said Gytha, longing to be off the boat.

'Yes, my lady. But danger lurks there, too. The forest is not as woodlands of your home. There are bottomless meres and wild beasts that would hunt you. Boar and bear and wild ox lurk there, and no man lives who blunders among them.'

'Silver forest and smoking rivers! I fear you are spinning a seaman's yarn,' scoffed the Twice Scarred Thegn.

'What he tells is true,' said the axed and burnished Roni the Dane. 'I have heard it so from my kin who have travelled down river, to the storm-full sea they call black and the sun-hot lands. Yet danger is not from the bears and boars, but from the horsemen who ride out of the Wild Field and strike terror in the hearts of men.'

'Yes,' said Gytha suddenly. 'For they are born in the saddle and speak to their horses in the tongue of animals. They have no need of reins or saddles, and can shoot arrows in all directions at the same time. None miss their target. Edmund, do you remember the day we watched the scented Swetesot shoot arrows backwards from a galloping horse and crawl under its neck as it sped across the hill? And did she not speak to the horses in the horse tongue and they did her bidding? That is true is it not, Wulfwyn?'

'Yes, my lady,' said the Radknight, 'she would jump on the horse's back by sliding down its neck. Oh, it was a trick to see.'

Gytha laughed at the memory. 'Pig-boy would tell you about her if he could speak. Pig-boy, come here!' Pig-boy clambered over the thwart and stood in front of his lady. 'Did the scented Swetesot not grab a horse by its nose, pull its head down, slip her leg across its ears and sit upon its head?' Pig-boy brayed with pleasure, rocking back and forth, nodding his head at the memory. Then suddenly he clutched his heart.

'You miss her, don't you? said Gytha. 'And so do I. I wonder where she and her little baby Boniak are now? I pray for their safety.'

Save for the hollow groan and splash of oars and the crackle of ice in the rigging, there was grey silence. Gytha shivered violently, the warming oar denied her. All others – slave, prince and warrior – shared the tasks aboard: keeping the brazier lit, stirring the gruel pot, passing mead to the rowers. Only Gytha, princess bride, could not. 'I am strong as any man here,' she complained, 'I rowed twelve days without rest when we fled Flatholm Island for Flanders.' But it was to no avail. It was forbidden.

Time passed slowly as they rowed through the ghostly ice fog, working the longboats east. Sometimes a breath of wind would fool them into raising the sail, only to have it vanish. They cursed the gods that promised rest from their benches. In time, they did not bother, lest the rhythm of their rowing was lost.

His turn over, the Twice Scarred Thegn Eadric stepped over the thwarts and sat himself at the brazier. Gytha handed the old man a pot of mead. His hands, she saw, were wrapped in a bloody rag.

'Let me look, Thegn Eadric. Let me fetch the soothing balm.' But he pulled his hand away with a shake of his bearded head.

'Remember, my lady Gytha,' he said, looking into the cup, 'how we rowed in terror of the shores on either hand, and never rested from beyond the Tamar for fear of capture by the Bastard Duke's seamen? And how the west-storm delivered us to Count Baldwin at St Omer when we were starving and could row no more? Now I welcome any storm and any land to be off this serpent-headed knarr. Boats are for Dane-folk, I am done with them and the wave-road. I crave a horse, to hunt with hawks and nosewise hounds across the high down, and afterwards rest by the logs of your father's hearth.'

Those in earshot – her brothers, the Towering Mace Monk, the Radknight, and Pig-boy – nodded and were silent as they, too, remembered their home, far beyond the grey west sea, wondering if they should ever see it again and knowing in their hearts that they would not. It was lost, that place: those green, smooth downs; the leaf-carpeted beech woods; the unblurred trout in winter-born streams. And somewhere there, thought Gytha, my mother lingers in life where father lies buried.

Two more days and two long nights they rowed over the leaded Baltsea. Their bones ached, their hands were raw and their arses numb from the benches. Only the curling prow wave and splash and drip of the groaning oars showed they were moving at all. All prayed for wind, each to his own god.

The English, led by the Towering Monk Blaecman, prayed to the Lord God in Heaven; the Balt-folk to Austaras, bringer of wind; the spear Danes to the four dwarves; but none dared offer tribute to Perun, God of Thunder.

Gotland island appeared, rising from the water in the dawn. Ahead was the little town called Visby. The word was out and long before the knars' keels scraped, people lined the shore. Gytha stood at the stern, shawl pushed back, the circlet in her golden hair shining under the water-sun that had unbound them too late, from their fog-walled jail. Next to her was Godwine, his longsword tight-belted at his side, steadying himself as the steersman ordered the oars shipped. Until the anchor held, two Balts with long poles held the boat off the rocks that passed for the quay at Visby.

'Look,' said the Towering Mace Monk, 'they have a chapel on the shore.'

'Yes,' said the steersman. 'It is for the Christian River folk that come. These islanders know only their gods and human sacrifice.' At that, the Towering Blaecman made the sign of the cross and while a few of the watchers crossed themselves with him, most jeered.

'Good Father,' said the steersman, 'have a care. For they like no better than to send a priest to Odin's hall.'

'What is this place?' said Gytha, recoiling.

'It is the slave market, my lady,' said the steersman. 'All pass here from the north and west to the River land – slaves, amber, furs, even dancing bears – on the long journey to the lands beyond the forest. Where, too, the Norsemen rest before returning to their farmstead wives with hoards of silver dirhams.'

'And the daughter of an English King passes here, no better than a grinding-slave. I have more guarding me than a hundred slaves.'

'Look!' said the helmed Radknight, his war shaft pointing skywards. 'Look at their halls, with roofs like upturned boats, serpents at either end. How big they are! They must house half the town.'

'No,' said the steersman. 'They are the Jonjarl's store halls where all is kept before it is shipped away. The Jarl's dogs guard them day and night. His Balts will kill any who stray too close. All the Jarl's stores and homes of the people are ringed by the high earth, and the ditch you see there, for here too there is risk of sudden attack. Just as Hedeby was burned, so too was Visby by raiders from the Wend lands. Until Jonjarl made peace and Harald called Hardradr took Elisaveta as his Queen peace-weaver.'

'And now my vow-sister must go to that place and be married, to a River prince, such is the custom of the peace-weaver that benefits all,' said Godwine.

'Benefits all? What peace can our sister Gytha weave?' demanded Edmund. 'The king and that wife of his would rid themselves of us, that's all. What peace would we weave with this Vladimir? I wish we had never come to our Dane-kin. Much better we had stayed in Dublin. Who is this Jonjarl? I tell you; we are lost in a slavers' camp. All that was ours is gone and our vow-sister forfeit.'

'Yes, Edmund, we must be on our guard here, for I fear there are too many in this place who might take the Godwineson Hoard for their own and slit our throats. Come Thegn, come Roni. Cease your enmity and gather the Company, for we have a common purpose to stay alive. We will need lodgings and protection, not for my sister but for all my Companions of the Golden Dragon of Wessex. Take me to this Jonjarl.'

'There is no need, young Lord' said the steersman. 'Jonjarl awaits you and the princess on the shore. News of your coming is no secret here. He knows only two moods,

Lord. Courtesy and killing. If he chooses courtesy today, know you what tomorrow's choice will be.' The steersman chuckled as the Companions looked to where Jonjarl, ruler of Gotland, strode over the rough ground to the water's edge surrounded by a tattooed war troop, twenty strong. Hard, bearded men in red tunics over their ringed war-shirts, boldly patterned with embroidery at hem and sleeve, wearing golden face helms lined in fur. How drab the company of hearth-friends looked! Even the Frankish swords and thin caplet crowns could not hide the threadbare English wool they still wore beneath the fur coats gifted by the royal Dane for their journey.

PART TWO CHAPTER TWO

JONJARL'S ISLAND

'WELCOME, PRINCESS, I AM Jonjarl, Lord of this cloud-smoothed island. The west winds tell me of your beauty and they speak true. Our humble town is modest, but our greetings no less for it. All are sad to leave this place as you will be, fair Lady.' Then, turning to Godwine, Jonjarl thumped him bluntly on the shoulders with both hands so that the circlet crown Godwine wore in place of a helm slipped to his brow.

'So, Jarl Godwine, hatchling of the serpent's egg,' the shave-headed Jonjarl said loudly, the Thorhammer tight-chained about his sinewed neck, his blond beard jutting outwards at Godwine' s chest. 'It was your father who killed my friend Harald Sigurdsson Hardradr.'

There was a pause. Godwine said nothing, the steersman's warning lodged in his head. Slowly, he raised his gloved hands to straighten the coronet. A black raven harsh-cawed nearby. Nobody stirred. Then the shave-headed Jonjarl guffawed. 'Come, boy, don't be alarmed by Jonjarl. The gods know it was a fair fight, your father's trolls beneath the bridge as Hardradr the great king crossed above.' He made a gesture of thrusting a spear upwards, his face and body too close to Godwine's. The warrior laughed, and his company of gold helms, each tattooed from hands to neck with trees and figures, laughed with him.

Still Godwine said nothing, though from behind him the Twice Scarred Thegn fidgeted and cleared his throat. 'Kill him, Lord,' he mumbled in the dialect of his Essex farmstead.

Gytha, sensing most terrible danger from which only their death would follow, stepped forward, head up, back straight. 'Jarl Jon, Great Thegn of Gotland,' she exclaimed, as if to drown out the sound of her heart pounding in her chest. 'You ask my brother to scorn your welcome with words to defend our noble father's honour.' The savage Jarl turned his gaze from Godwine to Gytha, unused to have a girl address him so directly, but he did not hush her. 'Our truth is different to that carried here on the west wind. For the wind knows no names, no good nor bad, nor truth nor lie. It knows only to fail men when most needed. So, we thank you for your welcome. We are weary from the benches, and our small company needs rest.'

His fist relaxing on the grasp of his hammer, Jonjarl's tone changed. 'Yes, fair maid, bravely spoken. The wind did not fail if it blew you here.' Gytha winced at the man's festered breath and toothless leer as he looked at her, but she stood her ground. 'See, helm-brothers of Thor? I forget my hospitality so quickly to these girl-hairs!' he shouted. Then, turning back to Gytha, said, 'lady, you are as a mirror of your father, whom even bridge trolls obeyed. The horn of the slain-choosers sounded the welcome and Hardradr joined the einherjar in the Val halls justly, with your father's spear between his buttocks.' Jonjarl laughed loudly.

Now it was Gytha who was word-robbed. Was this a welcome or yet more insulting of her father?

Just then, as the sun dappled the strand with the heatless light of spring, fortune smiled. A comely silver-haired woman, wearing a thick red felted dress and a heavy silver ring at her neck, stepped forward. 'Forgive my lord and husband, fair guests from the green Island beyond the grey west sea.' Taking Gytha by the arm, she continued. 'Princes and princesses seldom step onto our strand and our welcomes gather moss. Follow me, fair Lady, to where you and your noble brothers can rest from the wave path that brought you here. Another journey awaits you and, until then, our humble hall here at Visby will be the last soft hearth you know.'

The fearsome Jonjarl and his helm brothers stood aside as the small, plump woman steered Gytha and the Companions of the Golden Dragon of Wessex up the steep slope to the first of the boat-roofed halls. Outside, blank-faced Balt guards stood by the slave pens with clubs and dogs, carved rune stones and poles, from which dead crows hung like bunches of black fruits, their ruined feathers fluttering in the chill breeze.

Within The Hall, a fresh logged fire in the welcoming hearth greeted them. Gytha and the others looked about them. The space was huge, the roof straked and stringed like an upturned boat held up by a forest stand of logs thicker than any man. All about were boxes and chests piled high; carpets in brilliant colours hung on every wall and, beneath them, countless weapons and rows of studded shields, each with the marks of long-fought battles. There were upturned benches, scattered tables, heavy with the remains of feasts and drinking. At the far end, on a raised platform, stood a great chair with a snarling wolf head carved into either arm. That was the chair of Jonjarl.

The Towering Monk looked about him, crossed himself, and said loudly as if entering the hell-hall of the Devil himself, 'Christ blind me.' The others too crossed themselves, open mouthed at the wealth that greeted them.

The woman told the companions to make themselves comfortable, pointing to a corner behind stinking bales of marten and squirrel pelts. She took Gytha to the far end, to a small chamber separated from the rest by a gold cloth, broidered in swirling strokes and lines of great beauty, unlike anything Gytha had ever seen. Quickly, a mug of sweet mead was put, steaming, in her hand. Seeing a crucifix set above the bed ledge, Gytha dropped to her knees. She gave thanks to the Most High who knows all secrets for the comfort he had found for them, joyful at being off that snakehead knarr boat and in a chamber that reminded her of home. Aching for a moment of peace, she slipped the crownlet from her head and shook her hair, a golden cascade on her shoulders. Overcome by a yawning that would not stop, she curled on the sheepskin rug and slept.

The woman was sitting on the bedding beside her as Gytha woke.

'Where am I?' she asked.

'My lady, there is nothing to fear. you are guests in this hall. No harm will come to the betrothed of the River Prince. My husband Jonjarl will see to it. Now let us go to the lashing baths, where we can talk.'

Gytha followed the woman across the yard to a small, half-buried shed with a sod roof. Friendly smoke curled above it, a thrall carried fresh birch branches and laid them outside, the low doorway. They had to crouch to enter. Inside, in the dimness, there was a bench on which they sat to remove their clothing and leather boots, and then naked, the two women stepped through into the tiny wooden cell. The heat hit them, and Gytha coughed. The woman picked up a ladle and, shoving it into a bucket, tossed water onto the fire stones which hissed furiously filling the little room with steam.

Then, as the sweat-shine flowed, she took the birch twigs and beat Gytha with them all over her body. The woman laughed at Gytha's protests.

'Here, you beat me!' Gytha did as she was asked, gently at first but harder and harder, laughing as she did it.

'Enough,' said the woman, 'let us sit now.' as Gytha grew accustomed to the cloying heat and darkness. 'What must I call you?' she asked the little woman, sweat pouring from her. 'Drottning? Jarlinna? Are you Queen of this land?'

'No, I am not Drottning or Jarlinna. The fair Lady of my kin, may call me Colwenne.'

'Of my kin?' asked Gytha, studying the woman's face more closely. 'Of what kin do you speak? My grandmother? She was Dane, kin of Knut, the Great King. Yet you speak as do the English folk, not Dane.'

The woman laughed. 'I am English as the bell of the great church at Canterbury from where I was taken, even as it peeled of danger.'

'You were taken from Canterbury by raiders?' said Gytha, eyes widening, all else forgotten. 'And now you are the queen wife of Jonjarl?'

'Not queen wife, not churched wife, nor handfast wife, but bed-wife,' Colwenne said, 'for you see I bear this thrall ring of melted silver dirhams.'

Gytha looked at her closely. 'And your father, was he Thegn or ceorl?'

'He was Thegn, Lady Gytha, a man of Kent, a mighty war leader as was your father. And now his eldest daughter is the bed-wife of the pagan slaver and mother to his sons. Not all his sons,' she added, with a mirthless chuckle.

Colwenne took water from the bucket and washed Gytha roughly, rubbing the tallow soap over her hair and body, then rinsing it off.

'Why don't you take your freedom, Colwenne?' said Gytha, spluttering, her eyes smarting from soap, but happy to be clean once more.

'Freedom for what?' Colwenne's voice sounded tired. 'Freedom for what? From what? I can never leave this place. He has me twenty winters his bed wife, to bear his children, feed him, clean his vomit. The daughters of many English folk have passed through this place highborn at their father's halls but thrall maidens here, where the fairest cost not eight ounces of silver, and men enough to buy them. Others they take to the huts and throw them to the night-dogs when they are spent.' She paused and emptied her bucket of soapy water. 'No, fair Lady, freedom would change nothing. Free woman or ring thrall, they stole my life the day the spear Danes came and killed my brothers and took me to their camp to sell me as a milk cow to a swine.'

Gytha tried to imagine the life of the Jarl's bed woman. There was something that confused her. 'But you called him husband, nor did he stop you when you took us from the shore. You scolded him before his gold helms and he said nothing.'

'Lady,' Colwenne explained, smiling suddenly. A knowing smile. 'A woman, grinding-slave or free, can have power over any man, but he must never know it.' Then, wrapped in their clothes, they ran barefoot and wet-haired back to the women's chamber in the boat hall and settled in front of the fire.

Gytha stared into the flames holding the cup to her mouth, thinking about Colwenne's words and feeling puzzled by them. Red flames in the hearth flickered across her lips, her cheeks, her hair, which Colwenne parted to the scalp. With a long, rhythmic motion, she slid a fine-toothed comb down the length of Gytha's tresses until, victorious, she picked a nit between her thumb and forefinger and flicked it into the fire.

Gytha continued gazing into the flames, flinching whenever the comb hit a knot of hair.

'I too am no freer than you now, Colwenne,' she said, shaking her head slightly. 'The River people have me for the nephew of their Great Prince. I must wait here until the Trader takes me to him.'

'Yes, we know him, he is the worst of them. He has left again for the mainland and will return soon with more slaves. Then you will make the long journey to the halls of the River Princes. Many dangers await you, but he is the greatest of them. Give thanks you have your brothers and the company of your hearth friends to protect you. Those who have not, do not live to talk of their humiliation.'

Gytha was looking at the Jarl's wife as she spoke. There was a beauty about her, an echo of something so familiar, it troubled her. It was as if she knew the woman, as if they had met. Yet how could that be?

'You shall have a finer hall to call your home than this one, Child.'

Gytha started; no woman had called her 'child' in so long. Unbidden, she reached out and took the other woman's hand. Colwenne smiled.

'You shall have jewels and gold and beautiful clothes of silk, the colour of the sky, to match your eyes.' Quietly, Colwenne's eyes filled with tears which she brushed away impatiently. 'I must live on this place with men's greed and thrall misery my daily bread, where rock and sea and sky share one grey between them.' She sniffed. 'I am sorry, but to hear your voice, child, has woken a hundred memories. I see my father and my mother in your clothes. Your brothers are as mine, fine, handsome and strong, and the Companions of the Golden

Dragon of Wessex are as my father's hearth friends.' With shaking hands, Colwenne patted down her skirt and wiped her eyes. 'You must think me silly to cry.'

Gytha could only shake her head, her throat too tight for words. 'No, I don't,' she whispered, and it was if she was looking at the herald of her life to come. Suddenly the likeness became clear: Colwenne was older – smaller perhaps – but in voice and face she reminded Gytha of her own mother, her gentle swan.

Just then, there was a cough outside the doorway. 'Forgive me, Queen,' said Godwine from outside. Colwenne called him in, using the English tongue, saying not to call her queen.

'Lady,' he began again, 'My men cannot sleep in the hall of your husband. We are too many. The trader has a dwelling hut nearby and we will make our camp there. But my lady, if it pleases you, you will care for my vow-sister here. The Radknight or one of the Companions will be on hand for her.'

'No harm will come to her, young Lord,' said Colwenne. 'She will stay with me and we will talk of home and of your grandfather, honoured guest in my father's hall when I was a free-running child.'

The Companions of the Golden Dragon of Wessex soon settled into the life of the island while they awaited the return of the Cold Trader, not knowing if it would be a day or a season, or whether they were passing through as travellers or prisoners. Jonjarl's men made them welcome at the spear hearth in the boat hall, but the company of brothers kept their weapons close to hand. They shared mead, meat and their minstrel's songs with these hard men of Gotland, but not their trust.

Meanwhile, Gytha spent her days with Colwenne and the other women of the island, some highborn thralls as she was, taken in their youth. The little chamber rang with their laughter as they busied themselves weaving, spinning and embroidering. Gytha, too, took her turn at the loom, wondering at the strange animals that formed beneath the darting shuttle that dodged between the threads. Sometimes she would sit on the floor with Colwenne's jewel cask and try on every bead and bangle. She had never seen such treasures as Colwenne kept in the box beneath her bed. In turn, Gytha would show the women her golden rings of Kings her mother had given her, which she had guarded since the day they had fled Waltham.

One afternoon when it was raining, one of the collar-women, the bed wife of Jonjarl's brother, killed but not mourned, brought a bulging leather pouch and tipped the contents onto the table. They were pebbles no bigger than a chestnut, but each was clear as honey. Within some, there was an insect.

'What is this enchantment?' said Gytha, her eyes wide with surprise as she held one smooth stone to the tallow light, the fly within glistening green, every vein on its wings visible. 'How does it live within this warm stone?' She picked up another and turned it round in her fingers.

The woman, stolen from her people's home in the great forest beyond, smiled. 'Once upon a time a beautiful princess called Jurate, daughter of Perkunas, God of my people, lived in a palace by the sea made of this amber. Jurate loved a lowly fisherman, but her father sent lightning to kill him. To this day the fishermen think of Jurate, and these stones, they say, are Jurate's tears.'

'Poor Jurate,' said Gytha, feeling the stones in her hand. 'It cannot be pleasant to have flies in her tears.'

The woman laughed. 'I'd never thought of that.'

In her waking hours, sometimes Gytha forgot the life ahead she feared. But at night, in her dreams, there were faces staring up at her from dark meres, wolves howling, the Cold Trader in a prince's clothes. She would wake, her heart beating at the terrors she had seen. Once she cried out so loud Colwenne sat with her as with a child, until she slept once more. 'Tomorrow, child, we seek the help of the wand-wed seeress, Groia. We must take gifts.'

A dish of animal hearts, an earthen jug filled fresh goat's milk, and fine bed-cloths from the store, were packed in a basket as offerings to the seeress. Colwenne and Gytha made their way past the lightless cabins where the thrall captives awaited their fate, and out of the settlement gate beneath the watchtowers. Pig-boy and the Radknight walked behind them in silence with the laden horse.

Gytha, still pale from her troubled sleep, asked how the seeress might greet them. Colwenne calmed her, saying that with the gifts of cloth, milk and a broth of the animal hearts the seeress might tell Gytha of her life to come beyond the great forest in the east.

'But why would she know about me, Colwenne?' asked Gytha. 'I am a stranger here. Can she see beyond the forest to the Red Fortress of the River people?'

'Child,' said Colwenne, 'the wand-wed seeress knows everything of stranger, enemy and friend. Groia does not need to journey to the land of your betrothal, when the spirits will reveal all to her.'

But this answer only made Gytha more alarmed. She stopped in her tracks. 'Colwenne, kin sister to my own mother, follower of Jesus Christ our Lord and Saviour, you take me to this sorceress to invoke the spirits of your husband's people. Oh, Mother of God, forgive me. Protect me from the devil and all his works!'

Seeing her distress, the Radknight stepped forward, but Colwenne waved him away. 'Child,' she said, 'let us pray here in the meadow.' Then Gytha and Colwenne knelt together in the spring-flowered field. The Radknight and Pig-boy, unsure of what to do, stood nearby, watchful heads bowed.

'Lord God in Heaven,' said Colwenne, 'Lighten our darkness we beseech thee, Oh Lord, and by thy great mercy defend us from the perils and dangers of the night, for the love of your only Son.'

'Amen,' said Gytha, crossing herself and brushing her lips with her hand.

'You see,' said Colwenne gently, standing up again. 'You have nothing to fear, our Lord will protect us. But in this place, the light and the darkness share the land equally, neither stealing from the other, and so it is with my faith. This is the land of Thor and, while your priest would not have it so, I have to live with my God and the gods of the island, and not anger them. This is how I must live, child, or my Lord Jonjarl would beat me like any thrall woman that no longer pleased him, casting me from his hall, and the crows would peck out my eyes.'

Gytha looked to the Radknight for help. 'Wulfwyn, you heard Colwenne's words. Will I be cast into the furnace and burn with the old believers, as the priest says, or should I go to the Seeress Groia? Pig-boy, you were schooled by priests, what say you?' But Pig-boy made no sound.

The Radknight spoke. 'My lady,' he said, pondering deeply, 'Colwenne is of our people yet knows the customs of this place.'

'Twenty winters,' said Colwenne.

'Yes, twenty winters,' he repeated. 'And your grandmother, Mother of Heroes, the Old Lady whom you loved and feared, she too believed in the old Gods and spoke with them in times of great trouble.'

Gytha remembered how her grandmother would call to the spirits of the sea and the sky, and no harm came to her.

'Colwenne,' said the Radknight. 'Gytha is the daughter of the lawful King of England and all English folk. I am charged to protect her life as mine. Let us go to the wand-wed seer, but if she is fiend-woman, you will be the first to die.'

They followed the track and soon arrived in a clearing. Here stood a small boat hall surrounded by a huddle of half-buried round bothies with animal skins for doors and smoke lingering above their sod roofs. There were a few draggled sheep in a fold. Sled dogs barked at their approach. Ragged women came out of the bothies to look.

Colwenne went ahead to the hall, greeting the Seeress in the Norse tongue, 'Spakona Vardlokur, last of the nine sisters, who sees beyond the nine worlds, we seek your guidance for a troubled daughter.' She waited a moment, from within came a voice, an old voice, asking who it was. Gytha stepped into the room and gasped. In a raised chair at the far end sat the oldest woman she had ever seen. She was wearing a dark blue cape, lined in cat's furs and decorated along its hem with stones. On her head she wore a lamb's fur cap. There were brightly coloured crystal beads strung around her neck and in her sinewed blue-veined hand she held a knob-head staff. From floor to ceiling, the walls of the hall were painted in runes, and pictures of Odin, Thor, the wolf Fenrir, Hel and Sleipnir – and gods, whose names she did not know. There was a bitter smell; around the hearth were piles of bones of long-dead animals – the fate of the forlorn sheep in the fold outside.

Disgust overwhelmed her and she hesitated. Colwenne stepped forward, reaching up to kiss the old woman's hand, then beckoned to the shaking Pig-boy to place their gifts among the offerings at the hearth. Groia gestured to Gytha to come forward. Keeping her head bowed, not daring to look, Gytha edged forward until she stood directly in front of the wizened old woman.

Groia gazed deeply into her eyes before her wrinkled face creased into a horrific, tooth-free grin. She stank. Gytha felt the vomit rise. Colwenne spoke then, her voice high, telling of Gytha's night terrors and her fears of what the future held, so far from home, so far from the lost land of her mother. How all she knew was loneliness and longing. 'Groia', she implored, 'you see beyond the bleak nights where green fires dance in the ice sky, beyond the everlasting forest where the stars vanish and the flames of hell leap towards the heavens. There she must make her home. Comfort her with your vision, I beg you, that she knows all is not lost.'

The hall had filled now with more women – thirteen in number, some old and some young – but no men gathered here. All were listening to the words that Colwenne spoke to the seeress. The old lady beckoned them to hold hands and make a circle, and the thirteen women began to keen. She drew Gytha next to her and, stopping only to chew henbane seeds she drew from her waist pouch, she started. Little bursts of speech, unconnected, interrupted the low song.

'The king lies dead … the child cries. The house burns. Horsemen … a thousand horsemen stand and bow … the bear dies but not the boy.' And so, it went on until, mid-verse, the old hag let her hands drop and she fell back asleep. Not knowing whether to stay or go they waited, but the woman Groia did not wake.

They returned to the hall in silence. Gytha, head pounding, tried to make sense of the seeress's words. 'The king … is that my father?' she wondered. 'She saw a house. Is that our home from which we fled?' Gytha's eyes filled with pain and incomprehension. 'What boy? What bear?'

'She saw you, child,' said Colwenne. 'You're the queen she spoke of – the mother to whom a thousand horseman bow.'

'Yes, but what about the bear and the boy? What happened to the boy?'

Colwenne shook her head. 'You must wait, child. What we do know is that the boy lives, but not the bear.'

The words continued to trouble Gytha. Something seemed to flutter in her stomach, so she hunched forwards, hugging herself, staring at the flames. 'We must go back,' she said. 'The wand-wed must explain.'

Colwenne shook her head. 'Child, we cannot.'

'Then I will go myself. I will take the Radknight to protect me and give her gifts of blood hearts, but I must know.'

The older woman tried to soothe her. 'Calm yourself, child,',

'I am not a child!' Gytha shouted, and with that she jumped up and ran outside the chamber, nearly knocking over the Radknight. He tried gently to halt her, but she dodged his outstretched arm. Colwenne followed a moment later, saying, 'Leave her, Wulfwyn. She will calm. Tonight, I will give her brew and place hops about her pillow and she will sleep where no night elf can harm her. She'll be well tomorrow.'

But Gytha was not. The next morning, she awoke with fever, shaking and soaked in sweat as news reached them that the wand-wed seeress had never woken from her sleep. Gytha's fever rose, and Colwenne called the Towering Mace Monk to her bedside. He listened stonily to her account of their visit. Standing over them, Blaecman pronounced that the Most High, who knows all secrets, had struck the heathen witch down and He was punishing Gytha. Striking Colwenne across the cheek as he might a thrall, he cursed her for her foolishness. 'Christ blind you, woman! You have led the girl to diabolical sorcery and her fate is in God's hands.'

Colwenne fell to her knees and begged the Lord's forgiveness. 'I deny the charms and potions of women,' she wailed. 'I
believe in the Lord God Almighty and in Jesus Christ his son.'

'Believe in the power of prayer, woman,' said the monk,
imposing a month's penance, 'or be denied absolution.'

Filled with dread, Godwine, the quiet and thoughtful
Edmund, the Twice Scarred Thegn Eadric, and even the axed
and burnished huscarl, Roni the Dane, knelt by Gytha. Only
the Radknight and Pig-boy were denied her bedside to pray
that she might live and stood heads bowed at the door to
the chamber. Colwenne, the monk said, was to blame, but
they were complicit in her sin. Pig-boy was distraught and
wept. The Radknight, his face the colour of ashes, gazed
at the floor in his agony, wondering, with dread, what fate
awaited him.

But they had not reckoned on Jonjarl. Hearing of the
monk's words, he barged into the room, sending the Radknight
flying. Godwine and the others leapt to their feet, but apart
from their wounding-knives at their belts they carried no
weapon. Jonjarl pushed his way past them and seized the
monk by the throat. Stunned by the speed and ferocity of the
Jarl, Blaecman, who stood a hand-span taller, felt the fist tight
around his gorge and began to faint. Jonjarl punched him in
the face with crushing force, flattening the monk's nose. Blood
spattered everywhere.

Cursing all Christians, Jonjarl left the chamber.

The spring came, melting the last of the snow. The flattened
brown meadows were green again. Bony milk cows and goats
wandered in the pale sun, freed from the darkness of the
wintering pens. Ships were drawn noisily up the strand. Amid
the heaving and shouting, the Cold Trader could be heard,
hailing the waiting men on the shore. 'I bring fresh cargo from

the west. I will rest here, till the west wind blows.' The slaves, shackled together, were led to the half-buried sheds, their fate weighed in silver.

There were about twenty of them, a mixed group. Some were painted women speaking Brithon, the tongue of the Celtprince Baladrddellt rac Denau, Splintered Spear of the South. But others were speaking English.

'The Lord have mercy on them.' Said Gytha when she heard.

'When I see them, I see myself,' said Colwenne, 'and my heart is filled with sadness for the life they have lost. I was no older than some of them and no fairer. I too ran free in the hall of my father until the Danes came.' She shuddered at the memory. Gytha continued to stitch on a broidered cloth. Saying nothing, feeling the cloth with her fingertips, plunging the coloured yarns tight along the patterns she had drawn.

Word soon went around one of the new English slave women was fair to see.

'No doubt the goat of Gotland will take her for himself, now Colwenne pleases him no longer,' said the Twice Scarred Eadric, thrusting his wounding-knife into a spit-fresh slab of meat. The others laughed grimly – all but the towering Blaecman. 'May God blind him!' he said, as he always did whenever cursed Jonjarl was mentioned.

Godwine, who said little to anyone, not even to his brother Edmund, since their arrival now spoke. 'We are all cursed – no better than those thralls. Even without the ring about our necks, we have no freedom, and all here would kill us. We have no home, no land, we are no better than outlaws in the forest once more. Our Hoard is spent, our number few, and no man fears the sons of Harold Godwineson.' He paused and they were all silent.

'We are as Israelites wandering in the wilderness.'

'No sister, they had hope. We left the land of milk and honey far behind us across the grey west sea. No promised land of Canaan awaits us,' said Edmund bitterly. There was a groan from the Companions.

'The land of Cain awaits us,' said the Twice Scarred Thegn, the fury and frustration there for all to see. All knew that he was right. There they sat around the hearth, staring into the flames and dreaming of the life they had once had.'

'To fight is better than to be prisoner of the Jarl,' said the axed and burnished Roni. 'My axe is eager to split his shaved head like a log.'

'To burn all the better in the halls of hell,' said the Towering monk.

'We will fight,' said Godwine, 'but not here. We are too few and we are sworn to protect our vow-sister. The Cold Trader has returned. She is in as much danger as the thrall girl of whom you spoke. We will bide our time until the moment is right. Until then, we will travel to this place on the River. The Great Prince has need of warriors. Hardradr, whom my father killed at Stamford, was the war leader to the Great Prince and riches flowed to him.'

'Yes,' said the Towering Mace Monk, 'and to that Wend queen. But no matter. The plan, young lord, is a good one. In the time of your grandfather, the exiled Edward found refuge at the hall of the Great Prince on the River and he too returned to England for the crown of Alfred.'

'Let my claim be more successful,' said Godwine grimly. 'He, like us, had no army to enforce his claim. History forgets him as we too will be forgotten.'

It was Pig-boy who noticed it. He arrived at the barn greatly agitated, hanging around outside Gytha's chamber until she came to ask him what the matter was. Pulling at the

Radknight's arm, Pig-boy pointed at Wulfwyn's face, then pointed to where the thralls were kept. Neither Gytha nor the Radknight understood what he was trying to tell them, and Pig-boy got more and more agitated. Pointing at the young warrior's hair, nose and mouth – even his ears – he gestured to the half-buried shed. Then once again at Wulfwyn and Gytha and back at the shed.

'Pig-boy is saying somebody in the shed looks like you,' said Colwenne. Pig-boy nodded furiously, jumping up and down.

'Somebody who looks like Wulfwyn?' repeated Gytha. Pig-boy nodded even more violently, honking in agreement, and tried to pull the Radknight.

'He wants you to go with him,' said Colwenne. 'But have a care. The Balts will not let you near the shed.'

'But they will not stop me. Come with me, Colwenne. Let us see what has Pig-boy so frantic. No one will question your right to inspect the new thralls.'

And so together, their shawls wrapped about their heads, the two women picked their way through the mud of the yard to the shelter that housed the English thralls. The Balt guards stepped aside as Colwenne announced herself. There came the sound of shackles scraping and a woman's moan.

Stepping through the low entrance after Colwenne, Gytha could see the shape of a figure on the floor shackled like a dog. Girl or woman, it was hard to tell. Ash lay cold as dust where a meagre fire had been. An empty pot and some beets lay scattered on the floor, scarce food enough for a cow, let alone human kind.

'Who are you?' the dirty figure called out in English, terror in her small voice. 'I am Colwenne, thrall wife to Jonjarl, ruler of this island. And this is the Lady Gytha, sister to Godwine Haroldson, rightful King of the English.'

The girl let out a gasp. 'I am Ailsi, sister to my lady's Radknight, Wulfwyn.'

Now it was for Gytha's turn to be word-robbed. 'Ailsi? … sister to Wulfwyn? He has spoken of you often! How are you here, a thrall?' she said, careful not to raise her voice above a whisper.

'My lady,' said Ailsi, 'a Norman burnt our father's hall at Thurgarton and put his head upon a spike. They stole our land, as they stole that of your father and mother also. We were cast out, all of us. My mother and all our household went to the Fenland to seek the outlaw Hereward, with only what we could carry in our bundles. We hoped for a ship to take us across the sea. But we were surprised by raiders, spear Danes who stole our meagre Hoard and seized me and those of our household who would fetch a price. Of my mother, I know nothing. If she lived or died, I do not know.' The girl's voice wavered, but she continued. 'We were carried first to Hedeby where they put the thrall ring around my neck. The Wend bought me for twelve pieces of silver. Now I am I don't know where and fear I will die.'

Gytha could barely grasp what this girl, maybe fifteen years old, was telling her. Whispering, she put her hand out to touch the ragged creature, shivering in the dirty straw stable. 'Yes, we fear the Wend too, Ailsi. He is an evil man; may Christ blind him.' Then, pausing, she asked, 'what do you know of my mother, Ailsi? You speak of her. What became of her and all at Waltham?' But the girl, sobbing, shook her head.

Turning to leave, Gytha said urgently, 'Ailsi, you must be strong. Your brother Wulfwyn is here.' Ailsi reached out to Gytha, clinging to her smock, but Colwenne pulled her away.

'We are in danger here, come.'

'Don't leave me here!' called Ailsi. Her sobs drowned only by the furious barking of the Balt dogs, as they hurried back to the barn.

The Radknight's joy at his sister in captivity, a few paces from where they sat, died when he learnt his father's head was on a spike, and possibly his mother dead too. He jumped up and would have run to Ailsi that moment had the Old Thegn not forced him to sit.

'We can do nothing,' Thegn Eadric said, 'think, boy, or you'll get us all killed, her fate is not ours unless we make it so.'

'Will they bring Ailsi to the River folk with us?' asked Gytha.

'Yes,' said Colwenne. 'her virgin price is greater there. The Trader will keep her close. He knows what the Jarl would do.'

'Jonjarl would do nothing the Trader would not do,' said the Radknight, his nostrils flared in fury. 'Either man would keep her for himself. Ailsi was a child when I left the hall, my father old. I thought them safe from the Norman swine. Now virginity has spared Ailsi her death, but it will hasten the end of her life unless I do something.'

The Feast of the Annunciation and Good Friday fell on the same day that year. Colwenne said it was an omen from which no good would come. In the village, there was great activity as villagers built a massive pyre in the shape of a longboat with serpent-head prow among the standing stones. On the pyre, they laid the body of the wand-wed seeress, Groia, freshly dressed in new clothes for her journey. Her body was wrapped in a black cloak edged in gems and, on her head, they placed a black lamb cap lined in white cat fur. Brass broaches were at her shoulders, strung with beads, an amulet on her head. Her knob-handle staff they placed in her right hand, as in life. Around the pyre, the thirteen women wailed and keened.

All day, men and women from the village came, some bringing gifts of henbane seeds and charms, others bannock buns and sheep's hearts in milk; one placed a narwhale tablet with runes on her chest. Sheep were led aboard the boat and slaughtered, their bleating clear on the wind. As the daylight ebbed and fires were lit, the men and women grew drunk on apple mead and berry kvasir, and danced, hailing their gods with oaths and boasting until they seemed possessed.

The Towering Blaecman would have none of it. 'He who denies that Jesus is the Christ, as does this Jonjarl, is the antichrist, the one who denies the Father and the Son. He is the devil, the burning tallow branches that smoke into the night sky, the fire of hell itself.'

He ordered all the company of Christians to the chapel. Shouting against the din from the shore, he led them in prayer, asking God's forgiveness for the heathen on the eve of Easter.

'On the twenty-fifth day of the month,' he bellowed, 'Gabriel first came to Our Lady with God's message, and on that day, she conceived in the city of Nazareth, like trees when they blossom at the blowing of the wind. And then, after thirty-two winters and three months, Christ was crucified on the cross that same day. And as soon as he was on the cross, creation revealed that he was truly God. And the sun grew black, and the day was turned into dark night, from midday until the ninth hour.'

Outside the chapel came the sound of shouting. Godwine crossed himself quickly, stood up and signalled the men to follow him.

There was Jonjarl, his gold-helmed hearthguard standing in a circle, swords, axes and shield-boards in their fists. In the middle stood the Cold Trader. Shackled on the ground was Wulfwyn's sister, Ailsi.

Holding his hand up to stop the companions as they rushed from the chapel, seizing their shield-boards and pulling knives from their scabbards, Godwine shouted, 'what is going on?'

The Radknight, seeing his sister upon the ground, leapt as if God had given him the wings of an eagle. 'They would take Ailsi to the pyre!' he yelled.

Jonjarl, a massive club in his hand, turned. 'Back away, Girl-Hair,' he said to Godwine. 'The grinding-slave shall be a fitting companion for my mother. The wand-wed lady lies ready to ride the flame-boat to Odin's Hall. But now I take this English maiden, and all who stand against me die.' Then, turning back to the Trader, he said almost softly, as if trying to placate him, 'come, good friend, you shall have her price in silver. A small token for your wares and your life. Now, step away from the girl.'

The Cold Trader swore in his language and both men slowly lowered their swords. 'How much, Good Jonjarl, will you give me for her? I sense there are those who would bid high against you.' With that, he glanced at Godwine, with the snort of a man used to bargaining with war-men of the north. But his contempt was short lived.

There was a scuffle behind Godwine and a muffled shriek. Pushing himself forward into the light of the fire, stepped the Radknight, his wounding-knife at the Lady Colwenne's throat.

'Here is our offer, Jonjarl. The life of one English thrall for another.'

Jonjarl growled. The hearthguard crouched, about to attack, outnumbering the English folk who now closed around the Radknight, ready to fight. The Cold Trader was now watching, his advantage seized from him. But the goods lay still between his feet. Snatching Ailsi by the collar, he dragged the sobbing girl to her feet. But Jonjarl burst out laughing, until he could barely catch his breath and had to lean on the club. And still he laughed. Finally, wiping his eyes and nose with a tattooed arm, he stepped forward.

'So,' he said, 'the girl-haired boy would have me trade this broken-down mare for a virgin.' And then, as if struck by a thought, added, 'A virgin thrall with a name. How so, boy?'

'Because,' said Gytha, stepping forward, 'she is his sister and for her he will take the life of your bed wife of twenty winters whom you now call a broken-down mare. Tell me, Jarl, you would let the blood mother of your sons die at the hand of this English man for the sake of a slave girl?'

Jonjarl shook his head as if trying to shake the haze of mead from his eyes. 'Huh,' was all he said, turning on his heel, his men following, leaving the traders, Ailsi, the Companions, and the now-choking Colwenne.

The Radknight let her go. 'Leave,' she gasped. 'Leave the island. He will kill you, all of you – you too, trader. He will be drunk tonight and tomorrow, after they have fired the ship, but when he wakes with murder in his heathen heart, he will seek revenge. Every Christian will die.'

'The Most High, who knows all secrets, will protect us,' said the Towering Mace Monk. 'And what of you, Lady Colwenne? Will you come with us?'

'No, Father,' she said, adjusting her cowl around her face and absently tucking the loose end into her thrall collar. 'Pray give me absolution. I will stay with my Lord Jonjarl, for I am the mother of his sons and I cannot leave them till they are grown.'

'And what of this Ailsi?' said Godwine, turning to the trader. 'Now you know who she is.'

'Yes, now I know who she is, I know no harm will befall her because you shall guard her as you do your sister,' said the trader with a sneer. 'We will leave at dawn – the boats stand ready. And put any thoughts of treachery from your head.

My men have orders to throw this girl into the sea, should any harm come to me.'

Colwenne wished them Godspeed. For Gytha, she had a special gift. Standing half-lit by the pyre that had blazed behind them, Colwenne took a honey-clear amber stone, set in gold, from a tiny pouch beneath her cape. Holding it up between thumb and forefinger, Gytha saw a perfect spider sitting within, as real as if it lived.

'Take this gift, most precious princess, take it,' Colwenne said, her eyes moist. 'Look on this honey amber and remember Colwenne. For you, child, have become a daughter to me and you will always be in my prayers.' She hugged Gytha. 'No matter where the Lord leads you, may my spider always bring you luck. Be strong, for our blood, Gytha, is the English blood of our green-holm beyond the sea. Our hearts are of oak, our bodies sturdy as the ash. We survive, you will survive.' She paused, holding Gytha by the shoulders, and gazed at her face. 'You, Gytha, are the daughter of a great king. You are the sword gift, in you is the courage of the English.'

Gytha buried her head into the fur at the little woman's neck and hugged her. 'I hear your strong words with my ears, and in my heart. I wish them to be true, but I fear that I am trapped as the spider in the stone. You are as a mother to me, Colwenne, but to whom will I be wife or mother? I hear only the wrinkled corpse now burning on that pyre. She saw into my future and I shudder at the meaning of her words.'

'Yes, child. My heart is heavy. I sought only to help you. Forgive me, child. I meant no harm and I suffer damnation for it in God's eyes,' said Colwenne, her face full of tears.

Gytha touched the other woman's arm softly. 'It is for the Most High, who knows all secrets, to forgive. But I feel no ill towards you. You – more than any person – have showed me kindness and love, when there were none but you who understood the pain in my heart. Of course, I forgive you!'

'You had better go,' said Colwenne. 'The boat waits. Be strong, my lady.' Then, with her thumb, Colwenne made a little cross on Gytha's brow, as her mother, Edith Swan-neck, had done as she settled her for bed. Arms tight round each other, Colwenne walked Gytha to the shore where the Companions of the Golden Dragon of Wessex waited, oars in the rowlocks and the long ropes stowed.

PART TWO CHAPTER THREE

DARK HEARTS

THREE DAYS THEY ROWED and three days it rained. Water dripped off the rigging, until all were sodden, even beneath the hide shelter. Grey above and grey below, the oars splashed unceasingly as they made their slow way east. There were five boats, two bearing Gytha and the companions; three with the Cold Trader's slaves and other cargo. Occasionally, the shout of a Balt guard or a whip crack told its own story. Gytha rejoiced for the Radknight, for Ailsi was on their boat, though the thrall collar was still around the girl's neck. Even the Twice Scarred Eadric mumbled something about the Lord moving in mysterious ways. He had raised the matter of purchasing the girl's freedom, but the Cold Trader cautioned them that if the fate of slaves troubled them, so her price must rise still more.

Boredom and fear were Gytha's journeymen. Her appetite gone, she sank into the melancholy once more. She would pretend she was at her home, her mother talking gently as she brushed her hair. She dreamt of riding free with Magnus and Edmund beyond the smooth green ridge behind her father's Hall, Edmund's saker high in the vault. Magnus, ever their laughter-smith. Beyond them, the sparkle sea, before the beacons burnt and her years in purgatory began.

But here, no beacon burnt its warning. Danger was the Wend himself. How she feared and hated him! She saw how he would look at Ailsi and knew he might take her, so Gytha had Ailsi sleep at her feet as a dog sleeps at the feet of its master. Sometimes the girl would cry out as Gytha herself had done. Knowing full well of what she dreamt, Gytha had no need to ask. Nor did she know the words to do so, understanding only that if she asked Ailsi to speak of her dreams, then she must speak of hers too, and she could not. For all were of her mother, the death of her father on that field, the loss of her home and of the beardling boy Magnus, her brother. Was that, she wondered, the fate of all the English Companions, even Colwenne too? Were they of one story? Gytha could only pray, as she knew her Aunt Gunhild would have her do, and beseech the Lord to lighten her darkness.

The shore was still a way off. It lay, featureless and low, on either hand. Gytha saw black trees to the water's edge and patches of white snow. No village, no smoke; nothing stirred. It was colder, too. Lumps of ice floated near them in the grey water. 'River ice,' the Cold Trader called it. The steersman swore and doubled the look-out.

They reached Ladoga after another day of hard rowing up the river. To Gytha, the strand on either side closing in on them was as if being sucked into the jaws of a serpent, from which there would be no release. The village lay on wedge of land on a lake, surrounded by still more forest. Nearby was a river, its mouth bunged with logs and ice. There was a watchtower at the gate to the water's edge and a high palisade around the outside of a tight huddle of reed-thatched cabins. The Companions were housed twenty in each, save Gytha and her brothers, who were given a separate dwelling by the headman.

The cabins were dirty, hurriedly vacated. Everywhere, water lay in puddles so deep that the slippery walking logs, laid end to end, were themselves awash. The place stank of mud and tar, and of flesh and the bales of pelts which lay stacked ready at the shore. Here, ragged collar thralls moved cargoes from the longships to serpentless river boats for the journey south. It was into this world that Gytha and the Companions of the Golden Dragon of Wessex arrived that spring, treading the path into exile, with collar thralls bound for the slave market in Constantinople. .

Distrust was everywhere; a man would not piss without three to guard him. Mead, beer and fire-water flowed freely, in a town where women were scarce, and fighting men had time to while. All waited for the spring flood to ease: silver merchants; slave dealers from the south with curved scimitars; River people; tall Wends, the Cold Trader's kin; fearsome blond-bearded Varangians, as they called the Dane folk, with hammers of Thor about their necks; and fur-wrapped Chud, Ests and Maris. These last were high-cheeked trappers in bark shoes, their log canoes barely afloat with the piles of finest winter beaver, white fox pelts and amber to barter for silver, tortoiseshell, food, coloured beads and swords. Fearing the strangers who would kill them and steal their daughters, these forest men vanished as quickly as they came.

Beyond the town lay the low, round burial mounds – hundreds scattered about in the meadow, some new, some with trees growing from them. In the middle of this grove of the dead stood a grizzled oak tree, its dark branches shading a sanctuary of wooden idols to the Balt gods. There they performed ceremonies, sacrificing live cockerels and casting lots on how they could best please Dazhbog, god of sun, the life giver, Svarog, god of fire, Stribog, god of wind, and Perun, god of thunder.

It was there the Cold Trader went the day following their arrival. Under the watchful eye of the shaman, he made offerings of bread, curds, meat and wrinkled onions, saying loudly, 'Oh my lord, accept these gifts. I return from a distant land with a glorious bounty of unimaginable worth – an English princess bride, her brothers and their hearthguard, and a slave girl, a thegn's daughter, also from beyond the grey west sea. For whom, with your blessing, I will receive many silver dirhams.' And then he listed all the things they had brought from the Danefolk, and for which he hoped to be well rewarded.

This might have passed unseen by the Companions had Pig-boy not followed the Wend and observed what the others had not. And so, through a mixture of mime and scrawls on the wax board, he told the Radknight. 'And we thought him Christian,' Wulfwyn said to Gytha as he recounted Pig-boy's story.

'We keep the company of the devil himself,' said Gytha fearfully. 'Let us find the monk and seek the Lord's strength in prayer.'

The wait for the flood of river melt to ease was broken by hunting trips into the forest. Stories of wild boar the size of bears filled the evenings around the hearth, but the silence between the Companions and the Cold Trader grew with each passing day. Ailsi's freedom hung in the air unsaid.

Drunk on mead and still mud-splattered from the boar chase, Twice Scarred Eadric called out to him one evening, 'Wend, come and eat with us. Or do you fancy yourself too mighty for us?'

'Are you mad? I'll not have the swine here,' said Godwine under his breath.

'Lord,' replied Old Thegn, 'I keep my enemy close and you should do likewise.' He then turned to the Cold Trader.

'Come. Make space for him at our table and let us show him the hospitality of the English folk.'

'I'd rather show him the hospitality of an English fork,' said the Radknight to nobody in particular. There was laughter, but no joy in it.

'So, Wend, there is little here save wolves, bears and hunters. Is this the land beyond the River you call home? Is our Gytha, daughter of our King Harold Godwineson, to be Lady of swamps, flies and fallen timber?'

The trader said nothing as he sat down amongst the English, who awaited his reply. 'Yes,' they murmured, grim-faced around the long table. 'And what of us who would fight for your Great Prince, brother to the Queen Elisaveta? What of him?'

'Speak, Wend,' said the axed and burnished Roni the Dane. 'You took the Bastard William's silver to bring us here to the end of the earth. Is that what King Sweyn Estrithson wanted? For us to be exiled here? Is that why you remained at Hedeby, to haggle coins for our heads with the agents of Normans, whom we saw come to his hall?'

Thoughtful Edmund spoke. 'Did King Sweyn Estrithson offer silver by the head? Or was it a lump sum for all the English, that you would lead our Earl Godwine, the Lady Gytha and the Companions of the Golden Dragon of Wessex here to this forsaken place?'

The Monk Blaecman stood, towering over the Wend, pointing his finger. 'Is the betrothal to this Vladimir a lie, Wend? Is the Lady Gytha a thrall like any other? May God blind you if you have tricked us!'

The Twice Scarred Thegn Eadric took up the note. 'You have the silver. What would you do now, Wend? Kill us and sow our bones in the forest floor for still more trees to grow upon and never more be heard of?'

There was uproar. 'Kill him now!' the Company shouted.

Godwine stood, holding his hand up. 'Quiet!' he shouted above the din. 'The man is a guest at our board, let him speak.'

'He's no guest of mine,' said axed and burnished Roni the Dane. 'I would kill him myself and cut him into squares as befits the oath-dog.'

'I think not, burnished warrior,' said the cold Wend, his face unmoved, playing with the folding scales as if weighing their chances. 'For Balt, Est and Chud, grandchildren of the father god Dazhbog surround you. You will burn in this hall if I am harmed. I pay them well for their furs, and should you try to flee, Leshok's wolves will fight over your corpse. His wood wives will embrace you in the marsh and hide you for ever. For this is not the copse and glade of the home of which you talk, where you hunt mice and rabbits with birds. This is the wildness. Nor can you return from where you came, beyond the grey west sea, for every man's axe and spear is turned against you English, bar one. My Lord, the Prince in whose service I visited the hall of the Dane King in search of a bride for his son, Vladimir. So, listen, English. Without me, you will never find your way south to the Red Fort at Smolensk and I will hear no more threats. For if I die, you die also. In these forests of the moist mother earth, the trappers and tree worshipers steal soft Christian souls to feed the spirits of the marsh.' He paused again to let his words sink in. Hearing no protest from the assembly, a slight smile crossed his sly face, never reaching his grey eyes.

'I welcome you, princes and princess, to the land of journeys, where the forests are rich with game and the rivers filled with plentiful fish. But I, too, will be glad to spy the River, the mighty Dnepr, and the Wild Field beyond, which I last saw a year or more back.'

The small hall settled as he spoke. Gytha, with Ailsi at her side, moved closer to where she could better hear the Wend speak. Edmund and the Radknight made space between them.

The Wend paused, looking at the group before him.

'But did you or did you not get paid to lead us here?' asked the axed and burnished Roni the Dane, his fury ill-contained.

'Yes, I received a good reward to lead you from the Dane King's hall. Though not as much as I was promised, so I took that slave girl at a bargain price and shall make a profit it seems. But remember this. I saved your lives, for the Norman's agent would have had you killed.' He paused, playing with them. Gytha felt the Radknight tense next to her; Ailsi's hand sought hers. 'But this promise I make to you and your company of hearthguard. I hold the betrothal parchment with the Dane King's great seal, which states in the Latin tongue of your priests that the Lady Gytha will be bride to Vladimir son of the queen's brother, Vsevolod, Prince of Chernigov, and you, little king without a kingdom, shall fight in his pay and become rich.'

One evening, as a spring wind blew and the catkins jiggled on the branches, they heard that they were to leave Ladoga for Rurik's fort at Holmgaarde, up river. By now, the dark night had vanished and the white night had come in its place. It was warmer too. Gytha pressed the black-tipped marten fur to her cheek one last time and bid it farewell.

Gytha, escorted by the Radknight, took the log road beyond the gate to the lakeside to see the loading of the flat bottom river craft for herself. On their return, they passed the slave huts. A group of honey-skinned men crouched, rags around their chains, while a woman stirred a pot at an open fire, the men's heads shaved save for a tufted knot of hair, the warrior mark of the Wild Field.

'Look, Wulfwyn, Qypchaq warriors from the Wild Field. those are the scented Swetesot's people,' Her face lit at the memory of her friend. 'You remember what Swetesot said about her people. Their home is the grass ocean, their people saddle-born, suckled on sour qumiz milk. They live, fight, eat, drink and die on the backs of stallions; Angry and quick-tempered, they fear nothing, but all men fear them.'

'They look wild enough,' said the Radknight.

A dog growled and flattened its ears as they passed; the ruffian Balt guard kicked it.

The women called out to her. Gytha stopped, remembering a word that Swetesot had taught her in Exeter, years before. 'Tinishlik,' she replied.

'Tinishlik princessa'. The woman fell to her knees in front of her, reaching to kiss the hem of her cloak. Gytha backed away. The Balt guard clubbed the Qypchaq woman across the head with a stick, but the woman didn't cry out. Gytha and the Radknight hurried on, taking care not to slip on the mud slick track. The exchange left Gytha troubled.

'Swetesot said Qypchaq women kill and die in silence.'

'what did you say to her, my lady?' asked the Radknight.

'I said peace in their language, as Swetesot taught me.' After a pause she spoke again, a determined edge to her voice. 'Wulfwyn, I shall buy those Qypchaq, to guard me.'

'Guard you, My Lady, they will slip into the night with your head, to make a drinking cup of it.' The Radknight was almost laughing at the idea, then seeing she meant it, stopped, .

'They will not harm me,' frowned Gytha. 'Go tell the trader to name his price.'

And so, the day before they left on the long journey south, Gytha bought the Qypchaq captives. Everyone tried to stop her, saying they were too dangerous, but she insisted.

We are prisoners of the trees and the marsh,' she said, 'I fear these forests and I fear the River folk more. But my enemies are the Qypchaq's enemies, my dangers are their dangers. They will know of threats that menace me, before I do and will warn me.'

'How?' said Godwine. 'When you cannot speak to them, nor they to you? '

'As dogs warn their master of the stranger. A hound, Godwine, does not know words. It barks and we listen.'

Godwine laughed. 'Sister, you have the guile of our grandmother, Mother of Heroes. You shall have these horsemen of the Wild Field serve you. God willing they will not part your ears from your neck.'

'They will not!' said Gytha, defiantly.

They rowed up river against the stream, the forest all about alive. Some of the little boats, bearing wax, furs, honey and slaves, were only tree trunks with planking on the side. In places, the dark pines withdrew; marsh was everywhere and owls flew on whisper wings low across the reeds. Wolves howled in the night. But sometimes, where the ground was higher, alder and unblemished birch stood in flowered glades, sunlight twinkling through their quivering leaves. Here, bees and beetles and butterflies went about their business.

The men, straining at their benches or poling the fat boats through the mudbanks, yearned to be freed for the hunt. For here there was a bear with a cub, there an elk, its antlers like wooden angel's wings, standing watchful, the current eddying between its long legs.

With feverfew and wild garlic balm on their faces – for the biting flies were everywhere – Gytha could forget her fate. Never walking where the sodden ground moved beneath their tread – for there lay drowning death – she and Ailsi stretched their legs, stiff from the day spent seated in the bottom of the cramped boat. They wondered at the beauty all around. Even the Qypchaq sang as they lit the cooking fire and prepared the night camp for the lady, they called Princessa.

One of those evenings as Ailsi wove Gytha a crown of white daisies and blue cranesbill, she asked what would become of her. Gytha took her hand in hers and gazed into her young face.

'Am I to be sold in a market again?' Gytha met her anxious gaze, but was loath to answer.

'As will I, Ailsi.'

But Ailsi shook her head, sobbing, 'You are to be a princess in the hall of a great prince, with collar-thralls to do your bidding and jewels on your clothes. I am a thrall, locked in and beaten, no better than a cow. Please help me, I beg you, Lady Gytha. You alone can save me. The Wend will not heed my brother, saying that he has other plans for me.'

'Yes, Earl Godwine and the Twice scarred Thegn Eadric have also spoken of you to the Wend. Godwine says that he has sold you, but will not say to whom.' She reached out and held the sobbing girl, the thrall ring hard against her arm.

The river narrowed and green bluffs rose at either hand. Ahead, they spied the swirl and eddy of hidden rocks. The stream grew faster, too strong for men to fight. Rowing for the shore, swearing and shouting, they dragged and heaved each laden craft up the bank to a road of smooth hewn logs that led through the forest to a place above the rapids. The volok road, they called it. The first boats to go were Godwine's and the Companions. Everyone – thrall and warrior – hauled the boats along the wood-road, pulling and pushing, yard by yard. The forest rang to their shouts and the screech of stubborn hulls on the timber lane. Some took mud and buckets of water to throw beneath the hulls to grease the keels, then as the road took them once more towards the river, the vessels gathered speed on the downward slope. Hands wrapped against splinters and burning rope, they wrestled to slow their crushing, grinding path. It was back-breaking toil, and with every step the risk of

death or injury. Only Gytha and Ailsi walked in safety behind
the boat. Behind them they could hear the thunder of the
rapids. Ahead lay the smooth river and calming rhythms of
the oars once more.

The ambush was so sudden that the brothers, the Burnished
Roni, the Old Thegn and their hearthguard had no time but
to shout a warning of river-pirates!

One moment, they were slipping and struggling, the next
fighting for their lives with whatever weapon came to hand.
The boat carrying the Hoard slewed off the logs and crashed,
splintering, against a sturdy tree. The river pirates surrounded
it, and at first the Companions were not aware that their quest
was anything more than seizing the precious cargo that lay in
the hull. But the pirates were after another prize.

By the time the Radknight could turn away from his
attackers, a second group who had lain low between the log
road and the river made straight for Gytha and Ailsi, cutting
them off as they fled. Wulfwyn could do nothing as men
grabbed them.. He heard Ailsi scream as she half fell, half
rolled through the rocks and undergrowth, but he could not
reach her. Another held Gytha by the hair. She felt for the
jewelled wounding-knife at her belt and, in one desperate
thrust, buried it to its hilt. The man crumpled beneath her as
rough hands grabbed her from all sides. One hit her. Another
punched her stomach. The breath flew from her as they tipped
her into a boat.

But the pirates were too busy to see the Qypchaq racing
down the slope. The nimble horse warriors from the Wild
Field, terrible in their fury, stabbed, thrusted and jabbed.
Most terrible of all was the woman, the one who had knelt
at Gytha's feet

The fight was over in a moment. The river-pirates died
swiftly, the Qypchaq slicing off their heads and holding them

up so the blood cascaded onto their faces. Unable to flee, the other river pirates jumped from their boats. In their terror, they tipped Gytha into the icy water, her cries for help muffled by the roaring rapids that dragged her under. The Qypchaq woman, Tulpan was her name, hurled herself into the river, grabbing at Gytha's clothing as she strained to hold her against the current that would pound them both to death among the rocks, as the Qypchaq men dragged the two ashore. Half drowned, Gytha coughed and vomited at the feet of her rescuers. Tulpan knelt by her, her breath coming in great gasps, a grin of victory fleeting across her broad face as Gytha stirred and opened her eyes.

Above them, fighting had ceased. Horns brayed loudly. Gytha, her clothes ripped and soaked, golden hair hanging sodden around her shoulders, was helped by the Qypchaq back up to the log road.

There, astride his horse, was a warrior in polished mail, a golden pointed helm on his head, a cape casually about his shoulders. He was young. Gytha guessed him to be about eighteen, no more. In his hand was a curved sword, unsheathed. Armed men stood behind him; two lay dead on the ground.

Gytha struggled to make sense of the scene that greeted her. The Radknight dragged himself upright and stumbled towards her. 'Thank God, my lady,' was all he could repeat. 'I thought you were lost. There were too many and I could not get to you. Where is Ailsi?' The Qypchaq woman pointed. The scratched and bruised Ailsi, covered in blood, was running up the log road towards them.

'Well,' said the gold-helm warrior in the Dane tongue. 'Who have we here? A Rusalka who rises half drowned from the river with wild savages and now a blonde thrall girl too.'

Gytha pulled her sodden cloak about her and was about to speak. The warrior laughed. 'Be calm, unquiet Rusalka,' he said, 'let us first attend to the wound on your head.' Gytha put a hand to her wet hair and felt the matted stickiness of blood. She half remembered the blow.

Further up the log road, Godwine and the Companions were gathered by the boat, slewed across the track, half lying on its side.

'The hull is cracked but the Hoard is safe beneath the oiled cloth. I feared we had lost both the Hoard and you, our vow-sister. God in heaven was merciful today.'

'Who are you?' said Prince Oleg to Godwine, looking down from his horse, the curved sword still drawn. 'Kneel before me. You speak with Oleg, Lord of Chernigov, son of Grand Prince Svyatoslav, ruler of Kiev and all Rus, brother of Duke Gleb, ruler of Novgorod, the new town,'

Godwine returned the fair-haired prince's stare.

'Prince Oleg,' he said courteously but still did not bow, 'we are travellers bound for the Red Fortress at Smolensk. We come in peace and thank you for your intercession. Now we must return to the river and, when we have patched our craft, continue our journey southwards.

Prince Oleg looked Godwine up and down. 'So, you are not Dane nor Rus. Not Wend, Est, Chud, Krivitch nor Balt. Your tongue is strange, your clothes ragged, but that is a Frankish longsword in your hand. You travel through this forest alone?' asked the prince. Then, gazing past Godwine, added, 'here comes a man who will give me the answers I need. For a price, no doubt.'

The Cold Trader was running along the slippery way. 'Earl Godwine, my lady Gytha, thank Almighty Perun and all the spirits of the forest that you are safe.' Seeing the prince, he fell to his knees and bowed his head three times to the ground.

'Ah,' said Prince Oleg. 'Zhiznomir! I might have guessed you would appear. Now the fun is over. So, you bring travellers not grinding-slaves. No doubt profit rewards your abstinence. No woman, young or old, slave or high born, is safe from Zhiznomir,' he snorted, addressing the company. 'So, tell me, trader, who is this Jarl and lady who you would bring us? Their clothes speak of the rotting mire, but their weapons tell another story.'

On his knees, the Cold Trader described his mission, introducing Godwine as a king without a kingdom and Gytha, his royal sister, betrothed to Prince Vladimir. Prince Oleg, son of Svyatoslav, listened intently, his eyes darting from Gytha to Godwine.

'Ah,' said Oleg finally. 'That explains the Frankish swords.' He stared at Gytha and, seeing the tilt of her chin, was amused. 'If she is to be married to my cousin, you had best wash her first. We shall make a camp here and tomorrow we will return to Novgorod, the New Town where, Lady Rusalka, you shall rest before you make the journey to the River to meet my cousin, Vladik.'

'Your cousin, Lord? Prince Vladimir, Lord of Smolensk, is your cousin?'

'Yes, he is the son of my father's brother,' he replied, adding boastfully, 'he follows my every move and wishes that he were me. But don't look so grave, my lady. Be not cast down by disappointment – he shall have wars enough to keep him from your bed.' And with this, Oleg son of Sviatislav and his companions roared with laughter. Gytha felt the colour rise to her cheeks and dared not look up at this arrogant young prince who would dishonour her so. But she said nothing.

It was then the Companions realised one of their party was missing. 'Twice Scarred, Thegn Eadric!' they called, but there was no curse nor growl to show his whereabouts.

They found him shortly afterwards on the steep bank above the river, his head near split from the chain shirt that he had worn each day since he was a boy. It had not saved him this day. Around him lay the bodies of Balts, silenced witnesses of the Old Thegn's fearsome axe.

Gytha stared bereft at the bloody corpse, tears streaming down her cheeks. Gently she stroked his greying cheek and eased the battered helm off his head. Godwine, Edmund, the Radknight and Roni the Dane knelt about him, their heads low as the Towering Blaecman intoned the Viaticum. *'Per istam sanctan unctionem et suam piissimam misericordiam, indulgeat tibi Dominus.'*

It was a sombre party that huddled that night on the bank of the Volkhov. Gytha stared into the fire, numbed by the loss of the Twice Scarred Thegn who had cared for her as a father, fulfilling his sworn oath to shield her as he had each day on their long road together since Waltham. Brave as a bear, the rasp-tongue Thegn of her East Saxon kin was no more among them. In her moment of direst need he had died as he lived.

His soul was commended to God in Christian burial and they burned the broken boat as befits a great chieftain of the north. Christians all, yet they hurled their lighted flares onto the pyre and wept. Oleg's men drove the captive pirates into the flames; others they speared, some they drowned. None lived, and neither Gytha nor The Companions of the Golden Dragon of Wessex cared of their heathen fate.

Then a black-beard priest in a high hat and robes, holding a painted icon of the Virgin, led Prince Oleg and his hearthguard in psalm fifty-one. The Towering Monk took Gytha's arm and, sinking to his knees, he folded his hands over hers. The deep harmonies in that clearing lifted Gytha's heart as she watched the embers fly upwards into the night sky and prayed for Twice Scarred Thegn' soul.

*   *   *

A kurgan mound to mark the burial site, a rough cross at the top, their journey to the New Town resumed. A light wind from the north helped them and made the rowing easy. The mood lifted in the sunshine, and the gash on Gytha's head began to heal under the poultice that Tulpan had wrapped over it. The Qypchaq, usually sullen, chattered amongst themselves, their reputation as warriors enhanced, their bravery confirmed. Ailsi, whom they called Aisulu, Beauty of the Moon, sat amongst them, smiling, while refusing the sour qumiz milk they all drank. Without them, they would now be dead or carried off. Gytha shuddered at the thought.

The river widened with a lake beyond. A palisade stood upon the high bank. This was Novgorod, the new town. Above the gates were square turrets with steep roofs and eaves, low as brows. Mailed bowmen watched their arrival. Boats of all sorts were dragged up onto a little beach, and children splashed and shouted at the water's edge. Fishermen were casting nets in the shallows and terns dived headlong into the brown grey water while, overhead, kites observed.

News of Vladimir's betrothed travelled quickly. Duke Gleb, ruler of the New Town, in boots and long coat, his round hat trimmed in mink, Prince Oleg making the introductions. Gytha wondered if Vladimir was as this Prince Oleg.

'Welcome to the settlement of our forefather Rurik, he announced proudly.

It was part market, part hunting camp, part stronghold. A half-built church towered at one end of the green mound overlooking the river. A bridge spanned the river leading to a fishing village. There were alder, hazel and pale willows along the water's edge, bees sipped at purple irises and the steep bank up to the palisade was a blaze of golden dandelions.

But for Gytha, the Radknight and Ailsi, there was no comfort in the warm sunshine. Ailsi's bondage pierced their every waking moment. They could think of no way of freeing her. Without a force to take her, their only hope was silver. But when they put it to the Company, The Companions of the Golden Dragon of Wessex were divided. Godwine and the Radknight argued heatedly. 'Lord,' he said, 'the Twice Scarred Eadric, proud Thegn, would have counselled to save my sister, no matter the price. She is kin, English kin, her life more forfeit than all English lives. But Godwine shook his head. 'Good Radknight, if we offer to buy Ailsi's freedom, the price will rise the more we barter till all the hoard is gone. Faithful Wulfwyn. We cannot pay the price and be left with nothing.' Wulfwyn was almost weeping with anger and frustration at his words. Gytha knew to keep her counsel.

'The trader wishes to sell her to the vain and boastful Prince Oleg, said the burnished Roni. 'I am sure of it.

'How do you know this?' asked the Radknight, aghast at the Huscarls words.

'It is plain, boy,' said Roni. 'He tells the prince she is an English princess. This is his plan.'

The hall fell silent; this thought was new to the companions. Edmund, who had barely spoken, said, 'so he would barter Ailsi to Prince Oleg, knowing that he would wish to have an English princess like his cousin Vladimir. The greater the effort we make to win her return, the more desirable she becomes. These are the devil's people, so help me God.'

'Aye,' said Roni. 'He has nothing to fear, he outnumbers us tenfold, our bleats, no more than the lamb to the wolf. He will take her if he wants her.'

'Enough,' said Godwine. 'I have heard enough. I will not risk the Company for the safety of one girl, even the sister to our brother Wulfwyn, friend and companion to my own sister, and the daughter of our own English kin. I fear the Burnished Roni is right. The trader holds us for fools. See how he has us guarding his precious cargo, and without any choice we protect her. There will be no haggling for her with the Trader, nor with the prince.' He held the Radknight's outraged gaze and silently bade him keep calm. 'We must think of a better plan to outwit this trader at his own game or lose her. Until then, we do nothing.' And with that, the Company broke up, divided.

Wulfwyn was distraught, and when Ailsi heard that his plea to the Companions had been refused, they both wept like children. For Gytha, it was hard to bear seeing her closest friend and now his sister so distressed. How bitterly she wished that the Twice Scarred Thegn Eadric still lived, or that she might ask Colwenne's advice. Leaving the mud-walled bothy that was her hall, where Oleg had housed her separately as was the custom, she went in search of the monk.

She found him sitting on the river bank with a rod, his mace idle at his side. Her voice startled him. 'Father, forgive me intruding in your contemplation, but I have prayed that Ailsi be delivered from her bondage. I cannot see the Radknight, who would give his life for me, so distressed. Nor can a daughter of our kin be sold while we look on, but do nothing.' Gytha sank to her knees. 'But the Lord will not answer my prayers. Ask, and it shall be given, is what the scripture says, but even my brothers have failed me.'

The monk shook his head. 'This is not time for prayer. Sit with me, my lady. I watch the swallows and count the clouds and wait in vain for a fish to take my worm. For the Lord is here, but heeds me not.'

'Father!' said Gytha, shocked, 'do you make light of my pain? Praying for a fish is not the same. How can you – a priest – say such a thing?' Gytha stood up and was about to walk away when she saw tears in the man's eyes. How old he looked, she thought, and why did his hand tremor so? She sat down again.

'My lady,' he said, 'St Paul in his letter to the Philippians said, *"In everything* by prayer and supplication with thanksgiving let your requests be made known to the Most High, who knows all secrets". Be it fishing or a life, we are God's children. He gives us what is best for us. "I will pour water on him that is thirsty and floods upon the dry ground".' He smiled tenderly at Gytha. 'Together we have travelled many miles and suffered much, but still we strive not to give up – to be as your father was, fearless in the face of an overwhelming force, a beacon to us all.'

'And he died for it and left me and my brothers without a father.'

'Yes, as Jesus died for us.'

'And without a home,' Gytha continued, 'without our country, so that now like Israelites we wander ...,' She paused, staring out into the lake, then took the old man's hand. How frail he seemed. Wrapped in her own woes, she had failed to see the punishment the years and the road had wrought on this warrior-monk. 'Oh, friend and tower of strength, I hear your hope but the Lord has abandoned us. Our prayers go unheeded in the Kingdom of God. I pay each day for our deliverance, but our lives become worse as we travel ever further from our home. What will happen to us? Will the English folk vanish into the wilderness? For that is what I believe.'

'Yes, my lady, but the Israelites' prayers were answered finally, and there shall be a land of Canaan for us and for your kin.'

'But what of Ailsi?' said Gytha, remembering her purpose.

'Ailsi,' said the monk, absently jerking on the line, a small fish jiggling in the sun. 'Ailsi is like this fish, caught by her thrall ring. She will go where the line takes her.'

Gytha could hear no more of this. She ran from the sunlit river bank and wept alone in her chamber until Ailsi came to see with news that there was to be a feast to honour the arrival of Godwine.

Two men seized Ailsi as she left Gytha's banya, one placing his leather glove over her mouth, the other picking her up, her legs kicking helplessly. Gytha, in the thick-walled hut, heard nothing, only raising the alarm when Ailsi did not return. Fearing the worst, she called for the Radknight. They knew that it was no accident.

Then Tulpan, the Qypchaq woman, who had saved Gytha on the river, rushed in and stuttered in her halting Dane tongue, 'the trader's men, the trader's men Aisulu Aisulu.'

Quickly a meeting was called, but Roni – burnished and axed once more – advised great caution. 'We are guests, one wrong move will make us prisoners once more,' he counselled. 'If the Trader has taken the girl to sell, he will not give her up.'

'She is no thrall,' said the Radknight, his fury hardly contained. 'She is my sister, the daughter of a thegn. Too long I have listened to others to do nothing and wait, and now I have lost her!'

Gytha stretched her arm to him and held it tight. 'Dear friend,' she said. 'Ailsi is as a sister to me also, and you a brother. But the burnished Huscarl Roni is right. If you demand her return, her price goes up and the trader will play with us as the cat toys with a mouse.'

'Yes,' said the Towering Blaecman, now returned from fishing. 'They will guard her well, at least better than we have guarded her. Nobody doubts your bravery and your pain, my son, but you will die, and what help are you to your sister dead?'

The Radknight struck his fist into the log sides of the hall, not once but again and again. until there was blood on his knuckles.

'I shall go to her?' Gytha asked. 'They will let me see her.'

'They will not, my Lady' said Wulfwyn angrily. 'and what good can it do if she is to be sold?'

'Because Ailsi would rather die than be sold so we must not delay. I shall send Pig-boy to see where she is held. That much we must know, and perhaps we can rescue her.'

So, Pig-boy was dispatched, only to return, miming that the place was crawling with the Traders' men and that he dared not try to slip past them for fear of having his throat cut as well as his tongue.

After mass, they made their way from the half-built church to the Duke of Novgorod's hall for the welcome feast. Godwine, Edmund and Gytha were wearing their circlet crowns. It was a sombre gathering, but the Duke was all generosity. 'Mead and kvas for our most honoured guest, Godwine Haroldson, the king without a country. And for the princess, soon to be our sister, and for the brave Companions who journey with her, though they know not where.'

The Rus laughed, but the English, uncomprehending, sat stone faced on the rugs, their weapons close to hand, under the gaze of the Duke's hearthguard,

Gytha looked about her. The Hall was full, next to the Duke was Prince Oleg, and many other warriors of the Ducal hearthguard each placed according to his status.

There was no sign of the Cold Trader.

'Can you see him?' Gytha asked the Towering Blaecman.

'No,' said the monk, 'the worshiper of trees and graven images is not here. Must we sit here long? My bones are stiff, with no bench or bord to lean on. Even Danefolk have a bench, but here we must sit upon the ground to eat as cows chew in the rain.'

With all the town present, the noise in the Hall was deafening. The Duke was at one end of the Hall on his carved throne; the peasant-men at the other. One man stood out, neither a priest nor warrior-handsome, like the vain and boastful Oleg. He was dressed in a long kaftan coat rich-broidered in gold, unarmed, save for a jewelled dagger. His thumbs were hooked into his sash, observing. Catching Gytha's eye, he gave a courteous nod.

More food and drink arrived. Hams, sour cabbage, hard eggs and jugs of kvas were piled on the ground before the Duke, who offered morsels to Godwine and Gytha as guests of honour. There was music and singing and a jesting fool playing his whistle. The crowd whipped into a frenzy, shouting out encouragements. Then, suddenly there was a hush. All eyes went to the back of the Hall. The bishop entered, in his golden cassock and domed crown, placing his staff rhythmically before him. A small procession followed.

'It's a wedding,' whispered Gytha, in amazement. 'Oh, look at the Bride, is she not beautiful in her robe? 'who is she and who is she to marry? 'Is she marrying the Duke? look, that must be her father.'

For a moment, Ailsi was forgotten, as Gytha soaked in the scene before her. The bride wore a stiff headdress with a thick veil that hid her face, a pale blouse broidered in the most brilliant red and green threads over a wide skirt with layered petticoats, covered in flowers of the finest needlework. She was led by girls dressed as she with flowers in their hair, and young men in billowing broidered flower shirts, baggy trousers tucked into the tops of their boots. A man paced to one side of the bride. Gytha was watching intently. No detail was too trivial. She too would be bride to a prince. The scene before her was magical and the air full of music and cheering.

The procession stopped in front of them. The man bent to draw back the bridal veil. Gytha's heart stopped in her chest.

This was no father ready to give his daughter's hand. it was the Cold Trader.

Ailsi looked up, her eyes wide as a cornered doe. Gytha gasped. A shout rang out behind her. It was the Radknight.

'No!' he bellowed. 'You shall not have her!'

Ailsi stood bewildered, tears streaming down her face. The other thralls wailed. Gytha was on her feet, but the Cold Trader, sword in hand, placed himself in her way. All the English were standing now, but none dared move. They were surrounded.

Prince Oleg laughed, delighted by the show; and all the Duke's hearthguard and the townsfolk laughed with him. 'Very good!' roared Oleg, clapping his hands. 'Very good, Zhiznomir, you rascal. To see the English oaf-faces is worth any price. I will take them all, have this one washed and bring her me, but first let us celebrate my marriage with my English friends!' And with that, he burst again into uproarious laughter and the hall with him. 'So, king of nothing, you enjoy my wedding? She's pretty, my English bride, is she not? How comely she looks in our clothing, and better still without.'

Godwine stood, stiff as plank wood, shaking with anger, as Oleg took his arm, switching into the Danish speech. 'Come, we are brothers, Let us drink.' He handed him a horn of mead.

'Drink, King!' ordered Prince Oleg, laughing still but there was menace in his face. 'Or fight and die. Better to drink than die, eh King Godwine,' he said staining his words with his sneer.

Seeing his chance, the Radknight lunged at the Prince, Gytha grabbed his arm, catching him unbalanced. 'Stop, Wulfwyn!' she screamed.

Quick as lightning, the burnished Roni and Edmund seized the crazed Wulfwyn and fell with him struggling onto the carpeted floor. Two others took the Radknight's legs and sat on him. 'Kill him,' ordered Oleg.

'No, Prince' said Godwine, 'get him out of here and bind him, he will get us all killed.'

The noise in the hall was deafening as the people of the New Town laughed at the joke played on the English folk. Only one man did not laugh at their humiliation. The man, in the long kaftan coat, embroidered in gold, who stood aloof from the orgy in the hall.

The Pig-boy crept back into the shed. In his hand he clutched a length of bark, silvery on the outside, pale within. Painstakingly, he scratched at it with the point of a blade, making small grunting noises as he did so. Then, spitting on his finger, he took a tiny amount of cinder from the fire and carefully rubbed it over the scratching. As if by magic, words appeared. Latin words that none but Gytha, her brothers, and the Towering Blaecman might read. For his message was most secret, and only they might know. On he went, writing and rubbing until the bark was covered in spidery black writing. Then, placing it carefully against his body, he went in search of the priest, the sound of feasting loud behind him.

PART TWO CHAPTER FOUR

THE JUDAS SHILLING

THE QYPCHAQ WOMAN TULPAN shook Gytha violently, saying 'lady, quickly, brothers.' It was pitch dark. Gytha was confused. She had only just laid down. She splashed the offered water on her face. The shock of what she had seen in the hall, vivid in her head.

Grabbing her shawl, she ran barefoot across the yard. Godwine was there, still dressed, the thoughtful Edmund bleary from the mead. The axed and burnished Roni the Dane was armed and ready, with the Towering Monk beside him. In the middle of them all stood Pig-boy.

'Oh, Lord in Heaven, what has he done that you drag me from my bed?'

Asked Godwine, handing her the piece of bark.

'What is it?'

'Read it, sister.'

'It's in Latin. I cannot read it quickly.'

'Then let me tell you and Roni what it says,' said the monk. 'Pig-boy was gambling, with the prince's men.'

'Pig-boy gambling, you wake me for that?'

'No, no,' said Blaecman. 'Pig-boy won, and received this.' The monk handed Gytha a silver penny, no bigger than a fingernail. Gytha took it and turned it round in her hand.

'Look at it carefully, Gytha,' said Godwine.

Gytha handed it back. 'It's a penny.'

'It is an English penny,' said Godwine. 'How do you think one of these serfs got an English silver penny, Gytha?' He paused as her mind worked to make sense of it. 'Let me tell you. He stole it off the body of a Balt who snatched you and Ailsi from the log road.' Pig-boy was nodding furiously. 'Now you have to wonder how a Balt robber in a forest came to have this coin.'

'Godwine, brother, you speak in riddles.'

'We believe,' said the Towering Blaecman, patiently, 'that the Balts on the log road were paid to attack us.'

'Paid by whom?'

Paid by The Cold Trader,' said Godwine.

'You mean the Cold Trader paid the river pirates to attack us, seize the Hoard, seize me?'

'Yes,' said Godwine. 'and ransom you back to us. The Bastard William's men paid him with this coin at the Dane King's court.'

Gytha was stunned. 'And he paid the river pirates with their English money! May God strike the devil, cast him to the furnace, let him burn forever.'

'Your Qypchaq foiled their plan,' said Edmund,

'And the Twice Scarred Thegn gave his life.'

She looked at Pig-boy. 'Pig-boy, thanks to you, we know the truth.' Pig-boy smiled his tongueless grin and bowed low, honking at her approval.

'But what use is the truth?' said Edmund. 'The Lord has given us the truth but we must use it wisely or the Lord will not reward us.'

'We tell the Cold Trader that we have proof that he set the attack. And, if he does not return Ailsi to us unharmed we will take this little coin to Prince Oleg.'

'He doesn't care, he knows this Cold Trader for what he is, yet trades with him and mocks us before all the people of this town,' said Edmund.

'Does anyone have a better idea?' asked Gytha.

'It won't work,' said the Burnished Huscarl. 'The prince wants Ailsi for his bed. He will think of nothing else, and the Cold Trader fears him more than us, with reason.'

'But we must do something now. We have no time. We must act quickly, while we can win her back!' Gytha stared at each of them, willing them to do her bidding.

Godwine rubbed his beard, just as her father had.

'Father would have wanted it so, yes, and the Old Thegn. We cannot let his death go unpunished.'

Godwine nodded. 'We will do as our sister Gytha wishes. Ready the Companions of the Golden Dragon, tell them to keep their weapons close and their eyes watchful, but say nothing of our plot.'

A challenge outside the door stopped him mid-sentence. Zhiznomir stepped into the room with a smirk and feigned a half bow at Godwine and at Gytha. The blood froze in Gytha's veins, such was her loathing for this man. She could not look at him. The English warriors stood in silence, waiting.

'I come from Prince Oleg,' he said, 'He would have you know he will let you fight for the girl.'

'Fight?' said Godwine,

'Yes, Lord, fight for the girl. He who would have her most, may fight the prince's champion.' Gytha's heart missed a beat. Wulfwyn to fight the Prince's champion?

'Aye Princess, it is Prince Oleg's wish that his champion fights this knave of yours. What shall I tell the prince?'

Godwine held the stare of the snake before him. 'So not content at humiliating us with your trickery, the prince would set his finest warrior on the crazed boy. Well, you can tell

your prince Oleg this, Zhiznomir – or not, as you choose.'
He paused and the trader waited, fingering the silver scales
at his waist. 'Tell him that we know it was you that paid the
robbers to attack us and left two of his warriors dead. Soon
to be joined by a third.'

The trader laughed. 'King without a kingdom, I have no
time for your foolishness.' He was all bravado, but a flicker
in his eyes spoke otherwise. 'What shall I tell the prince?
Will the challenge be met or shall I send the English virgin
to his bed?'

Gytha felt the silver still in her hand. Stepping directly
in front of the man whom she hated more than the tattooed
Celtprince, more than Jonjarl, or even the devil the Bastard
William – she raised the Judas shilling to his face.

'Do you know what this is?' She paused, watching the
dawning of recognition in his eyes. 'Of course, you do. Yes, it
is English sliver, given to you by the agents of Bastard. And
you know where it was found?' It was more of a statement
than a question. 'Yes, on the Balt you paid to snatch me. And
now I have it. Tell Prince Oleg that, trader – or should I say
Traitor! Tell the prince… or we will.'

The Cold Trader stared at the coin before him; only the
apple in his throat gave away the fear that clutched his heart.
The deal for Ailsi and the grinding-slaves was barely made,
no money exchanged, nor would be if the prince got wind of
his treachery. Instead, his flesh would be cut from his body, he
would be skewered on a stake, and roast on the fire like a pig.

'Give us the girl Ailsi, Zhiznomir, if you wish to see out
this day,' said Godwine. 'For either I will kill you or the prince
will. Either way, all the wealth your duplicity has earned you
will be for nothing. No kurgan grave awaits you. The birds
will pick your eyes from their sockets as you suck on your
own cock like a baby.'

The men laughed; Pig-boy honked with glee. 'Your threats are nothing to me,' said the Cold Trader. 'You have no proof. What good is a coin? It has a face but no voice, it knows not where it came from nor where it goes. You think you can frighten me, king of nowhere, king of nobody? You have taken a coin from your hoard – the last, I guess – and think you can blackmail me with this story.' His snake-eyes hardened. 'You have no evidence. You think Prince Oleg will believe you and not me, his friend? King of nothing, you are not so clever after all.'

'Show him, Pig-boy.' Pig-boy pulled the bark from his tunic. 'The bark speaks the truth. It is a confession from the prince's man who took your coin – this coin – Zhiznomir.' She spat his name. 'From the Balt you paid to attack us. And there are more where this came from.'

'You don't believe the evidence, Wend?' said Godwine. 'Then let us heat the brand in the fire, and blind you. For if your eye offends you, our Lord, who knows all secrets, tells us to pluck it out, does He not, monk?'

'He does,' said Blaecman. 'Matthew five, verse twenty-nine.'

The Cold Trader turned pale and steadied himself against the table. 'What would you have me do?' he asked, his voice hoarse.

'Give up all the money you received from the Bastard William in payment for the life of the Thegn Eadric, and have your men bring the girl here,' Godwine ordered.

'They will not free her if I am not there.'

'Fetch the Radknight,' ordered Godwine.

Wulfwyn, his hair dishevelled, appeared, wounding-knife in hand. He grunted as he saw the Cold Trader and lunged at him. The others retrained him.

'Wulfwyn!' shouted Godwine. 'You shall not kill him. We need you to guard this man until your sister is safe. Then you can kill him. Now, go with him to get her.'

Struggling to control himself, the Radknight obeyed.
'I will kill him, Lord Godwine, When Ailsi is free.'

'I have a better plan. I shall go. They won't question a
woman, I will have Thorgood the piper and Tulpan escort
me – she is brave as any warrior. And Pig-boy, too,

My lady, I beg that I too can come to free my sister, the
Balt guards will stop you,' said the Radknight.

'Very well Wulfwyn, come but dress as a woman.'

'Roni,' said Godwine, 'have all the men readied. We may
have to fight. Surprise is all that we have. If the prince gets
wind of this, we are lost.'

As daybreak broke, the little group made its way across the
courtyard in front of the church, past the duke's hall still loud
with the songs of drunkard, down to the dark cabins by the
bridge where the Cold Trader laagered his wares. Armed Balts
stood around, their dogs barking as soon as Gytha appeared. An
icy calm took hold of her as she and her companions walked
the last few paces. She held her head up, looking straight ahead
and hissed at the trader, 'wave them away, but say nothing.'

'Nothing,' repeated Thorgood, 'or my dagger will slip up
your arse till my fist reaches your balls.'

The Cold Trader gestured to his men to leave. Then they
continued to the first hut. The whipping pole stood outside.
There was blood on the ground.

'Ailsi,' Gytha called. 'It's me, Gytha Haroldsdaughter. I come
to say farewell.' Then to the Cold Trader: 'Bring her here.'

Behind him, Tulpan gave him a little nudge. 'Bring out the
English girl,' he ordered.

'That's enough,' said Gytha, shutting him up before he
could say another word. They waited, then Ailsi, her legs
shackled, stepped blinking into the light. Pouncing forward,
the Radknight, tossing his borrowed shawl aside, grabbed his
sister. A shout came from the top of the bank. Glancing up,

Gytha saw a group of men running down the slope towards them. The Duke's men. 'Wulfwyn, look!' she shouted. Forming a circle around Ailsi, the little Company of English drew their swords. The Cold Trader made a dash for it but Tulpan was quicker still.

'Kill him!' yelled the Radknight.

'No!' shouted Gytha, 'we need him!'

Frantically, they looked for a route to flee; the prince's soldiers were nearly upon them. In the nick of time, Pig-boy whistled and waved for them to follow as he ran across the bridge to where two men were pushing a fishing boat down the bank. Dragging the Cold Trader by his beard like a kicking goat to its slaughter, Gytha, the Radknight carrying Ailsi, Tulpan and Thorgood kicked the startled fishermen into the river, grabbing an oar each. Arrows hissed at them, striking the boat, or into the water about them.

'Stay down!' ordered the Radknight. 'May the Lord curse them all!' Then, pointing to where Godwine's hall stood, said, 'Look! They have fired the hall. See the smoke!' They watched as the men on the shore turned, pointing at the rising smoke. The bell in the half-built church rang out. Then Gytha saw Godwine and the Companions stream down to the shore, straight into the duke's men.

A furious fight erupted on the bank. Unable to get aboard the boats, Godwine's men formed a shield wall, manhandling the flat-bottomed fishing craft onto their sides for a barricade. Arrows lodged harmlessly in the planks, but the peril they were in was grave.

Gytha watched in horror.

'Come,' said Wulfwyn. 'We must row.'

Gytha grabbed one and all heaved at the sweeps. 'But where are we rowing to?' she asked, looking around her. She could see the fire raging in the hall behind them. Like ants, men were running on the beach. The last flowering of the English were fighting for their lives.

'We must save them! They are trapped, Wulfwyn. we must go back!' Gytha cried.

'And do what my Lady?' said the Radknight, still wearing his borrowed smock. 'Die there? At least you, my lady, and Ailsi are safe. I am not about to risk your lives again.'

Gytha banged the oar. 'We don't know where we are going or what dangers lie on the road ahead, but we do know that my brothers are dying on that beach as I speak. We must return.' The fury in Gytha's face left the others in no doubt that she would rather die with the Company than leave them. 'Turn!' she shouted. 'I made a vow at Waltham. I must go to them.'

The Radknight shook his head. 'No,' he said, 'I too made a vow to your mother to keep you from harm. I will not return.' The two of them, who had suffered so much together, the royal daughter and the young knight – mistress and servant, but above all friends – stared at each other. Gytha looked away first, clenching her fists, not daring to speak.

Wulfwyn put out his hand to her, laying it on her arm, and mumbled, 'my lady, your brother, Earl Godwine, would want you to save yourself, not walk into the fire for him.'

'Keep rowing, there is an island ahead.' shrieked Ailsi

'Only fools return to a fight.' The Cold Trader, lying bound in the bottom of the boat, spoke, Tulpan's foot on his head. 'The duke's men number four thousand, pray for their deliverance.'

'Make him shut up, Tulpan!'

Tulpan kicked the Cold Trader in the head, his round cap flying off into the bilge-water. A trickle of blood ran down his nose. She stuffed a dirty cloth into his mouth. He snorted and groaned, then was silent.

Unnoticed to them, the sky had turned purple. In the stillness that followed, the fighting on the shore, the screams of wounded men, the din of ringing metal on metal was clear to hear. Then, there was a mighty, blinding flash. A brilliant bright ball of blue fire hissed into the water a boat's length from their craft, followed by a deafening crack and rain so hard it bounced high off the surface of the lake. The world vanished as the deluge became a waterfall on their heads. Then the wind struck them, spinning the boat sideways and tipping them almost on their side. Frantically, they clung to the sides of the boat, praying that it might not tip over and send them to their death.

Gytha had no time for fear; her time at sea had taught her well. Grabbing an oar, she thrust it into the water, heaving as hard as they could, until the reluctant boat slowly came under her control. 'Bail! bail!' she shouted, the rain streaming down her face. She hung on, keeping the shrugging prow into the wind while the others scooped out with water with their helms. After what seemed an age, the furious gusts eased, but the thunder and lightning was all around them. Ailsi cowered, howling, knowing the chains about her legs would drag her to the bottom if they were to capsize. The Radknight, Thorgood, Pig-boy and Tulpan bailed as if possessed, while the Cold Trader half drowned in the bilge.

On they rowed, their hearts heavy, all that was left of the English kin. Here on a distant lake, the sons of Harold, King of the English, and the bravest men in all England would end their story at Novgorod. And what the future held for Gytha, only the Lord could know. Slowly, the new town grew smaller; a plume of smoke was visible until the summer storm hid it from their view.

The Cold Trader grunted and snorted again and at a nod from Gytha, and Tulpan removed his gag. Ahead was an island with a low hill, on which stood a carved oak tree of a giant man.

It was Perun, his great mace in his hand, knurled branches forming antlers. His head was silver, his moustache gold. As they drew closer, Gytha could see a decorated hall standing on the stony turf, surrounded by a grove of flickering, white birches. Its steep roof was thatch, supported by painted pillars topped with antler heads.

As they neared the shore, the boat filling fast as they could bail, the smell of rotting, burning flesh hit them on the clear air. They could see there were more pillars, each carved with the faces of the lesser gods, Svarog and Dazhbog. Fires burnt in braziers and men in cream capes and white robes came down to the shore. The Radknight drew his longsword and laid it ready in front of him. Pig-boy and Thorgood did likewise. 'Get these chains off me,' begged Ailsi. 'I will drown here!'

'What is this place?' said Gytha, covering her face with her shawl.

'It is a holy place. Not for you who pray to a god no man sees,' said the Cold Trader. 'It is where we true believers honour our gods.'

Gytha struck him hard across the face. 'Why is he here! Throw him over the side.' Needing no encouragement, The Radknight and the piper grabbed Zhiznomir. But Pig-boy frantically shaking his head, honking, pointing at the men on the shore and hanging onto the Cold Trader by his leather coat. Tulpan sat at her oar as the boat drifted into the shallow water. Bearded men, unarmed but for long carved staves, waited on the shore.

'Free me,' hissed the Cold Trader, 'or they will kill you.' Reluctantly, his arms were unbound and he shouted to the watchers, Gytha, uncertain if they would be killed, but too outnumbered to resist, let him get off.

The stench as they walked up the small hill grew worse. Everywhere were tethered animals, awaiting sacrifice. The fire burnt brightly in the brazier. Gytha looked up at the great forest tree, carved into the face of a man with a moustache. In his enormous fist he carried a mace and from it sprang flames. The Cold Trader threw himself onto the ground and signalled to the others to do the same. 'I will not,' said Gytha, remaining on her feet. Tulpan sank down, but the others followed their Christian princess, remaining upright.

The priests brought them food and made space in a hut. Such a pall of sadness hung over the group that they could not bring themselves even to share what they had seen. Gytha withdrew into another place, rocking in her grief. Even Ailsi's cries of pain at the hammering on her leg chains and thrall collar did not rouse Gytha from her melancholy as she counted all those, she loved who had died or been left behind, never to be seen again. Tulpan brought her food, but she shook her head. In her heart, she wished they had turned back, if only to die with her brothers. None of the others was surprised when she turned towards the hut wall and wept silently, her shoulders shuddering as the pain swept through her.

Ailsi, free of her shackles, came to Gytha and lay next to her saying nothing. The Radknight sat poking the fire with a stick, talking quietly to Thorgood. Without a boat, both knew they were trapped; to stay on this island meant death. Their luck would not last beyond the night. Outside, the night air filled with chanting and the anguished bleating and squawking of animals bound for the Cold Trader's god, Perun. 'Let's pray,' said Thorgood suddenly. 'The devil walks among us.' They knelt and the piper led the pair of them in prayer. 'Lighten our darkness we beseech thee, O Lord; and by thy great mercy defend us from all perils and dangers of this night; for the love of thy only Son, our Saviour, Jesus Christ.'

*　　*　　*

At dawn, the Cold Trader appeared. His smirk returned. He eyed the Radknight with caution. 'I have bought a boat,' he told them. 'And paid the priests too much for it. But we must leave now, for the duke will send a party out to find us.'

The little group gathered on the strand, waiting for the boat to come. Ailsi was distraught, asking why the Cold Trader was coming with them. Gytha did not know except to say that without him they did not know the way. 'The way where?' asked Ailsi. 'Where are we going? Not to this Prince Vladimir?'

'Where else might you suggest we go, Ailsi? I am betrothed, the bride price is paid, we are but five folk forsaken by God and without hope of rescue. Where else might we go?'

'Look, here comes the boat,' said the Radknight. Around the headland appeared a low craft, followed by another, then a third, a fourth and more, each with armed men.

'The duke's men!' said the Cold Trader. 'Follow me, we must hide.'

'No, we will remain here. I am the daughter of Harold, betrothed of Vladimir, prince of Rus. I will speak with them. Stand your ground.'

The Cold Trader bolted up the beach, but the English folk stayed. Wulfwyn, Pig-boy and Thorgood drew their swords; Gytha stood erect, facing the oncoming boats. Ailsi was shaking; Tulpan was muttering in the language of the Wild Field. A faint wind ruffled the surface of the lake. Gytha drew the shawl from her face and crossed herself. If she should die here on this island, she would die silently as the daughter of a King.

From the first boat to crunch up the shingle jumped the man Gytha had seen in the prince's hall. There was no sign of Oleg or the prince. Ordering the soldiers up the beach, he walked towards Gytha. The Radknight and Thorgood stepped forward, but the man raised his hand and said in the Danish tongue, 'I come in peace to speak with the princess.' He paused, bowing, and waited for Gytha to acknowledge him. She nodded curtly in return.

'Princess,' he said, 'I am Khristofor, Posadnik of Novgorod, the New Town, head of the Veche Council, representative of Duke Gleb, son of Grand Prince in Kiev. Your brothers and their hearthguard live.'

Gytha gave a little gasp, putting her hand quickly to her mouth, then to her breast. 'Thank you, Lord ... thank you Lord, my prayers are answered,' she murmured, crossing herself furiously.

'I will take you to them, but first we must search for the trader, Zhiznomir.'

'No, no!' said Ailsi, terrified. 'I don't want to go back! He will take me again. Please, lady Gytha, I beg you!'

'You will not have her,' said the Radknight, stepping between the man and his sister.

Khristofor looked at Wulfwyn with a half-smile. 'Young sir,' he said, 'we have no interest in the play toys of the vain and boastful Prince Oleg. The Veche Council have instructed me to provide you with safe passage to Smolensk to deliver your princess to Prince Vladimir. But we must find the traitor Zhiznomir who hoped to profit but will die instead.'

Gytha, still shocked to hear that Godwine and Edmund lived, could barely understand what this man was saying. 'But what if this is a lie, a trap to capture us? And my brothers lie dead in the lake.'

'It is no trap, Princess. No lie. Your brothers await you. We, the people of the New Town, have no fight with English folk. You are our guests.'

'But did we not burn your homes?' said the Radknight.

'No,' said the Posadnik. 'The rain came. Some here say it was Perun, God of Thunder, who doused the flame and saved the New Town.'

The soldiers returned then, dragging between them a stumbling Zhiznomir, his arms piniomed behind him, like one of Perun's chickens awaiting slaughter. Gytha felt no pity for the Trader; Ailsi spat him.

They were rowed back over the lake to the fort, now peaceful in the summer light. The boats were still pulled into a square, the arrows still in the planking. Little was left of the hall but black beams. The Companions of the Golden Dragon of Wessex, Khristofor told them, had been swiftly surrounded. Their escape was either death on the beach or death in the water. But the Council had no fight with the English, not over a slave girl for the prince's bed. Nor had they any love for the Cold Trader as the story of his treacherous ambush became known. So, as the storm sky had turned from black and the evening sun peeped through, the bell peeled and the fighting had stopped.

'And Oleg? What of him?' Gytha asked Godwine after they were reunited.

'Oleg has to obey the order of the Veche Council. All do, from thrall to prince.'

'What?' said Gytha, with disbelief. 'The vain and boastful Prince Oleg heeds a Council?'

Godwine nodded.

'And Ailsi?' asked the Radknight.

Godwine nodded again and looked to the anxious girl, now free of her shackles and thrall collar. 'Ailsi is a free woman. She is a leather-caped thegn's daughter once more.'

'Oh, Lord have mercy,' said the Radknight, grabbing Ailsi's hand, his face all smiles. 'I prayed this day might come but feared God had abandoned Ailsi and heeded me not. Now I need never to look on her anguish again, nor feel the fury of helplessness. Nor will the boastful sneering Oleg take her.'

'No, brother Wulfwyn. The Council has traded the trader to Prince Oleg in Ailsi's place.' The usually stern Godwine was laughing now. 'To do with him what he will, but I doubt to share his bed.' The companions jeered, shouting out what the prince might do to the Cold Trader. Others called for his god Perun to save him now. Amidst the uproar and the laughter, Godwine raised a hand for silence.

'Ailsi, you are freeborn once more, a Christian maiden, with all the honour that is due to you as the sister of our brother Wulfwyn, Radknight of Thurgarton, bravest of warriors who has defended my sister, the Lady Gytha, as my own mother wished it the day we fled from Waltham.' Godwine smiled again. 'In the sight of the Almighty and all the Companions, no man could be more prized than you, Thegn Wulfwyn of Thurgarton, Huscarl to Godwine Haroldson.'

The Companions cheered and banged their weapons on their shield-board, each clustering round to embrace the Radknight, now Thegn Wulfwyn of Thurgarton. Stepping forward, Wulfwyn bowed to Gytha. She took both his hands in hers and kissed his cheek. Pig-boy honked his joy through broken teeth, his gaping grin large as a crescent moon. Ailsi gazed in rapture at her brother, the horror of her days and nights forgotten for now.

The Companions drank mead, sang and ate late into that night. They drank to the joy of living, to Gytha's safe return, to Ailsi's freedom, to Oleg's revenge on the Cold Trader Zhiznomir who had brought so much misery and suffering since his arrival at the great hall of King Sweyn Estrithson. And at the insistence of the Towering Mace-wielding Monk, they gave thanks to God who had delivered them from the mouth of hell.

Watchful eyes observed the English folk and reported what they saw and heard to Khristofor and the Council of the New Town. They were pleased, for it was for them to provide safe passage for the Lady Gytha, betrothed to Prince Vladimir in Smolensk on the mighty Dnieper, still many days and dangers away. The fate of the king without a kingdom was of little concern to them. He and his Companions posed no threat now and would save the Council having to send so many of their own to guard the beautiful English princess.

Gytha hated to sleep on the hard benches. How she missed still the rug-warm bed she shared with her brothers in their home hearth Hall. her mother combing out her hair and singing to them; the sound of the wind in the elms overhanging the brook, the angry robin warning of the stalking cat, the din of wheeling gulls on the flats beyond. Here there was water too and boats aplenty, but they were not the great boats, nor was it the salt sea. This lake had no sheep-smoothed hills at its shore, or rough sailors with tales of giants and serpents to scare them. This was a dark land where even brothers were foes and a man's word counted for nothing. She shuddered, and turning onto her side, pulled her knees up to her chest. Her thoughts of what lay ahead mingled with the sound of men's voices outside. Ailsi cried out in her sleep and Gytha sought her hand to calm her. Tulpan fidgeted and scratched on the straw-covered floor.

As she lay there, Aethelflaed, Lady of the Mercians, came to her. Gytha felt awake, yet caught in a dream. The princess was wearing a red-and-blue dress. Red and blue, as the Virgin herself wore. Aethelflaed smiled. Gytha's heart leapt; she looked around and there was the harbour; her father returning from the island with her Uncle Girth, her mother – shawl loose, golden hair streaming – welcoming his homecoming with a kiss to his neck. And there were the boys, all of them – Godwine, Edmund, and the beardling Magnus too.

Each bowing low to the king, their noble father. Looking around, there were many others: leather-caped thegns of England and, with them, the greatest of all their number – Twice Scarred Eadric, the Old Thegn, his battle-axe across his shoulder like a woodsman.

Aethelflaed looked on and Gytha took her hand in her own. Then she felt the lady tighten her grip. She spoke in a low voice. 'Gytha, you will be Queen on the River and reign with wisdom and intelligence. It is your destiny.' Gytha stared deep into her eyes. Then came the sound of horses. Her father was riding away, his soldiers with him. Her mother was sobbing, but Gytha could not run to her, though she tried. She tried to call but could not. She tried to hold her arms out but could not. Of Aethelflaed, anointed Queen-daughter of King Alfred the Great, there was no sign, only the ring that was left to her.

Gytha stirred; the sound of horses and the curses of men could be heard outside wall of their cabin. Closing her eyes tightly she willed herself back to her dream. Her heart was beating as if she had been running, the lady's words repeating over and over in her head: 'it is your destiny, Gytha. It is your destiny.' Slaves were moving about now in the women's hall. Tulpan, her cape tight about her, nudged a log with her bare foot until the smoke turned first to embers, then flame. When Ailsi woke and sat up, Gytha started to tell her of the dream – how she had seen her family, and of Aethelflaed's words – but she found she could not.

She held the memory tight within her and prayed to God that in his mercy he would protect her on this the first day of her final journey to the destiny the wicked Danish queen had contrived. She shuddered at the thought of Elisaveta, and the soon-to-be Cold Trader who had snatched her and brought her to this place. Only the knowledge that Aethelflaed,

Lady of the Mercians, knew of Gytha's fate, even here, gave her the strength to carry on.

A brusque shout from outside startled the women. 'Gifts for the Lady Gytha from Prince Oleg.' Tulpan returned moments later dragging a wooden box. It was the most beautiful box Gytha had ever seen. Its lid and sides were inlaid with chequers of light and dark woods and precious stones, with swirling lines like curling worms worked in silver, and there were silver handles and a lock and key. Opening it, she gasped. The smell of scented wood wafted around her as she pulled a three-row necklace of amber and crystal beads, some green as a river god's eyes and some blood red as the tears of martyrs. Then she drew out two huge shoulder broaches of golden filigree with serpents' heads and a pair of tortoiseshell combs, before opening a linen bag. Inside, rich-stitched with golden threads, was a red and blue dress, trimmed at neck and wrist with minute golden coins. It lay, soft and heavy as a sleeping cat, in her hands, so rough against the smooth, warm material. Lastly tucked beneath was a pair of crimson slippers.

'Oh, my lady, it's beautiful!' said Ailsi, pressing the dress to her cheek. 'This cloth that shines, what is it?'

'They call it silk velors, it is made from worms,' replied Gytha.

Ailsi made a face. 'Soft worms! My lady,' running her fingers along the stitching, feeling each freshly polished coin.

Gytha thought back to the last time she had seen a dress as beautiful as this. It was Exeter in the scented Swetesot's bothie. Swetesot, her friend from the Wild Field, whom she had saved from the fire, never to see again. She pressed the warm cloth to her face, a bitter sweet memory of all she had lost since that happy day.

'Will you wear it at the feast tonight, Lady Gytha?' said Ailsi, so excited she could hardly contain herself. Bending down, Gytha drew another wrapped package from the chest. In it was a golden headdress adorned with tiny paintings, round pictures of the holy saints, as beautiful as the icons in the wooden church nearby.

'You know what this is, Tulpan, don't you?'

Tulpan's narrow eyes were round as saucers. 'Princessa,' the Qypchaq thrall woman said haltingly, 'for princess of Rus…'

'Yes, Tulpan, our princess beauty,' said Ailsi, 'has a dress, jewels and crown made for a queen.'

Gytha shook her head in disbelief, the words of Aethelflaed still sounding there. Was the prophecy true? Was this her destiny, to be a queen? But how could this Oleg, son of Prince Sviatislav, give her such treasures? She was not to be his anointed queen, nor he a king in this land.

'How can I accept this?' asked Gytha. 'Quick, run to your brother. Tell him I must speak with my brother, the Earl Godwine, and the monk. But let no one know of this lest word gets back to the prince. Have them come here, for we cannot carry the box across the yard.

A few minutes later, Godwine, the Towering Monk, Roni and Wulfwyn the Young Thegn were looking at the treasures laid out upon the bench. Even the normally talkative Roni was stunned by the beauty of the gift.

Godwine picked up the necklace. 'This would build one hundred strong sea boats,' he said.

'Yes, Lord,' said the monk. 'There is wood enough. We lack only a sea to sail them on.'

'But that is not the point, is it my lady?' said the Young Thegn, looking at Gytha. 'What should my lady do with it? It is a dowry for a queen, but this Oleg knows she is betrothed to his kinsman. What is his intention to give her such a gift as this?'

The English fell silent, shaking their heads. 'Return it,' said Godwine.

'We cannot,' said Roni. 'We have already snatched the
bed prize from the prince.' He glanced at Ailsi, who blushed
crimson and stared at the floor, her hand touching her neck
where the thrall collar had so recently sat. 'No, we cannot. I
do not understand the minds of these Rus, but I sense there
is a game afoot. And we are but the pawns.'

'Well,' said Gytha, seeing that her menfolk had no answer
either. 'There is one man in this town who will know what
to do. We have only to ask him.'

'Not Oleg?' said the monk in surprise.

'No, dear Father. Not Oleg, but Khristofor, the Posadnik
of the New Town. It is he who will decide.'

And so, word was sent to the Veche Counsel that the
English would have the Posadnik come at his convenience
on a matter of importance. After their courtesies, the box
was produced and the contents laid out on the carpet in the
English hall and they waited for the Posadnik to speak. The
man stroked his beard, and sucked in his lips. Then, with a
snort, he laughed contemptuously.

'Prince Godwine, Princess Gytha, there is much that I
know, and to tell you all that I know would take the summer
and half the winter to recount. But this much I can tell you.
Yes, it is a gift for a queen,' said the Posadnik. 'And with it
our prince Oleg makes mischief.' The companions waited
in respectful silence, sensing that that to heed the Posadnik
might benefit them. Even the normally contemptuous Roni,
whose hatred of these Rus was growing daily, said nothing. 'All
brothers are rivals,' Khristofor said, staring at the fire. 'It is the
law of Yaroslav that the crown journey not from father to son
but brother to brother. Thus, blood flows wide as the Dnieper,
when brother takes from brother that which each claims
to be his. To see is to covet, and the Lord's Commandment
is snapped as twigs in a broom. That which is Vladimir's,

Prince Oleg now desires. It has always been so among the Princes of the River.'

The Towering Mace Monk spoke up. 'Since Cain slew Abel … you are right, Posadnik. And this prince, denied the maiden Ailsi, seeks the bigger prize. The avarice of princes knows no frontier or consequence.' There was a rumble of nods from the Companions around him.

'Say you, Posadnik, that Prince Oleg, son of Sviatislav, would he take the Princess Gytha to be his wife?' asked Godwine, his concern apparent. 'Are we to be ambushed once more on this road to the Red Fort at the end of the earth?'

'No, Lord,' said the Posadnik with a dry laugh, shaking his head. 'The Prince Oleg, as I say, makes only mischief. He is young. You can rest, for soon he leaves the New Town to seek tribute from the east, his hearthguard with him. He will not return till the first flakes halt the summer raiding. Your sister is safe.'

'But there is a feast tonight and it is his wish that the Lady Gytha wears the clothing of a Rus queen,' said the Young Thegn.

'Forgive me, Thegn,' said the Posadnik courteously, 'but the Lady has nothing else to wear – only rags for her back. If she is as other women, she will welcome such a costume for the feast.' The Companions laughed at the Posadnik's remark, though none had seen their wives and daughters for longer than they could remember.

'Posadnik,' said Godwine seriously, 'the Lady Gytha is betrothed. She cannot be in a queen's raiment, even for a feast.'

'My lord, the prince plays with you. Humour him. He is young and headstrong and will quickly tire of this. His thoughts are not of queens, but bounty, coition and warfare.'

'Very well,' said Godwine. 'Gytha shall wear the clothes he has given her. 'And the golden crown hood of holy saints?' he added. The Posadnik, Khristofor, nodded.

'Posadnik,' said the Towering Blaecman, 'we thank you for your wise counsel. I sense you are not merely a builder of these wooden houses in the New Town.'

'No, Father, I am no carpenter!' said the Posadnik. 'I was raised in the court of the Great Prince Yaroslav the Wise, in Kiev.'

'I guessed so.'

'You are not the first English I have known. Edward, the exiled prince came to Kiev when I was a child, as you come now. He married the princess Agatha. They had two children, Edgar and Margaret, with whom I played. They lived among us till bishops of your land begged Edward to return to claim his crown. But another seized it.'

Gytha watched her brother intensely. The Posadnik went on. 'You should know also that one Harald – Hardradr as he was known – sought sanctuary in Kiev and, as chieftain of men, a mighty warrior, was charged by the Great Prince with the defence of the Rus lands. He too took a wife from the court – Elisaveta, sister to Agatha. He loved her and she him. I have his poems.' Gytha looked from Khristofor to her brother. The pair seemed to be locked in some game of sorts. Then the Posadnik continued, 'He too was a King who lost his crown and his head in your country, Earl Godwine. And the Danish King Sweyn Estrithson took Elisaveta for his own. But forgive me, Earl Godwine, all this you know.'

'You play with me, Posadnik,' said Godwine. 'As the vain and boastful Prince Oleg plays with us – like the cat with a mouse.'

'No, Earl Godwine, I tell you only that your father's fame proceeds you and that Prince Vladimir, whom we know as Lone Warrior, will prize the maid his aunt Elisaveta has chosen for him. The daughter of a true King.'

'Or punish our Lady Gytha each day for being the daughter of the greatest king all English folk have known.'

Roni was now on his feet. 'King Harold of England did not seize the crown from the Aethling Edmund, but was given it by the gathering of leather-caped thegns, by the Folkmoot.' Outraged, he was almost shouting at Khristofor, his face red as a beet. 'Nor would he have killed the thief Hardradr had the Norse king not tried to steal the land rightfully belonging to my Earl Godwine's father! I served him, Posadnik. The most lovable and the most merciful of all kings... he was civil to his relatives, generous to the poor, merciful to pilgrims and orphans and widows – a defender of the weak. The mildest and most clement of kings, he did injury to none, save when insulted, and was open-handed to all. Terrible in war, yes... but in peace, beloved. He died protecting what was his by right at the hands of the Bastard William of Normandy.'

'Calm yourself,' Blaecman told the shaking Roni. 'The Posadnik told us true. We do not come to this land as humble travellers, but proud as the exile Edward came before us. And one day, God willing, we too shall return to our Land where the seed of Harold of England will once more be kings. Now let us pray.'

Reluctantly, the Companions of the Golden Dragon of Wessex – who had been stirred to indignance by Roni's words – sank to their knees, crossing themselves as the Towering Mace Monk blessed them. The Posadnik bowed and, crossing himself many times in the manner of his people, left the Hall of the English.

They sat on carpets and matting, thrall slaves bringing food on boards and ale in earthen jars. A skald minstrel picked his way among them, singing nonsense and shouting riddles. The crowd, bellowing the answers, were laughing.

'I go into the bath black and come out red. Who am I?' the minstrel called to the throng of drunken men, their voices slurred by ale, shouted out each other's names to huge amusement. Until the minstrel called out, 'It's a Crayfish! A Crayfish!' but none listened.

The Companions grumbled, shrugging and cursing at the revelry around them, none of which they could understand. Gytha, still unused to sitting on the ground, sat silently with the women, apart from the menfolk. Her beauty was set like a jewel in her new clothes, but it gave her no pleasure. Nor did Prince Oleg, who was drinking and laughing with his closest warriors, appear to notice it.

'Why give the gift of clothes and now ignore me?' Gytha wondered in a whisper to Ailsi, who shrugged her shoulders. Only Pig-boy could not take his eyes off his lady; he was staring, slack mouthed in wonder from the side of the hall. Uncomfortable in her headdress, Gytha smiled at him. Pig-boy's embarrassment was plain, and Ailsi giggled. Gytha looked about her at the new hall. From floor to ceiling swirls and flowers covered the walls in brilliant colours, still yet to be dulled by smoke from the hearth. It was lit by a hundred lanterns that made the painted room dance. It was magnificent, so different from the English halls or the great Boat Halls of the Dane King, with their shields and weapons hung alongside great tapestries. But something about it disturbed her, and try as she might, she could not remember why. It was as if this was all familiar to her, as if she knew about these halls, where not one plank nor board was left unpainted and princes who made sport of guests.

Then Prince Oleg, favourite son of Sviatislav, the Grand Prince in Kiev, stood and shouted in the Dane tongue that he would hear an English riddle. The crowded hall echoed their encouragement.

'So,' said the Towering Monk, 'you have your challenge, Lord. What would you have in answer? These folk will not understand, so give them one we learned at Exeter. Thorgood, he said beckoning the piper, 'proclaim our English Riddle with a lusty tune',

Thorgood played as Godwine rose to his feet, ale horn in his hand. He raised it to the prince and saluted him. Then he paused, and the hall fell silent, awaiting his words. He swallowed. 'Go on, speak,' said Gytha encouragingly.

'So, the king without a country is a king without even a riddle,' said Oleg, feigning boredom to the amusement of all in the hall.

'King without a riddle!' they shouted.

'Perhaps,' Oleg continued, 'Your sister, the Lady Gytha, might give us a riddle in your stead.' And then, proclaiming to the assembly, he added loudly, pointing at Gytha, 'What is a bow without a stinging arrow. A soldier's heart beats beneath the lissom breast. She who is to be wedded to my kinsman, Vladik. Can the Lone Warrior tame the jewelled princess?' Some in the hall laughed.

Godwine cleared his throat and the hall fell silent. Beside him, the Radknight whispered, 'There is none here, Lord, that speaks our tongue.'

'Just as well,' said the monk under his breath, 'that our secrets find no welcome hearth in the stranger's ears.'

'Who will translate the English of my home, that all may hear my words?' shouted Godwine.

'I, Ragnwald, speak your tongue.' The words came from a massive Norseman, tattooed and bearded, who sat beyond the fire, a squirming thrall girl in his grip. 'For I have sailed the west sea to your island and slew those who did not make me welcome.' The Companions stirred. Hands darted to weapons as they jumped to their feet. The room went still. Prince Oleg looked to see the cause of the commotion.

'No stink-shirt berserker boasts of killing English folk,' snarled Wulfwyn, wounding-knife drawn.

'Sit, Thegn boy' said the Dane, laughing loudly. 'Fear not, we were welcomed by all, wherever we travelled.'

'Get on with it!' shouted Oleg.

'Prince,' said Godwine, 'I shall speak the riddle in the English tongue, and then this Dane will render it so all here will understand it.'

He gestured to his men to sit. He called to Thorgood to play another skirl. Clearing his throat again, he began

'A curiosity hangs by the thigh of a man, under its master's cloak. Pierced through in the front; it is stiff and hard and it has a good standing-place. When the man pulls up his own robe above his knee, he means to poke with the head of his hanging thing that familiar hole of matching length which he has often filled before. What am I Prince?' The hall waited as the Dane, Ragnwald, translated for the Rus.

'It is the manhood of Oleg Sviatoslavich!' shouted the prince, delighted, interrupting Ragnwald even before he had stopped speaking. 'A curiosity hangs by the thigh of a man, under its master's cloak. It is pierced through in the front; it is stiff and hard and it has a good standing-place. It is mine, mine is a curiosity, When I pull up my robe girls cannot wait to poke it!' Turning to his companions, the drunk prince guffawed at his brilliance. 'So, King of Riddles – that is what I name you, King of Riddles – you do me great honour.' He raised his mead cup. 'Come drink, drink to the King of Riddles!'

Under his breath, Wulfwyn muttered, 'puffed up princeling! Who is not a prince by birth but wears a crown?'

'A crowing rooster,' said Gytha.

And so, the English and the men of the New Town continued in their revelry as the evening turned to night. Embers glowed brightly in the roasting pits.

Khristofor appeared, bowed deeply to Gytha, then sat himself down cross-legged on the carpet at Godwine's request.

The others moved aside. He looked at the English.

'Tell me, King of Riddles,' he said, the hint of a smile at the corners of his bearded mouth. 'a riddle about the Prince's manhood? Godwine smiled as a man does when he outsmarts another. 'Yes, wise-thinking Posadnik, he said.

'Come now, Earl, I think not' When the man pulls up his own robe above his knee, he means to poke with the head of his hanging thing that familiar hole of matching length which he has often filled before?

'I guess,' said the Posadnik Khristofor, his tone measured, 'that you speak not of the prince's manhood but a humble key as might hang from any man's belt. Am I right?' Godwine nodded blearily. Gytha, The Priest, Roni the Dane and Wulfwyn looked on laughing. 'And you let the vain prince believe you spoke of his manhood.'

'Yes,' said Godwine, laughing for the first time since any could remember. 'I thought it prudent. For all his vanity, he has the ear of Prince Vladimir, to whom my vow-sister Gytha is betrothed. Who knows what fate awaits her in the Red Fort on the River? It is for her I threw a tasty morsel for the prince to chew. It seemed wise after we deprived him of our sister Ailsi in his bed.'

The Posadnik Khristofor leaned forward and thumped Godwine across the shoulder with the flat of his hand. 'You have my admiration, King of Riddles. You have flattered our prince and avenged your humiliation. The beautiful Princess Gytha is fortunate to have you for her champion. Tomorrow we make ready for the Wolf road to Smolensk, I will escort you and your sister and your Hearthguard Companions and ensure your safety.'

Across from the square, chained and shackled, the Cold Trader sat in a dank stone cell beneath the fortress wall, listening to the merriment. In his hand he held a vellum snatched in haste from his forfeit wares. Carefully, so the guard would not see, he rolled it tight into its oilcloth and thrust it for safe-keeping up his arse, until all had disappeared but the royal seal.

PART TWO CHAPTER FIVE

PIG-BOY'S DOWRY

THE NIGHT AIR WAS filled with the sweet scent of pine resin. The fire was uneasily bright; it crackled and spluttered, its smoke freeing them from the whine and bite of wicked flies. No square of uncovered skin was safe from their attack, the darkness providing a fleeting relief before the dawn sun meant a fresh assault. It made Gytha think of one of the minstrel's riddles at the feast – 'You barely see me but can hear my song. Who am I?' – but had no pleasure from the answer. Gytha and Ailsi suffered the most. Nothing, it seemed, would stop the biting till their faces were swollen and bleeding.

'This Prince Vladimir will lock you both in a nunnery when he sees you,' Edmund had said, having no sympathy, 'where even Pig-boy and Wulfwyn will never find you.'

'Do not mock us, for if the wind changes, your prophesy could come true and we will forever look as lepers,' said Ailsi.

'Nonsense! your head is filled with pagan talk.'

'Hell is not the fiery furnace,' said Ailsi gravely, 'but a forest – this one – and these flies are the devil's own.'

It was Tulpan, not God, who saved them, her secret, wormwood leaves and yellow marigolds that flowered in the marsh. Taking handfuls, she squeezed out the absinth juice, mixing it with precious qumiz milk over the fire. Each day, before the Companions set off, the thrall woman – half warrior, half mother – would wipe the sour liquid on their faces, to the amusement of the Posadnik's soldiers and Ragnwald, the tattooed Norseman who had joined them on their way to Smolensk. His presence was an annoyance to the Companions, but the black flies troubled them no more.

Yet there was a beauty to this warm, wooded land that had been their home for two gruelling weeks, as they dragged and heaved the boats down the log roads between the shallow rivers that flowed deceitfully through the swamps and the bottomless meres where a drowning man's cries went unheard except by countless croaking frogs. Bear, bison and elk grazed quietly on the lush grass or kept their distance. Even wolves were nowhere to be seen, and this time no Wendish ambush struck, with the Posadnik's men and the Companions of the Golden Dragon of Wessex to guard Gytha.

Occasionally they passed ragged peasant-men in straw shoes, toiling in the marsh meadows, scything the first hay, the women and children stacking it to dry, on the wooden pickets that hid their hovels. They looked fearful as the company passed. In this dangerous land where Qypchaq horsemen from the Wild Field, river pirate, and local lords in search of tribute would burst upon a settlement in the dawn, seizing the girls, killing the men, driving off the horses, stealing the only milk-cow or pig leaving smoking embers and the wailing of those not quick enough to slide beneath the black water of the marsh, breathing through hollow reeds until the raiders left.

But it was a plentiful land too, rich in fish and game. Godwine would take a hunting party into the forest to return with a boar or deer to feed them all. For they were sick of the rough oat gruel the Wend people called kasha, the boiled roots, and most of all the dried sprats that tasted of salted leather.

Once the Companions brought back a lynx, so fearsome that even in its death throes it ripped at Edmund's throat with claws that, but for his ring-shirt, it would have killed him. He kept that pelt as a reminder that death lurks clad in the softest fur.

The rowers cautiously eased the boats through the marsh rivers, hacking at undergrowth that blocked their way and often grounding their craft on muddy banks. Finally, they reached the last sluggard stream before the mighty Dnieper, home river of the Rus. Now the Companions could rest on their oars and let the listless Swinets carry them south.

'Go on,' said Ailsi as they gathered around the fire on the last evening of their journey to the River. 'Ask him.'

So Gytha asked the Posadnik Khristofor the one question that had been on her mind every minute.

'Posadnik Khristofor,' Gytha's wide blue eyes bored into his. He had no option but to answer. 'Prince Vladimir, whom you call the Lone Warrior to whom I am betrothed, what sort of man is he?

'Princess Gytha,' he said unfazed, honouring her high birth with a bow. 'I have long waited for you to ask. I have known Prince Vladimir from when he was a child. He is handsome, brave, kindly, just and schooled in the scriptures.'

'Is he as vain and boastful as Prince Oleg? Who spits men's lives as fish bones into the fire?'

'No, my lady. Prince Vladimir eases the burden of debt and servitude on the poor, gives to the orphan, protects the widow and permits the mighty to destroy no man.'

Gytha was relieved. A weight had been lifted from her shoulders, for now she remembered where she had heard of Prince Oleg. It was one evening in Exeter, in the simple bothy of the scented Swetesot. It was she who told how Prince Oleg had taken her virginity by force and fathered her child Boniak. Gytha paused, her heart filled with anger at the hurt he had brought on her friend, but kept her counsel. No good would come of mentioning Swetesot's shame and banishment from the palace at Kiev, when one day it might be her home.

'And does this Lone Warrior speak the Dane tongue as you do, Posadnik Khristofor?' she asked.

'Yes, Princess. Better than I. All the sons of Rurik, to whom the legend says this land was given, speak the Dane tongue. His father had him learn the five tongues.'

'Five tongues,' said Gytha wonderingly. 'I speak three if you count the words of the Celt folk I learnt at Exeter.' She thrust the memory of that quickly from her head.

'Princess, he speaks the Greek tongue of his mother Ana-stasia, to the purple-born daughter of the Christian Emperor Constantine Monomakhos.'

'His mother is an imperial princess, the daughter of the Christian Emperor in Constantinople?' Gytha gasped as she took this in,

The Posadnik went on. 'He is fair-faced, a mighty warrior and hunter.'

'But why do you call him Lone Warrior?' asked Ailsi.

The Posadnik smiled. 'In Vladimir, God has compounded imperial and princely blood. It is the name by which the Emperor, his grandfather was known, it means a man who fights alone. But...' he paused.

'But? Posadnik?' asked Gytha,

'But nothing, Princess,' he replied. 'I fear only that you will hold your disappointment against me when he is not, in your eyes, as I describe him. For what do I know of what pleases a lady? I know only of the qualities we men hold high, and he has those aplenty. I should best say no more and let you reach your own opinion.'

Gytha felt no comfort in his words. A mighty warrior who could read the scriptures, the grandson of the great Christian Emperor himself – what would he want with her? Daughter of a king, but now a tattered beggarwoman.

'I cannot meet him so,' she told Godwine that night in the camp. 'He will think me no better than the rudest grinding-slave.'

'Yes sister, he will think us all beggars – that much the Posadnik's spies will have told him. Two of his men left at dawn. Where else would they have gone but to Smolensk? We shall stop at a place they call Gnyozdovo, a trading post near to the red fortress at Smolensk. There, the Posadnik tells me, we will find rest and a banya to wash away the dirt of the journey. There, we can buy horses for the procession to meet your prince.'

And so, alder and the white-birch yielded to scented pine glades, alive with insects' hum. Low mounds lined the bank, hundred upon hundred, the home of warriors long passed. And beyond, overlooking a bend in the Dnieper, was the little fort and trading post with its crescent harbour. Here in the safety of stronghold walls they could eat and sleep at last without fear of attack, while the Posadnik went on to the Red Fort to prepare for their arrival. 'Await my return,' he had said.

Gnyozdovo, like Ladoga to the north, was a Danish outpost. Gytha was struck by the smell of resin. It was everywhere, for here men heated pine tar to smear their boats for the long journey; beyond the countless bends, beyond Kiev, beyond the rapids, the fearsome horsemen of the Wild Field, to the domes and cool tiled palaces of Constantinople.

Here were cabins filled with goods from the sun lands, spices and cloth, jewels and finely worked artefacts bartered for the riches of the Northlands: for slaves, honey, amber and furs.

Here too were warriors for hire: seasoned hearthguards of the prince at Kiev; others, who had fought Arabs and Persians in the Holy Land.

Summoning smiths and leatherworkers, Godwine gave orders that all the Companions should have their ring-mail shirts polished, the leather repaired, their weapons sharpened, and their ripped and tattered clothing, worn since leaving the hall of the Dane King, patched and mended. 'Replace them,' he announced, 'for when we escort the Lady Gytha to the Red Fort none must see a stained and weary rabble united only as men are when hardship and adversity is their ruler. Nor must they know we are without a home, without a land to call our own, without status or title except that which we know ourselves to be. Let us take pride in all we still possess, our weapons, the coffers and crates that remain of the Godwineson Hoard, and our faith in the Lord of Hosts.'

There were cheers from the hearthguard, the loudest from the most noble – the axed and burnished Roni, the fresh cheeked Radknight Wulfwyn, the Towering Blaecman, even the quiet and thoughtful Edmund. Thorgood the Piper played a merry jig.

Gytha, her problems more immediate, aided by Ailsi and Tulpan, ripped off the lice-ridden clothes for the washers to soak and beat and rinse in the Dnieper water, where the bubbled scum floated grey downstream. Next, she had them heat water for the wooden bathhouse and when it was ready, she ducked under the low lintel to tallow-scrub her body and comb the nits from her golden hair. Soon the hut was filled with laughter, and muffled shrieks as Tulpan, pouring water on the coals, beat Gytha and Ailsi with leafy birch twigs, turning their white skins pink.

*   *   *

'We can sell our services to Prince Vladimir, for who would not have English warriors at his side?' said Wulfwyn, to the approval of all that sat about hearth fire.

'A toast!' shouted Roni. 'To the Companions of the Golden Dragon of Wessex!'

'The Companions!' they shouted back.

Godwine held up his hand. 'Drink, my brothers, for we have travelled far and met many dangers. Now we see an end to our journey, but would you sell your service cheap to the first bidder? Let us not be hasty. Why serve a river prince when downstream,' he pointed a finger southward, 'lies Constantinople where the Christian emperor rules? It is to him we should go to win the tribute owing to us, not pick through scraps from these forests. You saw their half-buried homesteads. There is nothing here for us. I say we take my vow sister to the prince and then we continue south.'

Gytha could not believe what she was hearing. 'My lord, my brothers would abandon me here in this strange land? What of our vow, sworn on the Flinty Cross at Waltham, you, Edmund, Magnus and I together? That vow has sustained me through terrible adversity when all men were turned against us. In the name of our father, King Harold, whose title you now carry, you would snap it like a twig!'

'The pledge, sister, was to avenge our father, not to comfort you.'

The blood drained from Gytha's face; 'Godwine, my Lord,' she replied, 'it is the mead that speaks so cruelly, banishing me from your heart. Your words wound me gravely. I have asked nothing of you – least of all to comfort me when I am most wretched and sorrowful. We have lived five winters in the paths of exile bereft of friendly kinsmen– I was but a flat-chest girl and you a beardless youth when we left Waltham, and now you would lead the Companions beyond even the Wild Field.

Here, your vow sister is betrothed to the prince – here I can comfort and protect you Godwine, not you me.'

She glared at Godwine, her back rod-straight, nostrils flaring, and he stared back at her drunkenly.

The silence in the hut grew unbearable as the companions watched. Finally, the Towering Mace Monk Blaecman roared, striking his palm on his thigh, 'Yes, young Godwine, the brine-blood of your grandmother flows thick and strong in your sister. She has a point, aye, she does. Would you take the Companions on the road again, where here you have a haven for your men? They are without comfort, without women. Stay here a while. This Vladimir builds a great stone church to welcome all Christian souls. There is trade here aplenty with which to fill our coffers.'

'Trade,' shouted Godwine, 'You would have us be traders, father? We have had our fill of traders and their kind.'

Undeterred, the old monk went on. 'Lord what do we know of the great city Constantinople? Rumours and fantastical ravings; heathen mead-talk of a city of golden vaults? I too have heard there is a church so big, all the people on earth fit within the nave, and so high that the vault reaches to heaven itself, from where God and the company of holy saints and angels gaze down at the sinners beneath.' He crossed himself, then continued. 'It is blasphemy. The devil himself speaks.' He crossed himself again. 'He would tempt you and lure you from here, not to Constantinople but to extinction in the furnace!'

The Companions shifted awkwardly on their benches as they listened to the monk. They knew Godwine would not dare rebuke their towering confessor, friend of his grandmother, the Mother of Heroes, whose counsel and ministry had sustained them in their darkest hours. They loved this old warrior-monk, for whom the terrible journey had hastened the end of days. He could no longer lift the mace that had been his, he no longer struck fear into the hearts of sinners, but his love for Harold's children and all the Company of English souls shone bright.

Gytha tendered to his beaker. 'You are tired, dear Father. Rest a little, for I will have need of my champion again, I fear.' She smiled and the monk placed his hands on Gytha's brow.

'Yes, I am tired, child,' he said, half to himself. 'He lays me down in green pastures, he leads me beside still waters where I might be a fisherman until the Lord Jesus Christ calls me.'

Gytha glanced at Godwine, outraged. He hesitated, about to say something more, but then thought better of it.

'Very well, good father,' he said, taking the old man's veined hand in his. 'We shall remain here among the Rus in their Red Fortress on the river.'

The first they heard was the cry 'It's gone!' In a moment, all was uproar. 'Thorgood is dead! The Hoard is gone. The Piper is dead!' Gytha, roused from her bed, ran into the hall. There, his throat cut ear to ear, lay Thorgood, and where the great boxes had been stacked against the wall was a hole. It took a moment for the calamity to sink in. For without the Hoard, the shilling-coins, the silver and the holy ornaments they had carried from Exeter, they were lost.

Godwine was giving orders. 'They cannot be far!' he yelled. 'They must be in the village. The gate is shut.' The Companions, still half asleep, were buckling their ring-shirts and swords, seizing thrusting spears and shield boards. All streamed from the hall, shouting so loudly, every dog around was howling

'What would you do?' the Radknight called to Roni. 'They cannot get out till the gate is opened. The boxes are heavy, they must still be in the fort.'

'Unless there is another way out,' shouted the Burnished Huscarl. Then he and Wulfwyn circled back to the wall that faced away from the river. Here, among the mean huts of carpenters, bootmakers and smiths, they stopped in the moonlight.

'This must be where they've buried it, but where?' said Roni, the light of the torch shining on his ringed war-shirt, his newly sharp sword glistening in his hand.

'They'd have to have dug a hole before the raid.'

'Or maybe not,' said the Huscarl. 'Maybe the thieves are in their cabins and our silver in their beds.'

'But we cannot search each hut. Every man would turn against us and defend what is his.' They hesitated. 'Look Roni, look!'

Behind them in the shadows there was movement. 'Who's there?' called Roni.

'Ragnwald,' came the deep-voiced reply, and the painted berserker, naked but for the bear pelt cape, stepped into the moonlight.

Roni and Wulfwyn ran towards him. Ragnwald stood facing them. In his right hand, he held the blooded war axe, in his left he swung an iron-bound coffer.

'You!' yelled the Young Thegn. 'You stole the hoard!' Others joined them, until the Dane was surrounded by a dozen men, swords and lances pointed to his heart. Ragnwald gave a blood-cold howl. The berserker's howl. Nor did he stop. He bayed as a demon eager to loose the skull-splinter axe above his head. Froth and drool spewed from his mouth, the fiend-fire from his eyes. The howling grew louder and louder. More English came rushing. For they knew well of the berserker frenzy that had sent the hearts of countless English to their graves. Others saw not a man but a mighty bear. All feared the crazed warrior whom no edge could cut nor fire harm. Only the Burnished

Roni was unmoved by Odin's warrior. Calling on God and the Lord Jesus Christ, he seized a flaming torch and ran at him, thrusting the searing tallow into Ragnwald's face. The hoard-chest fell to the ground and the Dane crumpled on top of it.

'kill him!' shouted Wulfwyn, as ten leapt onto the massive man. Picking up the still-burning torch, he thrust it into the Dane's face again. Ragnwald let out a scream.

'Throw him over the earth wall. The hoard must be there,' replied Wulfwyn. 'I'll take more men and search.'

It proved to be fruitless. They returned to the spot as daylight broke, but found no trace of the precious Hoard amongst the huts and stores.

Word spread quickly that the English Hoard was stolen. Losing the last of his worldly wealth reduced Godwine to the embers of himself. He was a shadow. No worse disaster could befall him. For Gytha the loss of her dowry spelt an end to all hope of princely marriage. From being the richest of all England, they were beggars in a far-off land.

'Does Prince Vladimir know, Posadnik?' Gytha asked when the mayor returned from Smolensk.

'Maybe he knows, maybe not. He has bigger problems – a territory to protect. The horsemen from the Wild Field attack our villages and seize our people, and he must defend them.'

'How long will he be gone? Must we sit here and wait?'

'Princess, the days are long and the nights are short. Prince Vladimir knows only his duty before God to tend to the people of this land who pay him tribute and look to him in their time of need. He will return when the last horseman flees back to the Wild Field to warn any others that to enter the land of Rus spells certain death for all who would be foolish enough to try. You must wait.'

'Can we not ride with him?' Godwine asked. 'For my men are restless, and without money they fear the winter starvation. If we could fight, we too could receive tribute and by our swords change the bad fortune that besets us. Forgive me, Posadnik, that I speak plainly to you, but I fear for their future and my sister's.'

The Posadnik turned to Godwine. 'Lord, I have come to know you and the ways of the English these last weeks, and nobody doubts your fame-deeds or your faith. You are truly a king's son. You have risen to every challenge and adversity, even on this day, but hot battle or bloody skirmish with the enemies of Smolensk and Prince Vladimir would be but temporary relief. You may have lost your country and now your hoard is gone but you still have the Lady Gytha. Word of her beauty, piety, grace and courage had reached Smolensk before I arrived at the city, and many ask if it is true. Think not as brigand but as escort to a royal princess. In her destiny lies yours.'

Godwine scoffed. 'You speak of fate, beauty and piety. What use are they when all else is lost? The scripture says from the one who has not, even what he has will be taken away.'

'No, lord,' said the Posadnik. 'The parable of the talents holds another message for you. Be not the wicked slothful servant, but the good and faithful servant to whom five talents was given and make five talents more. Yes, Earl Godwine, for if you succeed, the Master will say, "Well done, good and faithful servant. You have been faithful over a little. I will set you over much. Enter into the joy of your Master."'

Godwine looked at the older man. 'Posadnik,' he said, shaking his head from side to side. 'I know you to be a good man and hang on the words of our Lord Jesus Christ, but without a dowry what hope can the Lady Gytha bring to us?'

'Trust in the Lord,' said the Posadnik.

'Come, brother, let us pray together. For who knows what tomorrow might bring.' Godwine snorted and reluctantly dropped to his knees.

That night as they gathered to eat, Gytha asked Godwine if the betrothal parchment with the seal of the Dane King had been with the hoard.

Godwine hesitated, shaking his head. 'No,' he said

'Where is it?' said Gytha, her voice low so the others should not hear.

Godwine shrugged

'You mean you don't have it?'

'No,' said Godwine, 'The Cold Trader held it, it was his to hold until he brought you to Smolensk and claimed his reward.'

'Lady Gytha,' it was the Towering Monk who called her. He was sitting, shaking slightly; his palsy growing worse daily.

Gytha crouched down next to him. 'Aye, Father, how are you?' Her tone was light but not her heart, which was in turmoil at her brother's words.

'The Lord leads me to where the alders and the willows bow to the stream, yet not a nibble did I have. Perhaps it is the tremor in this hand that greatly frightens them away.'

Gytha smiled. 'Father, you called to me to tell me of your fishing?'

'No, child.' Nobody ever called her that anymore. 'I have a message from the dumb Pig-boy who would speak to you, but only you alone.'

'Why?' Her tone was shrill. She had troubles enough. What would she do if the vellum was lost to her?

'He couldn't say why, child, but I promised to speak to you, for he has served you well.'

'I will see him, but with Ailsi and my thrall woman, Tulpan.

The priest nodded. 'After the mass tomorrow.' And so, on their return from the little church, the Companions gathered in their hall for their meal and Gytha told Ailsi to bring the foundling Pig-boy to her. The cruel tongue-cut smile marred his kindly face as he brayed and honked his wordless greeting, bowing deeply. Ailsi sniggered, but Gytha rebuked her instantly. Reaching out, she took Pig-boy's hand and pulled him gently to his feet.

'You asked to see me, Pig-boy.' The Pig-boy nodded.

Gytha waited. 'What is so important that you ask the Towering Priest to be your messenger?'

The Pig-boy hesitated. Then, as if not knowing what else to do, he pulled up his tunic, exposing his scrawny stomach and the top of his breeches. Gytha raised her brows, disconcerted. Pig-boy stood there in front of her. There was another pause.

Then the Pig-boy tugged at a thread till the stitching at his waist unravelled. Out fell a thin leather pouch shaped as a pea-pod, as long as the span of a man's hand.

Drawing her jewelled wounding-knife from her belt, Gytha sliced the threads. To her astonishment, and the amazement of Tulpan and Ailsi, out fell jewels, sapphires and rubies, twelve of them, each the size of a hazelnut.

Ailsi gasped. 'Where did you get them, Pig-boy?' she asked.

'Yes,' echoed Gytha. 'Pig-boy, where did you get them?'

Pig-boy knelt and scratched his knife tip on the earth floor. 'Mother of Heroes,' he wrote in Latin.

'My grandmother gave you these. To give to me?' Pig-boy nodded. He was smiling now. 'When we were at Bruges at the court of Baldwin?' The Pig-boy nodded again. 'And you have carried them ever since?' He nodded harder still, braying now.

'Oh, Pig-boy, I don't know what to say!' She took his hand in hers and pressed it to her heart. 'Thank you, thank you, my heart-dear friend,' she whispered, looking into Pig-boy's dirty face. They had been through so much together, the dumb urchin and her. She smiled at him and set his eyes alight with love for his mistress. She thought for a moment. 'Tell none of this, brave Pig-boy. No one, you understand, until I have spoken with my brother?'

'He is hardly likely to, is he?' said Ailsi. 'Have you any more of them? For me.'

'Ailsi! He has guarded these jewels on my grandmother's orders all this time, and now, knowing of our desperate situation, he is giving them to me,' snapped Gytha. She turned to the Pig-boy. 'I want you to take this gift from me, as I have need of these jewels now. Pig-boy, my most good and faithful servant.' Gytha handed him a sapphire as blue as her eyes. 'Tulpan, see he has everything he needs — new clothes, bedding, anything he requires — and I want him housed close by. His actions are beyond the thanks of man. The Hoard may be lost but here in this pouch lie twelve hoards. From now, Pig-boy, you are honoured.' After Pig-boy had left them, his joyful honking clear to her across the yard, Gytha gave instructions.

'Ailsi, we will send to the merchant for silk cloth. The seamstress shall make clothes for us and for my brothers. We meet the prince as equals, not beggars at his gate.'

The news of Pig-boy's gem-belt did not remain secret for long. Godwine called the Towering Monk to pray for their miraculous deliverance.

'I shall sing of Your strength.' He boomed the words of the fifty-ninth psalm.

'Yes, I shall joyfully sing of Your loving kindness in the morning, for You have been my stronghold, and a refuge in the day of my distress. O my strength, I will sing praises to You. For God is my stronghold, the God who shows me loving kindness.'

The feast that followed dulled minds and raised voices. Godwine, calling for silence, had to bang the table hard to get it. 'Friends, tonight we have much to celebrate. But it is the time for us to honour the Pig-boy, the joy of our deliverance.' Then, calling Pig-boy to stand by him, he took a Frankish longsword on a tooled leather belt that lay on the mead bench.

'Pig-boy,' he said, 'the Twice Scarred Eadric would have killed you that first day had not my vow-sister, the Lady Gytha, begged for your life. Today, like the good and faithful servant, you repay her with unweary stars plucked from the heavens.' He paused. 'Henceforth, carry this Frankish wound-fire, this jewelled scabbard, this belt and cloak – for no man is more deserving.' And with that, Godwine buckled the heavy belt and longsword around Pig-boy's slender waist. Holding Pig-boy's hand up high in his, he declared to the assembled Companions, 'Before this company of heroes, I declare your name Baldred Gembelt, a free man. Let no man forget the debt we owe you.'

The small hall erupted as the Companions banged anything they could find on the tables and cheered to the thatch. Pig-boy's eyes were wide as fish mouths, but no bray nor honk came from that cruel black gape. He stood gazing about him in wonder, a hand fingering the unfamiliar belt about his middle. Gytha stepped up to him, tied the leather thegn-cape about his shoulders and kissed his forehead.

Rumours swirled that the king without a kingdom was rich once more. The Posadnik, Khristofor, got to hear of it and came to see Godwine and Gytha at the hall.

'I am told,' he said, 'that all finest cloth is bought, seam-stresses are working through the white night, and rust dull swords gleam. Yet was your dwindled Hoard not stolen?'

Godwine wondered whether to tell the Posadnik. He glanced at his sister. 'Posadnik Khristofor, the Lord is with us.'

The Posadnik smiled. 'Aye Lady he is. He makes jewels fall from the breeches of the man who brays as a donkey.'

Gytha burst out laughing, the marriage vellum forgotten. 'Aye, good Khristofor, your ears have not deceived you. My servant, the Gembelt Pig-boy, carried treasure in his breeches for three winters on the orders of my grandmother. She knew that misfortune would befall us, as it has, and trusted him above all others.'

'Your grandmother was a witch?' 'She saw the future?'

'When all that she had was lost and all her sons killed but one who lingers as a captive of the Bastard William – in Gytha she saw our hope.' said Godwine.

'Yes, it is that I wish to speak of. Prince Vladimir has returned to Smolensk with tribute and slaves, and will come here, for he has heard much of the Lady Gytha and would see her for himself.'

The blood ran from Gytha's face – no terror they had faced was half what she felt now. So, at last, she would meet the man to whom she was betrothed. What would he be like, this man they called the Lone Warrior? As Prince Oleg – vain and heartless? Or like her father? There was no man in her heart fairer, or more gallant than Harold. 'Oh,' she thought, 'let him be like my father, the finest man God placed upon this earth!' She bit her lip and coughed to sniff away a tear as she remembered him, and her mother too. Nobody must see her distress. She must be strong for all the English Company. Their future was now in her hands. If the Lone Warrior, Vladimir, favoured her, she would ensure favour for Godwine, Edmund and all the Companions. And if he did not, then she and they were lost. Her heart drummed in her chest. It was all she could do not to run from the hall. What if she should fail, if she did not please him? She was no fresh-face maiden, soft from prayer and needlework, with silken skin and lips of summer fruit, but travel-worn from a distant land, the hard journey scored on her heart and in her face. Her mother's golden hair, the blue eyes of her father-kin were as ever, but she glanced at her calloused hands and thought them the hands of a thrall, not a princess.

'How long till he gets here?' Godwine was saying, but the Posadnik did not know.

'Maybe tomorrow, maybe not,' he answered. 'The prince and his hearthguard will feast to celebrate their victories and there are matters to take care of.'

'It does not leave us much time to make a fitting welcome,' said Godwine. 'We have nought but good fellowship and a beautiful bride. How many will come? We must prepare the betrothal feast.'

Again, the Posadnik had no answer. 'Perhaps he will come alone, or with all his hearthguard. We have a saying, "he who searches for his beloved is not afraid of the world". The young prince will do as he pleases, when he pleases.'

Gytha saw a moment of anger cross Godwine's face – or was its fear? He too, must wonder what the future held for him. The meeting with Vladimir would mark a beginning or an end to both their lives.

With no time to lose, Godwine gave orders to the Companions. Wulfwyn he sent into the forest to hunt; others were to seize or purchase provisions: mead for the English, with wine and samagon for the Rus. Roni oversaw that a hall was cleared of wares, and tables and benches laid out in the English style, with shields and weapons fixed on the walls, and a throne chair for Godwine with another where Gytha might sit to his side. Gytha, with the help of Ailsi and Tulpan, washed in the lashing bath-house and laid out her only dress, the one that Prince Oleg had given her. She had not wanted it then, but now she thanked him for it – for she had no other that matched its beauty, nor had she anything other than his gift of the golden bonnet for her head.

'Maybe it is better to look as they do,' she said to Ailsi as she arranged the outfit upon her bed.'

Ailsi laughed. 'Yes, for if we look as we do, they will think us washer-women and hand us their sweated clothes to clean in the river.' Nobody, thought Gytha, would think Ailsi a washer-woman for, despite the torment of her captivity, the youthful bloom was still about her. Gytha kept the thought to herself, though a sadness weighed over her at her lost youth, snatched from her by the Bastard William and never to be regained.

Sensing her anguish, as a father senses it in his own child, the old monk asked that Gytha might pray with him that evening before the Companions ate. Taking his precious Testament from its battered leather pouch, he unrolled it at St Paul's Letter to the Romans. 'Read for me, child, my eyes fail me.'

So Gytha read, 'The Apostle tells us our journeys are made prosperous or otherwise according to the will of God. We should readily impart to others what God has trusted to us, rejoicing to make others joyful, especially taking pleasure in communing with those who believe the same things as us.'

'Oh, kindly Father, friend and comfort,' Gytha said. 'Each day, I beseech the Lord to deliver all of us safely. There can be no turning back, but this night the Lord says I must step bravely, but he does not tell me what might befall me. My faith sustains me, but a girl's heart beats in my chest and I find no courage there.'

The old monk raised her chin in the cup of his hand, so she would look at him. 'Gytha Haroldsdaughter,' he said, 'a hundred warriors beat in your heart. Jesus Christ said, "My peace I give to you – not as the world gives, do I give to you. Let not your heart be troubled. In the world you have tribulation, but take courage. I have overcome the world.

This Vladimir too is Christian. Though his rights are not ours, God the Creator is his God too.' He looked into her eyes with a deep love and understanding. 'Gytha, long to see him. Impart your spiritual gift, be mutually encouraged by each other's faith. Now pray with me.' And together they prayed until the shouts summoning them both to eat became too insistent to resist.

Gytha's fears were swept aside by wild excitement. The Hoard was found in a drain under the wall, near where they had seized the berserker. 'And now he lies dead beyond the wall.' Said Gytha, happily.

'No, my Lady,' said Roni. 'His body is gone.'

'Halfdead perhaps, My Grandmother, the Mother of Heroes, talked of Berserkers. He can change himself to a wolf, a wild boar or bear,' replied Gytha.

'Nonsense, my Lady. We have nothing to fear from the halfdead,' said the Young Thegn with a shrug. 'I will not be frightened by heathen Dane legends. The Hoard is ours and God's grace shines on us. Tomorrow the prince comes and our mission will be complete.'

All was ready from Sunrise as they waited for word of the prince's arrival with gifts of bread and precious salt. In the dress Prince Oleg had given her, Gytha was a Rus princess, her golden hair peaking from beneath a veil, the long gold pendants hanging from her jewelled bonnet like golden plaits, a drop of scented oil in each. She was wearing cream and palest lime dress, so richly appliquéd she feared she must melt in the heat of that summer day, and the heavy necklace of the Holy Saints around her shoulders.

'When he comes,' said Godwine, the coronet forming a line about his brow, 'stay in your chamber until I call for you.'

'I will not, I shall greet him in the way of our people, not theirs. He shall see me as I am, the daughter of a great king, an English king and Ring-Giver.' Her eyes flashed proudly. 'if he thinks me a harem bride, he will be disappointed. We are warriors as he, and that is how he must see me too.'

Godwine was about to speak when the shout went up that that boats were approaching the small harbour below the settlement. He looked at his vow-sister and the Companions of the Golden Dragon of Wessex in their new clothes – helms, ring-shirts, axes, swords and thrusting spears gleaming, war shields newly painted – and he nodded.

'Come, Gytha, we will greet him together.' And with his jaw firm, he strode out to meet Prince Vladimir Monomakh.

'Wait, brother.' She turned to Ailsi. 'my wounding dagger?' Ailsi looked surprised. Gytha tied the dagger across her slim waist in the English style.

'Now,' she said, feigning laughter to hide her nerves, 'now I am dressed to welcome any prince.' The men cheered, striking axe and sword on the heavy shields, and the Company marched through the gate to the harbour beyond.

Coming towards them, eight men at the oars, was a sturdy river boat with a high dragon prow. Two slim young men stood amidships unhelmed, in the finest clothes, each matching the other but reversed. One had a red cape and black tunic, the other a black cape and red tunic. Both had red boots. Their arms were folded across their chests, and both bore crescent scimitars, golden jewelled, at their sides.

One they recognised, the vain and boastful Prince Oleg. Ailsi gave a gasp and edged closer behind Gytha. But Gytha's eyes were on Vladimir. She had never seen so fine a man.

He was taller than his cousin, with broader shoulders. Where Oleg had long fair hair and narrow mean face, Vladimir's was noble and haughty, his head was smooth-shaved

but for a fine moustache and a single side knot of hair. A ruby
and two pearls, set in gold, hung from one ear. His eyes were
brown, his features regular, the gift of his mother Anastasia,
daughter of the Christian Emperor in the East.

''The prince shaves his head.' said the Posadnik, sensing
Gytha's astonishment.

'Those who killed the father I hold dearer than any man,
shaved their heads. Give me the girl-hair of the English.'
she added.

The Posadnik glanced at her and held his counsel.

The boat was quickly roped to the pier head. The
Companions waited on the shore as Vladimir's hearthguard
in pointed face helms jumped onto the weathered boards,
followed lithely by the two princes and a black-hat priest.
Godwine stepped forward and nodded his head in greeting,
waiting for the shaven prince to do likewise – but he did not.
Gytha held out the bread and salt, offering it to him.

Instead of acknowledging the coroneted Godwine and his
sister Gytha, the prince addressed the whole throng. 'Brothers,'
he bellowed, in the language of the Danefolk, 'I come to
welcome you to the comforts and safety of the Red Fort at
Smolensk, where you and your Hoard will be safe from bandits
and berserkers.'

Gytha looked at the prince. There was cruelty and humour in his brown eyes, straight nose and firm chin. But, she
thought, this was no savage. There was something about the
depth and timbre of his voice and the measure of his Dane
speech that told her he was schooled. She glanced at Ailsi, who
returned her look, wide-eyed in amazement. Prince Vladimir,
the Lone Warrior, Duke of Smolensk, was handsome.

The air was thick with the heady smell of scented oil in
her pendants and the pitch used to caulk the boats. She took
a large breath. Perhaps it was the morning heat and her heavy

golden bonnet pressing on her brow, or the witching song of frogs in the meadows. She felt her heart thump within her breast and the roaring of the grey-green sea in her ears. She hurriedly tried to take another breath, as her legs gave way beneath her.

The prince paused as Gytha, the eldest daughter of Harold, King of the English, slid limp to the ground. Then, continuing to speak, he said, 'So make haste brothers, for on the tenth day of August the Holy Church celebrates the feast of the Smolensk icon of the Mother of God.'

At that, the black-hatted priest stepped forward and, in the tongue of the Rus, intoned at high speed, 'She is an intercessor before the Most High, who knows all secrets, for the whole world, and She has been granted special power, for in Her hands She holds the uncontainable God, Master of Heaven and Earth.'

The assembled crowd crossed themselves and bowed deeply three times at these words. The English, caught by surprise, hesitantly crossed themselves too, unsure if they should bow. Some did, others did not. Godwine turned to where his sister lay ashen on the grass, wondering how his welcome should have gone so wrong.

PART THREE

THE LONE WARRIOR

PART THREE CHAPTER ONE

KILIKIA

THERE WERE MANY WOMEN in the terem of the Red Fortress. With little to do until their warriors returned, the terem women would weave, visit the pine forest to pick berries and mushrooms or dance and sing to sweet lutes during the long evenings. It was as Swetesot had said. There were the royal women of the Prince's family and the free wives and daughters of his hearthguard. Most were Rus with silver torks, big earrings, coins on their clothes and veils for when they went outside. Then there were the bonded-women, fair Finns from the Baltsea, Mari from the tall-forest, elysian Chuvash, fierce Circassians and gracile Ethiopians. All welcomed Gytha with honour – but, as she remarked to Ailsi, more as a curiosity rather than the betrothed.

It was so different from all she had expected. The days passed. Gytha liked to explore the fortress at Smolensk. It sat atop a bluff so steep above the river there were wooden steps to climb down. Roofed battlements surrounded it, with mighty towers at every corner, and within these ramparts was a town of wooden houses, barns, stores, workshops and a church. It made her father's great hall at Waltham look like a farmstead.

The weary road faded and colour returned to plump her cheeks. Overhead, the crystal sky rang with the cries of geese heading south; swallows gathered in the eves and the stork chicks left their roof-top nests of sticks. Of Vladimir, there was no sign. Neither he nor the vain and boastful Prince Oleg had been at the fort since the Companions of the Golden Dragon of Wessex had arrived.

Gytha was speaking Rus, though it came hard to her and it made the children laugh, their smocks tinkling with tiny bells sewn on their hems.

One of them troubled Gytha. She wondered who the girl might be, who seldom appeared, and when she did, it was always with her mother at her side. She spoke rarely and then only in whispers, in a language Gytha didn't understand. She was not a slave nor snatched by raiders, but of noble birth, a child woman, with shimmering black waves of hair tied in a single maiden's plait to her slender waist, amber skin, enormous soft brown eyes. She was as delicate and beautiful as a flower in her silken robes, and her name was the Princess Kilikia.

The Posadnik Khristofor shrugged his shoulders and said nothing. Gytha, pale but composed, sat with Godwine and waited for their friend and Councillor to speak. He pressed his flattened palms to his lips in thought and his head shook slightly from side to side, as if struggling. Then, hesitantly, he said, 'it was his mother the Princess Anna's dying wish that he be betrothed to another.'

'And this other is the child, Princess Kilikia?' said Gytha a little too loudly.

'Yes, Princess Kilikia. the tribute bride, gift of her father King Gosdantin, who rules the last Christian mountain beyond the Black Sea.'

'A symbol of the trust between her father's people and the River Princes, a tribute bride, a peace-weaver?' said Gytha, the words leaden on her tongue. She paused trying to take in what the Posadnik was telling them.

'Tell me, good mayor, was the Dane Queen deceived as we, or did she know that Prince Vladimir was betrothed to another?' she asked. 'Did she act in good faith or conspire with the Cold Trader to take me away?'

The Posadnik Khristofor shook his head. 'I do not know, Princess. I cannot answer. But the trader, Zhiznomir, lies chained in the prison at the New Town, his wares and goods seized. I shall have him brought here and you can seek your answers with the burning iron.'

The Towering Priest, now stooped and leaning painfully on a stick, spoke faintly, so all cupped their ears to catch his words. 'The Lord hid his purpose from us and delivered us here. The Bastard William's men were at the Hall of the feeble-minded Dane King with gold to buy his peace. But there could be no peace between the Dane King and the Bastard while we remained. We were in mortal danger.'

'Good father,' said the axed and burnished Roni, 'we are delivered, for which we must give thanks, great danger lay in wait for us at the Hall of the Dane King, but not from the Bastard's spies, but from the queen herself. It was she who paid the Cold Trader to take us far away, to be killed on the log road, to rid herself of the sons of the man who killed her husband and his beautiful daughter too.

Gytha cried. For the first time since leaving England. Gytha cried. She cried at the betrayal, at the wasted journey; that instead of the high position in the court of Vladimir she had been promised, her destiny was to be a nunnery where the shame of being passed over for this Princess Kilikia would be her only companion for life.

But above all she cried for her home, and for her mother, her gentle swan.

In the silence that followed, broken only by the whining of nosewise dogs, there was such fury and hurt that each waited on the other to speak,

The quiet Edmund rose. 'My brothers, I thought myself numbed to all adversity. But my sister's pain breaks all hearts in two. We are the last of the English. We are deceived, my sister betrayed. The Bastard William, the Dane King's wife, sought an end to the English, to crush us. But they have failed. Every man has turned his edge against us, Hardradr, the Cold Trader, Prince Oleg, – but, my brothers, we live!'

The companions banged on the tables. Gytha smiled her encouragement, though she felt nothing but despair.

'My brothers, we stand in the shoes of the greatest of men, and great men need great deeds. Our destiny is to seize the crown of the English once more. Let us learn from this Harald Hardradr, whom our father slew at Stamford – for he too was a king without a kingdom, He served the Emperor in Constantinople in his Varengian Guard, before returning to his homeland in the north to became the greatest king the Northmen have known, since King Cnut the Great himself.' He paused 'Brothers, let us do likewise. Let us not remain here, humiliated. – we cannot turn the other cheek. Winter will soon freeze us to this place, then let us continue to Constantinople, where we will serve the Christian Emperor, and with the riches we gain we will return to England with an army to take back what is ours. This is not the end, but the beginning of our greatest undertaking.'

The Company banged their knives and fists on the tables and drummed their feet. 'And Godwine, son of Harold, rightful King of the English, will lead us!' he shouted, and the cheering grew louder still.

The Posadnik leaned closer to Gytha. 'My lady,' he said, 'shall I have the trader, Zhiznomir, brought here to Smolensk? He bears the betrothal warrant.'

'No, all is lost,' said Gytha. 'Have him thrown in the river with the Warrant'. I have no use for them. The Posadnik said nothing.

There was a commotion in the Fort. Their prince was return-ing from the summer warring. Everyone gathered on the wall to watch the mounted hearthguard in their metal shirts, flaglets fluttering from their lances. Behind them straggled horses laden with tribute and furs, cattle and the shackled fighters from the Wild Field. There was laughter, shouting and boasting as wives and daughters called out to greet them on their homecoming. One warrior caught sight of a young woman and threw her a golden necklace, drawing cries of admiration; a hag asked another where her necklace might be, to the guffaws of the crowd. There was great happiness as the men slipped from their saddles and threw their weapons to the ground, clutching their women folk and the offered flagons of samagon, one in either hand. But not all were smiling; some wore bloody rags that hid the wounds of their encounters with fearsome horsemen of the Wild Field. Vladimir, too, had not gone untouched: a blood-stained cloth bound his right leg. Not a battle wound, but a bear had sunk her jaws into the prince's knee in her dying moments. The wound was infected, and the prince was in pain as he called out to his men, 'I do not commend my own boldness, but I praise the Most High, who knows all secrets, and glorify His memory because He guarded me, a sinful and a wretched man. Now, let us purify ourselves, my brethren, from every corporal and spiritual blemish. And, as we call upon our Creator, let us say, Glory to thee, lover of mankind.'

Gytha turned to Godwine as they watched the home-coming. 'When will you speak to him?' she asked. Godwine was silent. 'I must have the Posadnik Khristofor explain the custom of their court. We are the prince's guests and we will achieve no victory if the product of our claim is to make him an enemy.'

Gytha's fought to hide her anger at her brother's answer. 'Godwine,', 'We have talked of this a hundred times. If you do not champion my honour, you will bring shame on us all. My betrothal to the prince cannot be undone – the Trader told the Queen Elisaveta he carried the warrant of this prince's father to seek a bride amongst the north-folk for his son, Prince Vladimir. It was I that was chosen by the Queen Elisaveta and her husband, the Dane King, and the betrothal carries their seal.'

'I know all this, Gytha,' said Godwine, irritated by his sister but knowing too that she was right, and he must seek to defend her honour. 'But we have neither warrant, if it ever existed, nor betrothal with its seal. They are with the Cold Trader and none thought to take them from him – not I, nor the monk, nor the Posadnik Khristofor. Even if we had the betrothal,' he added bitterly, 'their black-beard priests have made it clear enough that they would forbid the marriage of Prince Vladimir to the foreign heretic, over the wish of the prince's mother, the daughter of the Emperor herself, who betrothed her son to this Princess Kilikia before she died. So, we will lose our claim, Gytha. He will not take you as his wife, the Church forbids it and the will of his mother will over-rule any claim, legitimate or other, that we might have.'

'Then get silver, Godwine, that no matter where the Lord takes me, I should have about me the comforts of my rank as princess. We may be without a country, you and I, but I am the daughter of a King. A Sword gift, a Mother of Heroes, the Courage of the English – that's what Colwenne said.'

'Very well,' said Godwine. 'I shall let it be known we seek
the decision of the prince's Council to settle with silver, the
shame and hurt that this duplicity has brought to you and all
English folk of whom I am King and Ring-Giver.'

'Thank you, my lord and brother,' said Gytha, pressing her
head against his shoulder.

And so as soon as the prince was rested from the revelry of
their return, Godwine made his approach, and the next day
the Council was gathered in the painted hall of the Fortress.
The prince sat on his carved chair; his longsword propped
against his bandaged leg. He was wearing a high-collared
belted coat that came almost to his ankles, every part stitched
with threads of red and blue, gold and silver. On his head, he
wore a soft hat, his warrior plait hanging behind his ear. Vain
Oleg, a sneer never far from his lips, in baggy riding pants
tucked into soft boots, a Qypchaq scimitar tucked through his
waist sash, stood with the most senior of the hearthguard in
their mail and pointed face helms. High-hatted beard priests
in black robes were on Vladimir's other side, and behind them
the senior ladies were gathered, in the broidered robes and
drop-jewelled bonnets of their status. In the middle – head
bowed, frozen with fright – sat the perfect Princess Kilikia,
her hands folded on her lap, her mother next to her.

Opposite was Godwine, wearing his coronet and cape.
He too had his Frankish sword propped between his legs.
To one side of him, standing with the hearthguard, were
gathered the Young Thegn Wulfwyn, the Burnished Roni,
Blaecman the Towering Monk and Edmund. To the other sat
Gytha, her circlet covered by a shawl, with Ailsi as her handmaiden. Neither were dressed in the splendid clothes of River
people, choosing instead the red-and-blue woollen tunics of
the English. Only the shoulder broaches and the jewels about

Gytha's neck, which the Gembelt Pig-boy had carried all those months, left no doubt of her nobility. Ailsi's plaited hair fell from beneath her shawl, and more than once she felt Oleg's stare on her. The heat in the hall from the torches along the walls was intense. The mood was cold and formal.

They waited as the Rus priest blessed the company: 'The Lord gives righteousness and justice to all who are treated unfairly and who ask God to bring His justice. He will bring full justice to all who have been wronged. He will not stop until truth and righteousness prevail. Amen.'

As the soon as he had finished, the Towering Monk Blaecman, bent with age but still imposing, said in booming English, 'And the Spirit of the Lord will rest on him – the Spirit of wisdom and understanding, the Spirit of counsel and might, the Spirit of knowledge and the fear of the Lord. Amen.'

The groups crossed themselves. The Rus bowed deeply three times according to their manner and when the blond English did not bow at all, the black-robed bearded priests cast disapproving glances at Godwine and Gytha. Then the Posadnik, unweaponed, wearing his finest silk coat, trimmed in fur, over a belted tunic with a black-and-white pattern of crosses, stepped into the space between the two parties. He addressed the waiting hall in the Dane tongue, that all present should understand. He explained the purpose of the Council, and that there were before them not one but two betrothed women: the Lady Gytha, daughter of Harold Godwineson, King of England, a Christian land beyond the sunset; and the Princess Kilikia, gift-child of Gosdantin, friend and ally to the Christian Emperor, and to our Grand Prince on the River.

Each, the Posadnik said, had a claim to be the wife of their prince and mother to his sons. Gytha straightened her back, lifting her chin slightly, and stared ahead of her, calm and composed. The child-princess, Kilikia, stole a glance at the warriors about her and looked down at her hands again. Oleg laughed. What Vladimir thought, his face gave no clue. He leant forward to listen better, an elbow on his knee. The Posadnik Khristofor paused and waited for the hall to settle before calling on Godwine.

Godwine recounted the coming of the Cold Trader to the court of the Dane king with the warrant from the prince's father to find a virgin bride from among the Dane folk in the north. And how the Queen Elisaveta herself – Prince Vladimir's aunt – had chosen Gytha as the fairest of all. Then how, against Godwine's will, they had been sent first to Gotland, then to the east on the great betrothal journey that brought them to the Red Fort at Smolensk. He paused, weighing his words carefully.

'Prince,' he said, 'through the hardships of the journey, we know not if the Trader Zhiznomir spoke true he carried a warrant from your father to seek a bride among the people of the north. Nor do we have the betrothal with the seal of the Dane king as proof, all were with Zhiznomir, now prisoner or better still dead.' He paused, his pride rebelling against the need to press their case. 'Yet we have come in good faith with my sister as your bride. Now she is without the comfort or the safety of the married state. For which we ask this Council to grant her compensation according to her status.'

'Why?' exclaimed the prince. 'You come here and claim your sister is to be betrothed to me, without a warrant, without oath witnesses… as you claim to be a king, but have no country.' His Hearthguard laughed out loud at this. 'And now you would have me pay. I have heard enough.' And with that, he stood up.

The Posadnik stopped him. 'Prince,' he said, 'do not hasten from this Council. You shall speak that the English know your mind as you now know theirs. With God's guidance, it is for the Council to decide on the merit of the claim.'

Vladimir sat down, his face like thunder. Godwine's countenance was no better, and the two glared at each other. Gytha, head bent, not submissive so much as furious and humiliated.

Next, a priest was called to speak. On and on he droned, saying that the English were followers of the heretic excommunicant in Rome. Gytha sensed that the Towering Mace Monk was eager to reply, then the priest would shout and point an accusing finger at the English, then look towards heaven and cross himself, whereupon all the others would cross themselves too. Gytha glanced at Ailsi, whose eyes were closed, and nudged her. 'Wake up, Ailsi. They think we are devils.'

Then the Towering Monk had his turn and rose to his feet. 'No,' he told them, 'this is not the place to argue God's purpose for all people for whom Jesus Christ his Son had died.' Instead he argued that the River people and their prince needed to grant justice to the Lady Gytha, whose humiliation would be complete if they rejected her plea. The English grunted their agreement. Gytha caught the prince's eye and held it, challenging him to look away.

The monk went on. 'For those of you who doubt the purity of the Lady Gytha or that she, escorted by her brothers, has come to Smolensk in anything other than good faith – with or without the warrants and witnesses of which you speak – can be assured that this can be resolved. Send a message to your father's court, Prince, and let him tell of how he sent the Cold Trader north to find a bride among the Dane-folk for you. If he confirms this is the case, then my lady's claim is true and must be honoured, or payment made. This is your law.'

The Posadnik finished the proceedings, saying, 'Let us meet again tomorrow. The Council will decide whether to send a message to Prince Vladimir's father.'

PART THREE CHAPTER TWO

OLEG'S LIE

THE ENGLISH RETURNED TO their quarters in the Fort, out of earshot of the River people.

'I don't like it,' said Roni. 'Those black-beard priests hate us, and they are turning the prince against us.'

'Maybe so,' said Edmund, 'But they now have a problem they were not expecting. For if they receive word from the prince's father that he instructed the trader, then they must decide which betrothal is the more valid. The father's wish that his son should wed a north-woman, as was his own mother, Princess Ingegerd – or the mother's deathbed wish that he should be joined with a princess from the South.'

A furious debate broke out among the English Companions as Edmund's wise words sunk home. 'They will have to honour the Lady Gytha's claim,' said the Young Thegn with a grin. 'A father's wish must rule all others. It is for him – not the mother – to decide who marries Prince Vladimir. And if they do not wish to go against the will of the dead mother, Princess Anna, then they will pay all that we ask.'

The Companions of the Golden Dragon of Wessex nodded at the sense in Wulfwyn's words and even the Gembelt Pig-boy, who had sat quietly listening, brayed his pleasure.

Then Gytha spoke. 'My lord and brother Godwine, may I address the Companions?' Her brother nodded and Gytha stood up. She looked at their faces – so familiar to her – and felt a rush of love for these men with whom she had shared so many hardships. Often, she had hoped that, with God's mercy, their reward would be a home – a hearth to call their own – and enough booty to woo the prettiest maid. But that hope was forgotten now.

'I thank you for your faith and love. Truly, I don't know what I should have done, had you not been with me on this journey without end? Each time I lay my head I pray for a place to call home. As you do, too. Somewhere I will find peace that I have not known since we learned my father lay dead on the Senlac slaughter field. The strength to go on each day is the strength you give me, each one of you.' She paused a moment, as the Companions swallowed, their softer feelings undammed, which until now had been held in check. 'But don't be so foolish to think they will ever allow the messenger to seek an answer from the Prince Vsevolod. They know he sent the Trader north, but confirmation would set the wishes of Vladimir's father against that of his dead mother – and no son would do that lightly. No, they will seek a different course.'

'Like what my lady?' said the Young Thegn.

Gytha shook her head. 'We cannot ever know these people. The Rus are not as us, this much we know already. But I ask you, given the choice of a ragged woman from a distant island beyond the grey west sea, whose value is but the jewels she stands in, or marriage to the child peace-weaver whose father's soldiers are their shield in the south against the horsemen of the Wild Field, I fear the worst for me, whatever the truth.'

The Companions of the Golden Dragon of Wessex were silent at her words. Edmund placed a hand on Gytha's shoulder. Godwine seemed to be torn by a battle raging within himself, unable to rise to the occasion with the same clarity of thought both his sister and Edmund had showed. Once again, the English felt that God had turned against them, even as they had believed their torment to be over.

'Come,' said the Towering Monk, 'we have made plain our plea for the honour of our Lady Gytha, for whom every one of us would gladly die, and now we must trust in the Lord. So, let us pray that, tomorrow, truth and justice will prevail.'

Prince Vladimir, the vain and boastful Prince Oleg and their hearthguard came late to the Council. The Posadnik Khristofor, eager to proceed, said nothing, but his irritation was apparent as he glanced towards a door where all could hear raised voices. Gytha waited with Ailsi and her brothers. Opposite was the Princess Kilikia. For a second, she looked up and catching Gytha's eye, she smiled. A shy, child smile.

Ailsi tensed next to her, 'Did you see that? after all the trouble she has caused!' But Gytha felt only indifference. Her thoughts were of her betrothal to the Painted Celtprince.

'She is a flat chest child Ailsi; no curse blood flows. the storm that rages about her is not of her making. She too was wrenched from her hearth-home like a barnacle from a longboat, as were we.'

'but she has her mother,' said Ailsi bitterly. 'I would have her killed and that would be an end to it.'

Gytha said nothing,

It was Oleg who spoke first, switching into the tongue that joined the people of the River and the men from the north. 'I have heard much about these girl haired English,' he began. 'More than enough. And one thing reaches my ears, which troubles me sorely. This woman,' he said, pointing at Gytha, 'aged beyond her years and wise to the ways of the world, this false bride who moans that her life is ruined and would have my cousin Vladik pay her for her loss, has lost that which all women hold so dear… to another man.'

Gytha's heart missed a beat and there was a gasp around the hall as Oleg's words sunk in. Some hearthguard nodded, confirming the truth of it. Vladimir was staring at the ground, his shoulders hunched. For a second, he shot a glance of pure fury at Godwine. Gytha's breath froze in her throat. What could Oleg mean? What was the sneering, spoilt princeling trying to say?

'She is no virgin!' Oleg said, repeating it in the Rus tongue that all might understand. 'This woman comes to us defiled.'

Gytha's legs gave way and she clutched Ailsi for support. Godwine jumped to his feet, his hand on his longsword. 'Sit, Earl!' ordered the Posadnik as ten of the hearthguard stepped forward, lowering their pikes at the English.

Oleg was enjoying the effect his words were having; the smirk had returned as waited for silence. 'Yes, king without a kingdom,' he sneered. 'And the man who stole your sister's maidenhood stands by her. Her champion, Wulfwyn, whom you call Thegn. The warrior forever at her side lay atop her.' He turned to the assembled crowd. 'You can only wonder at how she might seek to convince a husband of her chastity. Though were she to substitute her handmaiden here on the wedding night, such a husband would be forgiving.' With that he winked at Ailsi, who burst into tears. Wulfwyn, who had stood slack-jawed while the calumny sunk in, now gripped the hilt of his longsword. Roni grabbed him. All around was uproar. Gytha could barely grasp what Oleg was saying and slumped to the ground in front of Prince Vladimir for the second time.

'But there is more,' yelled Oleg above the hubbub, as the Posadnik shouted for calm.

'Silence, let him speak!' ordered the prince and the hall fell silent.

'This woman who hangs her chastity like a bloody bride-rag on a thorn was betrothed to another, a prince likewise, who found her coupling this Wulfwyn in the midst of a battle.' At this, the Young Thegn struggled in the Huscarl's grasp, but still Oleg continued. 'Yes, while a great battle raged. A battle where this prince, whom all knew as the Splintered Spear from the South, died dishonoured. Aye, his heart splintered by this woman. And she talks of honour.' Oleg spat.

Godwine could take no more. Sword in hand, he stepped into the centre of the hall. 'These are lies, all lies. Who says these things? Wulfwyn was injured and the Lady Gytha tended to his wounds as the battle raged. Without her he would have died. God heeded her prayers and took pity on the beardling boy and granted him life. That is why Wulfwyn, her life-ward, is by her side each waking hour, to protect and guard her as she protected and guarded him.' He looked around the hall, as if challenging any man to gainsay him. 'My sister is chaste and pure as the Holy Mother herself. I will have no-one say otherwise. Before the Most High, who knows all secrets, Oleg, I will defend my sister's honour, as I defended her from this prince of which you speak. He did not die in battle. He was a traitor. I killed him with this sword as I will kill you.' And thrusting his longsword at Oleg, he challenged him.

Vladimir was on his feet in an instant and the hearthguard with him. The Companions stood too, the two sides face to face, a few feet apart. 'The challenge is accepted, and God will be the judge, not man.' Godwine gave a brief nod, satisfied, but then his face turned to outrage when the prince added, 'but the life of my cousin and kinsmen Oleg, who speaks true, is not forfeit. He shall name another, as is our custom.'

'What!' Godwine shouted. 'I will kill you, Oleg. Not another in your place!' He lunged forward, but one of the pike men knocked his sword out of the way, the sword edge a hair's-breadth from Oleg's ear.

The Posadnik Khristofor spoke. 'It is our custom that a man may choose another to fight in his place. The duel will be here at dawn tomorrow. This Council is over.' Slowly the warriors filed from the hall, neither looking at the other, all talk of messengers and betrothal claims forgotten.

The Companions of the Golden Dragon of Wessex hurried back to the English hall. The Young Thegn, his pink cheeks almost purple, was panting with rage at Oleg's slander. Roni, who had restrained the young warrior in the hall, was grim-faced. He shouted for quiet. 'Everything Oleg said was a lie! Companions, you must pay no heed to it.' He held out a hand as the hubbub continued. 'Eat and rest. For tomorrow if things go ill or well' – at this the English cheered – 'we must be ready to fight.'

Gytha ran back to her chamber with Ailsi at her side, her mind racing.

'Ailsi, where could this sneering prince have heard such things? Who would have spoken about me so? None of the Companions, that much I know. But who else? He even knew of the cursed Celtprince. Though now I wonder if life with him could have been worse than the life I now endure. But this was no time to question God's will. Tomorrow my brother Godwine defends my honour. But whom will he fight?'

She took a breath to calm her beating heart as her thrall woman, Tulpan, entered the chamber. 'Princessa,' she said, pointing towards the Terem door, where Pig-boy, at the threshold, was twisting his cap in his hands. Gytha waved for him to enter. The Gembelt Pig-boy fell to his knees in front of her, bowing low. Pulling his wax tablet from his belt, he scratched, 'Berserker lives.'

She didn't understand. Had Wulfwyn and Roni not hurled his body over the wall back at the settlement they called Gnyozdovo? Then all became clear. Ragnwald the Dane, whom they thought dead, lived. The prophecy was true – no man could kill a berserker, half man, half bear. It was he who had boasted he had been to their green island beyond the grey west sea. He knew of the battle at Exeter, and of her betrothal to the Celtprince. It must have been he who had told Oleg. Gytha closed her eyes, unable to believe that in England, her heart-home, her good name was shamed. What if her mother had heard this lie? What if all England spoke of her as Oleg had to the Council?

Ailsi was looking at Gytha anxiously, 'Are you all right, my lady?'

Gytha shook her head. 'If you only knew. I cannot even begin to explain. Come, let us find my brother.' Gytha rose from her seat but Pig-boy stopped her. Scratching once more on his tablet, he wrote, 'Berserker fights Lord tomorrow.'

'No! the howling bear warrior who returns from the grave.' Gytha sank back on to the stool. 'Godwine cannot fight a berserker.'

In the hall of the English Wulfwyn stepped forward. 'Lord, let me accept the challenge. It is I who am dishonoured, as is the Lady Gytha, by this lie. So, it is right that I should fight. Be it this sneering prince or his stand-in, I care not. For I shall have truth on my side and God will be.'

'No, she is my sister, Thegn Wulfwyn,' said Godwine, 'with whom I swore a blood oath at Waltham, under the Flinty Cross.'

'I swore too,' said Edmund. 'Let me fight.'

Godwine gipped his brother's shoulder. 'No, good brother Edmund, for if I die tomorrow, I will die knowing you will lead the Companions of the Golden Dragon of Wessex and champion our vow-sister, Gytha, as I have tried to do.'

'Better I die and you live to lead us,' said Edmund defiantly.

'Stop,' said the Towering Mace Monk, 'Edmund, if Godwine sees his duty is to fight, help him prepare. Trust in the Lord. He is your help and your shield.'

'So, it is settled,' said Godwine, crossing himself as Gytha burst in.

'No! You must not fight! Oleg has the berserker as his stand-in. He is not dead. He lives. It was he who told those lies.'

'But I swear, he was dead,' said the Young Thegn, 'Was he not dead, Roni?'

'Not dead enough,' said the axed and burnished warrior. 'We should have nailed the holy cross through his heart, for they say you cannot kill a bear-man with iron alone.'

'Then, Lord,' said Wulfwyn, turning to Godwine, 'I say again I will fight, let my longsword be the holy cross to pierce his heart.' He knelt at the feet of the Towering Blaecman, sword outstretched. 'Come, Father, bless this edge of mine. Arm me with the armour of righteousness that I might carry out God's holy will. I have lived for this day when I might fight, and if the Most High, who knows all secrets, wills it, I will die for my lady Gytha.'

Godwine's distress was plain for all to see. 'My father,' he said to the Companions, his voice low, 'on the eve of Senlac also faced a choice. Should he lead the English south to fight the Bastard, exhausted as he was from the battle at Stamford? Or send my uncle in his place, as my grandmother the Mother of Heroes, wished. He fought at the head of his army, as a king must. Therefore, I too shall fight.'

'Brother,' said Gytha, 'only God can know what might have been, but had our father sent our Gyrth in his place, we all might still be in England. Our Father, King and the

Bastard vanquished. You must not be guided by our father, for the decision he took has worked ill for us. You are the last. A king without a country, but a king.' She held her eldest brother's gaze, and an understanding passed between them. 'Let Wulfwyn fight, there is no dishonour in that. He is shamed, as am I. The berserker lives because the Young Thegn did not kill him when the chance was offered. Let him right both wrongs tomorrow, for there is no warrior in our sacred Company whom God has given greater cause.' Gytha turned her blue eyes to Wulfwyn, and he bowed his head to his Lady.

'What say you, brothers?' asked Godwine, 'will we draw lots and let the Lord chose our champion, I or Wulfwyn, Thegn of Thurgarton?'

'No, Lord,' said the Young Thegn vehemently. 'I will fight. The Lady Gytha speaks for all of us. You are our King. I have no fear of this Ragnwald – he is not half bear, nor returned from the dead as some here say. He is a braggart spear-Dane like any other I have killed. I thought him dead once. Now the Lord has given me a second chance to send the berserker's black soul into His furnace for the lies that he has told.'

The Companions banged their fists upon the tables, and Godwine called for quiet. 'Wulfwyn, Thegn, you walk in the shoes of heroes. The honour of my sister – of us all – rides heavily on your shoulders. Now, my brothers, we should rest. Tomorrow, with God's mercy, the spear-Dane will lie dead at your feet, Thegn, and you will make this wrong right and the English proud again.'

Ailsi sobbed and prayed, and Gytha comforted her as best she could, though her own heart was breaking. 'We must trust in the Lord,' she repeated so many times,

'yes, the Lord, who has failed you,' wailed Ailsi in reply.

PART THREE CHAPTER THREE

EXCALIBUR

FINALLY, AILSI SLEPT. GYTHA slipped from the room and climbed the creaking staircases to the highest rampart as the sun was settling onto the forest far beyond the river.

Somewhere beyond the forest lay the grey west sea, and beyond the grey west sea was her mother, her gentle swan. The sun was on its way to her. Perhaps it could take her too. She had only to ask, she had only to take a step, and the sun would carry her home. Gytha crossed herself, begging forgiveness for the sin she was about to commit. Carefully she edged through a gap between the brickwork battlement and stepped carefully onto the sill, far above the river. Shielding her eyes with her shawl around her face, she stared at the sun again, its golden carpet lying on the water. It reached to her. It beckoned her. A carpet to fly her home to Waltham and her father's hall. Her mother, her gentle swan would look up from her embroidery and, smiling, say, 'come, Gytha help me, your young eyes are sharper than any eagle's. What colour thread shall we pick next? Choose it for me please.'

Sobbing, trembling on the highest edge. There was another voice, her father's. 'Be strong Gytha, in your breast be bold. There is no golden carpet.' Her fingers strayed to her neck and the small amber stone in which a spider slept for all eternity. 'Take this gift, most precious princess,' Colwenne, Jonjarl's thrall wife had said, 'No matter where the Lord leads you, may my spider always bring you luck. Be strong, for our blood, Gytha, is of our green-holm beyond the sea. Our hearts are of oak, our bodies sturdy as the ash. We survive. You will survive. You, Gytha, are the courage of the English. You are our sword gift, you are the Mother of Heroes.' Something surged in her bosom, Aethelflaed' s words came to her. Aethelflaed whose ring she wore through all adversity. 'Gytha, despair is enemy to hope. You Gytha, bear my ring, you will survive, you must survive. You will be a great queen. Let hope fill your soul, banish despair Gytha.'

Clinging to the rough bricks, first with one hand then both, so that her shawl flew away, her golden hair catching the last of the dying light, Gytha stood firm as the rude wind tried to snatch her from the ledge, And then the carpet was gone; the sun set, the river turned to slate, the forest that stretched to the grey west sea faded into black.

As the cock crowed, Ailsi woke.

'I must go to my brother,' she said.

'Go Ailsi, He needs your blessing. Be strong, he must not see your fear.' Ailsi wiped her nose on her sleeve and went to where Godwine, Roni, Edmund and the monk were preparing the Young Thegn for the combat ahead. Gytha followed. Everything had been discussed, all options weighed. Plans made should he win or lose. Wulfwyn chose a short woollen tunic, no ring shirt, choosing speed to dodge the berserker's axe. On his feet he wore soft boots, the straps wrapped tightly over his leggings. On his arms were two wide bracelets, His sword hung from his belt, his wounding-knife too. His left arm was free for his round shield board. Pig-boy gripped a thrusting spear.

They all knelt as the Towering Mace Monk blessed Wulfwyn, making the sign of the cross over his bowed head. Then, each one embraced Wulfwyn. Ailsi, her eyes tight shut lest he see her tears, hugged him tightly. Then Edmund took his own silver helm and placed it on the Young Thegn's head. Wulfwyn bowed to Godwine and then, hesitating, sank to his knee again, 'My lady,' he said, 'with the Lord's mercy my lance and my sword will right the terrible wrong that was done you yesterday.'

'Heart-dear friend and champion, let the Lord deliver us from lying lips and deceitful tongues. God be with you,' Gytha's voice was husky. She kissed him on both cheeks. And pulled him to his feet. He was ready.

The dawn was cold; there was a hard frost underfoot as they left the hall. A grey water sky into which the sun now rose revealed the area outside the Council hall. Fur clad people had already gathered in a large circle, Prince Vladimir on a throne brought from the hall. Oleg and his stand-in had yet to arrive. Godwine, calling the Companions of the Golden Dragon of Wessex together, swaggered into the centre of the fighting place, in front of the prince. 'What keeps this Oleg? It is time to deliver his justice, for the wrong he has done my sister!' he shouted.

As he did so, they all heard the unmistakable grunting roar of a bear and dogs barking. The Companions waited, wondering what was afoot. More dogs barked, then the sound of roaring grew louder. The crowd parted and into the centre strode Oleg, his three hounds on a leash, followed by a giant of a man holding a furious bear on a choke chain with one arm and prodding it with his battle-axe in the other. The crowd gasped at his strength. The berserker was hideous to look at; bare-chested, a huge pelt around his shoulders, his tattooed face was horribly scarred from the firebrand that Roni had thrust into it the night of the Hoard theft.

Catching sight of Godwine, the berserker lunged, shouting in a strange tongue. Prince Vladimir held up his hand. 'Let the duel begin!'

Wulfwyn stepped past Godwine. The English cheered. Oleg laughed when he saw the Young Thegn, so small compared to his wild Dane. 'Kill the boy, Ragnwald!' he shouted.

Ailsi shrieked. 'A bear! It is Ragnwald, not a bear that he must fight. Stop the fight, stop it.' Pig-boy rushed forward, handing Wulfwyn his lance. Ragnwald released the bear and gave it a fearsome kick in Wulfwyn's direction. The bear charged. Wulfwyn stood his ground, then buried his lance into its neck, the handle splintering. The force knocked him backwards. The crowd cheered. It would be moments now before the bear tore him limb from limb. Turning, it paused as if unsure, then it rushed at him again, roaring, red gums and teeth bared. Quick as lighting, Wulfwyn rolled sideways, protecting his body with his shield, his longsword now in his hand. The bear struck him with a massive talloned paw, ripping his shoulder open and sending his shield skidding across the ground. Wulfwyn hacked at its head and muzzle again and again.

The bear was on top of him; it was all over. It rose onto its hind feet as if in triumph, towering over the young Englishman. Wulfwyn, with one last mighty effort, thrust his longsword between its legs and pushed with all his might. The bear seemed to freeze, then dropped its body, pinning the warrior helpless to the ground as it fell. It did not stir.

The crowd were crazed with excitement. The giant berserker stepped into the blood-soaked ring and kicked Wulfwyn where he lay. The Young Thegn groaned and tried to raise his sword one last time. The berserker walked once around the ring, acknowledging the cheering, and stopped in front of Oleg. The sneering prince gave a nod. Returning to the middle, the giant Dane lifted his massive axe above his head, savouring the moment he could split the boy's blond head from his broken body.

'Oh God no!' screeched Ailsi covering her eyes. Gytha snatched her wounding-knife from her belt. Quick as heron to a fish, she was across the open space in three strides and, with the shield maid's scream, leapt up and buried the blade with both hands between the berserker's shoulders. His head jerked back as she drove down to his heart. Pride turned to shock, and then, slow as a felled tree, the giant Dane toppled forward on to the bear. The buried wounding-knife rose from the Dane's body, as Excalibur rose from the lake. Its jewelled hilt caught the morning sun, a sparkling cross atop a mound of flesh.

PART THREE CHAPTER FOUR

'RUSALKA RUSALKA!'

UPROAR. OLEG WAS ON his feet, sword drawn. Godwine, Roni and the Companions dashed into the ring, but one person was quicker still, Tulpan. The Qypchaq woman grabbed Gytha, rushing her from the ring where the Qypchaq men surrounded them, knifing the howling crowd aside. The Companions, lifting the weight that crushed Wulfwyn, pulled him by his shoulders from beneath the bear and the still twitching berserker, and dragged him from the ring.

In the frenzy, there was a scream. Edmund spun round; Oleg had Ailsi by the hair. She was fighting, biting him like a lynx; Edmund lunged towards her and the sword tip caught her golden braid, slicing it off. Oleg stumbled back, holding nothing but plaited strands. Ailsi flew into his arms as Edmund steadied himself, about to slice off Oleg's head.

'Edmund! Come. Now!' The companions shouted, surrounding him. they ran full tilt to where horses waited. The men scrambled to their saddles. It was snowing and the heavy flakes hid them as they careered down the steep hill towards the river gate. Gytha at their centre, her Qypchaq about her. The guards were no match for the English as they fled the Red Fortress, thundered across the Dnieper bridge and made for safety back at the trading post at Gnyozdovo. By God's mercy, all were unhurt, save for the groaning Wulfwyn and the shorn Ailsi.

Ailsi and the slave Tulpan bathed the crushed and bloodied Wulfwyn smoothing healing balms over his limbs and flanks. Gytha prayed as she had never prayed before, she prayed to the Lady of the Mercians, Aethelflaed, she prayed to St Panteleon the Healer, she called to her father in heaven and on earth. By a miracle, Wulfwyn lived the first night and then the second until Gytha dared believe that her prayers might be answered and he would wake from the pain-deep sleep.

When he learned that Gytha had saved him, he tried to clasp her hand to his heart, but of all the words he knew none came. 'Shhh don't speak,' she said and brushed his tears away with a smile.

But the Companions knew that the trading post at Gnyozdovo was a temporary sanctuary. 'We are trapped,' said Godwine as they huddled about the fire pit in the hall they had left only weeks before. 'What choices have we? If we stay here, Prince Oleg will seek revenge and, with his cousin will burn and starve us out, no matter how well we defend ourselves. Or we flee to the north, the way we came.'

The Company shook their heads at that. 'No, Lord,' said one. 'the rivers and marshes freeze, the princes will kill us in the forest for sport.';

'Or wolves will,' said another. 'No, we must stay and parley for our lives.'

The answer came sooner than expected. Once more the Posadnik Khristofor stood before them, shaking the snow from his fur coat. 'I come,' he said, 'not as your friend but as the messenger of the prince's Council. Prince Vladimir has no fight with the English. You are trapped here at Gnyozdovo for the winter — you are too few and too weak. The Council has decreed that were it not for the Lady Gytha's madness, Prince Oleg's champion Ragnwald would have won in fair combat. Prince Oleg is entitled to compensation, and wergild, as your English call it, to pay to the berserker's kin.'

'He had no kin, save the devil,' one shouted.

The Posadnik went on. 'The decision of the Council and of the priests is that you forfeit your Hoard as tribute, and all of you including the Lady Gytha will serve Prince Vladimir in return for your lives.'

There was silence in the hall, but for the crackling of the flames in the hearth and the dogs quarrelling over a bone. Nobody said anything. The Posadnik looked about him, waiting. The Towering Monk struggled to his feet with the aid of two Companions. His fists shook.

'Good Christian friend,' he began, 'you have counselled us wisely these last months, yet your message today leaves us silent.' He paused and gained his breath. 'Please thank the Council and the priests, and the princes Vladimir and Oleg. Tell them we English would rather die here now than live as slaves.'

'You have no choice, Father.' said the Posadnik forcefully. 'It is not your choice. You are the captives of Prince Vladimir, to live or die at his whim. The Council decrees it.'

'Nor is the Godwineson Hoard forfeit,' the monk went on. 'The last of the jewels, gold and holy chalices blessed by the Archbishop in our mother church at Westminster and passed down to us from King Harold are not forfeit. The Holy Hoard is to be used in the service of the Lord our God, not heretics.' The Posadnik's face darkened in fury but the monk held up his hand. 'If Prince Vladimir would have no fight with us, then allow us to attend the Council once more.'

'Why so?' said the Posadnik.

'Because no duel took place.'

The Posadnik was about to speak. The Towering Mace Monk stopped him again.

'The bear was not the stand-in for the Prince Oleg, but the stand in for the cowardly Dane, whom the Prince nominated as his champion. It was never agreed that a creature from the forest be proxy.' He shook his thickly veined fist. 'The cowardly Dane, Ragnwald – the berserker, nominated by Prince Oleg did not fight. There was no duel.'

The Posadnik began to laugh. 'You may be old, Great Monk, too frail to wield the mace that breaks men's bodies, but nothing dims your heart and mind.'

'You are right, good Mayor Khristofor – I count seventy winters.' He coughed and wiped spittle from his mouth. 'The young Thegn Wulfwyn was attacked by a bear and killed it, suffering grave injury as any brave hunter might. The tail-turn coward Ragnwald sought advantage by low cunning and failed even to land one blow in combat. He paid with his life, lost to a girl. Tell the Council, there was no duel. Prince Oleg's challenge stands.'

The Companions cheered mightily, calling Gytha's name.

'And I,' shouted Godwine, waving a mead flagon, 'shall fight this Oleg, I shall kill him in fair combat, to defend my sister's honour from his vile insult. With the coward dead, Prince Oleg has no witness to his lies. Tell the Council that!'

After the Posadnik returned to the Fortress, the English argued. Some cheered the monk; others feared the Council would never let Godwine challenge in combat the vainglorious Oleg, son of the Grand Prince himself.

'Brothers,' said Edmund, 'the Prince will not take kindly to our defiance, and the Hoard is a prize he cannot resist.'

'Double the guard,' slurred Godwine, sliding from the mead bench to the floor.

It was Sunday. Gytha walked with Ailsi over to the small church across the market square. There was thick snow on the ground, the little harbour was frozen and it was bitterly cold. Hunger added to the bleakness of the scene. A few stalls were still selling honey, tallow for lamps, gnarled roots, single eggs, berries and brown-bruised windfalls. A pinch faced stall-keeper shouted when she saw them approach, another crossed herself. A black-robed priest stood at the church doorway; his arms crossed. Gytha pulled the cowl about her face and bowed her head to enter. But the priest blocked her way. Pointing at her, he shouted, 'Rusalka! Rusalka!'

Gytha stopped, unsure, Ailsi too.

In that instant, Ailsi cried out as an egg hit her, and another. There followed rotten apples and frozen turds hurled by the villagers at the stalls. 'Rusalka! Rusalka!' they shouted, and the two young women fled.

It was a sombre meal that evening. There was little food. But worse was to come.

'The people were saying you are not of flesh and blood, not a Christian woman but a Rusalka who brings famine to the people of the river,' said the quiet Edmund.

Gytha asked what that might be. He hesitated.

'The unquiet Rusalki are the tortured souls of dishonoured maidens, who come from the world beneath the marsh, Scorned and dishonoured by Prince Vladimir, they say that you rose from the mire to seek revenge for your rejection. No natural girl, they say, has the strength to kill a berserker. You must remain here, a prisoner in our hall, for your safety. The village is too dangerous, Gytha. They will stone you to death.'

Gytha was distraught. Were it not for Wulfwyn, growing stronger by the day, she wished she had stepped from the tower onto the golden carpet and let it carry her home.

The Dnieper river was hard frozen. Where in the distant warmth of summer, boats had carried the traders and their cargoes, now great sledges drawn by horses, were driven onto the ice by flailing, cursing men. The snow banks grew outside the hall, the well froze and the temperature kept dropping. They had never felt such cold. Their woollen clothes long discarded for stinking furs and felted boots they stuffed with straw. There was no food and no corn for the starving animals, so they slaughtered them, boiling everything down to a reeking jelly they sliced in portions. It was so foul, the Companions risked the menace beyond the turreted gate to hunt or eat bony river fish they caught through ice holes, washed down with evil fire water, as the scented Swetesot, daughter of horses, had described.

Madness took the villages. In their hunger men denounced wives, sisters and mothers for hoarding food. Women were dragged screaming from their hovels and sorcerers would stab them, drawing out grain, fish and honey from the bodies of the dead, but the woman they condemned was Gytha.

Gathering the Company of English around him, Godwine stared into their haggard faces. 'My brothers,' he said grimly, 'Lady Gytha is in most mortal danger. In the snow-covered settlements along the riverbank and deep in the forest around Smolensk, the people demand that Prince Vladimir bring her to them and end their suffering.'

'Never!' shouted the Companions of the Golden Dragon of Wessex. But Godwine stopped them.

'We are caged like rats. There is no need to fear Vladimir's hearthguard when the villagers with sticks can starve us out. We stand at hell's door.'

There was a growl of fury from the Company at his words. 'Lord, there is a way out,' said Roni the Dane. 'Not many days west is the fort at Polotsk. From there, a great river leads to the Baltsea. Then it is a boat-ride to Denmark to my father's hearth. Let us go now. The land is frozen. We can move fast. There will be meat enough for us in the forest. Let's flee from here tonight while we have the strength and before the prince sends warriors to kill us.'

But the rest knew the Huscarl's brave words were as empty as their stomachs. No man could pull the heavy sledges through the frozen clumps of marsh sedge that would hinder and trip them every step they took. There were no horses to pull them, no grain to feed them, nor settlements to plunder.

'We shall die as many have in the Pripet wilderness, with nothing to mark our graves but a cross of ice that melts come spring,' said Edmund quietly. 'And this place Polotsk. Is not that where the prince magician Vseslav rules as king by day and wolf by night?'

'It is said he does,' said Roni grimly. 'But he is the sworn enemy of the Prince of Smolensk. He will welcome us.'

The weather changed from Blizzards to cloudless skies. Birds flew in the glass hard air. The sparkle-snow was pockmarked by mysterious feet. The Posadnik returned. The Council would hear them, he said, 'but it is a trial; the accused is the Lady Gytha'.

Numbed by the drinking, the Companions groaned their anger and despair.

'What am I accused of, Posadnik Khristofor?' asked Gytha

'Princess,' he said, 'duel or not, as the monk maintained, you were not proxy to Wulfwyn. The Council will say you my Lady murdered the berserker and must seek the clemency of Prince Vladimir.'

'My vow-sister, daughter of King Harold Godwineson, King of England is to be tried like a common criminal,' said Edmund.

'Try the bear,' said Godwine, his bleared eyes and mead breath telling their own story.

'The bear is dead, Godwine!' said Gytha as she stood up and stepped on to a low bench.

'My brothers, I will not seek clemency! The berserker and Prince Oleg shamed me, before God, this company and the people of the Red Fortress. There is not one straw-shod peasant in this land who does not tell his hogs of my humiliation, not one mother of daughters who does not give the fate of fallen women a name. My name. Now our brother, Wulfwyn, lies groaning on a bed, crushed and torn in my defence. No, I will not seek clemency. The vain and haughty Oleg hoped to bait the bear with the heart of an English warrior, as a hunter throws his hound a bone.' Her blue eyes met those of the Posadnik, daring him to disagree. 'And that turn-tail Dane, who thought one blow would clinch the fight, now takes his evil to the abyss and every Christian Englishman he ever killed is avenged, by me.' The Companions of the Golden Dragon of Wessex rose and cheered her words, Gytha held out a hand to quiet them. 'Yes, good Posadnik Khristofor, I will stand trial before the Council and Prince Vladimir. But I do not seek his clemency, only the Lord's justice.'

The Companions cheered yet more loudly as she sat down.

'You know the people call you a Rusalka,' said the Posadnik grimly.

'And what do you think, Posadnik Khristofor?' she replied. 'Do you think I am an unquiet spirit returned from the marsh to seek revenge for my lost honour?'

'Lady Gytha, in time of famine the people seek answers for their misery and blame spirits in the devil's service.'

Gytha's fury spilled over at his words. Edmund was about to speak. She hushed him.

'Are you saying you believe I am a spirit in the devil's service? That I have brought this famine on your people?'

'My lady, seers and sorcerers move from village to village saying since you arrived there is famine.' They all fell silent again. 'They say God's anger will make the river flow backwards, unless they kill you. They say you are a stranger – a heretic – come among them. It is because of you the people must eat birchbark and lime leaves or have only moss to stir with corn husks and straw for soup.'

'Come, Posadnik! They are not seers but liars. The Devil deludes them.' Gytha was white-faced, her anger masking fear. 'I am no Rusalka. The Cold Trader's men captured me, but I escaped from the river and climbed to the log road where the vain prince Oleg waited. So, take these seers and sorcerers and hang them by their feet from trees and let them eat their entrails. For everything they say is a lie.

'Lady Gytha, the people believe if you cast the seers into the abyss, ten will appear in their place.' Said the Posadnik

'Tulpan,' she called, beckoning her slave woman. 'Tulpan, you saved me from the river pirates and pulled me choking from the water death. Do you believe that I am a Rusalka from the bottomless marsh, here to avenge those who dishonour me, as these sorcerers claim?'

Tulpan, to whom Gytha owed life not once but twice, kneeled and pressed her forehead to Gytha's hem, then standing up she spoke loudly, so all could hear. 'Princessa, beautiful princess. Your eyes are like the blue heaven of my home. your hair glows gold as wisps of cloud in the light of evening. You are not from the bottomless marsh but from the sky above, Then Tulpan turned to the shorn Ailsi. 'And you, Aisulu, are the beauty of the moon.'

Holding the Qypchaq woman's words in their hearts, Gytha and Ailsi and the Companions prayed together that night, asking the Lord for deliverance.

PART THREE CHAPTER FIVE

SEERS AND SORCERERS

SORCERERS ARRIVED SOON AFTER at the trading post. Standing in the yard by the church, they gathered people to them with chants and curses. They knew, they said, who caused the famine: it was a woman. Then, while the priest looked on, they challenged the village men to yield the woman who was to blame.

'Rusalka! Rusalka!' they cried. 'Bring us this Rusalka, so that we might kill her! For she has hidden bread and grain in her body and would let your babies starve!' And the hungry people snatched up anything they could find – sticks, cudgels, pikes and flaming tar sticks – and ran shouting to the hall that housed the Companions.

Vodka and kvas had made the Companions of the Golden Dragon of Wessex slow to the danger and, not understanding the shouts of the crowd, they were still buckling on their weapons as the first flares were thrown. Some struck the snow-covered straw, sliding off the roof harmlessly, but one landed unseen in kindling piled at the back of Gytha's cramped bothie. Within a moment, flames leapt up the dry wood walls, catching first the straw, then the wood-wormed beams. Screaming, Gytha sent Ailsi for her brothers.

Shaking themselves from their drunkenness, Godwine, Roni and the others ran from the building to see Tulpan and the Qypchaq men fighting to protect Gytha. Ailsi was cowering beside her.

Tulpan died that night. Seeing a man lifting his spear to hurl at Gytha, the little Qypchaq from the Wild Field stepped forward, to shield her Lady. The metal tip, grazing her raised hand, buried itself in the socket of her eye. She barely uttered a sound – a slight grunt, no more – as she fell against Gytha, before slumping onto the blooded snow. Now Gytha stood alone, the rabble round her, with not even the wounding-knife in her belt. Snatching the lance, she pulled it from Tulpan's head and stabbed at anyone who came close.

The tattooed fury of the Qypchaq men and English swords beat the rabble back. The villagers turned and ran, dragging their wounded from their rage. Famished bodies lay like dolls on the snow; one tried to crawl away, but they killed him.

The fire out, they waited for the rabble to return, thanking God for their deliverance, praying for the soul of Tulpan, cursing the River people and the unending winter night.

Stepping over the exhausted men, the Gembelt Pig-boy pushed his wax tablet across the table to Gytha. She took it from him and sounded out the words he had scrawled.

'Kill devil servants. In God's Name.'

'Kill who?' slurred Godwine.

'he means the sorcerers, don't you Pig-boy?' said Gytha. Pig-boy nodded.

'They are the prince's subjects. It is for him to kill them, not for us, Pig-boy,' said Godwine. 'And you heard the Posadnik – ten more will only spring up in their place.'

Pig-boy looked perplexed. But Gytha's eyes narrowed as a thought took shape as she turned to the old monk. 'May man kill man in God's name, Father? The Lord taught us to love our enemy but these sorcerers do the devil's work and would harm me.'

'Yes, child, man may kill in God's name,' said Blaecman. 'These are the Devil's servants. To kill them is to free the people from the one who destroy both body and soul.'

Edmund listened carefully. 'We accuse them of sorcery and they accuse us likewise, but they are the devil servants and we serve only Jesus Christ.'

Wulfwyn the Young Thegn, his crushed and shattered body not mending for want of food, was propped at Gytha's side. He roused himself to speak. 'Kill them, for only we in this land can end their tyranny. The people fear them, even the Posadnik. Kill them and let the prince be grateful to us and have mercy on us. Kill them.'

Gytha scoffed. 'Let us help the prince? As he has helped us? Why?'

'My lady, Prince Vladimir is not the sneering Oleg – he is merciful and just he is not the author of our plight, Oleg is,' came the reply.

Ailsi nodded in agreement. 'I saw it in his face as the bear attacked Wulfwyn. There was a frown that spoke more than words. I did not understand its meaning until now. I thought only of my brother's life, but Prince Vladimir was angered by the sneering Oleg's trick.'

The burnished Roni spoke. 'I have heard of a lady's instinct, my lady Gytha, but never that we should place our lives at the mercy of a frown. You know what your father would say. He would laugh and ask, "what if it fails?". What if God shows no mercy – nor this prince who showed Wulfwyn none, nor you my lady?' Roni was angry now. 'What then?'

'Then, good friend and brother to my father,' said Edmund, 'we are no worse than now.'

'Don't mock me, Edmund. I cannot let the lives of all who remain – and there are few enough of us – hang on a frown. I do not care who saw it. I love your sister as a daughter and would die for her. In her I see your mother's grace and beauty and your father's strength, fearing nobody but God. I trust your sagacity, thoughtful Edmund – whom I have known since you were at your golden mother's tit – we are of no use to these river Rus alive. Dead, they can steal our Hoard. They know no mercy or justice.'

Edmund ran his hand through his thick blond hair, so like his father but gaunt with hunger. 'So, we must decide between an icy cross and a prince's frown. I say hunt these sorcerers to their lair, and I for one will enjoy the sport.' He began to laugh; it was a chuckle at first, then a roar. the Companions laughed too, slapping each other on the back and taking great gulps of the mead that remained. Only the burnished Dane, Roni, huscarl and friend to King Harold, did not laugh, Gytha saw. Reaching out, she pressed his arm. 'Thank you, Roni, your heart is as mighty as one hundred warriors. I know you would do only what you think best for me.' Roni nodded, but said nothing, only a wetness in the corners of his eyes showed that Gytha's words had touched him greatly.

Wiping the spittle from his cheeks, Godwine quieted the Company with his hand. 'So, it is settled. Edmund will rid the frowning prince of his pestilence in God's name and seek his mercy by our deed. Where are these sorcerers?' he slurred.

Pig-boy pointed vigorously to the ground.

'They are here?' said Gytha, 'in the settlement? Do you know where they hide?' Pig-boy nodded; his gape-mouth open.

Once the Company had mocked and laughed as Pig-boy honked his tongueless cries, but no more. They trusted him now. He was their eyes and ears, who watched and listened, as the Mother of Heroes had foretold all those years before. How they cheered the Pig-boy, patting his narrow, bony shoulders; Gytha smiled at him. 'Thank you, good and faithful Pig-boy.'

Gytha had one more task that day. Leaving the hall, she went to where her Qypchaq thralls had built a round shelter of sticks and hides. The freezing air was heavy with the sweet smell of burning hemp. There was rhythmic drumming from inside. Gytha crouched low to enter, and coughed violently. The men sat in a circle, throat singing, the sound so deep and unvarying, as they rocked back and forth in the smoke, passing the sour qumiz milk between them. They took no notice over her. Tulpan's body dressed in pale blue cloth stitched with the symbols of Tengri, the blue eternal sky, the thrice bright Sun and the moist mother earth. The thrall ring was no longer about her neck. In death, Tulpan roamed the Wild Field where horsemen vanished into the ripple-long grass like fish into the waves.

Gytha shut her eyes tightly, remembering another from the Wild Field, Swetesot, daughter of horses, her heart friend, slave and princess. Where was the scented Swetesot now she wondered, and her son Boniak? They were lost to her with so many she held dear in her heart, high born and slave born, all lost to her. Gytha stayed to honour Tulpan, this little heathen woman who had traded her life with hers, until she became too dizzy and craved fresh air once more.

Edmund returned before dawn, so frozen that it was some time before his teeth had stopped chattering and could tell his tale. Nobody had stopped them as they followed Pig-boy into the narrow alley behind the hall. From the hut came the sound of men and women revelling. Pig-boy signed that the sorcerers were inside. The Companions gathered silently at the door and kicked it down. The room was full of food and flagons. Grabbing the men, they dragged them by their wild beards and matted hair to the middle of the village and forced them to their knees in front of the church.

The priest came out. Edmund grabbed him too.

'The Antichrist!' screamed one, pointing at Edmund. A small crowd was gathering, lit by bright moonlight on the snow. 'His sister brings famine to our people. She who lurks within the deepest marsh sucking on the bones of men,' the man continued.

'Rusalka!' shouted another, but the crowd of half-starved villagers stayed silent, crossing themselves over and over.

The sorcerer spat at Edmund, and the young prince shouted to the crowd, 'he lies!' 'The Lady Gytha, my sister, fears the Lord God in Heaven. A woman who fears the Lord shall be praised – she is no Rusalka but a gift of God. And as for you,' he said, kicking the man over. 'You shall endure torment here and in the life after death.'

Defiantly, the sorcerer shouted that Edmund had no jurisdiction over him, calling on Prince Vladimir to punish the English. But Edmund bellowed to the crowd, asking if these men had killed their wives and daughters. 'Yes,' they cried, one naming his mother, another a sister.

Edmund called on the people to avenge the deaths of their womenfolk in God's name. And they rallied to his call. They beat the sorcerers, ripping out their entrails while they still lived; there they found their grain and honey and fish. Then they knew them to be the devil's servants and threw them over the wall. By morning, the sorcerers had been gnawed to bones by animals.

When the prince learned that the English had freed his people from the terror of seers and sorcerers, he sent the Posadnik to them once more. Godwine and the Companions would be received at the Red Fortress and no harm would come to them. Gytha could return to the terem as princess not prisoner and the Council would hear her after the Feast of St Nicholas.

PART THREE CHAPTER SIX

JUDGEMENT

'BUT WHERE IS HE? Gytha was whispering, the fear in her throat strangling her voice. Godwine was late, and there was no sign of him. The Posadnik was waiting, the old monk, Wulfwyn and Edmund with him, ready to escort her into the Council, but Godwine was not there.

'Edmund, get him,' But in her heart, she knew where he was. Godwine was drunk. Gone was the fire in his belly that had held them together through all their hardship and misfortune. Now he would sit, morose and silent, calling for the vodka which sent men blind. His hands shook; he would shout, then fall unconscious to the floor. Gytha knew her shambling, cursing brother was leader no more and would not come.

'He sleeps and there is no waking him,' said Edmund. 'There is sick about his beard and his breeches too are wet. Icy well water will not wake him. He cannot come today.'

'How dare he do this to me!' Gytha's pain boiled over. 'Who will stand as my protector before the Council, or must I stand alone? What if the Council rules that I have sinned? I will be cast out, beyond redemption.' She faltered, burying her face in her hands. The threat of the morning hung over them and they comforted her as best they could,

'I will escort you,' said Edmund, taking her arm. 'We will not let our sadness at Godwine's torment be a hindrance to the task that faces us today, we are buffeted by storms but united in our common purpose.' The old monk blessed Gytha and Edmund, and they walked across the castle yard to face the Council together.

The painted hall was full. The black-beard priests, knights, nobles and hearthguard silent as they entered. At the far end sat Vladimir, and the Council around. The Posadnik beckoned Gytha and Edmund to the centre; the monk Ailsi and Wulfwyn to the side.

The Arch-Priest stepped forward and declaimed,

'The Lord says, "The devil takes delight in cruel murder and bloodshed and therefore incites quarrels, envy, domestic strife and slander". You,' he pointed at Gytha, 'have turned aside from My way and have committed many transgressions. Therefore, I will be a swift witness against My adversaries, against the adulterer, and against those who swear falsely by My name, says the Lord."

Gytha took a breath and dug her nails into her palms. She had promised herself she would not plead or beg, but remain calm, speaking only in a low voice. They would see no fear in her. She knew what she did was right, and she would do it again, but these words from the priest spoke only of her guilt, before she had even spoken in her defence. Willing herself to be calm, Gytha swallowed, feeling the dryness of her mouth, and glanced at the monk, Ailsi, wide-eyed, at his side. A smile of reassurance crossed his lined face, and the barest of nods. It was enough to slow the thumping in her chest and she smiled back nervously.

It was Oleg next. 'So where is he, your brother, the king without a country?' he shouted. 'So that the quiet one, slayer of seers and sorcerers must stand here in his place. I hear Earl

Godwine falls beneath his table and lies in his vomit for his dogs to lick.' Edmund coughed, unsure whether he should speak. Gytha said nothing, stiff backed and composed, staring at the weapon wall above the prince, her eyes unwavering.

'Come,' said the Prince, 'let the thoughtful Edmund speak in his brother's place. It makes no difference and I have no wish to stay here. Villages to the east have been attacked. Qypchaq run as grey wolves over the land, taking our horses, cattle and women and I will not let another village be torched and tribute stolen from under my nose while we conclude the business here. We listen, princeling. Break your silence.'

'Prince Vladimir,' said Edmund. 'The Lady Gytha will speak, as is the custom in our home. She has no need for me to speak for her.'

'Very well,' said Vladimir.

Gytha stepped forwards, holding up her crucifix that she had taken from the box beneath her bed at Waltham, with both hands. The Council observed her in silence. She had golden broaches at her shoulders, testimony to her noble birth, and the gold circlet in her hair, the distinction of her rank, but she stood before them, not lavished and adorned like the boyar Rus, but wearing the simple grey woollen tunic of the English and a blue cowl, the colour the queen of heaven's cloak.

'The Holy Cross frees from danger those who invoke it with faith.' Her voice rang out pure and true as she spoke of the terrible lie the berserker had told, and how he had defiled her honour. She spoke of her exile and of Wulfwyn and the promise he had made to her mother to protect her, and how he had honoured that vow and nearly died not once but many times. She spoke about her father, the King of the English, and of God in whom she put her faith. And she spoke of her betrothal to the Prince of the river People, by Queen Elisaveta, Prince Vladimir's aunt.

'I come among you, not as a stranger, but betrothed with you Prince Vladimir. I am the lady of your days.'

Vladimir was listening intently. He ignored his scoffing cousin Oleg, ordering him to be quiet and Gytha to carry on. She felt him looking at her, weighing her up, and she tried to address her words to the Council, rather than to him. But as she spoke, she could not help directing her gaze, her thoughts, her voice at him, and he watched her.

'Prince,' she said, 'I am at your mercy. But it was not I who thought to unleash the bear as proxy and break with the tradition of your fathers.' She paused, sensing Oleg's fury. It gave her strength. 'Your reputation as a just ruler is spoken of throughout this land. My father said that of all the things a man has within his soul, justice is the greatest good and injustice the greatest evil.'

'And your father was the learned Plato the Greek?' said the prince, breaking into Gytha's flow.

'No, Prince. His name is Harold, Harold son of Godwine, King and Ring-Giver, Minstrels sing of his daring, his mighty strength, his fair face and heart. They weigh his worth and achievements with pleasing words.' Gytha held the prince's gaze with her blue eyes, until he turned to Edmund. 'So, killer of seers and sorcerers,' he said, 'are you schooled in fighting and learning as your father?'

'Aye, Prince, and I seek justice for my vow-sister Gytha,' said Edmund unfazed.

'She stabbed my proxy from behind during a fair duel decreed by this Council,' shouted Oleg.

'No, Prince,' said Edmund. 'Our Lord intervened when he saw that it went ill for Thegn Wulfwyn; struck down, not by the hand of man in fair combat, but by a wild beast of the forest.'

'Are you claiming your sister is the hand of God?' thundered the Arch-Priest.

There was outrage in the hall: 'Eretiki! Eretiki!' they shouted. Then the Posadnik stepped into the open space, Vladimir raised his hand to demand quiet.

'The Lord saw the fight was not just. He bade his humble servant Princess Gytha kill the heathen Dane.'

'She murdered my proxy!' shouted Oleg.

'It was God's will that this cowardly warrior of Odin die at the hand of a Christian princess. Your proxy, Prince Oleg,' said Edmund, 'was a bear and Thegn Wulfwyn of Thurgarton killed it. The blemish you cast on the honour of my sister was lifted and justice done.'

'The heathen bear was proxy to your heathen proxy, Oleg,' said Vladimir, slapping his thigh, and with him the hall and Council laughed too.

Oleg jumped to his feet. 'I am not on trial here, she is!' he shouted. 'I demand compensation. Wergild for my proxy, whom this...' Oleg was about to say 'Rusalka', but stopped himself, '...this crazed shield maid slew from behind.'

There was a brief discussion, a nod of agreement from the Council, the Arch-Priest spoke. 'A fine is called for the death of the Dane Ragnwald.'

'Very well,' said Vladimir, keen to bring the matter to an end. 'How much will you accept, cousin?'

'The hoard,' said Oleg. 'The hoard is forfeit.'

Word-robbed, furious, betrayed, Gytha stared at the prince, willing a thunderbolt to strike him dead. 'No, Prince, I beg you, The Hoard is all that we have. It is all that I have.' I thought you to be a great man to whom reason and fairness might appeal, but I was wrong. Your Council is a sham, contrived to seize our hoard and throw us into slavery. It was your intention all along.'

Vladimir stared at Gytha, his anger that she should address him so brazenly, visible to all, but he said nothing.

'Prince Vladimir, None can put a price on a virgin's honour, but our freedom, our Companions, and the last of our Hoard are too high a price for my virtue. What is virtue without freedom, Prince? It is nothing.'

Edmund stepped forward. 'Prince,' he said, 'reconsider, in God's name.'

'No,' said Vladimir, cutting him short. 'This Council is ended. You have my decision. The Godwineson hoard is forfeit. All English now bear the helm and shield of my hearthguard. You are now in my service, bound by the laws of my pious and glorious grandsire, Yaroslav the Wise, answerable to none but me. And Prince Edmund, silence your sister, return her to the Terem, where her sharp tongue will serve her well with the women of my court.'

PART THREE CHAPTER SEVEN

AILSI

AILSI FOLDED HER HANDS over the velvet she was embroidering with tiny stitches, smiling but saying nothing as she worked.

Wulfwyn looked at her and then to Gytha. 'She is making a helm cap.' He said.

'Oh Ailsi, are you? For whom?' Ailsi blushed.

'For your brother Edmund, my Lady,' said Wulfwyn.

'It is a new bonnet to wear beneath his cold helm. See, here, on this lining, there is a falcon, a hare, green grass and buttercups, so as he puts it on, he will see our English home.'

Gytha took it in her hand to look more closely, 'Oh Ailsi, he will love it. He misses home as much as I.'

There was a long silence and Ailsi returned to her task. It was lonely in the Terem, Since the Council, Gytha was neither prisoner nor free. The Companions came and went at Vladimir's bidding and she and Ailsi, cared for the frail old monk and for Wulfwyn.

Wulfwyn's recovery was slow, but with Ailsi to support him and Gytha holding the priest, the four would walk the rampart, ignoring the women who sold fortunes and globs of honey for pennies. Their talk was always of home.

Wulfwyn spoke. 'Once again, I am a husk, cared for by womenfolk as I was on Flatholm Island. Ailsi, please embroider a bonnet for me too, that I can remember our home at Thurgarton.'

'Good and faithful Wulfwyn,' said Gytha, moved by the sadness in his voice, 'I shall embroider you a bonnet with dandelion stars. For dandelions are blown by the wind and where they land is where they must make their home, and grow strong wherever they are. And like dandelions and buttercups that tell of spring while the nights are still cold. My flowers will cheer you until the days grow longer – buttercups for Edmund, dandelions for my loyal Thegn and life-ward.'

'My Lady,' said Wulfwyn, his melancholy turning to laughter 'I will hear bees buzzing in my bonnet with so many flowers.'

One day, Edmund drew Gytha aside and asked her about Ailsi. Gytha giggled and struck him in the ribs with her elbow. 'You like her, don't you? She grows bonnier by the day.'

'And she is wellborn,' said Edmund earnestly,

'Oh Edmund! Would you marry her? said Gytha, hugging him. A flush reddened Edmund's cheeks. 'Ailsi is like a sister to me and I would give her to you grudgingly. Treat her well or you'll have both me and Wulfwyn to answer to. But Edmund, Ailsi too was snatched from her mother. She knows only hardship and nothing of being mistress of the warriors' hall. Ambush and treachery are her life, not bringing up children in fear of God. If this is to be your home, then Ailsi must first be schooled in her obligations. Say nothing for now, and I will turn this raw girl into a bride fit for a king.'

* * *

But fate had other plans.

Vladimir and Oleg strode into the Terem one day, drunk after long days in the saddle.

'Prince!' said Gytha, jumping to her feet, both arms up, 'you may not enter here.'

'This English maiden orders me from my Terem, Oleg' said Vladimir, his voice thick and slurred.'

'And here is pretty Ailsi too,' said Oleg, grabbing Ailsi's arm and pulling her to him to kiss her. Ailsi screamed as she tried to free herself, but the more she fought, the harder Oleg held her.

Gytha shouted at Vladimir, 'Prince, tell your kinsman to leave her be. Now!'

'What will you do, Rusalka, kill me too?' said Oleg, gripping Ailsi so hard she squealed in pain. The little chamber was now full of those terror screams of women, where moments before there had been only peace.

Without thinking, Gytha pulled the jewelled wounding-knife from her waist. 'Yes, I will, you snivelling snot-boy coward! I should have killed you and your berserker.' With that, she lunged at him, the cowl slipping from her head.

Vladimir grabbed her by her long blonde plait and snapped her head backwards. 'Stop,' he ordered.

But Gytha would not. The shield-maid fury was on her. Vladimir grabbed her other arm and twisted it up behind her. But Gytha was strong. She fought on, the dagger still in her hand. 'Prince,' she snarled, her head arched back, arm pinned behind her back, 'have you not dishonoured us enough? Now you come to the women's place. With what purpose? To rape us? Shame on you, Prince.' Her breath was coming in gasps and she struggled to free herself. Vladimir held her more tightly, as an eagle holds the venom-snake in its talon. 'My brother Edmund says you are a noble man, brave beyond measure, intelligent and honourable. But no honourable man would come here. Only a drunk with his fool.' She elbowed him with her free arm, catching him in the ribs. He gasped loudly. 'God, your stinking breath would drive hornets from their nest.'

Still holding her in his grip, Vladimir laughed. 'Hornets? You are the hornet, Gytha Haroldsdaughter. Will you sting me if I let you go? Will you?' he tugged her hair back.

'Yes! Unless he lets Ailsi go.' Vladimir eased his grip and she turned to face him. 'Make him let go of her!'

Vladimir looked into her face and could see no fear in her. 'Calm yourself, woman, before I hit you with my fist.'

'Strike me, Prince, if you must. I fear neither you nor pain. You have robbed me, now you demean yourself. Go on, do it. Strike me.' The pair glared at each other. She, the fearless daughter of a blue-eyed English king; he, the warrior prince, son of an imperial princess of Byzantium. Giving a kind of low grunt of resignation, Prince Vladimir Monomakh, the Lone Warrior, ordered Oleg to let Ailsi go. Then he pushed Gytha away and the men left the chamber, cursing all women.

'God forgive me,' said Gytha, shaking. "I hate him, I hate him with every sinew in my body. He and his sneering cousin have robbed me of my honour and my future. Robbed us of all that we are and all that we have. And now worthless and forgotten, they would violate us.'

'I hate and fear Oleg,' said Ailsi, sobbing, rubbing at her bruised arm. 'He frightens me so, Lady Gytha. He will defile me, I know it! you saved me this time, but there will come another and another.'

'We are neither of us safe, Ailsi Why else would they come into the women's house? It will happen again, and the next time we might not be blessed by God's protection. Ailsi, we cannot be alone, but must always have one of the Companions close by, even here in this place.'

*   *   *

'I'll kill them both!' shouted Godwine when he heard, staggering against the table. 'From now on, neither the Lady Gytha nor Ailsi are to leave the hall.'

'No brother,' said Gytha. 'Vladimir will consider my admonition. We are not to be prisoners in our own hall. We will double our guard when we go out and never be alone where they can find us.'

'Ailsi's danger is the greatest,' said Edmund, 'Oleg will seize her, knowing that she has only her weakened brother to defend her. You, Gytha, have all the Companions.'

'Companions who are now subject to the prince,' said Gytha, 'Oh, my brothers, sometimes all strength leaves my heart!'

Thoughtful Edmund looked at her, quoting the bards. 'Vladimir is a warrior lucky in all things. He does not know what we endure, nor does he care.'

The rag-haired Godwine fuddled by the vodka, said nothing.

'Edmund,' said Gytha, 'there is a way that Ailsi will have the Companions as her shield. Marry her now!' Edmund coloured, but Gytha went on. 'Let us make the marriage pledge between you, today!'

Godwine's head came up and he stared blearily at Gytha. 'You talk of betrothal?' he slurred. 'Only I, Godwine, Thegn of Wessex, of the house of Harold Godwineson, leader of this English company can grant the betrothal. A wife to Edmund must have a dowry fit for a king's son. This Ailsi has nothing. Not even her clothes are her own.'

'Brother, you speak of her as a foundling,' said Gytha. 'Ailsi is daughter to a Thegn, sister to Wulfwyn. Her father was a friend to our father. Her plight is our plight. My dowry too is lost but let us grant her our safety, for that is still ours to give. A dowry fit for a King's son can wait. Ailsi cannot. Unless she is betrothed to Edmund, Oleg will take her for his own.'

Godwine shook the empty flagon in his hand, then hurled it across the table at a sleeping hound. 'I forbid it. I am the head of this house,' he declared, giving a great belch. 'I am head of this house and I command you to drink with me. Bring me more.'

Edmund and Gytha shared a look. 'No brother, we won't join you. A drunk man is bad enough, a drunk woman has no place in the world. But I see no other way. Nor would Ailsi want it otherwise,' she added with a smile, 'she is smitten with Edmund, and he with her.' Edmund blushed and coughed. 'Let us not talk of such things,' he said, 'I am a warrior and know little of what you speak. But she is fair to look at and her need is great.'

Gytha gestured Edmund to a quiet corner where she could talk without being overheard. 'You talk of need. Ailsi is pretty as any girl on God's earth, Edmund. What she lacks in wisdom, she will learn from you. And as God is my witness, she is in need of your protection as never before.'

'But what of Godwine? Without his permission, I cannot proceed.'

Gytha looked at her drooling brother, his powers no longer his to wield. 'He leads in name only, Edmund. I will speak with the Companions. You are our heart of English oak now, not Godwine.' I will seek the advice of the good monk.'

Assured that Ailsi and Edmund were not prohibited according to the laws of the Holy Church, the Towering Blaecman agreed the marriage should proceed without delay, even talking Godwine into grudging acceptance. So Ailsi in a blue woollen tunic, with snowdrops for her crown, married Edmund, not in the church in case the black-beard priests prevented it, but beneath the Holy Cross hastily erected and blessed in the English hall.

After the ceremony of the Loving Cup. Ailsi dropped to her knee in front of Gytha, all memory of Oleg's attack erased from her joyful face.

'Oh, Lady Gytha, may all God's blessings rain down on you for this most joyful day!'

'I am no longer Lady Gytha but your sister, Ailsi. Your joy is my joy.'

Ailsi gazed up into her face, then leant forward to kiss her hand. 'I pray that you too will press the Loving Cup to your lips as I have this day.' Gytha nodded, a sadness sweeping over her looked at Ailsi and Edmund, so happy, and saw what fate had denied her.

PART THREE CHAPTER EIGHT

THE HAPPIEST RETURN

THE RIVER MELTED. BOATS reappeared; their hulls fresh-smeared with tar. In the fortress square, boards were laid to cover puddles, deep enough to drown a child. Spring turned swiftly into summer. The storks returned and mud tracks dried to choking dust.

Gytha woke to a great commotion: protests, groans and rough shouts. Stepping out on to the staircase, she looked across the church square to the market, its stalls laden with fresh produce. To her delight, there were camels. She could hear them clearly over the hubbub. The first caravan from the south had arrived after the winter, and the fortress square was packed with warriors, blackbeard priests, mothers and their children – everyone watching as the belching, groaning camels knelt, then dropped to their haunches.

There were Persians, Arabs and yehud Radhan, with turbans and scimitars at their waists, hawking salt, silks, oils and fragrant spices. Camels and porters milling about. It was the best of sights. Gytha was enthralled at the noise, the dust and the smell carried to her on the breeze. She longed to rush outside to the square, but dared not descend alone from the terem. Then something caught her eye. A small woman wearing a belted blue silk riding tunic, knee-high boots and a coned cap. At her side was a small round turbaned man. Their prosperity was evident. She was holding a boy by the hand and pointing at great bales of saffron, cinnamon and sweet-smelling camphor.

Gytha watched. Then her heart skipped a beat in her chest. Her breath stopped; her hand came to her open mouth. She waited for the little woman to turn. Then, before she could contain herself, she shouted, 'Swetesot! Swetesot!' And as fast as she could, Gytha ran, clattering down the stairs, and flew across the fortress square to where her heart-friend stood.

The scented Swetesot looked startled and then cried out with pleasure, holding her arms in welcome. Her eyes vanishing into the widest smile. 'Pond Eyes!' she cried. How they hugged, uncaring at the looks of those around. It was her: the same round face, but older now. When they had stepped back, still laughing in joy, the turbaned stench-man bowed deeply to Gytha with a flourish of his hand to his heart. Swetesot introduced her son. Boniak bowed as young boys do and Gytha hugged him too.

The group made a strange sight in the square, as Gytha's Qypchaq slaves gathered around the scented Swetesot, kneeling at their princess's feet, pressing their foreheads to the ground. Swetesot said something sharply in her tongue, and they rose bowing and backing away. Then the English ran up to them, with Pig-boy in the lead. Unsure what to do, Pig-boy nodded to Swetesot, squeezing all life from his cap, but she held out her arms to him and hugged him, his braying adding to the commotion. Then came the burnished Roni, Wulfwyn, dragging the old monk, till the English surrounded the little Qypchaq princess, who hugged them all.

'Come,' said Gytha, tugging Swetesot's sleeve. 'Come now with us to our hall and let us make a special feast of welcome. We are not many, but my joy today is greater than that of a thousand men – no, ten thousand men!' And while the turbaned stench-man supervised the unloading, Swetesot and Gytha walked back across the square, arm in arm. Looking up, Gytha hesitated in her excitement. The prince was watching them from the battlement; then, seeing he was observed, disappeared.

'What brings you here?' Gytha asked as they settled in the hall.

'The little merchant has business with Prince Vladimir. We are sent by his uncle, the Grand Prince in Kiev. But, Pond Eyes,' said the scented Swetesot, her face screwed up with laughter, 'I had heard of your arrival here in Smolensk and had to see you. For we owe our lives to you.' She looked round. 'And Pig-boy. And Wulfwyn too.'

'Yes, I remember the terrible night they fired your home in Exeter, as if it were yesterday. There is so much to tell and we have time enough. Here is my sister, Ailsi, wife to my brother Edmund. She has heard me talk of you more than once. Ailsi, this is the scented Swetesot, my heart-dearest friend, princess of the Wild Field.

'So, you are Wulfwyn's sister? I owe him my life.' said Swetesot, holding both Ailsi's hands. 'We were in mortal danger in Exeter. Your brother saved us and smuggled us to safety on a boat.'

'Swetesot's father is a mighty Khan, and she was taken from her parents as tribute-daughter to the Grand Prince. She was defiled by the sneering Oleg and bore his child. This is Oleg's child.

Ailsi's eyes brimmed over, unable to speak. Swetesot put her arm around her.

'I have heard the stories of what he did to you, Ailsi. You are blessed that you have Gytha, Wulfwyn and now Prince Edmund to defend you. Rescue comes in many forms.

Mine was a turbaned perfume merchant, who saved my life and my child but not my honour. I, Princess daughter of the Khan, Ruler of the Grass Ocean, was bartered to him for odours.

'I know,' said Ailsi, through her tears. 'I know the story, but it was no comfort to me. I hate this Oleg, with every tissue and fibre of my being. But I fear him more.'

Then suddenly a smile appeared on her tear-stained face and she sniffed loudly. 'But now we must be happy. I have Edmund, and Gytha is overjoyed that you have returned to us. Wulfwyn says you are the daughter of horses, the best rider in all the middle world. Will you show us how you slip beneath the horse's neck and climb back into the saddle? He talks of it often.'

The scented Swetesot shrieked with laughter. 'I was a child then. And my horse is a camel now.'

'Oh, please show us!' begged Ailsi.

'Perhaps Ailsi, perhaps. You know your name Aisulu means, beauty of the moon, in my tongue. It is perfect for you' said the little Qypchaq princess.

And so, while her turbaned husband did business, bringing news of Kiev, where Oleg's father the Grand Prince ruled, and of Chernigov, fortress home of Vladimir's father – Swetesot and Gytha talked and talked.

'I thought you were dead,' said Gytha

'I thought you were dead,' said Swetesot. 'Then when I heard that you had come to Smolensk with a betrothal claim, my heart was filled with such a longing to see you. All Kiev spoke of little else. Your brother Godwine, the king without a kingdom, and you, Gytha, the princess without a claim – shamed, slighted and humiliated. It was more than I could bear. It was then I begged the little merchant that as you had saved us, we must come to you.'

'We are without hope and it is all my fault. My brother Godwine is drunk with honey vodka. Because of me, our hoard is lost, Edmund has not the Morning Gift for his betrothed, nor Ailsi a dowry. The Companions of the Golden Dragon of Wessex must break their lances on the borderlands, and I am without a husband and grow old,' said Gytha.

Swetesot looked at her forlorn friend. 'None is more beautiful than you, Pond Eyes Gytha Haroldsdaughter. You are a queen. All of Kiev talks about your beauty and how you killed the berserker when Prince Oleg took the bear as proxy.'

Gytha shook her head. 'Oh, that sneering Oleg. I wish I had killed him too. Now the common people call me a Rusalka and would rip my guts from my body for bringing famine on this land.'

'Don't heed Oleg or the people who wish you ill, Gytha. There is only one man here to whom all submit, and that is Prince Vladimir. Maybe my husband can help get the Hoard returned to you,' She paused, lowering her voice, 'but Pond Eyes, you must kill this Kilikia'

Gytha paused, weighing each word. 'Ailsi would have me poison her; the thought of revenge fills my heart daily. But were I to harm Kilikia, would I be any better than a Rusalka from the bottomless mere?'

The scented Swetesot said nothing. Instead, giving a little laugh, she jumped to her feet and said, 'Come, Pond Eyes, Princess of Wessex. Fetch Pig-boy and Wulfwyn and we will ride as we rode before in Exeter. Put all talk of sadness and revenge away, for the day is beautiful. Aisulu, you and my son, Boniak, shall come too.'

The ponies, wild, small and shaggy, answered instantly to Swetesot. She had a quiver of arrows across her shoulders, a bow hanging at the saddle hip, and no sooner were they across the drawbridge, she set off at full gallop with a whoop, challenging the English to follow. At the feasting meadow, its air heavy with the summer scent of new-cut hay on wooden frames, Swetesot stopped.

'Show us, please!' said Ailsi. 'Show how you slip forward, gripping the mane with one hand, and swing under the horse's neck.'

'No, Aisulu, beauty of the moon,' said Swetesot, laughing. 'I am too old for such tricks. Boniak will show you as I showed him. But first let us see if I can still shoot an arrow backwards straighter than you.' Tossing a horse-rug over one of the hay-men, she challenged them to hit the bullseye at a gallop. Round and round they went, loosing arrow after arrow at the target, but try as they might, the English could not match the skill of the little Qypchaq princess or her son.

Gytha could not remember feeling such happiness. Then, suddenly, a madness took her. Looping the rein around the saddle horn to brace herself, she pulled up her stirrups like a Qypchaq warrior, and kicked the little horse on, shouting, 'Watch Boniak! I can do what your mother will not!'

Gytha set off across the meadow. She rose to her knees, steadied herself, and then stood up at the moment both Prince Vladimir and Edmund – saker falcons on their arms – entered the meadow on the far side. It was too late: Gytha's horse would not stop. It charged on through the prince's men. Gytha shrieked in fright as she tried and failed to keep her balance, leapt from the horse and crashed to the ground. Over and over she rolled. Winded, she struggled to her feet.

The prince stopped. Turning to Edmund, he said, 'Mother of God! Now she learns horse tricks from the Qypchaq princess. Edmund, there is no taming her. Take your sister to the Wild Field and let her scatter her blood over the feathergrass ocean.'

Edmund, taking the prince at his word, thought Gytha banished from Smolensk. 'No, Prince,' he protested, 'my sister is as wild as ten falcons but she has beauty, piety, grace and abundant courage. Let her remain, prince.'

Vladimir glanced down at Gytha, standing puce-faced, clutching her ribs with her arms, the pony grazing nearby. A rivulet of blood ran down her face from beneath her golden hair. 'Wild, she is Edmund and courageous. Would that she carried the lance of my hearthguard. Take your shield-maid sister whom God gave a woman's beauty and a man's courageous heart. Hobble her in the terem before she breaks her neck.'

Edmund and the others breathed again. The prince turned his horse away and, followed by the hearthguard, as Swetesot slipped from her horse to tend to Gytha's brow.

'So, Pond Eyes, you knocked the breath from the prince and yourself.'

But Gytha was in no mood for chatter, such was her anger at herself. 'I am of the blood of Shield Maidens, the daughter of Hervor who carried the sword Tyrfing, and of his wife Brynhild, with the body of a woman but to whom nature gave the soul of a man! That is what my Grandmother, the Mother of Heroes once said. But he thinks me a man.'

Swetesot took her by the arm. 'Precious friend, no man thinks that you are a man. You have the heart of a man, the strength and courage of ten men, but no man thinks you are a man.' Pig-boy brayed his agreement and Edmund ordered them back to the Fortress before there were any more mishaps.

The incident faded, along with the bruise on Gytha's forehead, and was not mentioned again until Swetesot visited again with news.

'He speaks of you,' said Swetesot.

'Who?' asked Gytha.

'The prince. He asks how we are friends. My husband told him; about Exeter, and how you saved our lives. And then he asked about the England and the Bastard William and how your father died.'

'So?' said Gytha.

'Think, Gytha. Why does he care who you are or why we are friends? He cares because he cares.'

'He does not care, he mocks. He is betrothed to Kilikia. It was his dead mother's wish.'

'But not his father's!' said Swetesot. 'His father wants a northern maiden for Vladimir. A high-born girl, as fair as his grandmother Ingegerd, daughter of the Swedish King. He sent a messenger to his sister, Queen Elisaveta, but hearing nothing, his wife, the Imperial Princess Anastasia, chose this Princess Kilikia to be wife to Vladimir instead. Kilikia is young and they ripen her as an apple on the branch. The betrothal will be in Kiev in the autumn, after the Pokrova harvest. My husband must make the arrangements for the feasting with the merchants of Kiev.'

Gytha tried to take all this in. Her head was spinning. 'What you tell me is true?' was all she could say at first.

Swetesot nodded. 'The little merchant told me this an hour ago. I came immediately to you.'

Gytha was shaking. 'Swetesot, you are sure? The prince's father sent a messenger to his sister, Queen Elisaveta, to find a maiden in the north for his son?'

'Yes' said Swetesot. 'The fairest maiden in the north for the one they call the Lone Warrior.'

'So, my betrothal claim is true and all that was said against me by the Council was false. I must speak with my brothers. We must send a message to the Posadnik in Novgorod to find the evil Cold Trader who brought me from the Dane King's hall. Then I wished him dead and burning in the furnace of hell. Now I pray he still lives. Only he can swear my claim is true. We have no time; we must do it now.'

'But what of Kilikia?' asked Ailsi. 'Her claim is true as yours. You should have killed her when you had the chance. Anyway, you hate the prince, you say it always. He has shamed you and robbed you and now he mocks you and thinks you a man fit for his hearthguard, not as a chosen bride.'

'I don't know what I feel any more. Of course, I hate him. Yet to be without a husband is worse than hate. I can guard my hate, hold it where none but me can find it, but to be without a husband can be seen by all. A woman spurned, as I am, can never find peace, nor do I seek it.' Ailsi looked confused. 'I seek justice Ailsi, and what better way than to cleave the prince from his mother's choice and force him to do his father's will. Here is my only chance to escape a slow death in a barren nunnery and be that to which I was born – a princess, daughter to a king and wife and mother of kings. Can you see that?'

The scented Swetesot, daughter of horses, a princess torn from the Wild Field, nodded in encouragement. Gytha ran to her brothers and told them all that she had heard.

Edmund listened carefully, feeding his new Saker morsels of meat from his wounding-knife.

'What choices do we have, I know this prince best of all of us and he has honoured me with a new Turul. So we must move cautiously. I cannot confront him with the word of the merchant, and his shamed wife? He will have them killed and that will be the end.'

'Then the Posadnik must bring the Cold Trader here,' said Gytha.

The Burnished Roni spoke. 'No, my Lady, we cannot send for the Posadnik, though he is our friend. All here will learn the purpose of our quest and it will go badly for us. Do not speak of this to anyone.'

Gytha let her anger brim like the surging tide. 'And you would rather we did nothing! Here, a chance to right the wrong done to me and for us to earn our freedom, and you would do nothing. You an axed and burnished huscarl? Would that my father, your King and hearth-friend, could hear you speak of doing nothing.'

'My lady,' said Roni, dropping to one knee. 'I counsel caution.'

But Gytha was not listening. It was the Young Thegn Wulfwyn who broke the silence. 'My lords and brothers, I will go north to seek the Cold Trader. If he lives, I will bring him here, in a sack if I must. He will swear before God and their Council that the Queen Elisaveta sent the Lady Gytha here as her brother had requested, to be betrothed to the Lone Warrior, Vladimir. Let me take the Gembelt Pig-boy and some men and we will move swiftly up the log roads and the rivers to Novgorod. I will find the evil Cold Trader. And should we be stopped by the prince's men, none will tell of our mission – not Pig-boy, whose love for you Lady Gytha exceeds even my own. And if they should ask me, I shall say I seek another bear to fight.' With this, he laughed loudly but Gytha sensed its hollowness and thanked him from her heart for his undertaking.

And so, choosing busy market day, Wulfwyn and Pig-boy prepared to slip away from the Fort. That last evening, Gytha summoned her two most faithful attendants to sit with her and Ailsi that they might say their farewells where no eyes or ears could spy on them. Slipping the golden ring from her finger, that she had worn since her flight began, she handed it to Pig-boy. 'Good and faithful Pig-boy. This is the golden ring of Queen Aethelflaed daughter to King Alfred. My father wished me to have it to remind me of my English blood, the

Royal house of Wessex and to be mother to many English sons. Take it to my mother, Edith Swan-neck where ever she is. Go first to Waltham and seek her there. And when you find her, it is by this ring she will know you to be true. Tell her I live, and of our journey. And how, with every waking breath, I pray for her. Now go, most faithful Baldred. I wish you Godspeed, for we will never meet again.'

Gytha put the ring in a leather purse and had Ailsi sow it into the waistband of Pig-boy's breeches. Great tears rolled down Pig-boy's cheeks, soundless sobs from his open mouth, as he clasped Gytha's hand to his heart. Gytha wept too. Not since that icy Christmas night in 1066 as the serpent headed knarr surged, banged, shuddered its way over the night-sea to Exeter had she wept so uncontrollably. Of all men on earth, no other would succeed but Baldred, her foundling Pig-boy. From him, her mother, the fair Edith her gentle-swan would know that her daughter Gytha lived. Then she summoned the frail Monk to bless them. Ailsi clutched her brother one last time and they were gone.

Gytha and Ailsi were on their knees; Godwine and Edmund were standing with heads bowed. On the straw, his mace by him, his face lit by a yellow tallow lamp, lay the once towering monk Blaecman. His breath came in shallow panting gasps as Gytha dabbed a damp cloth to his mouth.

'Fetch the priest,' she said. 'He is slipping away.'

'What priest?' said Godwine. 'He denounces the black-beard priests who would anoint him. None know the Latin mass. He'll not hear Greek or Rus spoken at his last breath.'

'A priest waits,' said Edmund, 'you cannot withhold the sacrament, Godwine.'

'Have him come!' said Gytha sharply. 'Hail Mary,' she began. The old monk stirred, opening his eyes. He mumbled something and Gytha leaned forward. 'Yes, dear father,' her lips almost brushing his cheek. She felt his faint breath. His bony fingers, delicate as parchment, tightened on hers. They were so cold.

'For me,' he whispered. 'For me are the joys of the Lord. Not for me, this dead life, fleeting, on the land.' The breath caught in his throat.

The welling tear rolled down Gytha's cheek. 'Go in peace, good monk. Fly to your heavenly home, your exile is at an end.' The Companions of the Golden Dragon of Wessex all knelt and the black beard priest performed the ultimate unction in Greek. The Towering Mace Monk Blaecman of Abingdon – friend to their father and grandmother, whose wisdom, courage and understanding had sustained them in all their darkest moments, was gone.

As she prayed, Gytha recalled their last conversation. They were talking about Godwine. Gytha told him of her torment at what her brave and noble brother had become. A once proud prince —now a violent rag-beard. The vodka flagon never far from his hand, who raged and swore at God and all about him. Rus and English, freeman and serf. All felt the fury of his fist tying him with rope until he was sober. Then, red eyed and miserable, he would cry like a child, railing at the injustice of his life, wishing for death.

'It is not for us to judge, child, *Quos Deus vult perdere prius dementator*,' he had said. 'The Lord has seen fit to rob him of everything, and his mind too.'

'Father, he must never drink their fire water again. It will send him blind and kill him.'

But the old monk shook his head. 'what else does he have? The king without a country, no wife, no hearth nor home. Let him drink. Edmund leads us now.'

PART THREE CHAPTER NINE

MIDSUMMER'S NIGHT

'COME, THE PRINCE WILL judge the prettiest maid,' said Ailsi, exited at the coming feast. It was midsummer and shrieking swifts chased down flies in swoops and circles high over the market. 'On the night the ferns bloom, there is wrestling and swordplay, juggling and drinking – all kinds of games and pranks, singing, dancing and plenty of flirting. In the centre they build a fire in a circle, and the young men and women jump the flames, two by two, under the stars.'

'The Towering Blaecman said it is a heathen feast,' said Gytha, 'and a sin to attend.'

'Not to attend Ivana-Kupala night insults the prince and his people,' said Edmund, glancing at Ailsi, 'and it is a celebration of love, fertility and mischief.'

'Swetesot, daughter of horses is a heathen, and she is your heart-dear friend', said Ailsi as if that resolved it. Gytha said nothing. Her thoughts were not of pagans, but of what the night held.

Gytha and Ailsi, dressed in the embroidered blouses. white and red skirts and petticoats of the River people, led the English down the steep slope from the Fort and over the bridge. As they entered the feast-meadow, near where Gytha had fallen at the prince's feet, the scented Swetesot waited in a split orange and blue silken Qypchaq dress, soft boots, and a pearl, garnet and lapis breast plate. Around her head was a woven golden band on which hung her perfumed oils in hollow pendula by her ears. The air was rich with her scent. Boniak was dressed as a little Qypchaq horseman, with arrows, shield and silver mask. Her husband stood proudly in his white turban and black kaftan with a stitched hem, cuff and neck, in gold. His pointed shoes turned upwards at the toes, a curved dagger at his waist.

Gytha gazed in wonder at the warrior princess from the wild field and the rich merchant.

'I marvel at your wealth and beauty, and Boniak how fierce you look,' she said laughing with delight. 'If Wulfwyn and Pig-boy could see what became of the washer-woman and the blind boy...,' she remarked.

Swetesot, serious in her reply, said, 'I thank you sister though, there are those who would rather the ravished tribute daughter had not returned.'

'Not I,' said Gytha.

A peasant woman, pulling at her arm, offered Gytha a garland crown of woven meadow flowers, daisies, St John's wort, marigold and mint. Removing her cowl, she placed the petaled wreath on her head, her golden hair falling below her shoulders. Around her neck was Oleg's necklace, the one with three-rows of amber and crystal beads, some green as a river god's eyes and some blood red as the tears of martyrs. She wished she had not chosen it to wear on this night.

'Beautiful Princess, cast this crown on the river. If a handsome prince fetches it before it floats away, he will be your husband.' said the woman.

'I should have such a crown of petals,' said Ailsi, frowning a young girl's frown.

'You have a handsome prince, Ailsi! One is enough,' said Edmund.

Swetesot and Gytha laughed at Ailsi's disappointment, then Edmund broke her mood. 'Speaking of handsome princes, we must greet this prince.' Gytha gritted her teeth, steeling herself.

'I have suffered God's judgement and must now endure a judgement of stares. I pray for the end to this night of embarrassment.'

The Lone Warrior was seated on a throne mound beneath an ancient oak tree, his Arab stallion tied nearby, a jewelled Frankish longsword hanging from the tasselled saddle. One hundred flags flew from lances pressed into the black soft earth in a circle around him. A young man was playing a lute. On his right sat the princess Kilikia, child bride, green garlanded like Gytha. Prince Oleg stood talking with the knights, nobles and commanders of Vladimir's hearthguard, their sons wrestling for prizes.

Holding her head up and straightening her back, as St Perpetua facing the lions, Gytha walked toward him, knelt, bowed her head low as was expected, then greeted the noble ladies in turn. Gone were his warring clothes. Now Prince Vladimir had on his finest tunic of deep purple silk brocade, with golden clasps across the front. Around his waist was a leather belt with golden studs, from which hung a small satchel. He wore light rawhide boots and pale blue leg cloths. His great head was smooth-shaved but for his warrior plait and thick black moustache. His dark and noble features, his brown eyes and the ruby and pearl earring, the gift of his Imperial mother Anastasia, daughter of the Christian Emperor in the East, were lit by the warm evening sun.

He looked magnificent, Gytha thought. He was as handsome as the first time she ever lay eyes on him. She would not faint again, though the necklace about her neck was so tight she feared it might strangle her.

'Greetings, noble Prince,' said Edmund, bowing down low, hand to heart.

'Ah, English, you have plucked the finest flowers from our meadow.' The prince was all smiles. 'Join us and watch the fun. Sit here to my left,' he said, waving Gytha, Edmund and Ailsi to an Isfahan rug, leaving Swetesot, Boniak and her husband to stand. The sneering Oleg stared ahead. Gytha prayed the feast would pass quietly, wondering if Oleg knew or cared that Swetesot's son was his.

'Edmund,' said Vladimir as more food and drink arrived, 'what news of the Lady Gytha's champion, the limping Wulfwyn and the braying one? Their bear hunting takes them far to the north, I'm told.' Gytha's heart skipped a beat. She glanced at Ailsi.

Edmund shrugged. 'They hunt to the north. Would that I could fly your Saker gift with them.'

'Eat,' ordered the Prince, and waved to the trestles of golden roasted geese, wild boar, and river fishes, zander, sturgeon and tooth-grin pike, and to the pastries and pies that spilled from heaped baskets.

'Eat, eat, eat!'

'Prince,' said Edmund, 'First, let us challenge you to an archery contest, before the vodka blurs our aim.'

'Oleg' called the prince, taking two flagons and handing one to Edmund 'come, we will show this girl-haired princeling how vodka makes the River people shoot straighter.'

The challenge accepted, Edmund passed the flagon to the burnished Roni, and the four men stepped onto the game-field to swig and draw their bows at the distant targets.

'He plays with you,' said Swetesot, in Gytha's ear.

'How?' said Gytha, the petal crown uncomfortable on her head.

'The prince. He plays with you. He has his betrothed to his right and you, Pond Eyes, to his left. He speaks only with your brother. Take care.'

'You should have killed that Kilikia,' Ailsi whispered.

'What do you mean, Swetesot? He plays?'

'He does. Who knows why' said Swetesot, 'Though I will wager you will know as the night draws in, Gytha?' Gytha was unsettled by Swetesot's words.

Night fell, the flares were lit, the cooking fires hissed and spluttered. The air was full of stinging smoke, laughter and music. In the centre of the feasting field, young people gathered in a great circle, singing, holding hands, ready to jump the flame. Kilikia and her mother sat unmoving.

'Come,' said the prince, standing up. 'Who will jump the cleansing flame with me?'

Gytha did not move, waiting for him to take the child Kilikia. But he did not, he was looking at her. The blood rushed to her cheeks. 'Prince,' she stammered, 'do not shame me again in the sight of your people.'

'Gytha! I come at you! You will jump the cleansing flame with me,' he said, seizing her arm. 'Come,' he insisted, pulling her up roughly.

'Prince stop!' Gytha cried, 'you hurt me.' But he would not stop. Instead, making her worst fears real in front of the blackbeard priests, the noble wives and the Princess Kilikia's mother, Vladimir pulled Gytha protesting, toward the river bank. Edmund, Roni, Ailsi and the Companions looked on. There was nothing they could do.

There was a gap in the trees, a strand where willow, wormwood and alder stood aside for cattle and sheep to drink safely at the shore. The river moved darkly silent under the moonlight.

'So, Lady of my Days!' he said, spinning her around to face him, still holding her arm tightly. 'Cast your green crown on the water, that this handsome prince may fetch it before it floats away.'

Gytha froze, her blue eyes wary, brow furrowed, her face and hair gilded by countless tallows. 'What do you want with me, Prince?' she asked, trying to free her arm, shouting to make herself heard above the singing. 'Your betrothed sits at your side, yet you snatch me. You play with me as a cat with a mouse. Or will you ravage me here under the riverbank as Oleg would ravage Ailsi were Edmund not here? I am no mouse, Prince, nor would you ravage me and live. All fear you but I do not.' She paused as he let go of her arm. 'Do you forget Prince Vladimir!' She spat his name. 'You are betrothed with that child-woman, Kilikia.'

Vladimir, his deep brown eyes finding only anger, changed his tone. 'Call me Vladik, Gytha. I pray that it was not so – that you, not Kilikia, were my betrothed. I have observed you these months.' He was slurring slightly. 'Your beauty and spirit, Gytha, are like no other. You are more dangerous than the Qypchaq wolves that stalk the borderlands and yet your girl-haired English love you and would die for you.' He put his hand up to her cheek. 'I would die for you Lady of my Days. I would.' And then added, with a sort of laugh, 'were I a girl-haired English.'

Gytha brushed his hand away and took a step back, a branch stopping her from slipping down the bank. She was speechless. The singing grew louder. The branch was digging painfully into her back. Should she reveal that she knew about his father's wish, and the real reason for Wulfwyn's journey north? What if Wulfwyn never returned, or without the Wendish devil, the Cold Trader. Without proof to press her claim, the Council would never accept her. She would just be another woman of the Terem.

She needed time. But he was giving her none. She had to think. This might be her only chance to speak with him alone. Did he really mean he would die for her? Or was he mocking her? She knew so much, and so little of men's ways. The panic was rising again. She called on all who lived in her heart to guide her, to her father and mother, to Colwenne, even to Queen Aethelflaed for the words that she must speak before this Prince tired of her silence and left.

'Prince,' she began. She paused. Then, suddenly, she knew what to say.

'Prince, I know your words of love to be a passing truth. The vodka moulds the meaning of your breath. I thank you Prince, but you would not die for me, even if you had Samson's locks to your shoulders. The Princess Kilikia is your betrothed. It was your mother's dying wish. Now you humiliate and shame her, as you humiliated and shamed me before the Council, the knights, the noble wives, the black-beard priests, the hearthguard and the all the people of this land. Please speak no more of dying for me or wishing circumstances other than they are. The Lord's will be done. Return me to the mound under the oak tree and carry Kilikia over the cleansing flames, as is your duty.'

Vladimir was suddenly stern again. 'And now you tell me my duty! God help me were I to grant you power over me, Gytha. No, I will not carry that child over the flame, do you understand?' He crossed his arms across his chest, the golden bracelets gleaming, tipping his bald head up, daring her to speak again. But Gytha held her tongue, defiant, her eyes never leaving his.

'Come,' he ordered, 'throw the green garland crown into the water and if I snare it with my sword before it floats away, you, Gytha, will be my handfast wife as your mother with the swan's neck was handfasted to your father the King.'

'How can you say this?' said Gytha, shocked. Pulling the wreath off her head, she hurled it far out onto the stream where he could never retrieve it or drown in the attempt.

'There!' she said, 'fetch that, with your swan's neck.' She was shaking with anger.

Such defiance cannot have gone unnoticed, but Vladimir barely paused. Gytha did not care.

'I know this from the khan's daughter Swetesot,' he said, his tone icy.

'Prince,' she said, 'You speak of my mother Lady Edith Swan-neck as a bed wife. But my mother, my gentle swan, was rich in land, noble born and beautiful to behold. My father chose her, but she chose my father, Prince. They loved each other always and she is mother to his five children. It was my mother that my father sought to lie with before marching to fight the Bastard William, never to return. No Prince, you will not take me as your handfast wife only to cast me out when the child Kilikia is ripe to pluck.'

'You hate me, Gytha,' he said, more as a fact than a question.

'Yes,' she replied. 'I hate what you have done to us. Godwine is a drunk, our Hoard is taken, the Companions of the Golden Dragon of Wessex break their lances in the borderlands at your whim. And, as if you have not shamed me enough, you abuse my father's love for my mother to take me into your bed. Yes, I hate you.'

There was a heavy silence between them. Vladimir seemed to struggle for words, all swagger gone. 'What can I do to make you hate me less, Princess Gytha? Return the Hoard as your Morning Gift if you will be my handfast wife?'

'Oh, you think yourself so clever, Prince. Now you bribe me to your bed with what is mine, which you have stolen. You think you can steal my pride and virtue too?' Gytha wanted to run away, as far and as fast she could – but she knew not to turn her back on this prince, here in his lands, among the watching River people.

'I'll tell you what you can do for me. There is somebody I hate more than you, Prince. Your treacherous cousin, Oleg. Send him to the borderlands to break his lance on the wolves of the Wild Field, for if he stays my English will tie him by his feet to a wild horse's tail, as the Qypchaq do, and let him dance over the steppe.'

'But he is my cousin, and brother in arms. And Gytha you may call me Vladik.'

'He is treacherous, Vladik. You do not see it. He would kill Edmund to take Ailsi from him for sport. Just as he ravaged the scented Swetesot, and left her with a child. Her boy is his son, Vladik.'

Vladimir thought for a moment, frowning, his boldness gone. 'I remember.'

Gytha waited.

And if I grant you this? If I send Oleg to the borderlands, and order him to redress the wronged and ravaged daughter of horses, whom you love as your sister, then will you be my handfasted wife Gytha?'

'No, Vladik. I will not.'

He paused, shaking his head, as if her answer was beyond his understanding. Then he gave her a kind of half smile, a shrug of resignation. Perhaps the night air had cooled them both. 'Very well Gytha, I grant all you wish and ask for nothing in return. Except,' grasping her hand, 'except your beauty, against which I have no clashing weapon. You make the proud foolish and the strong weak. Lady of my Days fly with me now over this cleansing flame, for all to see.

'And the fervent I make mad, it seems, Prince,' she replied, sensing his confusion, her tone mocking.

'Lady of my Days,' he repeated, a little huskily. 'The two of them were looking at each other, lingering, their eyes tracing each feature, then quickly looking away.

Gytha, her anger withering, sighed. Was it acceptance, or exhaustion, she was not sure? But it was not defeat. Maybe there was no need to fear him, maybe she did have power over him. This prince, on whose whim all lives depended, this Christian man who gave to orphans, protected widows and brought death to his enemies, was asking, no, begging her, and it was hers to grant.

'Vladik, if I jump the flame with you,' she faltered, her words lost to the sound of the singing. 'we cannot jump back.'

Vladimir curled his arm across her back, pulling her to him. She did not resist. This was her moment, the Lord might never grant her another. Flinging hesitation, like her garland to the unregarding river, she slipped her hand under his belt, the heavy silk of his tunic bunching in her grasp. She pressed her blonde hair against his chest. Her heart was pounding so loudly in her ears, she was sure he must hear it. Then, their bodies locked side by side, they set off across the meadow to lead the young people, two by two, to leap the midsummer blaze.

PART THREE CHAPTER TEN

'THE HILL IS IN YOUR HEART'

'RUSALKA! RUSALKA!' THEY CHANTED.

Inside the terem, Gytha and Ailsi were trapped, terrified. It had started after the feasting, as Gytha knew it must. Kilikia's mother demanded Gytha be banished, saying she had bewitched the prince. But Vladimir refused. Instead, he left for the borderlands taking Edmund, Roni and the Companions. To Gytha's dismay Oleg was left in charge of the fortress in his absence. Of the English, only Godwine remained, playing loud board games for money with shaking hands as the vodka destroyed him.

At first, only a few had shouted, pointing at Gytha in accusation. 'Rusalka! 'Rusalka!' Then more gathered. Some spat at her, some crossed themselves.

The situation was grave.

'Vladimir punishes me still, because I will not be his bed-wife,' said Gytha, wishing the night at the feasting field had never happened. 'He even makes his sneering cousin our gaoler, though I begged him to send Oleg to the border.'

Ailsi was crying, 'I don't know who I fear more, Oleg or this crowd who will drag us out of the terem and kill us.'

'No, they won't,' said Swetesot.

Ailsi still sobbed. 'How could he leave us in the care of Oleg?' She wailed as the voices outside grew more insistent.

'Ru-sal-ka! Ru-sal-ka!'

'Vladimir is wily, Aisulu, calm yourself,' said Swetesot, 'he shames Oleg by leaving him here to guard women. Charged with our safety, Oleg dare not let any harm come to you. Yes, Vladimir is wise and wily like his grandfather.'

'He's not wise,' Ailsi shouted. 'These river princes make misery from mischief. Don't you see, the three of us, yes and that child Kilikia too It is their sport.'

The chanting stopped. Gytha peered from the tiny window. 'Swetesot, Oleg is in the square, his men are ordering the people to go.'

'I tell you Pond Eyes, the prince is clever, but he is a man.' said Swetesot. 'He wants only for you to grant him his wish.'

'You mean he meditates daily how he might enjoy delights that I deny him. I remember you said that about the turbaned merchant, many winters ago.

'Do it,' begged Ailsi, 'we will be killed if you do not. He will lose patience with you and the people will welcome it. My lady sister, be his bed-wife, I beg you Gytha.'

Gytha looked from Ailsi to Swetesot. 'So, saddle-born Princess from the Wild Field? Do I grant the prince his wish, but never wed in the eyes of God who knows all secrets?'

'*Oturğanım oba yer basqanım baqır canaq. Ol zengi,*' said Swetesot.

'What does that mean, my heart-dear friend?'

'Where I sit is a hilly place. Where I tread is a copper stirrup bowl.'

'Don't talk in riddles of hills and stirrups. Tell me what I should do?'

'Ride to the top of the hill, stand in the copper stirrup to see what lies ahead. From here you see only the waving grass.'

'And where is this hill Swetesot?'

'The hill is in your heart, Gytha.'

How her words seared. 'If I climb your hill, Swetesot, daughter of horses, what will I see? The road taken or the road still to come? I am betrothed to Vladimir, that is my road. But unless Wulfwyn returns with proof of my claim, there is no road. The Prince must wed Kilikia and I will not be his bed-wife. That is the hill in my heart.'

It was a year since Gytha first laid eyes on Vladimir. July slipped into August. It was hot and humid. In the fields beyond the walls, broken barley, flattened by summer hails was gathered in by bending peasants. Scythes and sickles glinting the measured rhythm of the harvest. High above the marketplace, hungry stork chicks clacked and teetered on perilous nests, waiting for their parents to return with a frog or cricket, while below the shouts and smells and dust of beasts and traders, heralded each arrival.

Sometimes Gytha, Ailsi and Swetesot dared browse the bales of silks and spices. Oleg's watchful guards close by to silence the cries of Rusalka that followed her. Even within the terem, she was among enemies. Kilikia's mother would curse at the sight of her. Only Ailsi and Swetesot were her friends, guarding her day and night, a thrall testing each dish before she ate it, in case of poison. Of the vain and boastful Oleg they saw little. Mercifully for Ailsi he chose to toy with the daughters of lesser men.

It was Swetesot who said it, when Ailsi paled and stumbled from the room, the sound of her retching plain to hear.

'The stork has brought more than a frog. That one is with child,' she said with the knowing woman's smile that accompanies such prophesies. And so it was; Ailsi was pregnant. Gytha's joy was true and heartfelt. The English would, God willing, have a royal heir of the finest English blood. But her predicament, the one that consumed her waking day and each tossing turning night, was still unresolved. Where was Wulfwyn? Had he found the Cold Trader? Had he got the evidence of her betrothal? Or was he dead? Another uncrossed grave on the log road? And so, as Ailsi's breasts and stomach rounded, Gytha became thinner and thinner.

Early one morning, news reached them that Prince Vladimir, Edmund and the English were returning, driving before them hundreds of captive men and horses seized on the border. The day of joy she dreaded most, had arrived.

'We must see that our English warriors have such a feast to welcome them, said Ailsi, shouting at the kitchen thralls. 'Mead and barley beer for every man, have the cooking fires lit. Hurry, hurry, they arrive.' Then she and Gytha climbed up the wooden steps to watch as the returning warriors crossed the fortress bridge. Gytha scanned the horizon in vain for her fresh cheeked Radknight Wulfwyn. Ailsi, one hand idle across her stomach waved furiously when she sighted Edmund and the Companions, the clatter of their horses and their homecoming cheers reaching to their high eyrie on the battlement. But Gytha seeing Vladimir riding at the head of his men, his war-shirt off, bare chested, looking about him, victorious, his side knot flicking back and forth, felt only wild beasts invading her belly. Once again, her life rested not with God, but with this River Prince, this Lone Warrior.

That night, as the English gorged on tender venison, capercaillie stew and sweet berries baked in pies, the prince entered the hall alone. His head was freshly shaved and oiled, the ruby and pearls gleaming in his left ear. He had on a fresh white linen shirt, embroidered with flowers, held closed with a broad sash, and new leather trousers loosely tucked into doe skin boots. Gytha froze mid word. He had the lightness of a man well pleased. If he was weary, it did not show, except for the helm-marks that made his face look thinner, she thought, and haughtier. He looked about him as the minstrel fell silent. Then he began to speak, his voice rich and clear, even those at the back could hear him. He started by thanking God for his safe return from Christendom's edge and mourning the dead in the words of his ancestor Svyatoslav, "Let us lay down our lives and fall in battle. The dead have nothing to be ashamed of", and then he thanked Edmund and the Companions, honouring their deeds, saluting their endeavour, praising all, naming some.

Gytha watched him terrified, fascinated - the nobility, the piety, the power of the sun-dark River prince, addressing her ruddy, round-faced English, with their matted beards and hair to their shoulders. The finest fighting men on God's earth, he called them and how they roared back at him, but he had yet to look at her.

Edmund, then commended the prince in turn, thanking him for the spoils of their skirmishing, for the bounty that was theirs, weighing his worth, his mighty strength and many achievements with pleasing words. For a moment, Gytha was in her father's hall, on her bed, playing 'the Lord I marry' with her gentle swan. 'The Lord I marry, what will he be like? and Edith Swan-neck would think a while and say, 'well dearest child, he will be fair faced, tall with blond hair to his shoulders, a mighty warrior, the bravest in the Kingdom, with bright blue eyes, a loving heart, and maybe the scent of honey-mead on his breath.' Gytha swallowed hard and hoped that no one could see the tears that welled, blinking them away like a stinging cinder from the hearth.

Then Gytha, most noble maiden in the English Hall, rose to offer the prince the brimming welcome horn, its silver rim crafted into coiling curling monsters by the finest English smiths.

Vladimir, creator of all her misfortunes, looked down at her and smiled broadly.

'So, Lady of my Days,' he said, 'my home-coming is complete or nearly so. We left matters unresolved, as I remember.'

No sooner had he spoken than the turmoil of the feasting field threatened to engulf her, but she forced herself not to show him the disorder in her heart.

'Prince,' she said feigning calm, holding the horn up to him with both her hands, 'it was my prayer each day that you and my brother return to us from the heathen border. The Lord has granted me that wish. I know nothing of other matters that need resolution.'

Was he irritated? She saw the impatient flick of his warrior plait. She held his gaze. Taking the cup from her, the prince, loudly wishing joy to Edmund's fruitful bride, 'mother of many English sons', tossed his head back and drank the whole horn in one, bellowing at the last gulp, as men do.

'Princess,' he said, wiping his moustache with the back of his hand, his belching mead breath sour. 'Shield-maid sister from beyond the grey west sea whom God gave a woman's beauty and a man's courageous heart. I wish I had you in my hearthguard.'

'Hearthguard and bed-wife Vladik? Not even Oleg seeks such a companion.' Her voice was low, but he heard her clearly.

The prince shook his head. It was the same look he gave her on the river bank; surprise, incomprehension, but mostly awe. 'You fear no one, do you Gytha?' he said. It was not a question, nor did Gytha feel the need to answer. Then the Prince guffawed and the hall laughed with him. The moment passed, the feasting and drinking began anew, the singing louder than before.

*   *   *

Beneath the walls a graver issue was unfolding in the slave sheds by the river. It was here that Vladimir's captives from the borderlands were housed. Hundreds of Pecheneg, Pole, Mari, Wallach and Torq, men women and children awaiting shipment to the great slave market in the south. Now they were running crazily, howling as if attacked by monsters. Death, when it came was swift and merciful.

The gate was sealed. All gathered in the church, noble and thrall prayed together for the intercession of Panteleon of Nicomedia, the saint of healing. To no avail, within days more captives were dead, bewitched, some said, by river sprites that bit them as they slept.

It was Ailsi who spoke up. 'I have been held in sheds, abandoned by God and all hope lost. My prayers were answered when you, Gytha, saved me. We must answer their prayers now. We cannot leave them in the sheds to die.'

'What prayers?' snorted Godwine. 'They are heathens. Let their Gods save them.'

Gytha thought carefully. 'Ailsi is right. If no others will go to the sheds then we will, it is our holy duty not to walk by on the other side. Ailsi you are to be a mother soon, you must remain. I will go.'

Godwine and Edmund's plea for her to stay in the safety of the fortress, fell on deaf ears. Gytha descended the hill with her Qypchaq thralls, the wailing growing louder as she approached the sheds. Putrid greening corpses lay everywhere. The still-living were scratching at swollen, blackening blisters, vomiting, and writhing at the terrible burning in their limbs. A few stood praying to heathen gods, others danced crazily, or stared into eternity as mortals do when all hope on earth is lost. Gytha neared a group of watching peasant women, unsure if she should take another step, or turn to flee back to the fortress.

'Princess, the kasha broth is blighted, it is the purple mould that kills them.' shouted a straw-shod woman, the same one who had given her the flowered wreath on midsummer night.

'The kasha broth?' said Gytha, holding her cowl tight across her face, 'Where is the kasha grain stored?' Beckoning, the woman led Gytha to a shed, overgrown with wormwood. A musty stench soured their noses even before the door was forced.

'What is your name? asked Gytha kindly,

'Fevronia, Princess' said the woman, showing no fear of the Rusalka princess, about whom all had heard so much.

Inside was a mound of unmilled grain, higher than a man. Scooping a handful, Fevronia showed Gytha the purple-black kernels, picking them out with her finger tips and holding them up for Gytha to see.

'But this grain is all blighted,' said Gytha in surprise, recoiling at the smell. 'This is why they die. This is not pestilence but St Anthony's Fire. That is why they dance and howl. Fevronia, I will save those not yet dead. I can make the sickness go. No more will die.' Turning to the captain of the guard, she pointed an accusing finger at him. 'It is you who has killed these people, it is you who feeds them blighted kasha. You have cost Prince Vladimir dear and will surely die for it.

'No Princess, I beg you,' the man replied in terror. 'It was Prince Oleg who gave orders to feed the prisoners old grain.'

'Princess,' said Fevronia, 'Prince Oleg sold our good grain to merchants, but we were never paid.'

'Then I will see you are paid, Fevronia, said Gytha, 'Prince Oleg has much to answer for.' Then, addressing the captain, she said, 'burn this grain and the slave sheds. See all are new housed and receive fresh gruel, made with clean kasha meal, every day. When the Prince asks why the captive heathens died in your care, pray he spares your life.'

Quarters were found, the sheds and the old grain set alight. Lifting each corpse to the pyre, the Qypchaq thralls sang for the departed spirits, the air heavy with hemp and charring flesh. The inferno licked all night at the fortress, casting the massive walls in an ungodly light as if lit from within, red as the unquenchable fires of Hell. Those captives who still lived, were given sour qumiz milk, absinth broth made from the wormwood leaves, hogweed and fresh kasha meal. Soon, as Gytha had foretold, all were well again.

No longer did the people in the fortress talk of a foreign Rusalka, but of the English princess who heeded the cries of the dancing dead with Christian mercy, and returned them to this life. The knights, the noble wives and merchants left gifts for Gytha at the terem. Slaves pressed their foreheads to the ground on which she walked. Minstrels sang of the beauty from beyond the grey west sea. They gave the song a name. All the River people, from the sedge bogs in the north to beyond the rapids far far to the south, knew it. They called it Gytha's Miracle.

'So, Pond Eyes,' said Swetesot, watching Gytha decorating a swaddling cloth for Ailsi's baby, 'now all would have you as their queen.'

'And holy saint,' said Ailsi, humming the tune.

'Don't speak so Ailsi. They hated me and called me Rusalka, now they love me. Only Kilikia's mother still spits on my shadow.'

'And prince Vladimir?' asked Swetesot, 'does he love or spit?

'Do not mock me, Swetesot. His silence is formidable. He awaits my answer. Just say yes and my future is secured until this lone warrior tires and seeks a different vessel. So, my answer is no. I will not be his handfast bed-wife. He called me the 'Lady of my Days', but how many days before he casts me from the Terem as you were banished from the palace at Kiev.

'You will not be bartered for odours to a passing turban, Pond Eyes. I was a new-blood maiden, pitilessly ravished and with child.' said Swetesot, rebuking her.

'Oh, forgive me, I meant no harm nor trim your sorrows. Few have been so wronged as you my heart dear friend. Only, I too have suffered since my father was killed and everything, everything that was ours was lost to one arrow from the sky.' Gytha picked up the embroidery and bent to it once more, choosing brightly coloured threads and stitching minutely while the light lasted. 'Oh, Swetesot,' she said, after a little while, 'Where are the good? The Lord takes them all, one by one, but I need them, here, with me. If only the Lord would grant me one prayer. To leave this lonely strong-hold, and fly to my father's hall. I yearn for my gentle swan to fold me in her arms or to hide beneath the mead-bord at my father's feet. He would ask "Where is Gytha?" And when I could no longer breathe for giggling, I would jump up and he would say "Oh, so I have a dog for a daughter, good dog, come gnaw on this tasty shin-bone." Oh, how I loved my father and miss my brother Magnus and my sister Hilde too. Our home was happy and I was loved, but's its all gone. Now I am alone.' She sighed. 'Lord grant me just one day to walk the soft green meadows among the farmhands or sit with the fisherfolk and listen to their telling in the accents of my English home. I tire so of exile, of strangers, never knowing who is a friend or an enemy, or what will happen to me next. Am I never to be the mistress of my destiny, unless my destiny is to be his mistress? I command nothing, not even beauty is mine to order, yet it is what he prizes. Many years ago my aunt Gunhild, cautioned me, though I was too young to understand. She said men's passions overwhelm them. They worship what they desire only until it is won. Little did I know

that I would suffer hatred and lust in equal measure on account
of this beauty. I am cursed, as Eve in the garden.'

'Gytha, a woman is a guest in this life. Men welcome us
joyfully, but men have long hands. Why do you care what
he desires?' asked Swetesot, her almond eyes watchful as the
half-sleeping cat.

'I don't, but he desires my beauty. But beauty is a blessing
given by God. I am more than beauty, yet he measures my
worth as he measures a man. He honours my courage and my
spirit. He sees a shield maid. He wants me in his hearthguard.
But as a woman he desires only my beauty.'

'You mean he does not see within?'

'Swetesot, I am a woman, with a woman's compassionate
heart. I would sooner love than hate. I look at Edmund and
Ailsi and wish only the same for me. I yearn to cradle a good
man to my bosom as my mother cradled my father in life and
in death. I yearn for a child. Is that wrong Swetesot, to need
gentle words not rough demands?

'And that is what you want from the prince?' asked Swetesot

'No!' Gytha replied, no!'

Swetesot looked at her for a long time.

'I don't know,' said Gytha awkwardly.

'I know,' said Swetesot. The yearning you feel within you
is love. You have only felt loss. For you love is loss, love is
grief. Love is the cold doorway to your past. This yearning
is another love, the love that sings like the sweetest bird. The
love that comes to fill every corner of your heart with warmth
and joy. Let this love in, not as a thief to rob you of all you
hold most precious but as the friend that makes broken hearts
whole.' Swetesot waited, and then added quietly, 'Gytha, you
love Prince Vladimir.'

'I do not,' she interrupted, 'I hate him with every fibre of
my being. All I see is Kilikia as Vladimir's betrothed and lawful

wife. I am destroyed. My last hope was my life-ward Wulfwyn. But it has been too long, His body rots beneath an uncrossed mound out on the log-road.

'My heart dear friend, you speak these words, but your brimming Pond Eyes could tell another story. Set your pain aside and listen to me Gytha, you love the Prince. You talk of his rough hands and lust and demands. The man is a warrior, feared by all, he is not a poet. What does he know of women? So do not think of the warrior, terrible and ferocious, but of the boy within. He too has a hill in his heart and that hill is you. He too searches the road ahead and sees only the wild field. Vladimir is not the painted Celt Prince, nor sneering Oleg. Vladimir is noble and he is good. He honours his mother's dying wish to marry Kilikia. But he calls you the Lady of his Days. He jumped the flame of destiny with you. He wishes the world was otherwise, with you. These are the words and deeds of love, Gytha! The prince is lost, in you!'

'Oh, I rejoice at everything you say. It is true I love him but it cannot be. Say no more. I am bleeding and when my heart is empty, I will toss far into the river to the tooth-grin pike, where it can never trouble me again.'

'And be the lady of your days alone, with the child Kilikia to rule over you, here in the terem! No Gytha, give offering to Tengri, the blue eternal sky and to the thrice bright Sun and to the moist mother earth. Your heart is a fruiting tree. You will be the mother of heroes.'

'Swetesot!' said Gytha, 'enough of your pagan talk. I will not give offerings to your spirits. The Lord is God in heaven above and on earth below and there is no other.'

'Gytha,' said Swetesot, very earnestly, 'your grandmother, the Mother of Heroes, keeper of the old ways, whispered prayers to many gods.'

PART THREE CHAPTER ELEVEN

ARDENT

'ACCEPT THE TRUE FAITH.' Vladimir was insistent.

It was a crystal day edged in autumn's gold. Gytha was riding next to the Prince. Behind them rode the Companions, Edmund, his saker dozing on his arm, Ailsi, Swetesot and Boniak, some nobles and their wives. The prince was in high spirits, serious one minute, joking the next as the small party picked their way past fallen trees and bottomless meres.

'Forswear the excommunicant creed and accept the seven sacraments,' he said, keeping his voice low.

Gytha's excitement at this invitation to visit the prince's stud-farm turned to shock. This was a new demand. What should she say? In her head she heard the Towering Blaecman chiding her to resist such talk.

'Why, Vladik?' She replied, trying to make light of it. 'Now you think me a pagan?' And she laughed.

'Gytha, you are no pagan, the daughter of horses is a pagan, but your Latin rite is heresy. Now that your mace monk scolds us no more, the Arch-Priest commands all English grafted, as apple branches in the orchard, to our communion. Renounce the heretic path of Rome and follow the True Faith to sit on the right hand of our heavenly father.'

Gytha bit her lip. The joy of the morning ebbed from her. What did he mean by 'heretic path?' The dark forest yielded to a sunlit meadow where a hundred or more horses grazed peacefully under the watchful eyes of men and dogs, the threat of lynx, wolves and bears ever present. At the far end was a moated square palisade of rough logs, an old frontier fort, its gate topped by a steep roofed watchtower.

Vladimir eased his horse close to hers as if nothing was amiss. 'Gytha.' She stared straight ahead. 'Lady of my days, I have a surprise for you,' he said.

They dismounted and the prince led Gytha to a pen. A mare whinnied. Her broad-dished face, wide brown eyes and high tail marked her as the finest Arab breed.

Behind her stood a chestnut foal, watching them approach.

'This is my beloved Sfandra, and this is Saheem.'

'Oh, he is beautiful!' gasped Gytha.

'Yes, exquisite, just a week old. His father is Habib, my clean-blood stallion.' Vladimir crouched down slipping a strong arm around the colt's chest, and the other around its rump, cuddling it like a girl to his heart. Forgetting his comments on the ride, Gytha knelt down close beside him.

'Saheem, Saheem,' she murmured. her shoulder brushing Vladimir's arm. The foal, teetering on wobble legs, suckled at her finger, uniting them in limpid eyed inspection.

'See, he loves you already,' said Vladimir, 'you have melted his heart.'

'And he melts mine,' she said, a smile welling from within.'

'Then he is yours! Vladimir announced. 'I give him to you, The Lady of my Days.'

'Oh Prince,' said Gytha in delight, moulding the warmest words to free the bonds of gift and giver. 'He is perfect. He is the most beautiful present I have ever received and Saheem is a fine name. Saheem,' she repeated it. 'It has the sound of the rushing wind and the earth beneath. What does it mean?'

'It too is perfect. It was my choice. Mine alone.' Vladimir laughed so loudly the little horse bounded away in alarm. 'Saheem means Arrow. It is perfect, is it not?' His face was alive with satisfaction. 'He will be the swiftest arrow, and you will be the envy of all the River people.'

'Oh,' said Gytha.

Vladimir's delight died. 'You don't like it?'

Gytha glanced to where Swetesot and the others were watching.

'No, Vladik, you are right. It is a beautiful name and I thank you for the gift from the bottom of my heart. He is perfect.'

'But in your blue eyes, rain has returned where I hoped only for sunshine.' He stood up. 'I command sunshine.' He lifted Gytha's chin with his gloved hand, but she drew her head away taking his arm instead, holding it in both her hands, trying to read his face as she spoke.

'I cannot love an arrow. An arrow killed my father, an arrow destroyed my life.'

'An arrow brought you here, to me, straight and true.'

'Prince... Vladik, don't, don't make light of it. I thank you, but I cannot accept Saheem. It breaks my heart but I cannot accept him.

His surprise turned to anger. 'You cannot accept him? A clean-blood Arabian stallion! The most priceless jewel in all of Rus. I bred him. His seed will flourish for one thousand years, Gytha!'

'I'm sorry, Vladik.'

Not another word was spoken. The Lone Warrior went to his hut in the rough palisade and Gytha to hers.

'I cannot accept his gift!' she explained to Ailsi and Swetesot. 'And it is worse. It's not only the colt. He says the

Holy Father in Rome is heretic. He orders me, all of us, to accept his Eastern rite.'

Ailsi was wide eyed. 'What? Cross yourself, bow three times and kiss the icon of Blessed Virgin. Tell him we too believe in God, the Father Almighty, Creator of heaven and earth; and in Jesus Christ, His only Son, our Lord: Who was conceived by the Holy Spirit, born of the Virgin Mary; suffered under Pontius Pilate, was crucified, died and was buried. That is his faith and ours.'

Gytha smiled at the clarity of Ailsi's youth. 'If only it was bowing three times and kissing the holy Icon, Ailsi. I am distraught with his demands and priceless gifts.'

Swetesot listened. 'Demands and priceless gifts are for princes to give and for others to accept. It was always so. Give the foal another name. It does not care.' The scented princess chuckled, 'any more than I care if your Christian god visits from the east or the west, north or south.

Gytha paused, picking her words, 'I hate it when you speak so, heart dear friend. You know nothing of my faith as I know nothing of stallion's names, must it be Arabian?'

'Then let him carry a name that lives in your heart, Pond Eyes,' said Swetesot reaching out, apologising with a look. 'The colt is the Prince's gift to you, not its name. It is his most prized possession, after you. You are his Terem favourite.'

'What will you name him?' said Ailsi, excited, relieved the moment had passed, not seeing that Swetesot was distressing Gytha still more.

'My father Harold is always in my heart.'

'No! you cannot! Edmund says our son is to be called Harold after his grandfather.'

'Then I name him Ardent,' said Gytha, after a long moment. It was how the prince had cradled the little horse in his arms. 'I will call the colt Ardent,'

'Ardent?' said Ailsi. 'Can we not call him Wingfast, sire of a thousand Wingfast foals?'

'No, Ailsi, I am calling him Ardent; if the prince permits.'

'What does it mean?' asked Swetesot.

'Ardent? It means passionate and strong.'

Swetesot smiled, 'let us name him tomorrow.'

Next day, while the men hunted in the forest, Gytha, wrapped against the autumn cold, took Ailsi, the scented Swetesot, and Boniak to see the foal. Swetesot, chanting to Tengri, the blue eternal sky, the thrice bright Sun and the moist mother earth helped Boniak tie the blue silken ribbon around its neck in offering, as was their Qypchaq custom. Gytha rubbed the colt's ears, whispering its new name with kisses. Ardent suckled her fingers, its little nose soft as feather down. Sfandra, his mother, watched, flicking her high tail.

'He likes his new name.' said Gytha, kissing Ardent more.

'Here comes the prince, let's see if he likes it?' warned Swetesot quietly.

Just back from the hunt, Vladimir was striding over to the pen, his bow in hand, quiver still at his belt, his fur jerkin open to the waist.

'Gytha,' he said, vaulting the gate. 'I have decided! If you do not like his name, then you must give him a new name! That is a good idea, is it not? He is your gift. He will not mind, he speaks neither Arabian nor English.' The prince laughed loudly, delighted as much by his joke as his solution.

'Thank you, Vladik,' said Gytha relieved. 'It is a very good idea and very generous too.'

'So, what will you call him? Not a pagan name, I hope,' he gave Swetesot and the ribbon a furious look, but nothing more.

'Ardent,' said Gytha,

'Ardent! Hmm, Ardent is a very good name. I name you Ardent, stallion of our English shield maid! So, that is settled.

Come, we feast. The ruff-foot gluxhar turns on the spit and
the smells torture me. Ardent,' he repeated. 'A very suitable
name. What does it mean?'

'Passionate and strong, Prince,' Gytha replied.

The attack was sudden. Gytha, Ailsi and the scented Swetesot
leaving the men to their drinking, were asleep in the women's
hut. The singing could be heard far off in the forest where
the Qypchaq waited, animal skins over their backs. Silently,
they crept to the palisade, others to the mares in the meadow.
Too late, the horses' heads rose, sniffing the night air in
alarm. 'Bear!' shouted a guard. 'Wolves!' shouted another.
A third, seeing a crouching Qypchaq dart towards him,
died before a warning left his mouth. Dogs were barking
everywhere now. The brood mares, whinnying in terror spun
to face their attackers, their escape blocked by the moat and
palisade behind them. In moments, more raiders with spears,
bows and whips circled the horses and drove them into
the forest.

Gytha was sleeping when the gloved hand closed over her
mouth. She woke, eyes wide, in an instant, A voice in her ear
hissed to stay quiet. It was Swetesot, bending over her, dressed
in warm riding clothes, fur hat, boots, a blue silk scarf about
her neck. Boniak too.

'Shh, Pond Eyes, keep quiet, Ailsi sleeps.' Gytha nodded.
Swetesot lifted the glove from her mouth.

Gytha sat up. 'Why are you dressed? What is happening?'

'It is a raid, but listen. I have come to say goodbye. I am
leaving, now'

'A raid? Leaving, where?' Outside the hut, there was uproar,
the drunken singing had faltered. Dogs were barking. Gytha
could hear Vladimir and Edmund. Gytha was confused, feeling
for her wounding knife with her fingers.

'My people are taking me and Boniak to my father the Khan.'

'Now?' Gytha's mind was racing. 'to your home?'

Swetesot nodded, 'yes to the Wild Field, where sky neither ends nor earth begins. Where a million flowers bloom and riders steer by heaven's unweary stars.'

'Wait, wait wait,' Gytha was trying to jump up, 'I will come with you. I must dress.'

'No', hissed Swetesot, pressing her down, 'you must stay.'

'No! I'm coming, wait for me.'

'Gytha you must stay!'

'Why, there is nothing here for me. He marries Kilikia before the snow.' She glanced at Ailsi and for a moment remembered the day she had left Waltham, leaving Hilde asleep without saying goodbye.

'You cannot live among us,' said Swetesot

'Why not?'

'You are not saddle born, you are not a daughter of horses, you are not my people.'

'I can ride as well as you. I will be happy. Let me be happy. These are not my people either.' Gytha was shouting in whispers.

'They are your people now. But Pond Eyes, I come to say farewell not to fight. I must go!'

Outside a watchguard lay kicking and shuddering on the ground, his throat cut. Others lay close by – some dead, some groaning – shot with arrows to the back, never seeing their attackers until it was too late. Vladimir strode past them, cursing the living and the dead for the loss of his brood mares.

Gytha could hear him shouting 'I want my mares back, hurry. Sfandra and the foal. Have they taken her?'

'Swetesot!' Gytha repeated, but Swetesot was at the doorway, where a Qypchaq thrall fully armed, waited. Swetesot pushed her son towards him.

'I must go with them. But listen, years ago in my wretch-edness I begged Tengri to return me to my home dead or alive. But he sent a white bird, a goose to carry me across the grey west sea. My life was over. I was a slave bartered to a fragrance seller. But Tengri was leading me to you Gytha, to give me another life.'

Tears were pouring down Gytha's cheeks at Swetesot's words.

'Tengri is here, Gytha, to give another life to you.'

Ailsi stirred, half opening her eyes.

Swetesot crouched, pulling her knife silently from her belt. Ailsi closed her eyes again.

'Why must the good go? Gytha sobbed, 'Please take me.'

The Qypchaq coughed at the doorway.

'Gytha, the greatest journey begins by standing still. Take this.' Crying, Swetesot slipped the pale blue shawl from her neck, and put it around Gytha's, just as she had placed the ribbon around the foal's neck. 'I love you, Pond Eyes.'

'I love you Swetesot, my heart dear friend. You are my blue eternal sky, the thrice bright sun, the moist mother earth.'

Gytha hugged Swetesot one last time and she vanished as Ailsi woke.

'Prince, Prince,' Gytha called from her hut. 'Swetesot is gone and Boniak and my thralls too.'

'It was all planned,' Vladimir shouted. 'They took my mares to distract us from their purpose. I will send Oleg to barter with the Khan for her return, if that is what you want?

'No Prince!' said Gytha amazed at his suggestion. 'Swetesot will slice off Oleg's manhood and ram it down his throat, before she lets him barter for her!'

'Then the Khan's tribute daughter is gone.'

'What about Ardent?' asked Gytha

'He is safe in the foaling pen with Sfandra, a Qypchaq lies kicked to death beneath Habib.' He paused as a new thought struck him, 'Of course! That is why she marked the colt with the blue ribbon, so they would not steal him from you.' He shook his head in disbelief, cursing all Qypchaq. 'I want my horses back and every one of the thieving Qypchaq riding a wooden stake by morning.'

'Did she really plan to flee?' asked a weeping Ailsi,

But Gytha had no answer to fill the hole that Swetesot had left in her heart.

'Where are the good? The Lord takes them all, one by one,' she murmured, clutching the pale blue scarf to her bosom.

'Will she return to us?'

'Never Ailsi. Swetesot, my heart dear friend will never return. She has gone. We must send word to the turbaned stench-man. He will grieve for her as I do. She is like no other.'

PART THREE   CHAPTER TWELVE

THE SERPENT

BETWEEN VLADIMIR AND GYTHA there was now a silence. He had not called her the lady of his days, nor made demands nor had he seen Ardent, since the raid. Instead he and Edmund hunted elk, aurochs and curl-tusk boar, while Gytha rode the clean-blood stallion Habib, ever mindful of his flat-eared fury. But what Gytha liked best was to sit with Ardent, stroking him, whispering of the scented Swetesot who had vanished into the rippling grass, as fishes slip into the waves. All the while Ardent suckled at her fingers or sometimes kicked his tiny heels skyward like his father.

Three days they waited at the stud for word that every mare was found and the thieves pulled onto the sharpened stakes that awaited them.

Then, to Gytha's relief, Vladimir ordered the return to the fortress and to hunt for beaver along the river banks on the way.

'Gytha I must speak with you,' The prince pulled his horse next to hers, nodding to Edmund and Ailsi to fall back, out of earshot.

Gytha suddenly shy, smiled at him. Chances to speak alone came rarely.

'Good men died. Did you know?'

'That she was planning to escape? No Vladik, I did not.'

'Ailsi told Edmund she heard you talking.'

Gytha hesitated.

'I begged her to take me with her, far away from here.'

Vladimir looked surprised.'Why?' His tone more troubled, than angry.

'I cannot say. Please do not ask.'

'But she refused to take you to the Khan?'

Gytha nodded.

'She was right, you cannot live among the saddle born. Here you are a princess in the Terem, there you are nothing under the sky.'

'I cannot live here Vladik.' Once again tears were rolling down her cheeks. She brushed them away angrily with her glove. 'how can I explain? You ask too much of me and I ask too much of you. I am denied what is my right, nor can you have what you desire. Yet both are ours to grant each other.'

'Woman! You talk in riddles,' said Vladimir, 'I would have you as the lady of my days.

'Only as your bed wife! Vladik, you are betrothed to the child. And now you demand I disavow my Christianity for yours. I cannot Vladik. Don't you understand?'

'Take what is given. I gave Ardent to you. My most pre-cious possession is yours, All the gold on the dome of the new cathedral in Kiev cannot buy him? He is beyond price. How is that not enough? Do you want more?'

'Vladik, Vladik, stop. I know you to be a great prince, God fearing, good and generous to all. Ardent is enough, too much, but I too am the daughter of a Christian King, not a bed-wife who denies her faith and virtue for horses. Have I not said this, are my words of no value?'

They rode on in silence, chewing the sourness of angry

words, neither yielding, yet knowing the time to speak again ended at the fortress gate.

Gytha could suffer it no longer. What had Swetesot said? A warrior, not a poet, who knows nothing of a woman's heart. She must reason with him in a manner a mighty warrior would surely understand.

'Vladik!' she said, 'may I ask something of you? Vladik, would you grow your hair for me?'

His hand went to the thick side knot that hung over his jewelled ear. 'No,' he answered curtly.

'Samson grew his hair and his strength returned tenfold,' said Gytha.

Vladimir laughed. 'Delilah did not ask him to grow it, she cut it.'

'But your side knot is heathen, not Christian.'

'I will not grow the girl-hair of your English men, if that is what you want?'

'Then look at the icon of our Lord, Vladik. See how his hair falls to his shoulders.'

'What! you taunt me now, Gytha, with heresy and a woman's cunning words.'

'No prince, but you ask me to follow your path of right-eousness, yet will not grow one hair on your head in return. That is why I begged the scented Swetesot to take me to the wild field, because you ask so much, too much.'

'And she refused and you will remain here,' said Vladimir, a flash of triumph on his face, 'We have talked enough. Return to the terem. I hunt.'

'Women!' he cursed, as he turned his horse to the river, his hounds nosing here and there beneath the banks, sniffing tell tale gnaw-marks on fallen logs for the freshest scent. Gytha cursing herself for angering him still more, when all she wished was to explain.

They were passing tangled branches left by the floods, when the dogs ceased their running and pointed to a thicket. The party waited, as Vladimir and his hunters slipped from their horses, lances ready to poke whatever hid there, before it could flee into the water.

Suddenly, the hunt was stopped. Vladimir was bending down. Then, grim faced he stood, called to Gytha, waving her to come forward.

'Look,' he said, lifting the branches aside.

Gytha peered amongst the greying logs and grass and there, wedged beneath, half in the water, not a beaver but a drowned man. A turban unravelling in the stream.

Gytha gasped, her hand over her mouth. 'Lord have mercy, is it...?' she faltered.

Vladimir nodded. 'Yes, your turbaned stench-man!'

'Who? Swetesot's husband?' asked Ailsi, frightened to dismount. She burst into tears, wailing, clutching her belly, 'God have mercy on his soul'

Carefully, they dragged the little merchant onto the bank and laid him down.

'Did he fall in?' sobbed Ailsi.

'Maybe he was murdered for his gold,' said Edmund. 'Others tried to kill him once before, in Exeter.'

A money satchel was still on his shoulder, secured by a strap.

'If he'd been robbed and thrown in the river, he would no longer have that,' said Vladimir.

'Maybe grief murdered him?' said Gytha, observing this little man whom she knew so well. 'His wife is gone and his heart is broken. He loved her as do I.'

Vladimir was bending down. 'This satchel is heavy, heavy enough to pull him under.' He undid the buckle, running his hand under the flap. 'Its full of rocks.' Suddenly he bellowed, jerking his hand back. A black viper was hanging from his glove by its fangs. He shook it off, yelling furiously with terror. The serpent dropped to the ground and slithered quickly back to the water.

There was mayhem. Gytha was by the prince in an instant as Vladimir sank to his knees, howling like a wild animal, ripping off the glove, clutching his bitten hand to his mouth.

'Quick! Take your knife,' he said 'Now, do as I say.'

Gytha swiftly pulled her jewelled wounding-knife from its sheath.

Vladimir's hand was swelling scarlet. He was panting with the pain. 'Gytha,' he said, 'take your point and cut deep between the fang marks.'

Gytha swallowed hard, she could barely see for tears. 'I cannot, Vladik!'

'Do it, woman!'

'He's right. Do it.' Edmund was by her side. 'He'll die here if you don't.'

Gytha uncurled Vladimir's clenched fingers, exposing two white dots. Edmund took the fallen glove and thrust it between the prince's teeth. 'Bite on that Prince. Go on, Gytha, do it.'

Still Gytha hesitated, the knife tip an inch above the wound. 'Do it, I beg you.'

'I will hold his arm' said Edmund.

'I want only that you live, Vladik,' and with that Gytha pushed the knife into the flesh so hard the narrow wounding-blade sliced through his hand. Vladimir grunted in pain but said nothing as blood gushed and the venom with it. Gytha dropped the knife, grabbed his bleeding hand and sucked at the wound. 'Get water!' she shouted, spitting blood; her mouth, her chin, her hands, her tunic smeared crimson. 'We must wash the poison away. We have no time!'

Next, she bound the wound, and tied a leather band above his elbow, but things were going badly for the prince. He tried to stand. His legs gave way beneath him. His breathing was laboured as the venom began to kill him from within. He vomited, his face ashen, his lips blue.

'We must get him to the Fort! We have no time!'

'Tie him to me,' ordered Edmund.

They lifted Vladimir onto the horse, wrapped his arms around Edmund's waist, and lashed them together. The prince's blood was dripping on the horse and saddle. They galloped full speed along the track until the Fort appeared ahead. Vladimir's head was lolling back and forth now. On they sped, past the draw-gate, up the trackway and into the square. Vladimir slipped from the horse, dragging Edmund on top of him as he fell.

'Take him to his chamber, send for the Arch-Priest. Bring Fevronia the peasant woman here now, I need venom salve, maythen, waybroad, willow paste, and fresh cow piss for a poultice. And well water to cool him. He is on fire.' The orders given she ran back across the square. But her way was barred by guards.

'You may not enter,' they said, blocking her with lances.

'Get out of my way, I have no time. Stand aside. Move!'

'Prince Oleg has ordered that you be denied entry.'

'Prince Oleg! Your Prince is dying and prince Oleg denies me entry, stand aside' But the guards would not stand aside. Gytha screamed 'Stand aside, get out of my way,' She hurled herself at the men in front of her, as Oleg appeared in the doorway.

'Return to the terem Rusalka!' he ordered, a dagger blade in his hand, 'Vladik has no need of you. You poison him enough.'

Gytha was sobbing, 'Oleg, let me pass. He is dying. I must go to him.'

'Try, and you die here,' said Oleg.

'But who will care for him?' she shouted.

'Not you. The princess Kilikia's mother is practiced in healing. She comes to tend him now.'

'Oleg, I beg you.'

A hand gripped Gytha firmly. It was the burnished Roni, 'Come my Lady,' he said, his axe at the ready in his fist. 'He will not let you enter, come, we will pray for the Prince here.

Gytha was inconsolable, as Kilikia's mother, chief wife of King Gosdantin and the child princess Kilikia entered the Prince's chamber, leaving her weeping on her knees in the fortress yard. Roni stood guard over her. Soon others joined, then more until the square was filled with Rus and English, slave and free on their knees praying for the Lone Warrior in his mortal struggle with the Devil. The black beard priests intoned the prayers of intercession, calling on the Guardian angels, the Holy Trinity, the most Holy Lady Theotokos and all the Saints. The walls echoed the fervid professions of the crowd as they crossed themselves over and over, bowing their foreheads to the ground. Lanterns were lit. Rumours sped, growing with each passing hour. His life is hanging by a thread. The Princess Kilikia tenderly wipes his brow. The drawing poultice smokes with Satan's flame.

Gytha too, called on all she knew, the quick and the dead, willing him to live and not to leave her. There in the half dark, Gytha vowed to build a great church to the Virgin if she would intercede. She dared not hope – she dared not even think of hope – but, little by little, life stirred in Vladimir.

Oleg was standing at the door. She heard Ailsi's sharp breath of alarm.

'The poison subsides and Prince Vladimir lives.' The crowd rejoiced, some praying, some shouting, some reaching to heaven in gratitude.

'Vladik lives?' Two words to burst Gytha's heart. 'Vladik lives!'

'So, sister, the little fat merchant drowned. But what ever became of the serpent?'

'You are the serpent, Oleg. My eyes are opened. You hoped to gain his title and his lands. If Vladimir died, you would be Duke of Smolensk. That is why barred me from his bedside. But he has not died. And the turbaned merchant, of whom you speak so insolently, raised your son, Oleg! Your son by the helpless girl you ravished and cast out. He died for love of her, Oleg! He died for the loss of her. – There will be no loss, no tears when you die, Oleg! with my wounding-knife in your dark heart.'

'*Prince* Oleg,' he shouted, raising his arm, striking her brutally. Gytha fell to the ground, blood streaming. 'Get to the Terem, where you belong. Never show your face outside again. The Princess Kilikia is the Lady of his Days.' Oleg swore a terrible oath at Gytha. 'And nights,' he added.

PART THREE CHAPTER THIRTEEN

BENEDICTUS

SHE WAS ON THE chalk road. She had fallen from her horse. Her Radknight Wulfwyn was kneeling over her, pressing a bloody wad of tussock moss to her head. Gytha cried out in her dream.

'My Lady, I have returned.'

Gytha was struggling to understand.

Her bruised head was throbbing from Oleg's blow. She opened her eyes, blinking. It was daylight. Wulfwyn was standing over her, his clothing ragged. With him stood another man, a young monk in the black habit of St Benedict, and the Posadnik Khristofor.

'Oh, Wulfwyn! I thought you dead, in an uncrossed grave out on the log-road.' Forgetting all custom, she hugged her faithful Radknight until Ailsi begged to hug him too. Godwine, Edmund, Roni and the Companions clustered around, thumping him across the back.

'My lady,' said Wulfwyn, 'this welcome leaves me breathless. I bring with me brother Tancred of Waltham.'

'Waltham, you come from Waltham?'

'Aye my Lady,' said the young monk.

'Sent by whom?' She could barely speak.

'By the Abbot at Waltham, my Lady. To seek you. To know how you and your noble brothers fare and to tell of the savagery we suffer under King William. The King stops at nothing to hunt his enemies. He makes no effort to control his fury, punishing the innocent with the guilty. He orders crops and herds, tools and food be burned to ashes. Three thousand English folk have sailed to Constantinople to serve the Christian Emperor in his Varangian Guard.'

'But have you seen my mother?' Gytha was barely holding herself together.

'My lady, I have not. I have followed you from Flanders to Cologne, then to the Danes, who sent me to heathens. Wendish river pirates who wished me ill, until Thegn Wulfwyn and the Posadnik Khristofor found me, near death, at Novgorod.'

'Well you are among brave English here and most welcome to our exile. I too was rescued from the river pirates. Then, turning to Wulfwyn and the Posadnik, she said, 'let me prepare a great feast of welcome, for you and for brother Tancred for his deliverance from the heathens. Prince Vladimir too has wrestled mightily with the Devil and lives. Let us rejoice. Now take Brother Tancred to the bathhouse.

'My lady,' Wulfwyn lowered his voice, shielding his mouth with his hand, 'we must speak urgently.'

'Oh, Wulfwyn I delight so at your homecoming but I weep for myself. Your monk brings nothing of my gentle swan. The scented Swetesot rides free over the Wild Field and I am confined evermore in the Terem,' said Gytha, reliving Oleg's harsh words.

'My lady,' Wulfwyn's voice insistent, 'we have the Cold Trader Zhiznomir here, bound and gagged beyond the wall.'

'Let me kill him,' said Ailsi, standing close. 'eight silver pennies he paid. Collared and chained to pleasure Oleg.'

'He confirms the betrothal! My lady, your claim is true, but he demands much payment.

'How much?'

'His weight in silver!' said Wulfwyn, his voice rising.

'His weight in silver!' hissed Gytha, 'he will be lucky to weigh his breath in silver. Bring him here.'

'Princess, heed me. I must advise against it,' said the Posadnik. We must summon the Prince's Council to hear his testimony.'

'But the Prince lies near death in his chamber,' said Gytha.

'Then we must wait,' the Posadnik replied. 'Thegn Wulfwyn guard the trader well, or he will be dead by sunset. There are those here, who will not wish him to tell his story.'

'How long must we wait?' said Ailsi, voicing Gytha's thoughts.

Gytha shrugged, 'The Council will never believe the trader's testament without the Dane King's seal. Zhiznomir barters brides for silver, why not the truth as well? Is that not right Posadnik Khristofor?'

The Posadnik nodded gravely. 'Without proof, the Council will seek confirmation from the Prince's father in Chernigov. But only if the Prince wishes it. He may not.'

'See Ailsi, I am lost.' said Gytha, 'I fear for my life, Oleg and Kilikia's mother conspire against me. I will renounce my claim.'

'My lady,' said Wulfwyn, 'there is still more.'

'Oh Wulfwyn my mind is numb, this wound to my head is throbbing. What more?'

'My Lady, the Gembelt Pig-boy, whom you sent to your lady mother, gave me this.' He drew a wrapped birchbark from a bag. 'We parted. Our company cut north on the log roads to Novgorod. The Pig-boy struck west as a pilgrim seeking way-fare from the Holy Church, through the great marsh of Pripet to the fortress of Polotsk and onward to the Balt Sea.'

'Alone? How, he cannot speak?'

'Aye, my lady. He carries a halter and a rope that they might think him in search of a lost horse.'

Despite everything that had happened; all that had gone awry, Gytha had to laugh. Cheered at the Pig-boy's pluck, she returned to her chamber to unpeel the birchbark. In tiny lettering he had written.

'You knew, my lady, what I could not say,
that I have loved you each and every day.'

It was signed Baldred. The name his mother, defiled, alone, a virgin of fourteen winters, had given him. Gytha sat quietly, holding the birchbark in her hand, before rolling it and carefully placing it by her heart. 'God speed you, my Pig-boy. May the Lord protect you and watch over you.'

And so, they waited. A day went by, Oleg and Kilikia's mother refusing all requests to let the prince leave his chamber.

To pass the hours, Gytha would ask the monk Tancred for news.

'Spare nothing, Brother Tancred of Waltham, no detail of my home is too slight for my ears to hear, my tongue to taste, my nose to smell, though my eyes will never see England again except through yours.'

'My lady, your father's estates, God rest his soul, are seized. Waltham is occupied by the Breton, Count Ralph de Gael, who took your lady mother and holds her prisoner at Mentmore.'

'at Mentmore?

'The last I heard, my lady. She mourns your father with each passing night.'

'And what of my sister, Gunhild?'

'She fares better than some.'

'How is that?'

'Your sister Lady Gunhild was sent to the nuns at Wilton, my lady,' said Wulfwyn. 'Many speak of her great beauty. A Norman knight, Alan Rufus, came to the Abbey, seized her and carried her off.'

'And you say she fares better than some?'

'Aye, my lady,' said Tancred, an edge of disapproval in his voice. 'She lives at Richmond, in the new castle as his ring-adorned wife. She defies the Archbishop at Canterbury and will not return to Wilton to finish her noviciate.'

Gytha laughed, relieved. 'Forgive me Brother Tancred, but Gunhild has the spirit of our grandmother, the Mother of Heroes. She is no more suited to holy orders than I. I pray only that this baron treats her well.'

'It is said that he loves her,' said the monk.

'He loves the lands he stole from us more,' said Gytha.

Finally, Oleg and Kilikia's mother could resist no longer. The prince's Council was convened. Gytha could not sleep for dread of what the morning would bring, dozing fitfully as dawn broke.

'Oh, Swetesot, we have the Cold Trader Zhiznomir. He alone can tell how he came in search of a bride to the Dane King, at the request of Prince Vladimir's father. And how the shrill trophy Queen, Elisaveta chose me. But he demands his weight in silver.'

The Qypchaq princess looked at her heart dear friend, her honey face crinkling as she laughed. 'Oh, Pond Eyes, my turban will give you all the silver you need to loosen the tightest tongue. He loves me and will do anything I ask.'

'But the turbaned merchant is dead, is dead, is dead.' said Gytha waking 'Swetesot!' she called. The chamber was empty but for the bright morning sun.

She dressed, picking her clothes carefully. Deciding on the simple grey woollen tunic of the English that she had worn at the last Council, she placed the golden circlet of her rank on her blonde hair and wrapped the blue cowl about her head,

The prince stepped over the threshold into the painted Warrior Hall, supported by Oleg. Behind him came a dozen knights and nobles of his hearthguard. Gytha's joy at seeing him was short lived. The pain from his bandaged arm was written ash grey on his face as he shuffled slowly to the throne chair. His leaden eyes cast about resting for a moment on Gytha but no smile hinted of a past affection. She dipped her head. The English clustered around her, bowed. One empty place remained. The Chief wife to King Gosdantin, mother to Kilikia had yet to enter. Gytha watched her cross the crowded Hall. On her head she wore a crown of pearls and coloured stones. Golden icons of the Apostles hung about her neck. Her silken tunic, deep yellow trimmed in blue, billowed as she walked.

'Look, a serpent-headed knarr boat.' whispered Ailsi. Gytha squeezed her hand, too anxious to speak. The Arch Priest blessed the assembly and the Prince, summoning his strength, announced the Council in session.

'Come forward, Edmund Harold's son, come forward to be heard.' His usual voice lost to a whisper.

'Good Prince,' said Edmund, 'we rejoice at your deliverance from the Devil's servant. All our prayers were answered.'

But Vladimir brushed Edmund's words aside, pointing at Wulfwyn. 'So, the bear you hunted was the slaver Zhiznomir. And you hold him here in my fortress?'

Wulfwyn hesitated, his red cheeks scarlet. 'Great Prince,' he stammered 'I am the life-ward of my Lady Gytha of Wessex. She wishes to speak with the trader and I have brought him to her.'

'So, it is the Lady Gytha's bidding you do?' He looked at Gytha. 'Speak,' he said, curtly. 'What business do you have with this Wendish trader, that you send your life-ward north.'

'Prince, only he can swear I am betrothed to you, as your father wished it. This Zhiznomir was at the Dane King's court and bartered my betrothal with your Aunt, Queen Elisaveta before all Spear Danes and our Companions of the Golden Dragon of Wessex.'

'Cousin she lies, she has no proof, where is the betrothal writ, the Kings seal. Where?' shouted Oleg.

'Quiet your mouth, Oleg! I address Prince Vladimir not you.'

'And you address Prince Oleg, heir of the Grand Prince in Kiev.'

'And you address King Harold of England's daughter.' replied Gytha. The shield-maid fury sparking in her blue eyes.

'A dead king without a kingdom,' sneered Oleg, turning to his laughing followers.

'My vow sister will swear on the True Cross,' said Edmund trying to calm the moment. 'The Council has doubted her claim, and this prince who answers for you, shamed my sister's honour before your people but not in the eyes of God who knows all things. The writ and seal are lost, the Trader alone can swear to its existence.'

'Yet,' said Vladimir, his voice faint, 'the trader will not speak the truth unless you loosen his tongue with silver.'

'Of course, he will,' interrupted Oleg. 'This heathen slaver, whom all know at Novgorod, will speak all the Babel tongues to free his chains. Chains and deceit are the tools of the slaver's trade.' He smirked at Ailsi. The hall was silent. 'Cousin, it was your imperial mother's dying wish that you be betrothed to the Princess Kilikia.'

Murmurs of agreement filled the hall, the black beard priests and the hearthguard nodding.

'Look there,' he continued, 'The Princess Kilikia's honoured mother sits before you. She snatched you from the Devil's grasp and returned you to us whole? Would you dismiss her now? Cousin, this Council ruled the English claim false and their paltry hoard forfeit. These girl-haired English are vagabonds. They bring nothing, have nothing but would steal everything. Prince, cousin, with friendship between the people of the River and King Gosdantin, there is much gain.' The nodding around the hall increased.

Edmund was about to speak, but the prince held up his finger to silence him, his brown eyes locked on Gytha's. All waited. The hall silent again. Finally, Vladimir spoke. 'You claim still it was my father who sent this trader to find me a royal bride among the Danefolk?'

Gytha gave no outward sign but her heart missed a beat. Was this the moment she had prayed for? Was he weighing her betrothal claim again? She searched his face, his brow, watching him twist his moustache, the set of his mouth. The mouth she had never kissed. Would the Lone Warrior, brave and just, heed Oleg for the good of all the River People or another call, the call of love for the English girl who stood before him?

'Prince,' her voice was strong, her manner proud. 'No man should rule unaided between the wishes of his father or his mother, for they are both sacred. Seek the Lord's guidance, as we are taught.'

Vladimir nodded, holding her gaze and she his.

'Cousin!' said Oleg sharply, 'the Rusalka bewitches you!'

'Prince,' Gytha continued, 'have them build a fire in the square and place on it the iron ploughshares. The Cold Trader shall walk the flaming road and you will know the truth. Trust in the Lord!'

'Nonsense! said Oleg. 'Is the last scream of the liar truth or lie? Only he that dies can know. Enough of this, Cousin. This Council has ruled. Take the child-gift of Gosdantin as your bride, and if you wish, then it is your princely right to pleasure on that unquiet spirit from the deep.'

Gytha sensed English hands reaching to their swords. Would Vladimir be swayed by Oleg's cruel words?

'Wait,' she said stepping forward into a single dusty shaft of sunlight, her cowl loose and her golden hair turned molten as the circlet on her brow. She must speak, not to the warrior but to the boy within.

'Would you have me walk the flaming road in the heathen's place? I, a Christian maiden. Would you believe it then, Vladik?'

A gasp went around the hall. 'What are you saying, Sister?' said Edmund, Ailsi grabbed at Gytha's arm, but she freed herself. Her body was taut as a drawn bow. Her breast rose and fell in slow breaths, her nostrils flaring, but her mind was clear and calm. Kilikia's mother was on her feet, shouting in her tongue and pointing at Gytha who stood before the assembly as a Queen.

'You would walk the flame road to death to prove your claim?' said Vladimir.

'I seek only what is my holy right – to be your wife. The Lord will protect me.'

The Arch Priest rose, pointing at Gytha. 'The Lord's name is Holy. Take not the name of the Lord in vain. The Lord will not hold guiltless those who take the Lord's name in vain.' There was spit on his black beard. 'Those who take the Lord's name in vain shall perish.'

'She is Rusalka. She will not die on the flame road,' shouted Oleg, 'She is un-dead. Do not heed her. Do not heed her.'

Vladimir, rejecting the hands that helped him, stood up unaided.

'I will not permit it. Tomorrow the heathen trader walks the flame road. Posadnik see to it.' He left the Hall without another word. Oleg and his knights in their pointed face helms followed after him, leaving the Warrior Hall in uproar.

PART THREE CHAPTER FOURTEEN

THE KING'S SEAL

THE COLD TRADER DIED that night, his body at the bottom of a well. If he jumped or was pushed no one knew. Only that he was dead and Gytha's last chance died with him. While Kilikia and her mother rejoiced, the English despaired. Gytha remained in the Terem awaiting the Arch-priest's censure for her blasphemy. She had nothing to fear from Oleg and Kilikia's mother now.

Some gathered idly in the square to watch as well-diggers were lowered on ropes to lift the trader, tipping him on the ground. A priest blessed the well, cleansing the water fouled by his heathen corpse. Ailsi and Edmund found comfort watching Wendish thralls toss the sodden body on a cart. But not Wulfwyn.

'My Lady, I have failed again in your time of greatest need.' he began. 'We handed the trader to the Prince's men, to await his morning fate. He cursed me when I last saw him, committing me to the flames of hell and I him, but in my heart I hoped he would speak only truth as he walked the flaming path.' Wulfwyn was close to tears, his distress as great as Gytha's. But she could find no words of comfort for him nor for herself.

'Hope? What is hope? My mother, my gentle swan, whom you served, lost all hope. Godwine lived in hope of a kingdom and drowns in vodka. Pig Boy was wordless in hope.

'I lived in hope for Ailsi, my Lady.'

'Good Wulfwyn, look at me and witness the death of hope.' Queen Aethelflaed came to me on Athelney. 'Despair is the enemy of hope,' she said. 'Let hope fill your soul, and banish despair. You will be a great queen.' But she was wrong, Wulfwyn! Despair makes me its home.' Gytha sat staring at the window. Wulfwyn waited.

'My Lady, I failed to see the berserker Ragnwald buried with a picket in his heart. Let me go now to where they bury the Cold Trader and be assured, he is truly dead. Things have gone so ill for us since he came to the Dane King's court.'

'Go to the pagan burial place, if you must. Hammer the Holy Cross through his dark heart, and come away. The Cold Trader cannot harm me further. It is over.'

They took the Cold Trader to where the grizzled oak tree stood, its dark branches shading the stone idols of his Balt gods. Wulfwyn watched from afar as tranced shamans performed the seven rituals, offering live cockerels and bleating goats in bloody sacrifice. He saw how they stripped the trader, sewed his body into an old animal skin and dragged him deep into the forest to a shallow grave marked by a horned cow skull. Then the shamans danced wildly calling out to Dazhbog, god of sun, Svarog, god of fire, Stribog, god of wind, and Perun, god of thunder.

Wulfwyn waited until the shamans were snoring where they fell. Then, taking a cross handled dagger from his belt he ran, half crouching, to the grave side. The Cold Trader lay face down, the animal skin half open. Crossing himself several times, he lowered himself in, stepping on the corpse.

The trader, odious in death as in life, groaned. Taking the dagger in both hands, he buried the blade to the cross hilt in the Cold Traders back with a grunt of effort and satisfaction. 'I commend this dark heart to the Lord God who sits in judgement. May he burn in the eternal flames of hell,' he said, crossing himself again. As he stood, about to clamber from the pit, his eye was caught by something. He looked closely, ready to jump away. Taking his wounding knife in his hand, he prodded it. It was a waxed disk, a red seal, and a ribbon between the trader's buttocks. Carefully, he tugged, drawing the seal and a tight rolled vellum writ from the trader's arse. Wulfwyn dared not hope. Quickly he left the foul burial place. Only the sound of bleating goats followed him as he galloped back to fortress before the gate was closed.

The Companions of the Golden Dragon of Wessex were at the evening meal, all sounds of laughter and minstrels absent when Wulfwyn entered, breathless and red cheeked. Catching Brother Tancred's eye, he beckoned him to come.

'Brother Tancred, is this what we thought lost forever?' he asked, passing the writ and seal to the monk, his hand shaking.'

'Have you read it? asked the monk

'No, Brother I cannot read.'

Tancred held it between thumb and fingertip. '*Sigilum Swenum Rex, Elisaveta Regina.* The seal of King Sweyn and Queen Elisaveta.' Then he unrolled the vellum. 'It is hard to read, the water has spoiled it, but see here, this protocol invokes God and the pious considerations of the betrothal. And here, it names Gytha of Wessex and Vladimir whom they call the Lone Warrior, and here it invokes God's wrath on any who fail to observe it.' He paused. 'Wulfwyn, Thegn of Thurgarton, yes, this is your Lady's betrothal writ, witnessed and sealed by the Dane King Sweyn.'

Wulfwyn was unsure whether to laugh or weep. 'For which so much blood had been spilled and honour shamed, may the Lord be praised,' he spoke as if enchanted by a spell.

'Come, let us show it to the Lady Gytha.' said the monk.

'First, let us seek the wisdom my sister Ailsi and my lord Edmund. I fear another rebuff will send my lady mad.'

Suspicion for the trader's death first fell on Oleg. Then, whispers spread about the Fortress that the Princess Kilikia's mother had ordered the Cold Trader's water grave. As any mother would, they said, to spare her daughter from dishonour.

The Prince ordered the Council re-convened, and the charge of murder be put to the chief-wife of King Gosdantin, who sat full veiled un-moving, the Princess Kilikia beside her. The Posadnik spoke, commanding the attention of the Hall.

'If the charge of murder is upheld, the Council must overturn its ruling, and judge the betrothal writ of Gytha of Wessex with our gracious Prince, to be binding.

Oleg was on his feet. 'The deathbed wish of the imperial daughter of the Christian Emperor in Constantinople is more binding than a Dane king's jottings. Would you bring the fury of Byzantium down on us for a,' he struggled for the word, 'for a forgery from a slaver's arse? Would you spurn both the princess Kilikia and your own mother, for that woman!' pointing at Gytha who stared at the floor. Vladimir, his head heavy on his hand, silenced Oleg's protest.

'Continue Cousin, and risk confirming your complicity in the trader's death.' Oleg quickly sat.

The Arch Priest rose. 'St Paul in his letter to the Ephesians says; Wives, submit yourselves unto your own husbands, as unto the Lord. For the husband is the head of the wife, even as Christ is the head of the church: and he is the saviour of the body. Therefore, as the church is subject unto Christ, so let the wives be to their own husbands in every thing. Thus, neither Imperial rank nor mortal circumstance amends the wish of Prince Vsevolod, son of the Grand Prince Yaroslav to seek a royal bride for his son from among the Danefolk. For this, the trader Zhiznomir was sent to the Princess Elisaveta, ring adorned Queen of King Sweyn.' The Arch-Priest glared about him. 'The word of God is flawless; He is a shield to those who take refuge in Him.'

The Council deliberated, noble and priest, quarrelling and conferring, their voices rising and falling until, finding no greater motive, nor stronger suspect than the Princess Kilikia's mother, the verdict of murder was inescapable. Calling for order in the Warrior Hall, the Prince then required the Council to deliberate on the Dane King's writ. By overwhelming majority, the Council ruled it to be valid. Gytha, daring a shadowed smile, breathing as if reborn, looked up just long enough to catch the Prince's glance.

Prince Vladimir's betrothal to the Princess Kilikia was forsworn, her dowry forfeit, and mother and daughter banished for ever from the land of the River Princes. If any thought the prince himself ordered the Cold Trader dead, and blamed the child's mother for his murder, none dared say it. Nor did they speak of the bales of sable and marten furs he sent to Kilikia's father with an escort of his hearthguard, that no harm should come to the child princess or her mother until they reached King Gosdantin's palace on the last Christian mountain beyond the Black Sea.

Standing at the terem door Gytha watched them go. Kilikia waved at her shyly as she rode by on a camel, half hidden beneath a silken shade. Her liquid eyes told of recent tears. Gytha raised outstretched fingers in gentle salute. She bore the child no ill will. She wondered if Kilikia even understood.

The wedding proclamation was sent the length of the river that Prince Vladimir known as the Lone Warrior, Duke of Smolensk would fulfil the wish of his father Vsevolod, Prince of Chernigov, and accept Gytha of Wessex, eldest daughter of King Harold Godwineson of England as his betrothed. The marriage, after the Pokrova feast and before the first snow, would be in the new cathedral of St Sophia in Kiev.

PART THREE CHAPTER FIFTEEN

TESTAMENT

AS STRENGTH RETURNED TO Vladimir, Gytha would sit with him, telling him stories of England before the Bastard William destroyed her life. He would ask about her father, and she would say 'He was warlike, greatly feared, the most handsome man in all England!'

'And who is the most feared, the most warlike, the most handsome prince on the river?' he would ask, and Gytha, laughing, would name every prince she had ever heard of, though never Oleg. And the prince would look crestfallen until Gytha said, 'I forgot, there is one other, brave and just, and yes, very very handsome.'

'And your mother?' Vladimir would ask. 'Tell me of your gentle swan.' Gytha would pause, sadness filling her blue eyes. 'My mother is beautiful, good and kind. She is the gentle swan who swims the sea of tears since my father was killed.' Her voice would trail away and Vladimir would comfort her, solicitous of her wishes. A great burden had been lifted from his shoulders and now he would lift all burdens from hers. He had the finest chambers in the Terem prepared for her, with thralls and point-helmed hearthguards always at her call. He ensured the haughty nobles bowed to her and that she sat in the painted Warrior Hall where only senior wives sat. The Companions too enjoyed her fortune. Edmund, Wulfwyn and the burnished Roni now wore silver helms, new ring-shirts and jewelled scimitars, hand crafted by the finest armourers in Baghdad. Only the black beard priests exhorted her to renounce her Latin impertinence and truly accept the Lord Jesus.

Gytha sought Brother Tancred to hear her confession and ask his advice.

'The estrangement between Christians east and west, Byzantium and Rome, rests in Might, Creed and bread.'

'Might, Creed and bread, Brother Tancred?'

'Yes, my Lady, Creed and the Eucharist, but mostly Might.'

'But will heaven be denied me, if I abandon my faith for the Prince's?'

'The Lord Jesus teaches all Christians "I am the way, the truth, and the life, and no one can come to the Father except through me." Do as the Prince asks my lady and no harm will come. Would that all difficulties of the heart could be resolved through scholarship alone.'

'But, Brother Tancred, our Towering Mace Monk Blaecman, whose body is still not cold in the grave, would shout at these river people as they went to Mass, saying, "Strive to enter through the narrow gate, because many, I tell you, will try to enter and cannot".'

'In Latin, I hope, my lady,' said the young monk.

Reassured that eternal damnation did not await her, Gytha studied the Eastern rite as Vladimir wished, in his language. Her teacher, the most venerable Sergius, the Chronicler, described to her how the Gospels had overflowed the Rus lands and how, together with all Christians, they glorified the Holy Trinity. He taught her of St Andrew, and of the Virgin's compassion and of the immeasurable depth of the mystery of Christ's incarnation. She learned the Holy Icons, and the sacred history of the River people; of Libed and Olga, and of the Passion-bearers, Saint Boris and Saint Gleb, at whose tombs they would pray before the marriage procession continued down the river to Kiev.

'This is for you, Lady of my Days.'

'What is it?'

'Instructions for our sons,' he said, 'if I am killed or die the next time.'

'You nearly died this time.'

Vladimir scoffed. 'The peasant woman Fevronia cured me with herbs.'

'Fevronia? Your cousin Oleg said Kilikia and her mother tended you ceaselessly and returned you to us.'

'No! I sent them away. It was you and the pious and good Fevronia who saved me. She told me you were praying outside my chamber throughout my struggle with the Devil's servant.'

'I honour and celebrate Fevronia,' said Gytha, 'I prayed as all the people of the Fortress prayed. Now, what are these instructions for our sons?'

'It is the tradition of my forefather Rurik that our sons receive nothing but a sword to make their way in the world. Ensure that our sons eat without unseemly noise, remain silent in the presence of the aged, listen to the wise, live in charity with their equals and their inferiors. They are to be moderate in language, not insult others, laugh excessively or converse with shameless women. They should cast their eyes downwards and their souls upwards.'

'I wish it too. And here is my instruction for you, Vladik. Write this down. Love Your Wife.'

'But I will grant her no power over me,' he replied with a hint of a smile.

For a moment neither moved. Gytha heard Swetesot's words, 'Gytha, the greatest journey begins by standing still.' As much as she had once hated this Lone Warrior, her exile was over. There was no need to resist any more. Vladimir was hers and she was his to love cherish and protect. There was no place she would rather be, yet she knew there was more. A stirring that made her want to grasp this moment forever.

She leaned forward and kissed him, cautiously at first and then more passionately. Vladimir slipped his still bandaged arm around her and drew her to him. Her head was on his broad chest, with its haze of hair. Her hands caressed him. She marvelled at the feel of his body. Every sinew, every muscle, every curve and angle smoothed by cool skin. She could feel his heart, his breathing warm in her ear, the way his moustache tickled, every kiss, every hug, each yielding of their bodies, smothering him, biting his neck, kissing his lips, his ears, his chin.

He too was consumed, enraptured by her. A thrill rushed through her as he needed to touch her, to stroke her, to bury his face in the flat softness of her belly, in her neck behind her ear, in each breast in turn, each rose pink nipple hard under his tongue, and then how she shuddered, threw her head up, eyes tight closed, her back arched, and a low moan which started deep inside her escaped her open mouth.

PART THREE CHAPTER SIXTEEN

BEHOLD THE WILD FIELD

THE DAY TO LEAVE the red fortress at Smolensk arrived. Boats pulled up on either shore to carry Gytha and Vladimir south to Kiev. Vladimir's father would meet them at the Tomb of the Passion-bearers Saints Boris and Gleb. The whole town came to the river bank to see them off. The Posadnik was there.

'Good Posadnik Khristofor, I wish you were coming with us to Kiev,' said Gytha.

He smiled at her, bowing. 'My princess, I cannot. I must return to the north, to my home and family before the first snow.'

'Posadnik, you knew my betrothal to be true. You believed me. Take this as a symbol that my bond of gratitude cannot be cut.' Gytha pulled the jewelled wounding-knife she had carried at her waist since Waltham and offered it to him, with both hands.

The Posadnik got down on one knee. 'I will treasure it, nor draw it from its sheath save only to tell my children and their children the story of the English maiden, the heathen Berserker and the Holy Cross. Farewell Princess of Wessex, farewell Gytha Haroldsdaughter.' He kissed her hand, lost for words.

At the waterside the fleet was assembled, slaves, goods, gifts and men piled aboard. The autumn rains granting ample water to rush them south. Six hundred vesti, they said, ten days journey at least.

Vladimir strode along the bank.

'This is yours,' he said, pointing to a hefty boat with an awning over fur-spread thwarts, a slave shackled to each oar.

They could hear Godwine's voice above the commotion.

'He doesn't think his boat is worthy of a king. Brother Tancred is trying to calm him.' said Edmund.

Vladimir was about to speak, but Gytha touched his arm. 'He shall have this boat, Vladik, I will travel in another. Let me choose one to my liking.'

'I will not hear of it,' replied Vladimir. 'The drunken king without a country will take the boat I give him.'

'Vladik,' said Gytha quietly, 'let him have this one. I have parted many waves in storm-grey seas. I am a child of the sea, at home to mud and gulls. My Grandmother, the Mother of Heroes, would say, you Gytha, are the daughter of Ran, the wave-strife will not trouble you, Brine is the blood of Northmen, the wet-cold sea is our road.' She pointed to a sleek vessel with a sweeping stern and dragon prow, drawn up on the bank. 'I will take that eight-oar!' She announced gaily, casting an expert eye over the clinkered hull. The sealing tar still shiny fresh, the planking and strakes the palest gold. 'She is new!' she said, delighted.

Vladimir knew to argue was futile, ordered the eight-oar readied.

'It is yours?' Gytha asked the young steersman.

'Yes, Princess,' he replied, pulling off his fur hat, kneeling and bowing hand to heart in his confusion.

'You built her?'

He nodded 'Tarred and launched a week ago, Princess.'

'Good. My brother Edmund, my lifeward Thegn Wulfwyn, the monk Tancred, the burnished Roni and four Companions will row and you will steer us. What is your name?'

'Piotr, Princess. I am the son of Fevronia.'

'Oh! I have much to be thankful to your mother for. Come, Piotr, make ready.'

Within the hour, painted shield bords slung along the sides, the fleet was pulling from the shore, turning in the current, and the long river journey south began. Leading, was Vladimir's boat, then Godwine's, and the Companions of the Golden Dragon of Wessex. Behind her was Oleg's boat. Behind him the hearthguard boats brought up the rear. Gytha glanced around her. Edmund and Wulfwyn were manning the first bench. A thrill ran through her. Piotr at the helm, was calling out the stroke. She felt the surging rhythm of the oars and saw how the prow lifted, eager to fulfil her betrothal at the cathedral of Saint Sophia in Kiev.

The black-pine forest passed swiftly on either hand. They were making good speed, faster than a man could run. There were few people in this land. Occasionally they passed a widow-village, or burned-out homestead which told of marauding Qypchaq. Evening fell and the river air grew cold. Deer came to the shore to drink, lifting their heads as the boats passed. None loosed an arrow, not wanting to delay their progress.

'Look who's coming,' said Wulfwyn. Gytha glanced around to see Oleg's boat surge behind them. He was standing at the mast, supercilious and defiant, arms crossed, legs braced.

'Edmund,' he shouted, now barely a boat length way, 'Edmund Girl Hair.'

'He wants a race, does he?' said Edmund, ignoring the taunt. 'Piotr, show him what your boat can do.'

Swinging the little boat over to the deep water on the inside of the gentle bend, Piotr called the pace. Faster and faster they went, but Oleg's boat, with twice the rowers, was still gaining. On he came, cursing the slaves to row faster; threats and cruel lash and splashing oars. Ahead was a spit of mud and at the end, a rock, around which the river split and swirled.

'What's he doing?' shouted Ailsi in alarm.

Standing now, her hair golden hair streaming, Gytha cried out, 'He's not racing us he is trying to force us onto the rock. Come on, let us show the sneering boy not to challenge the English! Piotr, take us through the gap.' Her cowl slipped, her golden hair streamed behind her. Never had she felt so excited since she and the scented Swetesot, the daughter of horses, galloped the green hills behind Exeter.

'Row, row,' she shouted, her hand raised, fist clenched, cursing Oleg. 'I am the daughter of Ran. Brine is the blood of Northmen, the wet-cold sea is our road. Row!'

'Princess!' shouted Piotr. 'Sit, I beg you! It is not safe.'

'Sit,' yelled Edmund.

But Gytha would not sit.

'Ready, ready. Starboard Hold!' Piotr yelled. Gytha braced herself. Oleg's boat was towering over them. Wulfwyn's side stopped rowing at this command. Heaving the steering sweep with all his strength, the veins and sinews in his short neck bulging with the power in his arms, Piotr slewed his nimble boat under Oleg's bow. Ailsi screamed, Gytha yelled her defiance, gripping the rigging with both hands.

Forced to alter course or run over the smaller boat, Oleg's boat tipped violently under the weight of men and oars. There was mayhem as the chained rowers fell onto each other, oars flailing, water cascading in over the side.

'Row, row, row!' shouted Piotr, swinging his craft back to safety in the deep water. But for Oleg's boat it was too late. With a great jolt that sent him and his steersman and crew flying, the heavy war-boat grounded on the shelving riverbed and stopped with a sickening crunch of wood as the mast fell, crushing the slaves beneath. Gytha heard their screams and crossed herself. But nothing could contain her glee. 'Brine is the blood of Northmen, the wet-cold sea is our road.' she called, 'Piotr, upon that rock I will build my church!'

On they rowed to join the fleet. Stopping for the night, cooking fires were lit and their story told.

'Have the steersman brought here.' Vladimir demanded. 'I shall put out his eyes myself.' But Gytha stopped him.

'No,' she said, 'Piotr did my bidding. Your vain and reckless cousin would beach us for his sport, knowing the rock could crush our hull to kindle wood.'

'Yes, Piotr's skill saved us,' said Edmund. 'That Oleg was beached is his fault alone. Have no sympathy for him. He sought to humble us and lost, again.'

'Very well,' said the prince. 'Tomorrow your boat will follow mine and Godwine will follow behind you.' Then he lowered his voice so only Gytha could hear. 'I beg you, Gytha, harness the shield maid within you. The Bible bids you to control your eyes, curb your tongue, moderate your temper, subdue your body and restrain your wrath. Cherish pure thought, Gytha, and exert yourself in good works for the Lord's sake.'

Gytha bowed her head. 'Yes, Vladik. When robbed, avenge not, when hated or persecuted, endure, when affronted, pray. Destroy sin, render justice to the orphan and protect the widow. But, Vladik, as the Lord bore a crown of thorns, Oleg is one thorn I cannot bear.'

Vladik softened slightly. 'We will pray together and ask the Lord's forgiveness for my cousin, but I want no more of this.' Gytha barely slept that night at his rebuke. But as the day broke and the birds began their singing, another voice within her rejoiced. No man deserved to eat the river mud more than the serpent Oleg.

They heard the beat of oars as they prepared to leave. Out of the dawn mist came Oleg, the face of thunder. His hull was patched, only a stump of mast remained. There was no bearded steersman at his sweep. Oleg had stabbed him as the keel surrendered to the mud's embrace.

Unnoticed at first, dark pine gave way to beech, oak and gold-leaf birch. Gone were the huddles of half-buried cabins; here huts had lime wash walls and thatch roofs. Straw-shoed peasant were turning the black earth with mules, their children waving as the fleet passed. The air was soft. A last breath from the sun lands, before the north wind came to paint the land with snow.

A fort appeared. Here was the Cathedral where Vladimir had brought the bones of the Passion-bearers: the warrior saints, Boris and Gleb to rest. Welcome tents lined the shore, decked with countless bunting flags.

Vladimir's father, Duke of Chernigov, waited with his knights and nobles. He was a stocky man with thick calves, a square jaw, and none of Vladimir's lithe beauty. Vladimir towered over his father as he kissed him three times, then presented Godwine, Edmund and lastly Gytha. Gytha dropped to her knees, pressing her golden circlet crown to the ground.

'Stand, Princess,' said the older man, pressing her hand to his lips. 'Word of your beauty and daring flies from mouth to mouth along our river.' Gytha kept her eyes on the ground. The Duke paused, turning to his knights and wives. 'Today, we welcome the children of an island far away beyond the grey west sea.' He paused, savouring what he was about to say. 'Their father killed Harald Sigurdsson Hardradr, King of Norway, then husband to my sister Elisaveta, Commander of my father's hearthguard and friend to the people of the river.'

Gytha glanced up to see only stony faces and quickly looked down again. Panic took her, the memory of her welcome at the Dane King's court, still raw.

'Sire,' said Edmund. 'Our father, Harold, King of the English, was a good man of war, handsome faced, detesting wrong and loving right, who died bravely in the defence of our English land and Holy Church. He sought no fight with your friend King Harald Sigurdsson Hardradr, but was attacked. There is here among us, one who fought under the red banner of the Golden Dragon of Wessex at Stamford Bridge. The axed and burnished Roni, life friend to my father and commander of this hearthguard. He will tell you that Hardradr died a hero's death and his name lives on in the story of our people and in the songs of minstrels for ever.'

The axed and burnished Roni stepped forward. 'Duke, Harald Sigurdsson Hardradr, husband to your sister, Warrior and King died in fair battle. I saw it and honour him,'

Fearing perhaps they had said too much, the quiet and noble Edmund waited, only the lump in his throat betraying the nerves he felt within. But getting respectful silence, he continued.

'Prince, at your command and by your sister's choice, this maiden, my vow-sister Gytha Haroldsdaughter, Princess of Wessex comes here betrothed to Prince Vladimir, to be a peace-weaver between Rus and Dane and English, that we should live in the tender mercy of God.'

'Well spoken, you are truly Prince of the English,' said the duke with a wry smile, taking the Edmund by the arm. 'Your words do you and your father great honour, but your sister weaves peace as the lynx weaves in pursuit of the fleeing hare.' He glanced at Gytha. 'Your peace-weaver thrust her wounding-knife between a giant's shoulder-blades at the Council of priests and knights. Your peace-weaver weaved beneath the bow of my nephew Oleg's boat and ten are dead. Maybe my sister Elisaveta saw something of herself in your sister, for a great warrior chose her too above all others, but as a peace-weaver, young Prince, she has yet to prove herself.'

'Father, this peace-weaver thrust her wounding-knife into my poisoned hand and saved my life. Her courage has sustained the Companions through their darkest days, her charity gave life to the dying, her nobility shone through when her virtue was tested.'Vladimir looked at Gytha gently as he spoke.'This peace-weaver, father, will be a great queen and mother to our people, revered and feared in equal measure. She is the Lady of my Days. Her beauty has captured my heart.'

'For which we will give thanks tomorrow when we pray at the tombs of the Passion-bearers,' said his father gruffly. 'Come, brave English warriors, we welcome you. Eat and rest, ready yourselves for your entry into our city of four hundred golden domes.'

The bridal party moved to the welcome tents, where Gytha received the solid golden collar, which the Imperial Princess Anastasia, Vladimir's mother had worn at her wedding. Gytha was surrounded by children, full of laughter and excitement as the Duke helped her put it on. It was only then, unpicking all the little fingers that would hold her hand, she fully realised she and her River prince would marry. She could not stop smiling.

'What's your name?' she asked a little girl holding back from the others.

'Parasha,' said the child, curtsying.

Gytha could hardly hear the whisper.

'Parasha,' the child repeated.

'Oh, Parasha! You are Vladik's sister. He talks of you, and now you and I will be sisters.' Gytha crouched down, the collar heavy on her neck, and hugged her.

The girl whispered something.

'Say it again, don't be frightened.'

'When I grow up, I will be a queen and wear the Imperial collar at my wedding,' said the child.

'But first, you will ride with me to my wedding, and hold my hand, or I may stumble under its weight.'

They gathered at the tombs of the Christian warriors, Saint Boris and Saint Gleb, to hear the hermit, Anthony of the Caves, welcome Gytha into their Communion. She wore a simple blue dress and cloak without hint of decoration, her golden hair hidden modestly with a veil, as she lay prostrate on the cold stone floor. Vladimir and the chronicler, the venerable Sergius, were kneeling by her. Terrified they might notice she was shaking, Gytha pressed her palms flat together in prayer with all her strength. Gathered around were Vladimir's father, Godwine, Edmund, Wulfwyn and the Companions. The River knights were in armour, golden pointed face helms in their hands. Ailsi and the noble women, dressed in damask, taffeta and brocades were in the gallery, as the frail monk intoned the words of Hilarion.

'This blessed faith spreads now over the entire earth and finally it reached the Rus nation, the fount of the Gospel became rich in water and overflowed upon our land. All lands, cities and men honour and glorify their teacher who brought them the Orthodox faith.' The English shuffled. His voice, little more than a whisper, rang out. ... 'behold Christianity flourishing!' Gytha rose, crossed herself, bowing continuously, marvelling at the hermit, one hundred winters old.

Piotr's sleek vessel was ablaze with flaming red berries and golden leaves to match the fresh planed wood as the bridal party gathered on the shore. Piotr beamed to burst with the honour of carrying the princess bride to her wedding in the city of four hundred golden domes.

Gytha, in her golden bonnet with the scented pendils, now wearing the imperial collar and the purple and azure wedding robe, clasped helping hands. The cloth billowed as it caught the breeze, threatening to tip her over the side.

'Careful, don't sink the boat,' said Edmund, with brotherly affection. They laughed as they set off, letting the mild stream carry them across trifling eddies, wavelets breaking at the bow. A light wind sprung up and Piotr had them ship their oars as the sail ballooned over their heads. It was a perfect day. In the distance, on its cliff commanding the sweep of the great river, the fortress appeared; to the right, the domes of St Sophia glistening; beyond, the new Cathedral of the Caves, and another and another. Painted churches tipped in molten gold. The English were awed into silence. Nothing on their long journey had prepared them for their first sight of Kiev on the River.

There were hundreds, thousands shouting, running and waving as the bridal fleet arrived at the landing place. Flags were snapping on poles, the citadel looming above them. Vladimir was waiting, erect, arms folded, unmissable, in black and gold silks, a scarlet cape hanging from his shoulder, the golden scimitar at his waist. His knights, an avenue of black and scarlet, raised their lances in salute.

'Look, look my brother! said Parasha 'Oh, he is beautiful!'

'He is,' Gytha replied, 'now hold my hand tightly please.'

Trumpets blared, shouting, drumming, cheering as Gytha rose, steadied herself and stepped onto the jetty.

'The Lady of my Days!' Vladimir bowed deeply in respect, admiration and welcome, but the crowd, clamouring for the English princess, engulfed them. Parasha screamed as she was knocked aside. Edmund and Roni swords drawn beat the throng away from Gytha. Vladimir shouted commands to his knights. The chaos was stilled, order brutally restored. A man lay dead.

Gytha, panting and shocked, comforted Parasha.

'My Lady, my lady,' It was Wulfwyn and Piotr, 'We have a lifting chair.'

As they climbed the steep slope they call St Andrew's Hill, she pushed the little curtain aside. A Saker falcon, its wingtip fingers quivering, hung next to her on the wind.

'Put me down,' she commanded. 'Help me, Ailsi.' Ailsi straightened her clothes, pushing her golden hair beneath the wedding bonnet. The thumping in her chest subsiding, she took a deep breath and walked the last steps to the cliff edge. Above her was the blue eternal sky, the bright sun reflected once, twice, thrice on golden domes, and as far as she could see, the moist mother earth.

A horseman stood on the distant shore, carved into the limitless horizon.

'Look Vladik, over there, a warrior, a lone warrior.'

'It is a boy,' said Vladimir, 'a Qypchaq boy.'

'It is Boniak' said Gytha, her jewelled hand shielding her eyes. The boy rose in his stirrups, lifting his arm high above his head in salute, then turned and vanished.

'Like a fish into the waves, go lone warrior boy, tell your mother, my heart-dear friend, that I have seen the Wild Field, where sky neither ends nor earth begins. Where a million flowers bloom and riders steer by heaven's unweary stars. Amid these suffering years, you have steered me through my wild field, far from my gentle-swan beyond the grey west sea.'

'Come Gytha. Let me be your lone warrior,' said Vladimir, taking her arm gently.

'Yes!' Gytha replied, the red banner of the Golden Dragon of Wessex thrumming above her. 'But no longer just my lone warrior Vladik. I carry our child.'

THE END

AUTHOR'S COMMENT

(IN CASE ANYBODY ASKS what I have been doing for the last five years.) Gytha was barely a footnote in the mosaic of medieval history, when I stumbled on a reference to her in a book on Russian church architecture. My first question was more in shock! 'What on God's earth was a little girl from the south of England doing all the way over there? It's miles away!' There followed a whole tumble of questions. How did she get there? How long did it take? Was she alone? And, the one question to which I had to have an answer. 'How did she feel, with her father dead, so far from her mother, so far from her home?'

Within days I was on an intellectual and physical quest that has taken me all over western and eastern Europe, but started in the ancient kingdom of Wessex, where she and I were both born, nine hundred years apart.

There is no record of her birth, nor do the English chroniclers of the time, mention her. But historians accept that King Harold Godwineson[1], described by the 11th century monk Orderic Vitalis as *'a very tall and handsome Englishman,'*

---

[1] Described by Orderic Vitalis in the 11th century as *'Erat enim idem Anglus maginitudine elegantia.'*

had a daughter called *Ēadgȳða* with his common-law[2] wife, a wealthy East Anglian noble woman, delightfully known as Edith 'Swan-neck.'[3]

With little evidence, Gytha's story quickly becomes a retrojection; frustrating the researcher, while liberating the inner novelist. To fill the lacuna, I am presuming Gytha was born around 1053, and was about thirteen when her father was killed at the Battle of Hastings in 1066. Where she was born is not known, but the choices are Waltham, north of London, where Harold had dedicated a church that stands to this day, or Bosham, her grandfather Earl Godwine's estate and safe anchorage near Chichester on England's south coast. The Bayeux Tapestry puts King Harold at Bosham shortly before the Norman invasion.

Gytha shared a first name with her hugely wealthy grandmother, *Ēadgȳða Þorkelsdóttir*, Earl Godwine's Danish (Viking) born wife, the sister-in-law of King Canute. After Hastings, Gytha's three brothers Godwine, Edmund and Magnus fled west with her to Exeter. It is probable, in view of later events, that Gytha was with them.[4]

Duke William 'the Conqueror' had good reason to fear the brothers could muster an uprising in Wessex. So in the dead of winter (1067/1068) he besieged Exeter. The town fell or was betrayed after eighteen days. Gytha's brothers escaped to Dublin to raise an army, while their grandmother

---

[2] Handfasted aka Danish marriage. She was also termed "*cubicularia*" lit. a bedchamber woman.

[3] Either from Old English *swann hnecca* (swan neck) or *swann hnesce* (gentle swan). A 12th century Waltham Abbey source titles her "*Editham cognomento Swanneshals*" Also known as 'pulchra (beautiful), fair and rich.

[4] Her sister Gunhild later attended the abbey school at Wilton, near Salisbury and was famously carried off by a Norman knight, Count Alan Rufus.

sought safety on Flatholm island in the Bristol Channel with *'many distinguished men's wives.'* Modern historians defer to the chronicled account that Harold's family fled Exeter by boat down the River Exe. This I question on the following grounds:

To escape down the Exe meant sailing into the English Channel, turning south-west into fearsome Atlantic swells and gale force winds to round Land's End. Then, having to double back towards the Severn Estuary, a distance of some 300 miles. This is not undertaken lightly in open boats, in winter, though it is conceivable they may have landed and crossed the Cornish peninsula further west. However, an overland escape-route north from Exeter towards the royal mint at Taunton and the family's Somerset estates near (modern) Weston-Super-Mare is only sixty miles. The River Axe flows into the sea close by and Flatholm island is visible from the shore. I cannot be sure, but the orthodox version may be due to a confusion of the Celtic river names, Axe and Exe?

Flatholm is not a place to await rescue. It's a barren, gull infested rock about 600m wide in a raging brown seaway, with no safe-landing. Yet they were there for at least a year, possibly longer while Gytha's brothers launched two failed attacks on the West Country, in 1068 and 1069. Her brother Magnus may have died during one of the raids.

Primary sources still make no reference to Gytha, the escape from Flatholm, or a dangerous sea journey to Flanders back up the English Channel with their enemy on either shore. We know Gytha's grandmother and aunts were with Count Baldwin VI at St Omer, but sanctuary was short lived. Count Baldwin, known as the Good, died in 1070. Gytha and her brothers went north to Denmark to the court[5] of their

---

[5] possibly at Aabenraa, Jutland or nearby Soederup where King Sweyn Estrithson had a farm.

aging Danish kinsman, King Sweyn Estrithson. (d.1076). One record (now possibly lost for ever[6]) says Gytha visited the St Panteleon monastery at Cologne on the way.

King Sweyn may have welcomed them out of pious duty, as Gytha's uncle had murdered his brother Bjorn twenty years earlier. Another brother, Jarl Asbjorn had just led a disastrous attack on England's east coast in 1069, losing a great many men and boats. King William was also bribing him to cease his raids on England, so we can guess that Harold's children were a political embarrassment.

Gytha, a high-born Christian woman, needed a noble husband. The average age for marriage, among the Anglo-Saxon aristocracy, was about fourteen or fifteen. For Gytha, now possibly eighteen, the matter was becoming pressing. Arranged marriages were not just for immediate gain, but a speculation. Being exiled, her father dead and her brothers dispossessed, she was of less 'worth.' However, there was a flourishing bride-trade between the Vikings and the newly converted Rus, a Nordic/Slav people on the Dnieper river centred around Kiev (now Kyiv, Ukraine). Nordic girls (children) were sent east on a gruelling thousand mile 'conjugal transit' never to return. Likewise, Rus girls were dispatched to western Europe and Byzantium, their familial status defining whether as queens with great dowries or concubines.

PREMISE ONE.

Professor Simon Franklin, co-author of *The Emergence of Rus 750 – 1200,* wrote that all Rus history comes with '*an implicit perhaps.*' What we do know is that Gytha's father slaughtered King Harald Hardrada of Norway and his invaders at the Battle of Stamford Bridge in 1066. Hardrada, the rival and enemy of

---

[6] Historisches Archiv der Stadt Köln destroyed in 2009

the Danish King Sweyn Estrithson had married Elisaveta of Kiev[7], a Rus princess, the daughter of the Grand Prince, whom he wooed, we are told, with his '*glittering achievements and poems.*'

After Hardrada's death, King Sweyn may have taken Queen Elisaveta as his trophy wife, as was the Viking custom. So, if Queen Elisaveta was at Sweyn's court when Gytha arrived, did she arrange for Gytha to marry her nephew Prince Vladimir Monomakh (born 1053), a junior Rus prince of the unruly Yaroslavichi clan? The 12th century Danish chronicler Saxo Grammaticus records[8] the betrothal of Gytha to '*Waldemarus king of the Ruthenians.*' This is the first evidence anywhere of Gytha's existence, but it provides no detail.

PREMISE TWO.

It is equally possible that a betrothal brokered by Queen *Elisaveta* in Denmark is a pleasing fiction. In fact, whether Elisaveta was even at King Sweyn's court or alive then is in doubt. One record says she died in 1067. Adam of Bremen suggests it was another of Hardrada's wives that Sweyn took as his trophy. All of which explains away my concern that sending emissaries back and forth from Kievan Rus to Denmark would have just taken too long.

This opens the intriguing possibility that if they had to flee Denmark, was the intention to join the many hundreds of

---

[7] Elisaveta's father Yaroslav the Wise, Grand Prince of Kiev was a dynastic marriage speculator *par excellence*. Her sister Anna was sent reluctantly to be the wife of King Henry 1st of France and her sister Agafia (Agatha) was the mother of Edgar the Ætheling and St Margaret of Scotland.

[8] The History of the Danes Book 11. Gytha is also named as King Harold's daughter in the *Fagrskinna*, which states "*Vall Vladikr Konongr sun Iarozlæifs konongs i Holmgarde*" – Holmgarde was the Norse name for Kiev, however Yaroslav (the Wise) was Vladimir's grandfather not his father.

English (Anglo Saxon) nobles who had fled to Constantinople after the conquest[9], to serve in the Byzantine Emperor's Varangian guard? The overland route to Constantinople via Kiev was familiar to the Anglo–Saxon nobility[10]. We never hear any more about her brothers, Godwine and Edmund so we just don't know.

Whichever premise is closer to the truth, the journey though *Garðaríki* (the old Norse name for Ruthenia/ Kievan Rus, now western Russia, Belarus and Ukraine) meant travelling nine hundred miles east across the Baltic to Ladoga near modern St Petersburg. Then, transferring to small flat-bottom craft for another four hundred miles to Novgorod and Smolensk, through a wilderness of shallow rivers, marsh, lakes, birch, pine, bears, boars, wolves and in summer, relentless flies. In winter, despite the bitter cold, the snow and frozen rivers made the journey faster. Between the rivers were long (10km) portages. Loaded boats and dug-outs were man-handled over log-roads, with the risk of serious injury or attack by river pirates[11]. The route is described in the (Russian) Primary Chronicle as 'from the Varangians (Vikings) to the Greeks (Byzantium)' and as a noble woman, Gytha will have needed a sizeable escort, and probably had her own confessor-priest.

At the fortress of Smolensk, now in Russia, the trade route crossed close to the headwaters of three rivers; the Volga to the Caspian, the Dnieper to the Black Sea and the Western Dvina to the Baltic, one of the most significant intersections of the northern medieval world. Slaves, furs, amber and wax

---

[9] The Icelandic Jatvarthr Saga says the English nobles 'would not abide under (William's) rule and left.'

[10] Kiev is where Edgar's father Edward the Exile had fled to forty years earlier to escape murder by King Canute.

[11] Ушкуйники -Ushkuiniki.

going south, Spices, silver, silks and weapons going north. Controlling it made the Kievan Rus princes fabulously rich.

Evidence of Smolensk's importance can be found in their excellent history museum, which houses the 11th century Rachevsky Hoard of 5000 silver Islamic Dirham coins and about 700 'short-cross' English pennies, some bearing the head of King Canute! The coins do not prove that there were Anglo Saxons there at the time, but it shows that transits were already well established a thousand years ago, incredible as that might seem, when you think how far away it is.

Smolensk was Prince Vladimir Monomakh's hereditary fiefdom and I think it is where he and Gytha met. They were about the same age and a noble woman of her rank would have been a rarity. I wonder what Gytha made of the warlike Rus with their exquisite Byzantine clothes, gold and jewelled artefacts, perfumes and silks, brought by traders up the Dnieper or on camels over the steppe (the Wild Field) from Arabia, India even China. In the fortress of Chernigov (now Chernihiv), Gytha's home for many years, I was shown the hollowed pendila (earrings that hang from a golden headband) to waft scented oils about the wearer's head.

We don't know when or where Gytha and Vladimir married, some sources say in Kiev in 1074. They probably conversed comfortably in Norse, the lingua franca of the age. Latin, Cyrillic, and Greek scripts, even Runes were used at this period. For paper they had the smooth pale inner side of silver birch bark, of which beautiful examples exist in the museum at Novgorod. This was the time of Schism (1054); the doctrinal pretext for a significant power struggle between Rome and the Eastern church. I suspect for Gytha, the problem was as much linguistic as dialectic. Then as now there were two rites, the Latin of the Roman church, and the Church Slavonic, translated from the Greek.

From Vladimir's own written accounts, it is evident that luxury and learning were not their daily fare. Life was harsh in the remote frontier forts of Smolensk, Chernigov and distant Pereyaslav. They had to contend with numbing winters, blistering summers, the constant warring with family members, and the ever-present threat from the bow and arrow horse-men appearing out of the vast Eurasian steppe. Kuman (Polovtsi), Qipchaq, and Pecheneg, were names as familiar then, as Apache, Cherokee and Sioux were to the settlers of the American West. After the fall of Chernigov in 1093 to a joint assault by his cousin Prince Oleg and the Kuman Khan Boniak 'the Mangy', Prince Vladimir wrote that just one hundred of his *druzhinie* (hearthguard) emerged starving with wives and children, and rode between Polovtsi[12] warriors who *'licked their lips like wolves.* I am sure Gytha was there.

Vladimir leaves us in no doubt that he was a great warrior, hunter and politician famed for his personal valour and skill at warfare. He *'compounded imperial and princely blood[13],'* his father Vsevolod being a descendent of Rurik. His mother Anna (Anastasia), was a Byzantine imperial princess from whom he took the family byname 'Monomakhos' (Lone Warrior/ Gladiator). He was devout. We are told he cried in church. He was notably literate, may have spoken several languages, and his Testament[14] is both lyrical and inspirational. Above all Vladimir was considered just, easing the burden of debt and servitude on the poor. *'Give to the orphan, protect the widow, and permit the mighty to destroy no man'* he wrote. Or, as the historian George Vernadsky put it, *'social legislation was for him an extension of Christian charity.'*

---

[12] The Russian term for the Kuman-Qipchaq steppe tribes.

[13] Saxo Grammaticus

[14] Поучение. The Testament of Vladimir II Monomakh.

In 1113 until his death in 1125, Vladimir was supreme ruler (Grand Prince) of an immense realm of forest, fortresses, family strife, steppe nomads and Slav peasants, stretching from the White Sea far to the north almost to the Black Sea. His descendants ruled in Russia for the next four hundred years.[15] His name lives on in Russia and Ukraine to this day, the jewelled and gold 'Monomakh cap' was worn by the Tsars at their coronations. There is even a Russian nuclear submarine named after him.

No pictures remain of Vladimir or Gytha, though there are stunning 11th century frescoes of his relations in the Cathedral of St Sophia in Kiev, which give one an idea of how they looked and dressed. Unlike the long-haired English, as seen in the Bayeux Tapestry, Rus warriors shaved their heads, leaving just a hanging side knot, a fashion termed *Oseledets,* which was subsequently popularised by the Cossacks.[16]

Gytha and Vladimir had five children, possibly more. Commenting on the birth of their first son Mstislav (christened Harold[17]), which the Russian Primary Chronicle states was in Novgorod in 1076, the Chronicler Saxo Grammaticus writes '*Thus the British and the Eastern blood being united in our prince caused the common offspring to be an adornment to both peoples.*' Other than that, we know almost nothing more about Gytha. Rus noble women past childbearing age moved in with their eldest sons. Their husbands took new wives. The 'Russian' chronicles, written by monks, rarely mention women at all.

---

[15] He was also the father of Yuri 'Long -Arm' - by another wife - who founded Moscow.

[16] See "The Reply of the Zaporozhian Cossacks" by Ilya Repin (1844–1930) State History Museum, St Petersburg.

[17] After his maternal grandfather. It was common to have both a Slavic and a 'Christian' name.

There are myths of Gytha's last years. One story tells of how she prayed to the healer, St Panteleon to save Mstislav when he was nearly killed by a bear. The cult of St Panteleon being popular among the Rus at that time. It makes an interesting link to the story of Gytha's earlier visit to the St Panteleon monastery at Cologne.

Some sources say she died in 1099, others say 1107. Some say in Smolensk, some say on pilgrimage to Jerusalem[18], and some that she was buried in the new St Sophia Cathedral in Kiev where Vladimir's sarcophagus still survives.

Prince Oleg, Vladimir's first cousin, formed a murderous alliance with Boniak, the Kuman Khan for control of Kievan Rus. Princess Evpraxia, (Parasha, who appears fleetingly in my story), Vladimir's little sister, wed Henry IV, the Holy Roman Emperor in 1089. The marriage was annulled by Pope Urban II, in extraordinary circumstances; a truly 'tabloid' scandal of the 11th century. According to a reference in our Domesday book, Gytha's mother, Edith 'Swan-neck' may have lived out her days at Mentmore, in Buckinghamshire[19], England.

Gytha's descendants include Prince Alexander Nevsky, Tsar Ivan 'the Terrible' and, most excitingly, through her son Mstislav's marriage to Princess Christina Ingesdotter of Sweden (another conjugal transit), a trace of her Anglo-Saxon blood flows in the veins of both the English and Danish monarchs to this day!

But, to get an inkling of what Gytha may have been like; my favourite clue comes from Grand Prince Vladimir's Instruction to his sons. He writes *'Love your wives but do not grant them any power over you.'* A hint that Gytha may have

---

[18] after the First Crusade 1095-99 to give thanks at the Holy Sepulchre for Mstislav's life - most unlikely.

[19] From the Domesday book. After 1066 Edith's many estates were seized by Ralph de Gael.

inherited her Aunt Edith's [20] '*tendency to offer unsolicited advice.*' It makes me smile every time I read it and leaves me in no doubt that Gytha, King Harold's daughter, was an amazing English woman, so deserving of a place in our sunlight.

JTCS 2020.

---

[20] Queen Edith, Harold's sister and wife of King Edward the Confessor.

FURTHER READING

Anonymous (2007) The Anglo-Saxon Chronicle. 20070424th edn. United States: Echo Library.

Avtamonov,Y. (2013) Simvolika Rastenij V Velikorusskih Pesnyah. United States: Book on Demand Ltd.

Bardsley, S. and Bardsley,Y. (2006) Venomous tongues: Speech and gender in late medieval England (middle ages series). Philadelphia, PA: University of Pennsylvania Press.

Barford, P.M. (2001) The early Slavs: Culture and society in early medieval eastern Europe. 1st edn. London: The British Museum Press, London.

Barlow, F. (2003) The Godwins: The Rise and Fall of a Noble Dynasty. 1st edn. United Kingdom: Longman.

Blair, J. (2002) The Anglo-Saxon Age: A Very Short Introduction. United Kingdom: Oxford University Press, USA.

Bosworth, Joseph. An Anglo-Saxon Dictionary Online. Ed. Thomas Northcote Toller and Others. Comp. Sean Christ and Ondřej Tichý. Faculty of Arts, Charles University in Prague, 21 Mar. 2010. Web. 5 Nov. 2013. <http://www.bosworthtoller.com/>. (2011) Available at: http://bosworth.ff.cuni.cz/

Castor, H. (2011) She-wolves: The women who ruled England before Elizabeth. London: Faber & Faber.

Chambers, R.W. (2013) Beowulf: complete bilingual edition including the original Anglo-Saxon edition and three modern English translations and extensive study of the poem and footnotes index and alphabetical glossary. . Edited by Alfred J Wyatt and M Heyne Socin. e-book edn. (C) E-artnow .

Christopher, D. (1994) Everyday life in medieval England. United Kingdom: Hambledon Continuum.

Clarke, P.A. (1994) The English nobility under Edward the Confessor. United Kingdom: Oxford University Press.

Cokayne, G. (1953) The complete peerage of England, Scotland, Ireland, Great Britain, and the United Kingdom, extant, extinct, or dormant. Edited by Geoffrey White. London : St Catherine Press.

Cross, S.H. and Shobowitz-Wetzor, O. (2012) The Russian Primary Chronicle. Cambridge, MA: Medieval Academy of America.

Davies , R. (2012) Wooden churches: travelling in the Russian North = Dereviannye tserkvi: puteshestviia po russkomu severu. White Sea.

Dmytryshyn, B. (1991) Medieval Russia: A Source Book, 850-1700. United States: Wadsworth Publishing Co Inc.

Douar, F, Durand, J. and Giovannoni, D. (2010) Sainte Russie: l'album de l'exposition, Paris, Musée du Louvre, 5 mars-24 mai 2010. Paris: Somogy.

Douglas, D. and .. and George W. Greenaway (1981) English Historical Documents: v. 2: 1042-1189. United Kingdom: Oxford University Press.

Fennell (1983) The Crisis of Mediaeval Russia, 1200-1304. United Kingdom: London; Longman.

Figes, O. (2003) Natasha's Dance: A Cultural History of Russia. United Kingdom: Penguin Books Ltd.

Franklin, S, Lecturer, Studies, S, Shukman, H. Shepard, J., Franklin, S. and Shepard, J. (1996) The emergence of Russia 750-1200. Harlow: Addison Wesley Longman Higher Education.

Franklin, S. and Shepard, J. (1996) The Emergence of Russia 750-1200. United Kingdom: Longman.

Freeman, E.A. (1871) The History of the Norman Conquest of England: Its Causes and Results. Vol 4 edn. Oxford: Macmillan & Co.

Freeman, E.A. (1913) William the conqueror. London: Macmillan & Co Ltd (Project Gutenberg ebook 2013).

Grammaticus, S., Davidson, H.E. and Fisher, P. (1998) The history of the Danes, books I-IX. United Kingdom: Boydell & Brewer, Limited.

Grekov, B.D. (1947) Культура киевской Руси. Edited by Pauline Rose. CCCP: Out-land languages publishing house Moscow .

Hall, J.L. and Anonymous (2012) Beowulf, (the standard translation). United States: Createspace.

Hamilton, G.H. (1992) The Art and Architecture of Russia: Third Edition (The Yale University Press Pelican Histor). 3rd edn. New Haven: Yale University Press.

Harrison, M. and Embleton, G. (1993) Anglo-Saxon Thegn AD 449-1066 (Warrior). United Kingdom: Osprey Publishing, Limited.

Hosking, G. (2002) Russia and the Russians: From Earliest Times to the Present. United Kingdom: Penguin Books, London, United Kingdom.

Knobloch, E. (2007) Russia and Asia: Nomadic and Oriental Traditions in Russian History (Odyssey Passport). Hong Kong: Odyssey Publications, Hong Kong.

Kulik, A. (2012) 'Jews from Rus' in Medieval England', Jewish Quarterly Review, 102(3), pp. 371–403. doi: 10.1353/jqr.2012.0025.

Levin, E. (1995) Sex and Society in the World of the Orthodox Slavs, 900-1700. 1st edn. United States: Cornell University Press.

Leyser, H. (2002) Medieval women: A social history of women in England 450-1500 (women in history). 2nd edn. London: Weidenfeld & Nicholson history.

Lytton, E.B. (1848) Harold, the Last of the Saxon Kings (The Works of Edward Bulwer-Lytton (19 Volumes)). Classic Books.

Martin, J.L.B. (2007) Medieval Russia, 9801584 (Cambridge medieval textbooks). Cambridge: Cambridge University Press.

Mason, E. (2004) The House of Godwine: The History of a Dynasty. United Kingdom: Hambledon and London.

McLynn, F. (1999) 1066: The Year of the Three Battles. United Kingdom: Random House.

Miller, T. (2014) History of the Anglo Saxons. Didactic Press.

Moreton, R.D., Matilda (2011) Wooden churches: travelling in the Russian North = Dereviannye tserkvi: puteshestviia po russkomu severu. White Sea.

Morillo, S., North, W. and Sharpe, R. (2008) 'King Harold's daughter ', The Haskins Society Journal: Studies in Medieval History, 19.

Morris, M. (2012) The Norman Conquest. United Kingdom: Hutchinson.

O'Brien, H. (2006) Queen Emma and the Vikings: the woman who shaped the events of 1066. London: Bloomsbury Publishing PLC.

Obolensky, D. (1988) Six Byzantine portraits. Oxford: Oxford University Press Reprints distributed by Sa.

Obolensky, D. (1994) Byzantium and the Slavs. United States: St Vladimir's Seminary Press, U.S.

Ostrowski, D.G. (2002) Muscovy and the Mongols: cross-cultural influences on the Steppe frontier, 1304-1589. 1st edn. Cambridge: Cambridge University Press.

Pelenski, J. (1998) The Contest for the Legacy of Kievan Rus'. United States: Distributed by Columbia University Press.

Perrie, M. (2006) The Cambridge History of Russia: Volume 1, From Early Rus' to 1689: v. 1: From Early Rus' to 1689. United Kingdom: Cambridge University Press.

Poole, R.G. (1998) Anotated Bibliographies of Old and Middle English Literature: V Old English wisdom poetry. Cambridge: D.S. Brewer.

Pouncy, C.J. (1995) The 'Domostroi': Rules for Russian households in the time of Ivan the terrible. United States: Cornell University Press.

Ramsay, J.H. (1898) The Foundations of England; or, Twelve Centuries of British History, B.C. 55 - A.D. 1154 Vol 1. Available at: www.books.google.con .

Rathbone, J. (1998) The last English king. United Kingdom: Abacus.

Reid, A. (2015) Borderland: A Journey Through the History of Ukraine. United Kingdom: Weidenfeld & Nicolson.

Rex, P. (2014) The English Resistance: The Underground War Againt the Normans. United Kingdom: Amberley Publishing.

Robert, M. (2013) The chronicle of Novgorod, 1016-1471. United States: Hardpress Publishing.

Schaus, M.C. (ed.) (2006) Women and gender in medieval Europe: An encyclopedia (Routledge encyclopedias of the middle ages). 2nd edn. New York: Routledge.

Schultz, J.A. (1995) The knowledge of childhood in the German Middle Ages, 1100-1350. United States: University of Pennsylvania Press.

Sixsmith, M. (2011) Russia: A 1,000-year Chronicle of the Wild East. United Kingdom: Ebury Press.

Stafford, P. (1989) Unification and Conquest: A Political and Social History of England in the Tenth and Eleventh Centuries. United Kingdom: Distributed in the USA by Routledge, Chapman, and Hall.

Stafford, P. (1997) Queen Emma and Queen Edith: Queenship and Women's Power in Eleventh Century England. 1st edn. Malden, MA: Oxford : Blackwell Publishers, 1997.

Stenton , D.M. (1957) The English Woman in History . First edn. London: Unwin Brothers Ltd .

Strickland, M. and Matthew, S. (1996) War and chivalry: the conduct and perception of war in England and Normandy, 1066-1217. United Kingdom: Cambridge University Press.

Swanton, M. (2000) The Anglo-Saxon chronicles. United Kingdom: Weidenfeld & Nicolson History.

Thomson, F. (2000) The reception of Byzantine culture in Mediaeval Russia. United Kingdom: Aldershot : Ashgate, c1999.

Toller, N.T. and Campbell, A. (1972) An Anglo-Saxon dictionary: Based on the manuscript collections of Joseph Bosworth supplement. Edited by Joseph Bosworth and T. Northcote Toller. United Kingdom: Oxford University Press, USA.

Vernadsky, G. (1975) The Origins of Russia. United States: Greenwood Press.

Wade, T. (1998) Russian Etymological Dictionary. United Kingdom: Bristol Classical Press.

Walker, I. (2004) Harold: the last Anglo-Saxon King. United Kingdom: The History Press Ltd.

Wanton, M. (2000) The Anglo-Saxon Chronicles. United Kingdom: Weidenfeld & Nicolson History.

Welcome to the digital edition of the Bosworth-Toller Anglo-Saxon dictionary (2011) Available at: http://www.bosworthtoller.com

Wheeler, M., Unbegaun, B.O. and Falla, P. (2015) The Concise Oxford Russian dictionary. United Kingdom: Oxford University Press.

Whitelock, D. (ed.) (1955) English historical documents Vol 1. London : Eyre & Spottiswood.

Wiener, L. (1979) Anthology of Russian literature. S.l.: Yesr Co Pub.

Williams, A. (1995) The English and the Norman Conquest. United Kingdom: The Boydell Press.

Williams, A. (2004) Eadgifu [Eddeua] the Fair. Available at: http://www.oxforddnb.com/view/article/52349

Zenkovsky, S.A. (1963) Zenkovsky serge Ed.: Med. Russia'S epics, chronicles, & tales. 2nd edn. New York: Penguin Books.

ABOUT THE AUTHOR

Johnny Stonborough lives in London with his American wife, Jane. After a successful career which included serving in the Metropolitan Police, over a decade on national TV & Radio as an investigative journalist, founding a ground-breaking crisis communications agency, and being the media adviser to the Speaker of the House of Commons, he is now semi-retired, an enthusiastic researcher of early Russian and Anglo-Saxon history, and a novelist.

ACKNOWLEDGEMENTS

My heartfelt thanks to my family, Jane, Eloise, Hugh and Carolyn, who tolerate my obsessions, with wise and patient counsel. Also to the many people who have been delightful in their support, advice and encouragement, in particular: Wanda Whiteley, Johnny Burrow, Holly Dawson and Katya Galitzine (a descendent of great princes, who corrected my Russian); the two artists, painter Lincoln Seligman for the beautiful painting of the Wild Field and Emma Thornton for the cover design; also Professor Oleksandr Kolybenko (Director National Historical and Ethnographic Reserve, Pereyaslav, Ukraine), Dr Taras Nagaiko (State Pedagogical University Pereyaslav, Ukraine); Dr Yehor Brailian (Kyiv University, Ukraine), Margarita Mudritska (Chernihiv, Ukraine), Liubov Prokhorova and Director Pavel Timashkov (Smolensk History Museum, Russia), Peter and Kristin Hell (Soederup, Denmark) also Vikingskibsmuseet, Roskilde, Professor John H. Lind, University of Southern Denmark; The Danish National Museum, Trelleborg, Dr Christian Raffensperger (University of Wittenberg, USA), the Isaev family (Chuvash Republic, Russia), the musical Varshavski family (Tatarstan, Russia), Alexander Tyulkanov (Moscow, Russia), Ed Wood, Nick Laing, Richard Ross, Johnny Rank (Bosham), and Gytha who told me to stop researching and jolly well write something.